Larissa -

May your Golden Bowl
overflow with
praise + Thanksgiving!

Blessings!
Maeve

A Ring and A Prayer

The Golden Bowl Series (Book 1)

by

Maeve Christopher

www.lachesispublishing.com

Published Internationally by Lachesis Publishing Inc.
Rockland, Ontario, Canada

A catalogue record for the print format of this title is available from the National Library of Canada

ISBN 978-1-927555-92-7

A catalogue record for the Ebook is available from the National Library of Canada
Ebooks are available for purchase from
www.lachesispublishing.com

ISBN 978-1-927555-93-4

Editor: Joanna D'Angelo
Copy Editor: Debra Glass

Please Note the following Copyright Notices
(and continued on next page)

DEDICATION

To Jeanne Paglio with gratitude and joy.

ACKNOWLEDGMENTS

My thanks to Joanna D'Angelo, Janet Hitchcock, and Chris Senechal for helping me make this book the best it can be.

Erna Harris, for your expertise in the restaurant and food service industry and patiently answering my many questions.

Brian Scully, for conversations on weaponry, so I know what weapons Annie's security team uses, though Annie still hasn't a clue.

My Tuesday Friends: Linda Delaive, Jan Lowell, Judy Nichols, Mary Wiersma, and Sue Wolfe, for your prayers, encouragement, and frequent reminders that God is in charge.

A RING AND A PRAYER

PROLOGUE

~ ANNIE ~

My favorite summer days were spent with my grandmother, painting, and chatting on my parents' back porch. When I was in my early teens I told her I wanted to be a professional chef. Within fifteen minutes Grammy had painted a big old farmhouse overlooking the rocky coast of Maine. "This is the restaurant you'll own one day, Annie."

I looked over her shoulder in wonderment.

Then she painted a large gold bowl on the front porch. "It's called The Golden Bowl."

"The Golden Bowl?"

"Yes." She turned the canvas over and scribbled *Rev. 5:8*.

Although my adoptive father was a pastor, I had no idea what that verse was.

Grammy could tell from the look on my face. "*They held golden bowls full of incense that are the prayers of God's people.*"

It was like she'd switched on a light. From an early age I was a firm believer in the power of prayer, having experienced it over and over again. That day, I decided it would be my mission to feed people—body, soul, and spirit. To let them know about the power of prayer by experiencing it themselves.

I'd kept a small gold bowl Grammy had given me in my bedroom for my special prayers. Why not do the same for my future customers?

And then I met Russ Brewster, who became my college

sweetheart and knight in shining armor. Within a week of my graduation I married him. Russ was handsome, smart, and industrious. He'd do anything for me. I could confide my deepest thoughts and dreams, and he'd not only listen, he'd support me in any way he could. His belief in Grammy's "painted prophesy" of my future, his ready smile and tender blue eyes, made me grateful every day.

He often teased me about my hair—it was so blonde it was white—and pale skin. He said I looked like an angel you'd put on top of a Christmas tree. Then he'd comment on my "baby blues," and I'd blush bright red every time. I think he got a kick out of that.

Since we both had nothing but debt, our honeymoon destination was an hour drive from my hometown of Ripple Lake to the Maine coast. It was Russ who decided we should meander around the town of Marberry, and our eyes lit up at the same time, when we discovered the old farmhouse that would become The Golden Bowl.

Since it had been on the market a while, and had fallen into disrepair, we were able to work out a great deal to purchase the property.

Russ was a talented woodworker who crafted cabinetry and furniture to pay his way through college. He took on the job of renovating our farmhouse while establishing his woodworking business. With his attention to detail and customer service, he attracted a high-end clientele. It wasn't long before we settled into a cozy apartment on the third floor. Then he set about renovating the rest of the building so I could open the restaurant in the future.

Meanwhile, I worked in the food service department at Marberry Academy and started my master's degree a few years later. Two days a week, Russ would drive me to Boston for my classes, then deliver furniture to local clients before picking me up for the long drive home. It was a grind, but we both had a sense of mission. When I finally graduated, I made a good income working at the local hospital and counseling private clients in nutrition.

Years went by and no children arrived. We were disappointed, but we both trusted God to know what was best.

I returned home from work one day and found my husband by the beautiful stone hearth he'd created. He'd died of an aneurism. Devastated by his loss, I think I fell into a depression, but I didn't let on. I couldn't give up on our dreams. His legacy. I threw myself into my work, knowing helping others would help me.

Four years after his death, I opened The Golden Bowl. A bittersweet day without Russ. But I had customers from day one. Eventually, I expanded the business with a bakery and food prep facility in the converted barn.

God had more in store for me. Early last summer, at the age of forty-seven, I received a phone call. The sister I thought I would never meet was coming to Marberry.

In fact, Debbie Lambrecht was a world-renowned fashion designer, an artist who'd obviously inherited Grammy's phenomenal talent. She brought with her an extended family of rock stars and celebrities, along with their security team. In the whirlwind of summer we bonded. We discovered we were full sisters. And we also found our birth father.

Then she bought the Miller Estate, a sprawling circa 1850 farmhouse overlooking the Atlantic, where they were staying. It was mine to live in—a far cry from my cramped third floor apartment above The Golden Bowl. Our birth father, Dr. Craig Westcott, now shared it with me, and our own security team.

My world had changed dramatically since Grammy painted The Golden Bowl so many years ago in Ripple Lake. But God had more surprises in store . . .

CHAPTER 1

~ ANNIE ~

Everything is different now. Everything is exactly the same.

I made my way through the crowd filling my restaurant, The Golden Bowl, and pushed through the back door onto the porch. Another mob of people. The beauty of the sea and sky called to me. Waves plunged against jagged walls of granite, splashing intrepid visitors, creating a distinctive roar that somehow always soothed me.

The Maine coast at its best.

Above the din of my patrons, the sea breeze carried a voice. "That's Annie Brewster! She looks just like she does on TV. It's like a Cinderella story, isn't it? A rich and famous sister comes out of nowhere."

A sister—my sister—had indeed come out of nowhere, and now she was gone again.

A bracing breath of fresh salt air was what I needed today. Normally, the last of the leaf-peepers were gone by now. But on this weekday in late October, The Golden Bowl was as packed as any weekend in July. The crowd on the back porch with me nibbled appetizers or enjoyed a late lunch. Waitresses jostled me as they worked through the diners, carrying trays loaded with buttery lobster, fried clams, and scallops wrapped in bacon, our specials of the day.

More people milled about on the rock-sheltered beach below, enjoying the sugary sand, the kind that begs you to take off your shoes, and sink your toes into its soft, comforting warmth. Some were walking off their meals, while others were waiting to be called to their tables. I thanked God for the sunshine and balmy temperature. We weren't usually so lucky with the weather this time of year. It could have just as easily been below freezing.

My mind filled with my sister and her family, glad they had a perfect day for travel back to Salzburg, Austria. Debbie and I had met for the first time this summer, and we'd formed a deep bond in those short weeks. My heart was breaking already, and I knew hers was, too. She'd called me three times since they left this morning.

Blue sky reminded me of her beautiful blue eyes. I must have blushed realizing we both had the same coloring. Debbie was twenty years younger than I, but the resemblance was uncanny. I'd known all about her through my grandmother and then the media, as she was now a world-famous fashion designer. Debbie never knew I existed until our birth mother made a deathbed confession. Within weeks of her funeral, Debbie arrived here in Marberry, accompanied by her extended family of rock stars and celebrities, not to mention a crack security team. The town was soon overrun with tourists and fans. It had stayed that way since.

In the midst of all that craziness, we sorted through our pasts and discovered our birth father, a retired cardiac surgeon, Dr. Craig Westcott, known to all as Doc. It was hard to believe, but Debbie and I were full sisters, even though twenty years separated us.

My contemplation ended when Ashleigh, my first shift manager, shouted from the back door. "Annie, you have a phone call."

"Is it Debbie?" As I turned, I saw Ashleigh was gone, sucked back into the busyness of the afternoon. I made my way through the crowd to a tiny office tucked under a staircase. Ashleigh sat in the corner, tearing into a tuna sandwich, her light brown hair falling out of a ponytail in every direction. It was after 3:00 p.m. and neither of us had had a break since breakfast at 5:30.

Smiling, I went to the phone and locked eyes with Ashleigh. "Debbie?"

"It's your agent," Ashleigh said.

"When did I get into show business?"

She chuckled.

Butterflies took over my stomach. "Hello?"

"Annie, it's Joe Harris. Amanda James has a scheduling issue. She can't make it next week."

I heard him puffing on his cigar as relief consumed me. "That's fine. I need more time to get ready anyway."

"She's flying in tomorrow. Her camera crew will do some scouting around the area. Take some shots of The Golden Bowl and the beach, the town. Her producer will interview some of your people, some of the townspeople. That kind of thing. The weather's supposed to be nice, so that's a plus. I'll get there as soon as I can. Amanda plans to interview you the day after. So you'll have time to get acquainted beforehand. She likes to be prepared."

Knees shaking, I fell into a squeaky chair. *So do I.* "All right, Joe. I'll do my best." The phone went dead. Joe Harris was not one to waste time chatting. His next billion-dollar deal was probably waiting on the other line.

I looked over at Ashleigh. "He hung up on me."

She giggled around a mouthful of tuna. "You may have friends in high places, but you're just a newbie. He doesn't have time to listen to you fret about messing up an interview with a superstar journalist."

"He said Amanda's coming *tomorrow*. Not next week. I need a drink. I don't drink, but I need a drink." I held my gurgling stomach, knowing full well it wouldn't even take water at this point. "How did I get myself into this? *Amanda James Now* is the biggest thing on TV. The audience is worldwide. Everyone's gonna be watching. What if I make a total fool of myself?"

I swept wisps of hair out of my face. "I can't let Debbie down. She must pay Joe Harris a fortune to manage their PR. I told her I'd do it. I can't back out now. But how can I face Amanda James?" *America's number one news magazine show*! My mind was swirling with the famous TV ads of *Amanda James Now.*

Ashleigh put down her sandwich and looked me in the eye. "Did I tell you what Cat told me?"

"No, what did she tell you?" Nausea was in full bloom.

"She didn't want to freak you out. But we both know she's a modern-day prophet if there ever was one."

I took a breath. "She is."

"She said, 'Annie Brewster is the hands and feet of Jesus. Think what a difference she's making in this world. This is only the start.' That's what she said. *This is only the start.* And now they're somewhere over the Atlantic, and you've got an interview with Amanda James. Wow."

"Wow." I suppose Cat had been smart not to tell me her thoughts, because "freaking out" was putting it mildly. "This is only the start? She said that, huh?"

"Those exact words." Ash nodded, grinning, and more hair escaped that loose ponytail. I probably looked just as disheveled as Ash did, after the day we'd had.

I put my head in my hands. Cat Clemente was not only a rock star, and acclaimed lyricist, she had an incredible connection to the divine. I had the honor of getting to know her this past summer when she and her husband joined the rest of their extended family here for vacation. As Debbie said, Cat was her cousin-in-law, but more like a sister.

Orphaned at age five, Cat had grown up with Debbie's husband, David Lambrecht. Not many people knew the true extent of Cat's abilities, but it seemed with her incredible success in music, more people were seeing it. This past summer half the town witnessed a little boy healed of terminal cancer after she prayed over him.

I struggled to my feet. "I've got to get home. Is—"

A bold knock on the door pushed it open. Peter Fellowes looked embarrassed. "Sorry to barge in, Annie. Hi, Ashleigh." He closed the door behind him, and I gave him a hug.

"Good to see you, Peter. How's the construction going?"

A broad smile lit up his craggy features. "I brought pictures. It's going great. We're going for another round of funding, so I'm back to see my best gifting table member." He glanced at Ashleigh and corrected himself. "*Members*." The "s" sound carried in a long "z" as he gave us a sheepish look. "But first I want to show you." He skimmed his hand over dark waves of hair, then pulled his phone out of his jacket pocket.

Ashleigh and I huddled beside him, admiring his pictures of a resort-like building, taking shape on the wild coast of Maine. As a special education teacher, and vice principal of Marberry Academy, Peter was well-qualified to go after his dream—a school for disabled children—a place that would give them everything they would need to face their challenges, to live happy, productive lives. Peter's ambitious fundraising program was creative for sure, but it was working. He called it "gifting tables."

Members of the gifting tables gathered often at The Golden Bowl for socializing and recruiting new members who donated to Peter's charity. For a $1000 cash gift you joined the table on the Appetizer Level. Then as more people joined, older members on the table moved up to Soup and Salad, then to Entrée, and finally to the Dessert Level. The person at the Dessert Level got her $1000 back plus $7000 more. Most members took back $2000 and donated $6000 to Peter's charity.

"It's gonna be awesome," Ash said.

He beamed at us. "It's even better than I dreamed it would be. We'll be able to start with a hundred kids next summer. Then I'm thinking we'll have as many as two hundred during the school year. Once we're up and running—I'm thinking we'll be able to get funding to expand to five hundred."

"That's ambitious!" I said, but how could he do it all in such a short time?

Peter picked up on my concern. "I know it's a big dream,

Annie. But those kids deserve this. They need a break—a good education—and they need to know in their gut they're worth it. They deserve a great life. They may have disabilities, but it doesn't need to hold them back." He wiped a stray tear. "Sorry, it chokes me up every time I think how we can help these kids. And we're so close!"

I took another look at the picture on his phone. It was an impressive building. My nervous stomach settled with warm feelings. "I—I think I have a thousand in cash. I'll put it toward the gifting table. Here." I went to my desk drawer to retrieve the cash box, counted out a thousand dollars, and put it in an envelope. I'd remember to put a note in the box for my accountant later.

Ashleigh said, "I've been saving for another table. I had to spend the two thousand I got last time fixing my bathroom. When are you having another party?"

"It'll be soon. I want to ratchet up the membership. I know I can count on you ladies to bring more members in." He took my envelope and reached into his pocket for a well-folded sheet of paper. "Here, just initial this so I keep everything straight."

I found a pen on my desk and signed where he pointed. "Thanks. I have to get going. But keep me posted on everything. It's exciting to think you'll finally have that school ready for next summer."

"I will. Thanks!" He was out the door.

The thought of my upcoming interview with celebrity-journalist Amanda James flew into my mind again. "I've gotta run, Ash. Is Bree—"

"Don't worry. I'll be here till 5:00. Bree is due in any minute now, and we have enough staff for whatever madness comes our way tonight. Go home and relax."

"Thanks." I gave her a hug, took my bag out of the drawer, and headed for the door. Brianna and our postman were standing on the porch in front of the large golden bowl, the "trademark" of my restaurant.

As I weaved my way through the throng of people

waiting to get in, I noticed Bree pointing to two large mailbags. Ralph gestured toward the sign by the bowl that read *Leave a Prayer... Take a Prayer.*

"Annie! Glad you're here. Ralph is gonna put these letters right into the bowl. We don't have anyplace else for them." Brianna's sweet freckled face was all business.

Ralph handed me a stack of bills. "This here is your regular mail. I sorted through all this stuff in the bags. Took me a couple days, and there's more comin' in every day. Looks like Marberry Post Office is gonna be buried. It's all handwritten stuff that looks to me like it must be prayers. So I thought just dump 'em in the bowl. Right?"

"Thanks Ralph, but I can't be a hundred percent sure they're prayers until I open them. Besides, I want people to be comfortable leaving a prayer and taking a prayer, like the sign says." I smiled at the postman, hoping to enlist his help.

"Two huge mailbags full are going to overwhelm the bowl and make it tough for people to write out a prayer to leave in there. And they might be less likely to take a prayer that's still in an envelope. So let's just take these bags and put them in the trunk of my car. I'll sort through them first."

When the bags were loaded into the car, I remembered I hadn't taken a prayer from the bowl. It was a habit I'd started from my first day in business. I went back.

Brianna was talking to a heavyset young woman holding a baby. I could see Bree was anxious to hand the woman over to me and get to her work. "Annie, this is Lisa. I told her she can start Monday—dishwasher. Then we'll see." Brianna turned on her heel and disappeared inside.

Lisa smiled up at me. "Hi, Annie. Thanks for the job."

"Lisa! Great to see you. How are you?" I took her baby's outstretched hand, caressing it with my thumb. Lisa must have gained thirty or forty pounds since the last time I saw her. She was a pretty young girl with large Bambi brown eyes and straight brunette hair that skimmed rounded shoulders. I smiled at the baby's big dark eyes. "What's her name?"

"Rosie."

"How sweet." Rosie was smiling and alert. Obviously, this baby was well fed and loved. Her smile fueled a twinge of regret that I hadn't been blessed with a child of my own.

"You heard I got divorced?"

"I'm so sorry."

A voice on the loudspeaker summoned a couple to the dining room. As they vacated their wicker chairs, I nudged Lisa in that direction.

We'd barely landed in our seats when she blurted her world of hurt. "He was the kind of guy that lives on cigarettes, beer, and big dreams. He *was* a hard worker. He just didn't have much of an education or much of a job. When we met, I thought I could make him into a good husband. I tried to push him to go back to school, get a good job. But he decided he could make more money gambling. That didn't work out. Then I thought our baby girl would change him. Nope. That only made things tougher. He'd take it out on Rosie and me. Especially when she cried. He hated when she cried. Then he got into drugs. That was the end for us. It was dangerous being around him."

I reached over to hug her. "I'm sorry."

Her brown eyes were wet, but she forced a smile. "So it's time for a job." She swiped her sleeve over her face. "This is such a beautiful porch. I love big old houses with wrap-around porches. While I was waitin' for Brianna, I watched people at the bowl. I thought I should write something and put a prayer in there, too."

I smiled and squeezed her hand.

"I went over and peeked at some of the notes. Most of the prayers are the same: help me."

"I think you're right," I said.

Her lips trembled, and she took a shuddering breath. "The sign says, 'leave a prayer and take a prayer,' but mostly people left them. They probably thought like me. My life is such a wreck I can't even take care of myself. How can I pray for someone else?"

"You can always pray for someone else. I want you to know it matters. It truly does. At the very least, a prayer can offer comfort—for us and for others. Prayer connects us with God. It's just talking to him."

Lisa cocked her head, giving me a skeptical look.

How could I make her understand? "Let's say someone has lost their job and they're frustrated because after so many months, they're still unemployed. But what if they've always had a dream to start their own business? But they never took the time to try because they were afraid of failing. What if they decide to take a prayer from the bowl, and it's your prayer. What if you wrote a hopeful Bible verse that you remembered? There's a proverb I really love: *Proverb 13:12—Hope deferred makes the heart sick, but a longing fulfilled is a tree of life.*"

Lisa nodded and gave me a tentative smile.

Encouraged, I continued, "Or you could just write a kind thought. That person might be truly moved and hopeful for the first time in a long time. They might feel a renewed sense of purpose, that they can change their lives for the better. Isn't that a wonderful gift that you could give? It doesn't cost a thing. And besides all that, nothing makes you feel better than getting out of your own head and helping someone else. Right?"

"I suppose you're right. Maybe I could do that for someone . . . and maybe someone's already done that for me." Lisa smiled.

"God does miracles every day, Lisa. Big and small. All kinds. Keep your eyes peeled, and you'll see." I stood. "I was just about to take a prayer for myself before I head home. Do you want to join me at the bowl? I'll hold Rosie while you write your prayer and pick one out."

Rosie grabbed my hair as Lisa handed her to me. "I don't think she's ever seen anyone with such bright hair."

I cooed and kissed her forehead. "She's adorable."

Lisa bit her lip in concentration, and wrote out her prayer. She folded the slip of paper and then leaned over the bowl, contemplating which note to take, as though she were picking a chocolate from a sampler box. A mischievous smile lit up her face as she tossed her prayer slip into the bowl and plunged her fist to the bottom, stirring it up. She came out with an oddly crinkled paper.

"Huh? It's hard inside." She unwrapped the prayer. "Oh!"

It was a large diamond ring. My eyes widened. This was a first for The Golden Bowl—at least as far as I knew.

"Can I—can I keep it? Can I?"

"What does the prayer say?" I was flabbergasted.

Lisa was breathless. "It—it says, 'Hope you have better luck with this than me.'" She jumped in place. "I can keep it! That's what it means. I can keep it."

I smiled with relief. "That's the way it sounds." The last thing I needed was more to worry about today. I needed to get home to think in peace and quiet. At least whoever was crazy enough to throw a diamond into the bowl attached a note giving it to the stranger who picked it up. My conscience was clear.

"I can buy a car!" She caught herself before her voice grew too loud. "I betcha I can buy a car with this."

The answer was not mine to give. "Maybe. You should go see Terri at Marberry Designs, the jewelry shop across from the police station. She'll help you, I'm sure."

I returned Rosie to her mother's arms and pushed my hand down into the bowl. The feel of fine linen paper intrigued me. It was definitely not the cheap paper a local office supply store donated to my cause. I pulled it out and put it into my pocket. "I need to get going now, Lisa. Do you need a ride?"

"No, thanks. My neighbor's picking me up. I'll see you bright and early Monday."

"Great! Thank you." I hugged Lisa and squeezed Rosie

between us. Her gurgles of baby talk prompted laughter from both of us.

Daylight was growing short, but I couldn't resist the urge to walk home along the seaside path known as Miller's Way. My old car would be fine in the parking lot overnight. Nothing in it but bags of prayers with nowhere else to go. I'd have to ask Dad about taking them to the prayer group at his church. They'd never fit in the golden bowl. Having a pastor as my adoptive father did have its benefits. I chuckled to myself.

I curved around the back of the building to the entrance to the dirt walkway. There were a fair number of people wandering the path—some sitting on benches or on the rocks jutting out into the sea. It was only a three-mile walk to the private beach of my new home, a perfect hike to get some fresh air and exercise. A perfect time to think and clear my head.

It had been a long, crazy day topped off with my newest employee plucking an extravagant diamond ring out of the prayer bowl. I hoped that ring would mean a new start to a life that had been so sad from the very beginning.

Lisa was the daughter of some former classmates of mine at Ripple Lake High School. Though Ripple Lake was a solid working-class town in the heart of Maine, the beauty of the town was marred by the presence of an unsavory trailer park that harbored drunks, drug-addicts, and a few nasty criminals. Lisa's parents had been alcoholics since high school, and both had been arrested for petty theft and drunk and disorderly conduct. Poor Lisa didn't have a chance. Now it seemed little Rosie was entering the same sad cycle, if Lisa's ex-husband was any indication.

I didn't have the energy to ask Lisa how she could maintain a dishwashing job with a forty-mile daily commute to Marberry then forty miles back to Ripple Lake. The salary I could pay wouldn't allow year-round housing in Marberry. She might find a winter rental, but even that would be difficult with the town's sudden rise to fame.

And what about child care? Her mother certainly wasn't a candidate for Babysitter of the Year.

It occurred to me my head was taking me down a path of negativity I didn't need. My heart prompted me to take that prayer slip out of my pocket. As I felt the heavyweight linen paper, it gave me a sense I was about to read something important. I stared at the elegant cream color momentarily, then unfolded the prayer. I stopped in my tracks. I recognized Cat's handwriting.

The Prayer of Jabez:
Oh, that You would bless me indeed,
And enlarge my territory,
That Your hand would be with me,
And that You would keep me from evil.
Chronicles 4:9-10

I gathered my new silk and wool skirt up and sat on a nearby rock overlooking the water. White-capped breakers belted the bluff, and the wind picked up, pelting me with mist. I put the prayer back in my pocket for safekeeping and wound my hair into a knot to keep it from blowing in my face. I repeated The Prayer of Jabez aloud. I didn't need the paper. The miracle of it was too much to bear, and I burst into tears.

How could Cat have known? The Prayer of Jabez was the subject of the last letter my grandmother sent me, shortly before her death. At the time, I was finishing up a graduate degree in nutrition, and she was so proud of me. She predicted that I would use my education to make the world a better place. She told me she prayed that blessing daily for me and for Debbie. I began praying it every morning, too. Now God was enlarging our territories. It was frightening and wonderful at the same time.

So many thoughts and memories were overtaking me—so much emotion that I lost track of time. A sliver of a moon in a deep blue sky and the deserted path told me I should go. I stood up and carefully shook grains of sand from my precious skirt and coordinated wool jacket.

The swirl of my skirt as I walked, the comfy supple leather boots—all my sister's designs—made me smile. This past summer, Debbie and her business partner had gifted me with an entire wardrobe I could never have afforded on my own. She was so excited she clapped and giggled as I modeled the clothes for her. I laughed when she told me I looked like a fashion model. Well, I was tall and slim like my sister, so I suppose that's why. At the age of 47, it was like a glimpse in a mirror twenty years ago when I looked at Debbie. We had the same coloring, same white-blonde hair and baby blue eyes. The same pale skin that blushed with every emotion. I was hardly a young woman anymore, but spending time with Debbie, her husband David, and my niece and nephews, made me feel that way.

Long before I'd ever met my sister, I spent hours online researching their company's fashion empire that clothed the rich and famous. Women all over the world paid outrageous prices for their designs, and I sure felt like a million dollars wearing them. But I also knew that my sister did a lot of wonderful charity work, and her clothes were made by well-paid artisans, unlike several other clothing lines I had read about that used sweat shops or child labor in poor countries.

I wondered if Grammy had told Debbie about the Prayer of Jabez. My sister had been blessed and became a blessing to others. She had certainly enlarged her territory. I suppose I really wasn't surprised that Cat knew how important that prayer was to me. She seemed to know everything of importance.

~ ANNIE ~

I'd just rounded the bend where the land jutted out to the sea when I saw him not far behind me. A shiver crawled up my spine. Maybe he was a paparazzo? The light was dim, and I couldn't see a camera. I picked up my pace and focused on my perfect walking boots. I could run in them as well as I could run in sneakers, if I had to. Without slowing, I felt inside my handbag for my cell phone. Then I remembered I'd left it recharging on my desk. "Crap!" I hoped my voice didn't carry on the breeze.

Concern gave way to anxiety, and I had maybe a quarter mile to go. I glanced over my shoulder. He was gaining on me. He was a scruffy character. Tall, broad shoulders—and he probably had close to a hundred pounds on me. I started to run, pressing into the wind. *Don't look back. Don't look back*! I looked back.

He didn't run. He had kind of a swagger. *A swagger. Like David . . .* "Oh God, help me!"

Is he one of us, or one of them?

My sister *was* an international public figure, and her husband certainly had accumulated enemies in his former career. And with all the events of the past summer, my innermost being suddenly understood the need for caution.

My mouth and throat were dry as the desert from running into the wind. From exertion and fear.

The gate to my property was right ahead. Billy, one of the guards, was posted there. He gave me a wave and his usual friendly smile, which allayed my fear a bit.

I slowed to a brisk walk and focused on him. It was hard to believe he was a former SEAL, with that California surfer boy look he had. As he opened the gate for me, I didn't dare look back.

Huffing and puffing, I managed to say, "Thanks, Billy."

Grateful I had Billy to deal with the approaching stranger, I ran up the lawn to the back porch and through the kitchen door.

CHAPTER 2

~ ANNIE ~

Something smelled good. I stood inside the screen door and took a few deep, relaxing breaths. Roast beef, roasted potatoes and vegetables, as only Mom could do.

My mother was at the stove. "Anne Auclair Brewster! You look as stunning as those supermodels you were hanging out with this summer." Mom smiled with her whole face.

I kissed her cheek, pulled out a chair, and dropped into it. "Thanks. I love this outfit. It's so comfortable . . . I didn't spill a drop on it all day."

"Well, you'll want to change for dinner."

"It's so sweet of you to be here today." I glanced around my new dream kitchen. "My first day without my sister in this mansion she bought for me." A long sigh rattled out of me. "I really appreciate you making dinner."

"That's what mothers are for. Your dad and I knew it was going to be a tough day for you. I thought you could use a home-cooked meal. And it's ready, so go get changed and I'll set the table."

"Thanks." I pushed through the swinging door and into a tall, unshaven man. Dropping my handbag on his boot, I tried to stifle an automatic scream.

"Sorry, ma'am, didn't mean to startle you." He grabbed me by the shoulders and my head rolled back. He was tall and scruffy, and I was pretty sure, he was the guy who'd been following me.

Embarrassed, I avoided his eyes. "I—I'm sorry. I didn't

mean to scream." I looked down at my bag draped on his foot. "I'm going to get a drink of water. Do you want one?" I stepped back into the kitchen.

He picked up my handbag and gingerly placed it on the countertop. "No, thanks."

Mom eyed him head to foot. "Mr. Rhodes, could you gather up all your men? It's time for dinner."

"Yes, ma'am. Thank you." He disappeared.

I fell back into my seat and took a gulp of water. Then another. "Mr. Rhodes?"

"He's the new man in charge of security."

"Do you like him?" I focused on Mom's furrowed brow as she spooned vegetables into a large dish.

"He seems . . . nice."

"Nice?"

Mom placed the roast onto a platter. "Well, what am I supposed to say?"

"*Nice*?" I propped my elbow on the table and rested my head. My eyes closed. "I thought he wouldn't be getting here until Friday."

A voice boomed beside me. "David Lambrecht doesn't take excuses."

I jumped in my seat. "No. No, I guess not."

Debbie's husband had hired an entire security team for me. He wasn't someone who would accept anyone in his employ getting a late start on a job.

"So here I am. Nathan Rhodes, ma'am."

I tilted up and stretched out my hand. "I'm Annie."

"Pleasure to meet you, Mrs. Brewster." He had a firm handshake. No surprise there.

"Nice to meet you, too. Please call me Annie.

He strode over to the stove and lifted a platter of sliced roast beef and a heavy dish of roasted root vegetables. "Let me help you with this, ma'am." His voice was a gravelly baritone, pleasing to the ear.

As he disappeared into the dining room, Mom beamed over at me. "He *does* seem nice."

I went for more water.

As I watched Mom, Dad, and our new Director of Security shuffle back and forth with serving dishes, my stomach gurgled from all the water. Nathan Rhodes was cut from the same cloth as my brother-in-law, David Lambrecht. Neither would take any excuses, if you dared offer one. Something compelling in their eyes commanded attention and exuded authority and confidence. Then there was that swagger. I wondered if they'd met through the secret organization that had employed David. He'd told me only that Mr. Rhodes was well qualified for the job. That was apparently all I needed to know.

"Annie!"

I turned to see Dr. Craig Westcott, my birth father, pushing through the swinging door. "Hi Doc. How was your day?"

Doc sat beside me at the kitchen table. "Difficult. I'm sure it was for you, too."

"Yeah. I wish Debbie, David, and the kids could have stayed for a longer visit."

He reached over and patted my arm. "Things will work out. Who knows, maybe they'll decide to relocate here."

"It'd be great, if that happens. But I'm not holding my breath. I'm just hoping I can afford a few trips to Austria, and that they really do come visit us in the summer."

Nathan reappeared to announce dinner was served. He took my cell phone out of his pocket and handed it to me. "It's important to keep this with you at all times, Mrs. Brewster."

"Thanks." I could feel my face heating up, as it always did when I was embarrassed.

His deep brown eyes held mine. "I apologize for the lapse in security today. From now on you'll have at least one guard with you at all times."

"O-o-kay." Now everyone knew I was flustered.

Doc gave me one of his raised eyebrows as we headed to the dining room.

~ ANNIE ~

It was sometime after dinner when Doc found me upstairs in Debbie's summer art studio. I stared out to sea, gazing at the sky, dimly lit by a crescent moon.

"We need to keep this room as Debbie's studio. Even if she never comes back, we'll have some of her art displayed here."

He put his arm around me and kissed the side of my face. "Don't worry, she'll be back. I firmly believe nothing will keep you two apart. Now that we've all managed to find each other—we're not going to let go."

The sound of a throat clearing turned us around. Nathan stood in the doorway. "Mrs. Brewster, Doctor Westcott, sorry to interrupt. We just received notice that Amanda James and her crew will land in Bangor at 12:30 tomorrow afternoon. We'll have her complete schedule in the morning. Your agent, Joe Harris, will arrive here around 5:00 p.m."

"Okay, thank you." I nodded politely. The thought of having an "agent" made me uncomfortable, to say the least. But Joe Harris had made himself indispensable to my sister and her extended family. He seamlessly orchestrated all of their publicity concerns and managed their entertainment deals. Now he was inserting himself into my business.

Nathan's voice took me out of my reverie. "If that's all, I'll be turning in now, ma'am."

"That's all, thank you. Good night." I nodded again.

"Good night." He walked soundlessly to his room.

Doc and I looked at each other.

"Why can't he just call me Annie like everyone else?"

Doc grinned. "I don't think Nathan Rhodes is like everyone else."

I suppose not. I had no idea what to say to that remark.

I knew 4:30 a.m. would arrive way too soon, but I couldn't get myself to bed. The window seat in Debbie's studio beckoned. Doc gently reminded me to get some sleep.

"Don't worry about me. I'll get to bed soon. Good night." I turned off the light, cracked open the window, and settled into the cushion, the window frame at my back. The sounds of the sea and the dim glow of moonlight lulled me a bit.

Amanda James. Interviewing *me*. What was I getting myself into?

It had been a whirlwind of a summer: meeting my sister Debbie and her extended family, finding out that Doc was my biological father, helping Debbie work through the death of her mother—our biological mother—and discovering that Debbie and I were full sisters. All in front of worldwide media attention and under the protection of an elite security force. It was mind-boggling. And sometimes frightening.

Now, The Golden Bowl, and my unique "business concept" would step onto center stage. When I started my little restaurant, I could never have imagined in my wildest dreams that Amanda James would interview me, and The Golden Bowl would be featured on television's number one news magazine show.

Since my new "family" of rock stars, secret agents, business agents, and fashion superstars had appeared, my restaurant was doing a soaring business. The trunk of my car was still stuffed with prayer requests for the bowl. The post office might explode with them. What would happen after the interview? I couldn't fathom it.

I sat at the window, gazing out at the night sky. What did God have in store for me?

~ DOC ~

I intended to get some sleep when I left Annie in Debbie's art studio. It had been a long emotional day after saying goodbye to my daughter, Debbie, her husband, David, my six grandchildren, and of course the rest of their extended family. Like Annie said, we expected to see them back here next summer, but that was a long time to wait. I wasn't positive Debbie would be in any rush to see me. But I would take what I could get.

Never in my wildest imaginings did I ever think I'd be reunited with Debbie. Never did I think she'd embrace me as her biological father. It had only been a matter of a couple of months since we'd met, but it was still tough to hear her call me Dr. Westcott. I wondered if we'd ever get to a point where she could at least call me Doc, like everyone else did.

I went downstairs to the kitchen and poured myself a cup of coffee from the perpetually perking coffeepot. I took a sip, gazing out the window at the white Adirondack chairs, and decided to go have a think out there. I filled a thermos with coffee and grabbed a blanket. Lights from the house and dim moonlight provided the right illumination. The sounds of the surf and the dark sky calmed me.

I remembered the day not long ago as I passed these very chairs unnoticed on my way to play ball with my grandsons. Annie, Debbie, and Cat were deep in conversation. "It's a God thing," Debbie said about how we'd managed to find each other.

I raised my thermos to the sky. "God, I guess it *is* a God thing. Thank you. Please work it out so I get to be a real part of my daughters' lives."

I reflected back over nearly forty years as a cardiac surgeon. I thought I knew everything about the human heart. But I was learning plenty of new lessons since I retired and moved to Maine. My plan to be closer to Annie, my eldest daughter, had blossomed in a way I never could have imagined.

I'd had months to think, alone on my patio overlooking the Atlantic Ocean. Annie was now forty-seven, tragically widowed a decade ago. Newspaper accounts of her husband's death were simple enough to locate. Russ Brewster had been a talented and ambitious woodworker with a thriving business. His greatest achievement, according to the local newspaper, *The Marberry Times*, had been his restoration of the old Maine farmhouse that would one day become The Golden Bowl, his wife's dream. A few years after his death, Annie opened the restaurant. By all accounts, she'd become successful, eventually expanding her business with a bakery and sweet shop as well as a food prep facility.

Annie's adoptive parents, Pastor Mike and Millie Auclair, had raised her as their only child in a strong Christian home in the blue-collar town of Ripple Lake. I'd decided to drive the forty-five minutes to attend Mike's church service and was welcomed at once. Any stranger in that town would stick out like a sore thumb—especially a tall, white-haired, well-dressed surgeon who'd come by way of California and New York. I immediately accepted the pastor's invitation to dinner at their home.

Since Annie owned a busy food service business in the coastal town of Marberry, she rarely made the forty-mile trip to Ripple Lake on Sunday mornings. Whenever she did, she didn't stay for dinner. I contented myself with glimpses of her, then more of a distant friendship as I became a donor to her charitable programs for the needy.

Mike and Millie were no fools. There was a definite physical resemblance—Annie had my coloring, my pale blue eyes, and fine fly-away hair. They knew I was her biological father. We didn't discuss it.

I believed Annie was just too busy and overwhelmed to even think about me—never mind wonder if I was her birth father. All that changed this past summer, when we both met my younger daughter, and Annie's full sister, Debbie. That's when everything exploded.

Yes. I had two daughters with the same woman, twenty years apart. Neither of them knew me. Their birth mother, Marion, was not my wife, but she was the love of my life. I let out a long rasping breath. Fool that I was, I'd always harbored the fantasy we'd end up together, somehow. That didn't happen, but another miracle had . . .

I was reunited with my daughters.

Now, here I sat in an Adirondack chair, thinking, reliving,

and gazing out over the Atlantic Ocean from the back lawn of the mansion Debbie had bought for us. As I expected, before she left, Debbie hugged me and called me Dr. Westcott.

She's still reeling from the shock of discovering I'm her birth father.

The moon disappeared behind a cluster of clouds. I took a sip of coffee from my thermos. It was hard to wrap my head around my younger daughter's life. Debbie suffered from an eating disorder, and had nearly died of a heart attack at the age of nineteen. Somehow, she'd managed to marry an Austrian who was an assassin for a secret government agency and then spiraled into the media spotlight when his escapades became front-page news. Now, seven years later, he was supposedly retired from that job, and busy being a devoted father and husband. Although I had a feeling he was still doing his secret agent thing. Meanwhile, Debbie had become an international sensation with a huge fashion empire. To say their life was crazy, was an understatement.

I'd take that crazy—as much as I could get. Hugging my daughters, playing ball with my grandkids, well, that had been sweeter than any accomplishment in my medical career. But they'd stretched their summer vacation well into autumn, so I couldn't ask them to lengthen their stay.

At least I still had Annie, along with the dream that I might have a real relationship with one of my children. The two of us, rambling around in this massive expanse of house, had enough security to keep us from worry.

Out of the corner of my eye, I spied Billy approaching.

"You okay out here, Doc?"

I checked my watch and let out a sigh. "Yeah, I guess. It's funny, when I was a surgeon, sleep was precious to me. Now, it's become a chore, a way to fill the time. I've been up almost twenty-four hours, but I've got nothing pressing to do and nowhere special to go tomorrow, so no need to go to bed."

He sat beside me. "Sure is quiet around here now."

Billy always made me smile. He was the furthest thing from a Navy SEAL I could have imagined. Everyone called him "Dude" or "Surfer Dude."

"Watcha thinkin' about, Doc?"

"Well, I watched yesterday's sunrise with Cat."

"Awesome. I can't believe I got to meet her. Got her autograph before she left."

I smiled. "Cat told me I'd appreciate some peace and quiet for a change."

"Ah, I dunno. Too much peace and quiet, maybe."

I chuckled. "It's been an experience, to put it bluntly. Rock stars, fashion stars, and secret agents make a strange blend." I remembered Cat's deep blue eyes. "I'll miss Cat. With all the craziness, she brought peace and hope. She made me think there is a God. A good God."

Billy's smile shone bright in the darkness. We sat in silence until the sun came up.

~ LISA ~

As I twisted around to find my jacket, the mirror on the closet door hit me, and I noticed the old brown plastic frame coming loose. Then I saw the jeans stretched tight over my stomach and behind. *I should throw that thing out*. I could still fit my hand into the elastic waistband. No holes in the jeans—I didn't need the stupid mirror to tell me that. I turned to face it head on, and it wasn't pretty. The ring stashed in my pocket made a funny bulge in the crease where my belly met my leg. I stretched my T-shirt over my stomach and pulled on a long jacket. I didn't look much better, but at least the ring was hidden. I slammed the closet door and went to find Peg.

She sat at the kitchen table with a cup of coffee and a pack of cigarettes in front of her. Kind of a guilty look on her wrinkled face. She knew smoking was bad for her and bad for the baby.

But I couldn't be mad at her. Peg was the only real friend I had in the world. She lived in the trailer next to mine, but she spent most of her time here. When we weren't playing cards or hanging out, she took care of Rosie. She was good at giving me advice, too. Her short, fuzzy gray hair reminded me she was more like a grandmother to me than just a friend.

I didn't have anyone else to babysit. And Peg was lending me her car. My last twenty bucks would go into the gas tank.

I leaned down over the high chair and kissed my baby girl. "Be good, Rosie Q!" She stopped pushing dry cereal around the tray long enough to giggle at me. *Eight months already*. My baby was born exactly eight months ago today. I hated to leave her, but what could I do? Maybe someday she'd understand. Maybe someday I'd understand.

Peg shoved a card into my hand. "Bring me back whatever you can from The Golden Bowl? Pretty sure it's roast beef today. Or beef stew. Beef somethin'."

"Okay. I might be late, though."

"No problem. We'll be here." She tickled Rosie.

Rosie's giggles almost broke my heart every time I left her. But her tears were way worse. At least she was happy with Peg. I hoped the place wouldn't reek of cigarette smoke by the time I got home. Rosie didn't need any more problems. A deadbeat dad was bad enough.

Peg's car started right up. "Thank you, God." I said it out loud. Now that I was gonna be working at The Golden Bowl, I'd need to remember about God and the power of prayer. Up until I got hired for a dishwashing job and pulled a diamond ring out of the prayer bowl, well, The Golden Bowl was just a place to get a free meal.

But as an employee, maybe someone would ask me about the prayer bowl. That made me kind of nervous. The manager, Brianna, had told me that all the employees have an orientation so they could answer questions about the restaurant and the prayer bowl, too. I wasn't sure what I could say to people about prayer. I wasn't going to tell them about finding a ring in the bowl. I decided I'd leave prayers and take prayers everyday. That could get me up to speed with it. Maybe.

None of my friends ever used the prayer bowl. But when we went into Marberry, we'd always get free food. Annie was a professional nutritionist and chef. Meals from The Golden Bowl were delicious—and healthy, too. Annie also had a soup kitchen in her dad's church right in Ripple Lake. You didn't have to go to church services there to get free food. Pastor Auclair seemed to know who needed help. I couldn't get by without it.

But that diamond ring scratching a hole in my pocket—maybe that would mean a new life for me and Rosie. Maybe.

I parked in Marberry Square and walked around, spotting Marberry Designs right away. I hoped Terri, the jeweler, would be in. My stomach had started growling before I was out of Ripple Lake, so I decided to walk down Shore Road to The Golden Bowl.

Annie was such a generous person, she'd never mind giving me breakfast, lunch, and dinner—all free. You could sit anywhere in the restaurant and rub elbows with rich people from Boston. Annie didn't care, as long as you were fairly clean and well-behaved. Everyone got great service at The Golden Bowl.

I'd go with my friends whenever I could. When we were finished with our meal, we'd give the waitress our cards and everything was free. Sometimes, I had some money for a tip or a donation. But most of the time I walked off without paying a dime.

Today I found a seat at the counter. Ever since the rock star, Paulo Clemente, and his family showed up in Marberry for summer vacation, the place was packed. All of a sudden, it turned out Annie was related to his friend—Debbie Lambrecht, the famous designer. Then, The Golden Bowl went crazy with tourists and reporters. I heard Amanda James, the famous TV reporter from *Amanda*

James Now, was coming to interview Annie. She'd probably get rich from all the publicity. It couldn't happen to a nicer person.

I didn't see Annie, but Brianna, the manager, waved at me. Made me feel kind of special. When I was done with breakfast, I had a dollar left from my gas money. So I left it for the waitress and went out front to the prayer bowl on the porch. As usual, it was overflowing with prayer slips, and I couldn't help skimming it with my hand. I guess I was hoping to feel for another ring, or something of value. But they were just prayers.

"Here, Lisa, write out a prayer and put it in the bowl."

I turned to see the elderly hostess holding a pen and small piece of paper.

I took them. "Okay. What should I write?"

"Whatever is on your heart, dear."

I wrote, "I'm all alone, and I have no money, and I want to give my baby a good life." I folded it over and threw it in the bowl.

"Now take one." She pointed a freckly, wrinkled hand at the bowl and smiled.

I hoped, as a dishwasher, I wouldn't have to help people at the prayer bowl. Why get so involved with strangers? But I pushed that thought aside, wishing for another diamond. I drove my fist to the bottom of the bowl and felt a paper that was different than the others. I pulled it out. It was expensive beige paper, but nothing of value with it. I read the handwriting: *Though my father and mother forsake me, the Lord will receive me. Psalm 27:10*

I stumbled to a wicker chair and sat staring at the paper. I tried to crumple it, but the paper was heavy, and it kept springing open. My eyes stung.

~ LISA ~

It was after 10:30 a.m. by the time I got myself to Marberry Designs. I tugged my shirt and jacket down over my belly and behind, opened the door, and cringed a little as the bell jangled. The thought of the ring in my pocket helped stifle my nerves.

"Are you Terri?" I interrupted her chipper greeting and walked toward a display case filled with dazzling jewelry.

"Yes, how can I help you today?" She laid her hands on the glass countertop. Fake red nails and probably a dozen sparkling rings grabbed my attention.

I spoke to her diamonds. "Hi. I'm Lisa Quinn. I work at The Golden Bowl, and Annie said you could help me." Even though I hadn't started my job yet, I thought telling her I was employed would help. Not sure why.

"Sure. Are you looking for something special?" She flicked back her dark wavy hair like she was doing a shampoo commercial. Terri the Jeweler seemed stuck-up from what I could tell.

"Yeah. I have a ring, and I need to find out what it's worth." I pulled it out of my pocket, along with some lint. That looked good.

I guess I didn't look like the kind of woman who'd wear a ring like that. Her eyes flashed as she took it from me. They got even bigger when she examined the stone with her magnifying glass.

"Is this your engagement ring?"

I was tempted to lie. But I remembered Annie's face, and she said Terri would help me. I guess honesty is the best policy. "I found it in the prayer bowl when I went to pull out a prayer. Here's the prayer that went with it. The ring was all wrapped up in the prayer paper." I pulled the paper out of my other pocket and handed her the crumpled ball. "Annie said I could keep it. She said you could tell me what it's worth."

She took the ring and checked it every which way she could. Finally, she put it down on a little pillow on the counter.

By now sweat rolled down my back, my heart pounded,

and my mind raced. The firm thousand I wanted gave way to a definite seven hundred fifty dollars, then five hundred. I couldn't get much of a used car for five hundred dollars. Burning started behind my eyeballs. *I need a car.*

Terri looked at me, and her cheek twitched a little. "I can give you forty thousand for this. I can't go any higher."

My knees gave out, and I leaned on the counter. "D—dollars?"

"Forty thousand dollars. That's my best offer."

"Sold," I said.

Terri wrote up the paperwork and handed me a check for forty grand. I couldn't believe my eyes. Shaking, I ran out of Marberry Designs before the woman could change her mind.

I was a little worried Terri's check wouldn't be good. But the lady at the bank next door couldn't have been nicer. She told me Terri was one of their best business customers. Then she helped me set up a new account, and I even got a portable shovel for my car as a free gift. I thought if Peg noticed it in the trunk, I'd tell her I found it in the road. She wouldn't have to know about my finances.

When I left the bank, my new savings account had thirty-nine thousand dollars, and I had one thousand in fifty dollar bills jammed into my bag and my pockets.

I sat in Peg's car, looking around the square, gawking at passersby, trying to think straight. I was in shock. I locked the door. No one was going to break in and steal my money. But Marberry was different than Ripple Lake, or at least my neighborhood in Ripple Lake. People here were better off. I bet a lot of them had a thousand dollars. Maybe even forty thousand.

What should I do? I couldn't buy a new car today. I was too excited and confused. Peg would want to know how I could buy a car. I couldn't tell anyone about this, especially anyone from Ripple Lake—all my friends included. They'd get it from me somehow, and forty thousand would go up in smoke or up their noses.

One thing I knew. I wasn't going to blow this. I was determined to give Rosie a real chance in life.

I remembered I had to get Peg's lunch from The Golden Bowl. I drove down Shore Road and parked in the lot. Off on the horizon sailboats floated on calm seas. *That's the life*. I got out of the car and went around back to sit on a bench overlooking the rocky coast. The warmth of the sun and the sound of the surf made me feel better. In one day, I went from bad problems to good ones. I was no whiz when it came to money, but I'd figure it out. Rosie and me would have that new life.

A breeze whipped up and my jacket flapped open. I remembered the prayer slip in my T-shirt pocket, took it out, and read it again. *Though my father and mother forsake me, the Lord will receive me. Psalm 27:10*

My father and mother—and my ex-husband—all left me. It was true. They did *forsake* me. But it looked like God didn't. I looked up at The Golden Bowl. The lunchtime crowd was in full swing. A little voice told me I could trust Annie Brewster.

CHAPTER 3

~ ANNIE ~

"You mustn't worry Annie, Amanda James is really very nice." My sister's voice was always such a joy, even if I had a hard time believing her. I sat staring into space, my cup of coffee set on the arm of my Adirondack chair. Although it was past lunchtime, I was in no mood for food.

"I can't help worrying, Debbie. We come from such different worlds. You're used to dealing with the likes of Amanda James. Not me. I'll just be glad when this is over." *I think.* For all I knew, this interview could spawn another crazy frenzy. I still hadn't opened the bags of letters in my trunk. Nathan had confiscated them for security purposes.

Debbie's sweet voice penetrated my fretting mind. "Just remember, you're not alone. I love you. Say 'hello' to Dr. Westcott for me. And Pastor Mike and Millie. I have to go now, but I'll call you later. I love you."

I put the phone on the arm of my chair, looked up at a perfect blue sky, and laughed. I wasn't alone. The prayer of Jabez floated through my head and out through my lips. God had a plan. I sure didn't know what it was, but it had to be good. I wondered just what territory would be enlarged in my life.

Then I wondered when Debbie would ever get to know and trust Doc enough to call him something other than Dr. Westcott. I couldn't blame her. It certainly had been a shock learning he was her biological father, and the man she'd called Daddy all her life was not.

Debbie had been born into a life of privilege. Our

biological mother had married a very wealthy man from a prominent family not long after I was born and given up for adoption. Doc had been in love with our birth mother, wanted to marry her, but that hadn't been enough for her. I don't know why.

It occurred to me, I almost never referred to my birth mother by her name. Perhaps, I'd somehow been affected by being given away. I'd known, from a young age, that I was adopted. But that never changed how I felt about my adoptive parents. My true parents. I adored them. And as I grew older, I rarely thought about my biological mother.

Even though Debbie had grown up with every material thing she could want or need, she'd been the one to suffer. It was important to me to help her through her trauma—the loss of *her* mother due to a heart attack five months ago.

I shook my head. Why would it be hard to understand Debbie's reticence with Doc, when I couldn't bring myself to refer to my biological mother by name?

I took a sip of cold coffee. I'd had a wonderful life growing up. It was strange to contemplate so many messed up lives around me. God had surely plucked me from the mess and set me gently into the arms of an extraordinary pastor and his loving wife soon after my birth.

Doc had never even known about me until he was in college in Boston. By the time Grammy informed him of my existence, he was on his way to a career in medicine. He'd become a highly respected cardiac surgeon in New York.

According to Doc, our birth mother had lived in luxury in Beverly Hills, miserable in a marriage she refused to leave. Almost twenty years after I'd been born, Doc returned to Los Angeles and met up with her quite by accident. Apparently the flame had not died. Debbie was the result of a brief affair.

Sadly for Debbie, she'd had a troubled childhood—with overbearing parents who had little regard for each other. As a result, Debbie had suffered from an eating disorder before meeting David. Then it was trouble of a different sort.

The kitchen door slammed and startled me. Nathan bounded down the stairs and across the lawn.

"*I don't think Nathan Rhodes is like everyone else.*" Doc's voice echoed in my head.

Nathan had cleaned up well, and now sported a handsome, dark suit. His salt and pepper hair was short, his face clean-shaven. Those brown eyes mesmerized me. When he looked at me, I felt like he could see something others couldn't. It made me blush—a trait I shared with my sister that made it too easy for others to read our emotions.

"Mrs. Brewster, Amanda James and her producer are in the parlor. Her crew is being directed to their rooms."

As he loomed over me, I knew my face was red. "Okay, I'm coming. God, help me get through this without making a fool of myself." I struggled to my feet, knocking the coffee cup to the ground. "Oh!"

He steadied me, and swept up the mug. "No worries. It was almost empty."

"Thanks." I tottered toward the back porch. "Coffee wasn't the best idea for me today, I guess." I was too embarrassed to meet his eyes.

"You're fine." His voice sounded different.

I looked up, and for a second, I saw a glimmer in his eyes, something like tenderness. Maybe I imagined it. He cleared his throat and the moment passed.

"Billy will be escorting the camera crew this afternoon. They have five locations they want to film. Should be pretty straightforward. You and Amanda James have time to socialize. Joe Harris is running late. He'll join you for dinner tonight." He was back in security director mode.

With all my jitters over Amanda James' impending arrival, why was I dwelling on Nathan?

"Okay, thank you, Mr. Rhodes." I nodded politely, not daring to upset the applecart and call him by his first name, as I did everyone else. *Nathan Rhodes isn't like everyone else.*

~ ANNIE ~

Amanda James was a consummate professional. Tall and slim, she wore a constant smile and perfectly coiffed auburn hair. She stretched out her hand and shook mine firmly. "I've got to tell you, Annie, I've been dying to meet you from the minute the news broke about you and Debbie. You look like twins!"

"Thank you. I appreciate the compliment. I'm about twenty years older than Debbie. And I'm a fan of your show. That first interview you did with Debbie and David . . ." My face felt like a furnace and my voice caught in my throat. I gasped for breath. "Well, it blew me out of the water. I haven't missed one of your programs since."

Her smile remained, but her voice softened. "I imagine it was the only way you could connect with your sister, when she had no idea you even existed."

Undoubtedly, Amanda had quizzed Debbie at some point. "Yes, it certainly was a surprise to both of us."

"I can only imagine the pain you went through. But I can see you're both doing well now. What a remarkable mix of business and charity you've created. I can't wait to experience The Golden Bowl and hear all about your adventures."

Amanda was quick about settling in. By the time I got off the phone with Ashleigh, and walked into the kitchen, I found Amanda chatting with Mom, Dad, and Doc, like they were old friends.

"Now, Dr. Westcott—Craig—I think it's wonderful how you've reunited with your daughters and become so involved in their lives. When did you first meet Annie's adoptive parents?"

Doc sat at the kitchen table, sipping coffee. "It wasn't that long ago. I retired to Maine not quite two years ago and lived only about forty-five minutes away. I didn't want to intrude on Annie's life, but thought I might be able to get to know her by visiting her dad's church. Mike and Millie were very welcoming. We hit it off right away. They invited me to dinner most every Sunday. Annie never stayed for dinner because she was needed at the restaurant. But I did learn about her work and tried to help support some of her programs."

"And you never told them you were Annie's biological father?"

"Annie didn't know. But Mike and Millie knew—though we never really came out and talked about it." Doc nodded at Dad, who smiled in agreement.

Mom turned from the stove, where she'd been checking on dinner. "It's not like we needed to discuss it. There's a physical resemblance—tall, same eyes and hair—and when Doc told us he was a heart surgeon from New York, we knew. What's to discuss? Annie seemed perfectly happy in her life. There wasn't a reason to discuss it then."

"But then Debbie's mother made a deathbed confession. And Annie and Debbie's world completely changed." Amanda interrupted in the way she always did on her show when she was revealing a mystery.

I realized all of America, and probably beyond, would stay tuned to hear the story. I had to sit down. It was only last May when our birth mother died of a heart attack. Shortly after, Debbie came into my life, and I'd focused most of my attention on helping her cope with it all.

Today was the first time I'd thought about it from my perspective. I hoped Amanda wouldn't push. I didn't want to start referring to my birth mother by her name. I wanted to keep a comfortable distance. Like Mom said, "What's to discuss?" I was perfectly happy with the way things were.

Mom placed a bowl of her hearty chicken soup in front of me and handed me a spoon. "You haven't had a bite today. Get this soup in you. Dinner won't be ready for an hour."

Amanda cast a hungry glance at my soup. “Is that homemade?”

“Of course,” she said. “Can I get you a bowl?”

Amanda flashed a big grin. “The coffee and blueberry cake you made, were scrumptious, but it’s not every day that I get to eat homemade chicken soup.”

Mom served it right up. Amanda leaned over her bowl and inhaled the blissful aroma of roasted chicken and hearty garden vegetables. Mom had been making this soup for as long as I could remember. When I was a kid, it never failed to soothe a cold or give comfort on a gloomy day. And it quickly became the most popular soup at my restaurant.

Amanda scooped up a spoonful with surprising gusto. “Mmm . . . that’ll cure what ails you.”

Mom chuckled. “Well, there’s plenty more.”

I could tell Mom was now Amanda’s biggest fan.

~ ANNIE ~

I threw my nightgown on and headed to the medicine cabinet for an aspirin.

“Mrs. Brewster!” Nathan’s voice knocked the pill down my throat.

“Just a minute,” I said, coughing. I sipped some water to help wash it down, then grabbed my robe. I flung it around me and opened my bedroom door. “Yes, Mr. Rhodes?”

“I’m sorry to bother you, Mrs. Brewster, but your *best friend*, Terri Monahan, is here.” He sounded a touch sarcastic. “Her name is on the list, so I allowed her into the house. She said the matter is urgent.”

“She’s a friend. You can send her up.”

By the time I ran a brush through my hair and made myself presentable, there was a quick knock, and Terri let herself in. “He’s not exactly friendly,” she said.

I tried to sound sympathetic, though it was tough at this late hour. “Yeah. I’m pretty sure friendly isn’t in his job description.”

Terri peered around the doorframe, obviously watching him walk down the hall. She peeled herself back again and closed the door behind her. "He *is* handsome—in a rugged sort of way."

I nodded. "Rugged *would* be in his job description." I couldn't help a goofy schoolgirl smile and quickly wiped it away. I didn't want Terri grilling me about Nathan.

"What brings you over, Terri?" *Probably an effort to meet Amanda James.* If there was anyone worth knowing in Maine, Terri and her husband would make it a point to introduce themselves.

She propped her stylish handbag on my dresser and mumbled a string of curses as she rifled through it.

I sat on my bed. Energy and patience was fading fast. Another knock at the door. "Come in."

Nathan reached around the doorframe and handed a ring to Terri. "Be careful with that." He cast a stern glance at each of us and left, the door clicking loudly.

"Thank God!" Terri kissed the diamond. "You really need to get some nicer employees. Or put them through one of your customer service trainings—something."

She sat on the bed beside me and carefully wiped the stone. "Must have landed in the dirt when they were interrogating me in your driveway. I had to show my driver's license. Can you imagine? Just to get in to visit you? Yeah, it must have popped out when I took out my wallet to get the license. They just wouldn't listen to reason." She pried off her too-high, red-leather heels, probably a pair my sister had designed.

"Terri, I need to get some sleep. Is there something you need to tell me?"

"Yes. I just got back from a dinner in Portland with my biggest client. He offered me a hundred thousand for the ring. If he offered me a hundred, I know I can get two. Just what I thought when that chubby girl showed up in my shop. It's unbelievable. Why would someone put that ring in a prayer bowl?"

I rubbed my eyes. "I haven't a clue. What did you give Lisa for the ring?"

Terri was suddenly coy. "A whole lot more money than that girl could ever handle. She probably headed straight to the liquor store."

I took her by the arm and turned to face her. "Lisa deserves a fair price for that ring."

"She got one. Honest." She quickly changed the subject. "So when is Amanda James coming to interview you?"

"She's here. I'm surprised you didn't see her crew out and about filming in Marberry today."

Terri's jaw dropped. "No! How did I miss that? Well, I was in Portland most of the day. You've got to bring them by my store tomorrow. And they have to interview Ted. Coastal Real Estate's served the Maine coast for more than two decades. Ted just opened his eighth office. He's the number one seller in the state—residential and commercial."

I had to stop the sales pitch before my head exploded. "Terri, they're just filming some of the sights—for background for her story. I don't think Amanda intends to do an in-depth study of Marberry."

"Well, change her mind on that. Marberry can use some great promotion. Since Paulo Clemente showed up this summer—and those yummy secret agents—and your sister bought this house, it's made an impact on our economy. People are looking to buy here. Tourists are coming and liking what they see. It's good for everyone."

Terri was on a roll and my head was pounding. "Okay. I'll see what I can do. Now I really need to get to bed. It'll be a long day tomorrow, and I didn't sleep much last night." I stood up and ushered her to the door. "Good night, Terri."

"Okay, but you better call me in the morning to let me know what time you'll be at the store. Marberry Designs is the quintessential—"

"I know! I know." I picked up her shoes and handed them to her. It occurred to me I should see her to the front door. Who knows where she'd end up if I let her wander the halls? I shut my bedroom door behind us and led her downstairs.

Billy stood in the foyer. "I'll see Mrs. Monahan to her car."

"Thank you, Billy. Good night, Terri." I heaved a mental sigh of relief and headed back upstairs. I turned into the hallway and almost ran into my agent, Joe Harris, the man who represented Paulo Clemente and most of the biggest names in entertainment. "Joe!"

"Sorry I'm late, Annie. I need to talk to you."

"Okay." I led him to Debbie's art studio and took a seat in the window, as he steered an upholstered chair to face me.

He dropped into the chair and took out a cigar. Joe knew there was no smoking allowed here, but every time he had a serious conversation, he had a cigar in his hand. I guess it was his little crutch. He inhaled the scent of it. "You're off to a good start. You're Amanda's new best friend."

"Really?" I couldn't imagine why he'd think that.

"Yeah. Just keep doin' what you're doin' and things will be fine. I'll be with you all day tomorrow, so if you have a question or Amanda oversteps her bounds, I'll take care of it."

"Thanks. That's great. I'm pretty nervous."

"No need for nerves, doll. Just remember we're here to tell *your* story. Amanda's gonna want to pry into David and Debbie's life, Cat and Cisco's life—anyone in the family she can find out about. Her producer was telling me she has a cute clip of a bunch of kids telling her Paulo's favorite ice cream flavor. That's what the public wants."

"Oh." I could feel my brow furrow.

"Yeah. It's a draw by the way. Blueberry and chocolate chip. So you'll need to stock up on those at the restaurant." He grinned. “Maybe do a blueberry chip sundae or something.”

“Okay.” While I wondered at the whims of the public, Joe sniffed his cigar.

“If ya wanna be proactive, smart, I’d say you need to think about packaging it up for online sales. That’d be a gold mine. His fans are fanatics.”

“Yes.” The thought of shipping ice cream left me cold. Yet another thing to add to my ever-growing to-do list.

“And speaking of food—now that Cat’s pregnant, word is she’s craving those lemon bars you make. Cisco said you sent a big box back with them, and they’re gone already. So you’ll have to get some more out to them. We’ll let that leak, too. Lemon bars would be a cinch to sell online.”

I wanted to feel flattered, but panicked was more like it. “Joe, I’m not really equipped to sell online and expand my business so quickly.”

“No worries.”

Easy for him to say.

He leaned forward. “I’ve got our makeup artist coming in from New York first thing in the morning. She’s the one who worked on you and Debbie for the shoot you did a couple months ago. We’re going for a professional look, and this woman can pull it off for you. No worries.”

Ugh. “I’m really not one to wear much makeup.”

“Yeah, but you’re gonna need it on camera. Pale skin, pale eyes, pale hair—you’ll look all washed out unless we do something.” He squinted at me. “Amanda’s hair dresser’ll be able to help you, too.”

He’s full of compliments. I never thought my coloring was a problem. And my fine, fly-away hair? It was best pulled up in a clip and left to its own devices.

“Now let me give you a few tips for tomorrow. Have you ever been in front of the camera?”

I sighed. It was going to be a long night.

~ LISA ~

I decided to look for an apartment and a used car in Marberry. That way I'd be close to Rosie, and I wouldn't have to wear out my car driving back and forth to Ripple Lake. The savings on gas would make it easier, too. And most important, I'd get away from my so-called friends in Ripple Lake and have a much better chance of hanging on to my money.

I wouldn't have to tell Peg about my money. I could tell her to chip in what she's paying now in rent and utilities, and I could make up the difference in my salary. We'd have a much better place together than we have separately. We could get most of our meals at The Golden Bowl. That would save us a lot of money right there. We'd probably be healthier, too. Both of us spent a lot on junk food.

Peg's stuff and mine could all fit into one new apartment. Since I'd be working, we wouldn't get in each other's way. She spent most of her time at my place anyway. If she wasn't babysitting Rosie, we were playing cards or something. She got a decent social security check every month. It could work out.

At six in the morning I left Peg and Rosie watching cartoons and pulled out of the trailer park. Soon we'd be out of here for good. I smiled and blasted the radio, singing along with Paulo Clemente's new hit. It was all about being set free. Between Cat Clemente's words and her brother-in-law Paulo's voice, they were totally amazing. It's like they read your mind and wrote it in a song. Rosie and me were gonna be free. I could feel it.

The parking lot was packed with cars and trucks, so I parked on Shore Road. As I hiked to the restaurant, hopes of talking to Annie disappeared. She'd be way too busy today to talk to me. There were license plates from New York, Maine, and everywhere else in between. It was a

Thursday in October, but it looked like a summer weekend.

Climbing the stairs, I saw a cute security guard standing by the prayer bowl. He looked like a surfer dude in a suit. "Are you a Marberry resident, ma'am?"

"Yeah. I work here. I'm Lisa." I pulled out my meal card. "Just came for breakfast."

He opened the door for me, and I tripped on the way in. There was a mob of people and bright lights everywhere. I made my way to the counter and called to the waitress, "What's goin' on?"

Then I could see Amanda James and Annie in the middle of the room in front of me. *Wow*. More guys in suits, keeping people from getting too close. Amanda was interviewing someone. She looked beautiful, just like on television.

I must have been sitting on the edge of my seat staring. All of a sudden, she caught my eye and smiled. Next thing I knew she was coming toward me with a cameraman. "Hi, I'm Amanda. Are you a regular here?" She put her microphone in front of me.

"Yeah. I'm going to be starting here as a dishwasher on Monday." I don't know why I had to blurt out about starting at the lowest job they had. Like it was a big deal. "I love your show." That wasn't much better.

"Thanks. What's your name?"

"Lisa Quinn."

"Nice to meet you, Lisa. Now, did you stop at the prayer bowl on the way in?"

"Um, yeah." It wasn't a real lie. I did stop and talk to the hunky guard.

She nodded. "Interesting. How important is it to you to have that bowl there? Does it make you think more about praying?"

"Um, yeah. I don't think I ever thought much about praying before."

"Interesting. Now, have you had those prayers answered?"

I sure wasn't going to tell her about the ring, and I didn't want to embarrass Annie and say the prayer bowl didn't work. "Yeah, some."

"Care to share any of those prayers?"

She shoved the mike back in my face. "Um, it's kind of personal."

Amanda gave me a sympathetic smile. Before I knew it, Terri the Jeweler barged in and draped herself over me, resting her hands on my shoulder.

"I'll vouch for Lisa, Amanda. She's had prayers answered, and I think there'll be more to come." I could see her wink right at the camera. Terri was a real self-promoter.

Amanda smiled. "Can you share a prayer with us, Lisa?"

"Well, a big one of mine is needing a house to live in so I can raise my baby girl in a nice place."

I tried to focus on Amanda's face, but Terri started motioning to a gray-haired guy in a suit and tie. He was huddled with us in a flash, beaming at the camera.

Terri spoke in a loud voice. "This is my husband, Ted Monahan, President and CEO of Coastal Real Estate. He has eight offices along the Maine coast, and he's the top seller in residential and commercial real estate."

Amanda shook his hand. "Great to meet you, Ted. Congratulations on all your wonderful success in Maine real estate. I think you'll be even busier since The Golden Bowl is bringing so much attention to Marberry."

Ted was soaking it all up. Terri couldn't have smiled any bigger. I tried to stretch my jacket over my belly. That'd look good on TV. I wondered how fat I'd look on the show.

Amanda reached for my hand. "I think we have an answered prayer in the making here, Lisa. It sounds like Ted is just the right person to help you find your dream house."

My mouth fell open. Maybe Amanda was doing a

giveaway show—like some of my favorite talk shows at Christmastime. Ted's jaw fell open, too.

Amanda had a glint in her eye. "Ted, how about showing Lisa and my audience around Marberry? I think you just might have the answer to Lisa's prayer here." She turned back to me. "What's your baby girl's name, Lisa?"

I smiled right into her microphone. "Rosie! I call her Rosie Q."

She chuckled. "I have a feeling you and Rosie will have a new home, soon. Another prayer answered, Lisa."

CHAPTER 4

~ ANNIE ~

By the time we returned home from The Golden Bowl, I was exhausted. The entire town had turned out today, and it felt like Amanda had spoken to everyone. Tourists jammed the streets, and there was chaos everywhere I turned. Amanda seemed to thrive on it. Not me. My stomach was in knots thinking about my interview to come.

While her crew prepared in the parlor, I headed outside to my Adirondack chair for a breath of air. Thankfully, we'd been blessed with a sunny, warm day. I wanted to enjoy a few moments of it. Cigar smoke hit me in the face as I came through the kitchen door.

Joe Harris grinned at me. "Nice going. Things are swimming along. Good job."

I stepped down off the porch and waved the smoke away. "It's not over yet. She's a lovely woman, but I'm still terrified of sitting in front of the camera with her one on one."

"No worries, Annie."

I bet he tells all his clients that. "Okay." I left Joe to his smoke and ambled down the back lawn, taking deep, relaxing breaths of fresh air. The Prayer of Jabez came to mind, and I remembered I wasn't alone in this.

"Annie!" Joe's gruff voice summoned me back to the house.

I thought the lights in my parlor would blind me. I blinked at Amanda.

"How does it feel to have the world's biggest power couple—Cisco and Cat Clemente—backing your business, Annie?"

Amanda didn't waste any time on chitchat. It occurred to me that petite Cat was the true "power" of the power couple, but everyone would assume it was her husband Cisco, the financial genius and self-made billionaire. I realized I was taking too long to answer a simple question.

I took a breath. "I couldn't be more grateful to have met Cat and Cisco through my sister, Debbie. Cat saw the need for The Golden Bowl—the importance of showing people the power of prayer—and our programs to help people in need. Of course, Cisco is a brilliant businessman. His advice and financial backing through his brother, Paulo Clemente's, foundation have been invaluable. Cat, Cisco, and Paulo are so incredibly generous. It makes my heart swell every time I think of them. And I think of them every day." My eyes began to water, but I didn't dare touch my shaky hand to my face.

"Why The Golden Bowl, Annie? It's obviously your life's passion. Is it the spiritual thing or is it a clever gimmick to get people to your restaurant?"

I blinked against stinging tears, hoping they wouldn't leak and ruin the makeup they'd put on me. My sister, Debbie, was well known for her quick tears. That was one trait I did not want to share. I swept a finger under my eye as I tried to keep my emotions in check. I took another deep breath.

This was the big moment. The reason why I was doing this, and the reason why The Golden Bowl existed. "There's a very real spiritual hunger in the world today. Personally, I believe we have a God-sized hole in our hearts. Only God can fill it. We're made that way. We need God. Scripture says to seek God with all your heart, and you'll find Him. Most people believe in God and pray. Prayer is a great way to seek and find God. I just want people to remember that. So, The Golden Bowl is not a gimmick. It's inspired by *Revelation 5:8*. '*They were holding golden bowls full of incense, which are the prayers of the saints.*'"

Amanda nodded. "Cat Clemente is known to be a great person of prayer, as well as the writer of astounding and inspiring lyrics. She told me, 'Annie Brewster puts prayer at the center of her life and business.' Is that true?"

"My dad is a pastor. I grew up in his church, and I've seen the power of prayer. Prayer is a way of life for me. I want people to know prayer can change your life. Many people don't know that."

"Can you tell us some specifics? How prayer has changed your life, Annie?"

"When I was thirteen or fourteen I told my grandmother that I wanted to become a professional chef because I loved cooking. She sat with me and painted a big old Maine farmhouse right on the beach. She added a large gold bowl on the front porch. I asked her why, and she said the restaurant is called The Golden Bowl. Years later when I found that huge house on the water in Marberry, I knew that's where I belonged. It was an answer to a painted prayer that day with my grandmother."

Amanda's eyes widened. "That's an amazing story. Is your grandmother the one you share with Debbie?"

"Yes, she was my biological mother's mother." I nodded, wondering if that made sense. "I was fortunate to meet Grammy as a child. She'd come to visit me as often as she could. She told me about Debbie. Of course, it became apparent that Debbie inherited her incredible artistic talent from Grammy."

Amanda tilted her head. "And what did you inherit from Grammy?"

"Hmm. Well, Grammy started her own business making custom draperies. So maybe I inherited her entrepreneurial spirit." I remembered to smile at Amanda.

"You've created a magnificent business here, Annie. The Golden Bowl is not just a restaurant, but much more.

You have meal programs for low-income people. You employ local people, many who've had some troubles in their lives. And today, when I spoke with your patrons, I could see the prayer bowl is a rallying point for the community. You've built a wonderful camaraderie, and I have a feeling that's going to spread from Marberry across the country. And beyond, now that Cat is involved."

I swallowed the emotion. "The response has been overwhelming, especially since The Golden Bowl has been in the news. People are sending prayers through the mail, merchants are putting small gold bowls in their places of business to raise funds for our programs, vendors are calling and asking how they can help. It's been amazing."

Amanda leaned forward in her chair. "I understand you had most of the bones of the business—most of the programs—in place before you met Cisco Clemente. He helped you with the structure of the business?"

"Yes, Cisco has been instrumental in creating and administering his brother's foundation, and so many charities and businesses that make giving back a priority, including my sister's design business. They do incredible work all around the globe. Of course, Cat has a big part in that, too. They really complement each other beautifully in their talents and passion for helping people. So when I had the honor of meeting them, and Cat asked me if they could help, I can't tell you how thrilled I was."

"You certainly have a common philosophy." Amanda smiled.

"Yes."

As Amanda led me down a garden path of personal questions, involving Cat and her pregnancy, my relationship with my "new" sister, Debbie, and what my "secret agent" brother-in-law, David, was up to these days, Joe gave us the high sign.

Relieved to have the break, I went to the kitchen for a glass of water and some privacy.

~ LISA ~

I hiked my shirt and jacket down over my rear end and tried to look interested. The last thing I expected when I woke up this morning was having a camera crew following me around Marberry.

Ted stood in the middle of his office, rattling on about his real estate business, what a great businessman and sales person he was, and how great his "team" was. Amanda's producer had to shut him up a few times.

Finally, we took off on a tour of Marberry. We drove in a real expensive-looking truck-like car, with me in the front passenger seat. The producer and cameraman sat in the back. Ted had to point out every last building along the way, and we ended up in front of Annie's driveway. The producer didn't look happy, and the guards sure weren't.

Ted turned to the producer with a big smile. "You know, Debbie Lambrecht purchased the historic Miller mansion for her sister, Annie. I handled the sale for them."

She gave him one of those fake smiles you use when you're not even listening. My favorite guard asked the producer what was going on. She just said, "Let's move along, Ted."

As we crawled along the road, I knew we were in a part of town I could never afford to live in. I bet *Annie* was surprised she got to live here. As long as I could remember, she'd lived in the little apartment on the third floor of The Golden Bowl. That wasn't so bad either. It had great views, and you couldn't get any closer to work.

By the time Ted finished his history lesson on the Millers and their mansion, we were back in the center of town. "I have a great two bedroom condo to show you. It's minutes from the beach and totally renovated. Move in condition!" He glanced at me for the first time. "It's in the Marberry school district, too. Perfect for . . . uh . . . Rosie."

"Now you're talking, Ted." The producer smiled.

A couple of minutes later we pulled into a driveway with a big stone wall on either side. An artistic sign read: Sandpiper Village. Even though it was October, the lawn was green, most of the leaves'd been raked, and some yellow and purple flowers sprouted up from the window boxes. When he stopped the car, my stomach got butterflies. I could *so* see me and Rosie living here. Everything looked so neat, like people really took care of this place.

Is this real? I didn't trust Ted as far as I could throw him. But maybe Amanda James worked a miracle. I kept dwelling on my favorite talk show, when the whole audience got a car for free. Could Amanda really get me a house?

Ted had a key, and he let us go inside. My heart pounded, I was so excited. He said it had an open floor plan. The kitchen had new appliances and beautiful granite countertops. Everything was so clean. Wood floors and even a fireplace and a little balcony where you could sit out in the sun. There were two good-sized bedrooms. Lots of light coming in. I started to cry. What if it was just a joke? Maybe Amanda wasn't giving me anything. I wanted this place so bad.

The cameraman came at me with the camera. I was probably a mess from crying. I rubbed my sleeve over my face and pulled my jacket down. "It's perfect," I said.

The producer smiled. "What else do you have for us, Ted?"

~ ANNIE ~

It was well into the Friday breakfast rush by the time I returned to The Golden Bowl to check on things. I intercepted Ashleigh as she ran from the kitchen on her way to a private dining room upstairs. Her hair splayed out of her ponytail in a mess around her head. *Another non-stop day*. "Ash?"

"We're getting hammered—we've got all hands on deck. Bree's coming in early. Don't worry. Okay? We've got it under control." She turned on her heel to head up the stairs, then turned back. "Oh! Peter Fellowes scheduled a gifting table party in the Miller Room. He wants you there—can't remember which night. It's in the book."

An elderly guest accidently jostled Ashleigh, distracting her.

I thanked the back of her head, then went to my tiny office under the staircase and flung the door closed.

"Mrs. Brewster—"

I let out a gasp as I swung around and slammed against the door. "Oh!"

"So sorry to startle you, Mrs. Brewster." He stood at my old file cabinet, a leather binder in his hand.

I swallowed the acid rising in my throat. A tall, elegantly dressed man with dark hair, who looked like he'd stepped out of a James Bond movie stood in my office. My teeny, tiny, messy office under the stairs! His crisp English accent, and that fancy leather binder, predicted trouble.

He stepped toward me and held his hand out, as though he might help. "I'm Buckminster Wynn."

I must have made a face. He took back his hand.

He tried again. "Buckminster Wynn of Brooke, Lewis & Wynn."

"Oh." I realized I now sounded rude. *Am I supposed to know him*? "Nice to meet you."

He must have thought I was daft.

He cleared his throat to start again. "Brooke, Lewis & Wynn is the premiere consulting firm to the restaurant and food service industry around the globe. I've spoken to Cisco Clemente—at length."

Since I didn't respond to this impressive information immediately, he carried on. "I assured Mr. Clemente that I can get your books in order and deal with these out of control salary and food cost issues—all the issues that are limiting your business growth. Mr. Clemente will be most pleased, I'm sure."

I thought my head would pop off. "*Mr. Clemente* does not own this business. *I* do. *I'm* the one you need to please, Mr. . . . Bucky—" *No, that's wrong*. "Buck—er—"

"Buckminster Wynn. Please call me Buck."

No doubt my face ignited to a brilliant red. "Mr. Wynn. I'm sorry. I don't have an appointment with you. If I did, I would have it written in my book. Under the circumstances, I don't think it's a good idea for you to be in my office. I'll call Cisco later, and if you leave me your card, I can contact you to schedule a more convenient appointment."

He reached into his suit jacket pocket and took out a thin gold case. I was sure I saw a diamond embedded in the cover. "Yes, Mrs. Brewster, I met with Cisco and Cat Clemente this past Tuesday at the airport in Bangor. We discussed your business over your delicious blueberry scones and lemon bars . . . although Cat took most of the lemon bars. For such a tiny thing she certainly had more than her share. I hear she's eating for two now, though."

I could only raise my eyebrows in response. Apparently he was more than a business associate of the Clementes.

He took a card from the case, stepped forward, and handed it to me. "Anyway, before they left for Austria, we had a plan. I knew you'd be busy with Amanda James—and congratulations on your feature on one of the world's top television shows—very impressive, Mrs. Brewster." He smiled his approval.

"Thank you, Mr. Wynn."

"Well, in the past few days I've taken some time to investigate Marberry and the surrounding area—get to know the inhabitants and the business environment here, you know. And since your interview is over, I thought you'd be ready to tackle the real work ahead."

In truth I was ready to tackle Buckminster Wynn, and not in a good way.

~ ANNIE ~

Despite the stiff sea breeze, I settled into my Adirondack chair with a steaming cup of coffee. My head spun with all the craziness of the past few days, and the anticipation of what was yet to come. Maybe the wind would blow away the cobwebs in my brain.

Now I had to contend with Buckminster Wynn of Brooke, Lewis & Wynn, with offices in New York and London. I took the most elegant business card I'd ever seen from under my phone on the arm of my chair. The silver-white paper felt like heavy silk. My muscles tensed in distress as I stared at the card. *Offices in New York and London*. My stomach gurgled in fear.

He looked like an expensive consultant all right. That suit must have cost a fortune. His starched white shirt couldn't have been any brighter. Gold cufflinks matched the card case he carried. It had to have been a Rolex watch on his wrist. Buckminster Wynn was tall, handsome, and impeccably groomed from his full head of sleek, dark hair to his polished shoes. "Very impressive," as he'd said to me in that crisp accent.

Then he drove off in a sports car that I couldn't name, but it turned heads and screamed money.

Yes, Buckminster Wynn was suave, charming . . . and dangerous.

My phone buzzed. *Why did I bring that thing out here*?

It was Cat. *Thank you, God*! "Hi! How are you?"

"Other than an addiction to your lemon bars, I'm fine. Auntie said she'd bake some for me if you send along your recipe. We promise it will be kept top secret. At least it would take some pressure off you posting them."

I laughed. It felt good. "Oh Cat, I miss you all so much!"

"We miss you terribly. Are you coming for Christmas? Salzburg is lovely at Christmas."

My heart sank. “I wish I could, but I doubt I’ll be able to get away.”

“Well, you think about it.”

“I will. But listen, I have to ask you about this consultant.”

“They call him Almighty Buck. But don’t worry, Annie. You’ll be able to help him.”

I’ll be able to help *him*? Cat must have eaten one too many lemon bars.

She kept going. “He met Cisco through the University Club. Very bright man. They played football together. You call it soccer. Cisco thinks he can solidify all your business systems and make things smoother. He’ll set up software that can keep things more organized for you. And an e-commerce website. Cisco says all this will allow for growth of your business and charitable giving without compounding stress and strain. I know this has been a difficult time for you.”

Most of my hair had loosed itself from my hairclip and now whipped around my head. I pried strands out of my eyes. “Yes. It has. I miss all of you so much. I really appreciate all the help with my business, but it’s daunting. It’s been crazy since the first rumors circulated that Paulo was coming here for vacation. I’m afraid to think what will happen when Amanda’s show airs Sunday night. She’s in such a rush to get it on the air. I wish they’d wait at least a week. Joe Harris even said we’d need to have blueberry and chocolate chip ice cream on hand, because someone said it’s Paulo’s favorite. And the thought of shipping that across the country?”

“Please don’t worry, Annie. Just do what you do best. Buck will help make things easier. It may take a bit of time, but that’s okay. You’ll get where you want to go. Think how many people you’ve already helped. Take a deep breath and another step forward. God is at work here—in so many wonderful ways.”

When I finished my conversation with Cat, I found my coffee had gone cold. A frigid wind gusted off the water. I pulled my jacket tighter around me and huddled in the chair, staring out into a darkening horizon. The shorter autumn days could be tough to cope with. I hadn't paid attention until now. I thought about the Prayer of Jabez and wondered how much angst it would take to "enlarge my territory." I'd never had so much attention, so many offers of help, and so much "family." So why did I feel so alone, so anxious?

Mom was at work on dinner for Amanda and the crew, Nathan and his crew, and our family, including my birth father. I couldn't be alone if I tried.

"Annie?"

I jumped out of my reverie. Amanda stood over me, wrapped in a long hooded wool coat and boots. She dropped a blanket onto my lap. "Mind if I join you?" She lowered herself into the chair beside me.

"Sure." I wasted no time in covering myself. "This blanket is perfect. Thank you. I love sitting by the ocean—even in the dead of winter. I can't resist the lure of the sea and sky. I have a heavy down coat that covers me to my ankles—and this heavy blanket. Woolen scarf and hat. The weather's been so unseasonably warm I haven't dragged them all out yet. But this is a great place to sit and think."

"What are you thinking about now?"

I had to laugh. "Always the reporter."

She chuckled. "Not really. But always curious. I think we've become friends over the past couple of days. At least, I'd like to call you my friend. I hope you know there are many conversations I've had with your sister that I've never shared—nor will I ever share—with the public."

"I appreciate that. I feel like we could be friends, too."

"Good. And Doc, too. He's a great guy . . . I heard he's divorced."

I smiled. Amanda didn't miss much. "Divorced long ago, from what I understand. And no kids from the marriage."

She let out a half a giggle. "That's probably because

he married the wrong person. From the way he talks, I can tell he still regrets losing your birth mother."

I wouldn't let myself go there now. It was enough to cope with moving forward with my new family members, never mind playing the "what if" game. For whatever reason, my biological mother decided to give me up and live her life with another man. She was gone now. There'd be no more explanations. The best thing to come out of all this was connecting with Debbie. And I thanked God that we were now in each other's lives. That was good enough for me.

I think my silence spurred a change of subject. Amanda cleared her throat. "I'll tell you what's on my mind. Your dishwasher, Lisa. My producer arranged for her prayer to be answered. Our sponsor, the largest home improvement retailer in the country, is donating a home to Lisa and her daughter."

I swung around in my seat, and the coffee mug dropped to the ground. "You're kidding! How?"

"They know my show this Sunday will draw a massive audience. They want some of the glory, and they'll get it. They can well afford it."

My eyes filled. "Oh, thank you, Amanda. That kid is finally catching a break. Thank you!"

"Lisa told my producer she was looking for a place to rent, and her neighbor from the trailer park will move in with her to share expenses and babysit little Rosie. That's her expectation. She said she's not going to tell the woman until she finds a place for them to live. Needless to say, we haven't breathed a word of this to Lisa. It'll be a big surprise. We asked her to join us for the farewell breakfast tomorrow at The Golden Bowl. She's going to bring little Rosie and her neighbor, Peg. We'll tell her then."

"Oh, that sounds wonderful! Thank you so very much."

"From what Debbie told me, it's not the first celebrity answer to a prayer at The Golden Bowl. But I don't think it matters where the answer comes from, as long as it comes."

I was speechless.

Amanda stared out to sea. "Cat once told me, 'God uses everything and everyone for his purposes. And God is good.' That stuck with me. I'm not a religious person, really, but that stuck with me. I've got to say it sounds crazy that everything can be worked out for good in this mad world. But that's what Cat believes."

"You can find that in scripture—in Romans," I said. "Some days it *is* hard to believe, but it's the truth." *Yeah, some days it is hard to believe.* Buckminster Wynn's face appeared in my mind's eye. Fear crept through me. If he was worth his salt, it wouldn't be long before he'd discover the mess I'd made of my business finances. What would Cisco say then?

Spiraling concerns of Cisco discovering my awful secret halted as Amanda rose from her chair. "My cheeks are frozen. Let's go inside."

Stepping into the kitchen, we inhaled the enticing smells of a roast turkey dinner. Dad and Doc assembled appetizers on the "good" china serving dishes, while Mom attended the pots and pans on the stove.

As I stashed my jacket and blanket in the closet, Amanda sidled up to Doc. "I could use a warm hug."

Doc turned red. "Oh?" He drew her to his side. They'd become fast friends.

I couldn't help laughing at everyone's confused faces—all but Amanda's. I imagine she'd done this a few times before. She winked at me as she took a sip from Doc's wine glass. Doc was maybe twenty years older than she was, but I suppose that was nothing in the world of show business. And he was fit and handsome for his age.

Nathan pushed through the swinging door, wearing the same sarcastic look my brother-in-law David often had. "Ted and Terri Monahan are pulling up the drive."

Amanda stepped out of Doc's loose grip and flung off her coat, tossing it in Nathan's direction. He caught it.

She smiled devilishly and took him by the arm. "This is going to be fun. Let's do show them in."

Though Nathan did not seem to find the humor in it, he allowed her to tug him into the foyer.

~ ANNIE ~

Mom's turkey dinner was scrumptious as always. We gobbled up creamy mashed potatoes with gravy, an array of roasted vegetables, a refreshing mixed green salad tossed with dried cranberries and almonds in a cranberry vinaigrette, and Mom's famous dressing along with the perfectly roasted turkey. Amanda and Doc kept us entertained with stories of life in the big city—one always outdoing the other. Terri tried to intervene with her New York story, but it fell flat. So most of us enjoyed the meal in relative silence. That was fine with me. I had too much on my mind to worry about entertaining everyone.

With dessert came a change of topic. Amanda served a piece of blueberry pie a la mode and slid the plate in Ted's direction. "Ted, I can't wait to show you the house Lisa will be moving to. It's the one on Shore Road—maybe a quarter mile from The Golden Bowl. Everything is completely renovated and new from the roof right down to the finished basement."

Ted processed this mid-gulp and coughed on his coffee. Surprisingly, he didn't choke, and he quickly put a smile on his lips. His eyes told a different story.

"Amanda, I never showed them that house. Lisa told the producer she loved that first condo, so we saw four condos. Lisa would be happy with any one of them. I didn't think you wanted to spend that kind of money. We'll have to film another segment."

Amanda smiled. "No need, Ted. You did a nice job

showing them around Marberry and getting a sense of what Lisa liked. We're going to spring the surprise tomorrow morning. I know she'll be ecstatic."

Stunned silent, Ted kept a fake smile plastered on his face.

Terri slammed her glass on the table. "That's not fair, Amanda. Ted worked hard on that tour for you. The least you could do is pick one of the condos, or film him showing Lisa the house."

Ted grabbed his wife by the arm to rein her in before Terri could say something they'd both regret. We both knew sometimes Terri was too ambitious for her own good.

"Terri, Ted, you've both been accommodating to my crew and me. I have every intention of airing Ted's segment. No doubt you'll get some good business from the publicity. You're being featured on the number one news magazine show in the country. You can't buy that kind of PR. But the owner of the house made a deal directly with our sponsor, with my approval. I want it to be a surprise for Lisa, and I'm sure it will be. Tomorrow we'll have our sponsor's agent take her through the house, and our cameras will be there."

CHAPTER 5

~ LISA ~

I was awake at the crack of dawn, wondering if Amanda James would really give me one of those condos. Instead of staring at the ceiling, I got up and dug around my closet for my best pants and a top that still fit. I went through a few tries before I found the right one. Rosie was sound asleep in my bed. There was a knock at the door, and I let Peg in.

"Cold out this mornin'. Make sure you wear a coat." There was a stench of smoke as she threw her coat on my chair. "Got some coffee?"

"No. I wanna get going. The Golden Bowl is gonna be packed, and we need to get good seats.

"Okay, we need to stop for coffee. Need my caffeine." She sat at the kitchen table. "Don't worry, we'll make it. Rosie's car seat is in the jalopy. We can leave right now if you're ready."

By the time we got to The Golden Bowl, the lot was full, and there was a line out the door, around the prayer bowl, and down the stairs. I almost cried. We might not even get in. I managed to park the car at the very end of the lot, not even sure it was a real parking spot. My heart sank when I saw the guard coming toward us. I rolled down the window and saw the same guy I spoke to the other day. Maybe he'd be nice. "Hi, I'm Lisa, remember?"

"Hi Lisa, we have a space reserved for you by the door. I'll direct you."

Huh? I didn't understand why, but I followed him, and we parked right by the porch. Then he helped us out of the car and led us past the crowd into the restaurant.

"Here's your table," he said. It was right by a beautiful stone hearth with a crackling fire. The best seats in the house. He took Rosie from me and lifted her into a highchair.

"Thanks—" I remembered I didn't know his name.

"Billy," he said, and his eyes met mine.

I pulled my jacket around me. "Thanks Billy, this is a great table."

He grinned at me. "Have a good breakfast." Then he walked off.

I dropped into the chair and craned my neck to watch him head out the door. Peg threw her coat on her chair and smiled. "Looks like Lisa's got a little crush." Before I could say anything, she grabbed the cigarettes out of her bag and handed it to me. "Watch my purse, I'll be back in a minute."

By now, pretty much every other table was packed. Ashleigh came by with a pot of coffee. "I'll leave this here for you. Is anyone in your party a tea-drinker? Or decaf coffee?"

"No, regular coffee is great," I said.

"How about some apple juice for Rosie?"

"Awesome. Thanks!"

Ashleigh went for the juice, and I could see Peg heading back with a couple that was probably as old as her. They were really well dressed—him in a gray suit and tie and her in a navy pantsuit with a pretty print scarf. As they took their seats at our table, I couldn't help notice the nice jewelry she wore—like something from Terri Monahan's shop. She smiled and shook my hand, and I forgot her name as soon as she told me.

Peg poured us all some coffee. "Jane and Mack own a furniture store in Portland. They're big fans of Amanda James, too."

Before I could make some comment, Rosie started fussing, and I remembered I didn't get her breakfast. I took a baggie of cereal out of my bag and dumped some on the tray. She went right to work on that. She really was a good baby.

Peg found Rosie's favorite teddy bear and handed it to me. "Oh look! There's Annie. Doesn't she look stunnin' in that outfit? I heard her sister gave her a whole new wardrobe. What a smile on her. I always loved her smile, but today she's more beautiful than ever."

Annie, Amanda James, and Ted and Terri Monahan headed toward us, and my stomach got butterflies. I couldn't stop thinking about that condo the past two days. I tried to smile at them.

Amanda took the seat beside me, after introducing herself and shaking hands with Peg. "This has been such a fun trip—meeting Annie and all the people of Marberry. Lisa, I have to tell you, little Rosie is such a cutie. I love her wispy curls."

I laughed. "I don't know where she gets those."

Annie stepped over to the fireplace and took the microphone Amanda's producer gave her. "Thank you all for being here this morning to share breakfast with Amanda before she heads back to California. It's been a whirlwind few days, but even in this short time, Amanda has become a great friend of our community. I'll let her give you some exciting news. Please give a warm welcome to Amanda James."

Amanda took the mike and hugged Annie. I don't think Annie was expecting that. She was red in the face when she sat down at our table.

Amanda had a way of grabbing your attention with her knockout smile and beautiful reddish brown hair that was always in place. Peg was sure she'd had it colored, but whatever she did, she looked picture-perfect for the camera. I guess show business came natural to her.

"Thank you, Annie—Millie, Mike, and Doc—for your

hospitality this week. It's been a pleasure getting to know you. And a big thank you to the people of Marberry and the staff of The Golden Bowl for making me feel so welcome. This is a beautiful town, but more importantly, it's full of beautiful people.

"As you know, Annie Brewster has given tirelessly of her time, talent, energy, and money to causes she believes in. And what inspires her, she says, is the power of prayer. Today, inspired by Annie, and all of you wonderful people, I want to give something to the people of Marberry. So I'm starting a foundation that will award a full scholarship to a deserving Marberry resident who has been accepted to the college of their choice. There are no age restrictions. One person will be chosen each year, based on merit, need, and a written essay. The decision will be made by a panel of five college administrators I've chosen and announced by June first each year. If you want to apply, you'll find all the information through the high school guidance counselor's office, as well as at the library and town hall."

The coffee cup shook in my hand as the room burst into applause. Then everyone stood up to clap. I could hardly lift myself out of the chair. I had to, though. I didn't want to look like I wasn't thrilled about this scholarship thing.

Tears started down my face. I thought for sure Amanda was giving away a condo. I thought for sure I was going to get out of Ripple Lake. Rosie and me would have a new life. I couldn't stop crying, but I guess people would think I'd be happy to have a chance at a scholarship. I wiped the napkin across my face as Amanda sat beside me.

Terri Monahan's voice came across the table. "This is so exciting, Amanda! Our niece is graduating this coming June. She's applying to schools now. She wants to study gemology. I'm so flattered. I'm the one who got her interested in the field. She works part time at my shop—full time in the summer. She's smart as a whip. We'll get the application in ASAP."

Amanda raised her coffee cup. "Terrific!" She took a little sip. "Let's order breakfast. I'm starved."

I checked my bag to make sure I had my free food card.

While Terrific Terri and Ted bragged about their businesses, and anything else they could think of, I stuffed down blueberry pancakes, eggs, and turkey sausages. Rosie had some oatmeal along with her dry cereal and apple juice. She was content to check out everybody around us and play with her stuffed toy. Peg was really good at keeping her from acting up if she got bored. There was always something else to pull out of the diaper bag.

I washed down my food with another cup of coffee and stifled a belch. Now that I couldn't jam in another bite, I wondered how I could leave without looking bad. Rosie was being an angel. Peg was talking furniture with the woman from Portland, her plate still half full. I wondered how Peg could survive on so little food. All she really needed was cigarettes and coffee. My ex-husband was the same way.

I just wanted to go home and have a good cry. Then I'd need to figure out how to make my forty-thousand dollar bank account get me and Rosie the life I wanted for her.

Amanda turned to me. "It's time to walk off some of these calories. Join me, Lisa." She motioned to Peg and got up. I tried to smile.

I hauled myself up. "I don't think the stroller is in the trunk."

Annie smiled at us. "No problem, we've got one here. Let's go."

I picked up Rosie, and we followed Annie and Amanda to the porch. Billy was at the bottom of the stairs with the coolest stroller I ever saw. I carried Rosie downstairs and put her in. "Thanks, Billy."

When I looked up, I saw everyone pouring out of the

restaurant. Amanda, Annie, and Peg walked alongside me and Billy, and the crowd followed us through the parking lot and down Shore Road. It was pretty weird.

"It's a great day for a walk." Amanda stretched her arms up to the sky. "The sun is shining. It's warming up. It's a great day to live by the ocean, isn't it, Lisa?"

"Yeah." This was really weird.

We rounded a little bend in the road, and I saw the sign. *Welcome Home Lisa and Rosie*! There were people cheering and clapping. *What's that sign*? I felt confused and a little strange as I turned to the noisy crowd. My head started spinning. Things went fuzzy. Before I knew it, I went down.

I woke up on somebody's front lawn looking up at Billy. He had nice blue eyes, and he was smiling at me.

Amanda's face came into view. "Are you okay, Lisa?"

The spell broke in a rush of embarrassment. I tried to get up. Billy took me by the shoulders. "Take a minute to recover, Lisa. You fainted. Rest a few."

"Too much excitement," Terri scolded.

There was a mob hanging over me. I thought the blueberry pancakes would come up any second. "I'm okay." I tried to roll myself to get up, but Billy had me pinned.

"Rosie?"

"She's right here with your friend. Still in the stroller. She's fine." Billy helped me sit up. "Just take a minute here."

Peg pushed her bony body from behind Amanda and Terri. Her raspy smoker's voice was loud. "You're okay, Lisa. Rosie's fine here in Annie's arms. You won a house! Get up, and let's go see it, baby! You won a house!"

I remembered the sign. "A house?" I pushed to my feet, and Billy steadied me. "I won?"

Amanda hugged me. "I think your prayer has been answered, Lisa."

"I got the condo?"

I noticed the cameraman filming us. She turned me toward the house, and I read the sign again.

"It's a four bedroom, three bath house overlooking the water. It's all yours. And Portland Interiors is furnishing it for you. I can't wait for you to see Rosie's room," Amanda said.

And then the truth hit me. I looked up at the big blue sky, and I knew. This was the beginning of something good. First the job. Then the ring. And now this house. But it wasn't just all these things. It was these people, too. People could be good. I glanced at their smiling faces. *Thank you, God.* I'd put that in the golden bowl.

"Thank you for answering my prayer." I grabbed Rosie right out of Annie's arms and hugged her close. "It's true, Rosie Q." I whispered into her little ear. "I'm gonna give you a good life, baby. I promise."

I turned to look at the house again. It was the most perfect place I'd ever seen. I could hardly see it though, I was crying so hard.

~ ANNIE ~

By midafternoon on Saturday, I was sitting undisturbed in my Adirondack chair. Reviewing the events of the past days, my mind was a blur. Amanda had stirred up all of Marberry, including The Golden Bowl, then had flown off to the next stop in her glamorous life. My phone continued to ring incessantly. I had to turn it off or go insane.

Mom, Dad, and Doc knew to leave me alone so I could think and recoup. Only a part of me was excited about the deluge of publicity The Golden Bowl had and would receive. I had a growing fear things would soon spin out of control. It wouldn't be long before my family would know just what an inept businessperson I was.

How could I have accepted help from one of the most astute and intelligent businessmen on the planet? It seemed like a good idea at the time. Cisco and Cat had made it so easy to say yes—a board of directors for The Golden Bowl. Cisco, Cat, Dad, Doc, and Debbie all meant the world to me. But it was probably a dumb idea to have them on the board of a company with me at the helm. How long would it take before Buckminster Wynn would report some devastating news? That is assuming he could locate any usable records.

How could The Golden Bowl fit into this grand business model Cisco had proclaimed? I was a chef and nutritionist with a soft heart and good intentions. I was incapable of doing my own taxes—or much of anything else that involved finances.

The pain of that thought brought me out of the chair and down the stairs to the beach. I picked my way around the rocks to the packed sand of low tide. Gusting winds pushed me along. Anxiety rose. *I'm no businesswoman.*

I looked up at the blue sky and fluffy clouds and remembered the linen paper I'd pulled out of the prayer bowl today. I knew it had to be another from Cat. I unzipped my hoodie and carefully pulled it out of my shirt pocket.

I'm thanking you, God, out in the streets, singing your praises in town and country. The deeper your love, the higher it goes; every cloud's a flag to your faithfulness. Soar high in the skies, O God! Cover the whole earth with your glory! And for the sake of the one you love so much, reach down and help me—answer me!

from Psalm 108, The Message

How did Cat do this? Laughter bubbled up from deep inside, and I let it go into the wind. Up to the puffy clouds declaring God's faithfulness. I couldn't stop laughing.

I had no idea what the answer would be. But there would be one. Some day.

I must have trudged a mile on the sand, the wind alternately encouraging and discouraging me, when I realized I was hungry. Mom was probably at work on another delicious meal. She spoiled me to no end, especially since Debbie left. She could see how tough that was on me—finding a sister, then letting her go.

I turned back toward home and there he was—Director of Security, Nathan Rhodes.

It was strange being on the edge of celebrity, especially the over-the-top celebrity of my new extended family. Cisco's youngest brother, our rock star Paulo, commented to me this summer, "You'll never be alone again." I guess he was right.

I approached Nathan and smiled to engage him in conversation. "I didn't realize how late it's getting. I hope Mom has something good for dinner."

His mouth quirked in reply. I had the feeling that was as much of a smile as I'd get. My brother-in-law was no different.

"Mrs. Auclair told us it's chicken pie tonight. I'm lookin' forward to it."

I couldn't help myself. "Why don't you call Mom, Millie, and me, Annie? It'd really be a lot more comfortable for us."

His eyes flickered with some emotion I couldn't read. "I'm here to keep you and your family alive, Mrs. Brewster, and protect your property. It's best to keep a professional relationship."

The cold penetrated my core. "Of course, Mr. Rhodes, I understand." I zipped the sweatshirt as high as it would go and started off down the beach as quickly as I could. Doc was right—Nathan Rhodes was not like everyone else. *Best to keep my distance.*

~ ANNIE ~

Mom and Dad left early Sunday morning, in time for Dad to conduct services at his church in Ripple Lake. I watched from the window as they took off in a black SUV driven by one of our guards, with another one riding shotgun. I briefly considered where that expression came from. Most likely the Old West.

Doc put his hand on my shoulder. "Well, I guess all the excitement is over. Debbie's gone. Mike and Millie are gone. Amanda James is gone."

I tried to be upbeat. "Now real life begins, Doc. But don't worry. I promise to be home every night. Mom's not the only one around here who can cook."

He chuckled.

"Unfortunately, I can't loll around here today. I've got to get to the restaurant to check on things. But I'll call you by lunchtime. I want to have some time to myself today before that show comes on tonight."

"Don't stress over it. You did a great interview. Cisco knows what he's doing, and when they get all the systems up and working, you'll be able to handle the growth and expand your business and charity work in a logical way. For now, just roll with the punches, and take care of yourself. You've been through a lot, and you need time to process things, time to adjust."

I exhaled a deep breath. "Yeah, you're right. It was just a couple of months ago when I lived in the attic of a restaurant. Now the world's my oyster, right?"

We both laughed.

~ DOC ~

I closed my laptop, got up from the kitchen table, and grabbed my jacket from the closet. I needed a walk to clear my head. Video-conferencing with my daughter, Debbie, and her two sets of triplets, was the highlight of my day. I had six beautiful grandchildren I never imagined I'd have the opportunity to get to know. Less than a week since they'd left, and I felt that loss deeply—an ache in my chest. The toughest part was the "hello, Dr. Westcott," and "goodbye, Dr. Westcott," from my own daughter.

I'd brought it all on myself. Debbie had paid the price for my negligence. Now that I was miraculously in her life, how could I expect her to welcome me into her heart in a matter of a few months? But I did hope.

As I walked across the back lawn down to the hedge overlooking the Atlantic, I remembered the many games I'd played here with my grandkids this summer, the laughter, the delight. High tide and gusty winds kept me from the beach. I started toward one of the many woodsy trails on the property. The colors were still vivid. The muffled sound of my footsteps on the downed leaves lulled me into contemplation.

My only chance with my youngest daughter would be to patiently wait for her to come around. Debbie would have to decide how our relationship would evolve. *All I can do is be there for her, as much as I can, in whatever way makes her comfortable. Just be grateful she's in my life somehow.* In the meantime, I'd focus on Annie.

It seemed her business would go on in chaos for a while. Who could cope with the hordes of tourists and reporters, all looking for a story and a celebrity sighting? Annie was strong and resilient, but I could tell this pandemonium was taking its toll. Anxiety was getting the better of her.

I hoped the consultant Cisco hired would bring her some relief.

~ ANNIE ~

Not surprisingly, I walked into an overflow crowd at The Golden Bowl. I found Ashleigh in our tiny office, her ponytail wilder than I'd ever seen it. She had coffee in one hand and a pastry in the other. "This is the first bite I've had today, and I'm desperate for the sugar."

I put my bag in the desk drawer. "Take your time, Ash."

"There were throngs of people lining up an hour before opening. I've never seen anything like it. I mean we've had lines for lunch and dinner—but *five* o'clock on a Sunday morning? It's nuts. There hasn't been one free table or chair since we opened the doors."

"Well, that's a good thing." *I think.* I flipped through a stack of papers on the desk.

"Those are all the new applications for food cards. You need to check them all. You might have to get stricter on the requirements. I think the world now knows you're a soft touch. They're comin' out of the woodwork."

I wrapped an elastic band around the pile and threw it in the top drawer of the file cabinet. "Okay, thanks. I'll look into it." It was 8:30 a.m. and I thought my head would explode. Maybe I wasn't ready for the world to visit The Golden Bowl. Maybe I shouldn't have my "territory enlarged." It was all giving me a headache. "I'm going to check on the kitchen. Take a little break and enjoy your coffee."

As soon as I made it through the door, I was embraced by a swarm of people. Everyone wanted to know if I was nervous about my appearance on *Amanda James Now*. Of course I was. But what could I do about it? I chatted with everyone as I politely pushed through to the kitchen.

Things were humming along. A momentary sense of pride filled me. At least I could put together an effective kitchen. I'd been fortunate to hire and retain outstanding key people. They made it possible for me to focus more on the charitable programs we offered. They made The Golden Bowl feel like family.

I poured myself a coffee and headed out the back door to stand on the porch. A cold gust of salt air greeted me. A few hearty souls sat by the rail, staring out at the water, sipping hot beverages. October was a big month for hot apple cider and cocoa.

I greeted those who met my eye and strolled around to the side rail. I looked over toward the big old barn we'd converted to house The Bakery & Sweet Shop, and a facility where we prepared meals and products we sold at retail locations within a fifty-mile radius. The bakery was doing a brisk Sunday morning business. Children and their parents, probably all on a sugar high, played tag on the lawn, laughing as they tore around the grounds.

They reminded me of my nephews, and thoughts returned to Debbie and her family. They were so happy together. I'd had such happiness with my husband, Russ. He'd supported me in all my dreams. An accomplished woodworker, he'd singlehandedly transformed the interior of The Golden Bowl long before it ever opened. He even planned how we could renovate the barn. But he never saw the grand opening of the restaurant or the transformation of the barn. He'd died suddenly of a brain aneurism more than ten years ago.

I'd come home from work and found him by the hearth he'd built with his own hands. I never had the chance to say goodbye. Tears welled up. What would he think of all this now? *Me* interviewed by Amanda James. He must be laughing in heaven.

Buckminster Wynn exited the bakery, and my breath caught in my throat. He took a seat on a bench near the ice cream window. Although the barn was a good distance away, I could see that leather binder was with him, and it looked like he began work on a tablet. My heart thumped. With a tap of those diligent fingers, Buckminster Wynn of Brooke, Lewis & Wynn could singlehandedly smash all my dreams and turn them into a nightmare.

CHAPTER 6

~ LISA ~

I didn't put Rosie in her crib our first night in my new house. There was so much room in my new queen-sized bed it was easy to let her sleep with me. I'd probably use it tonight, but I guess I was a little bit scared of being in a new place. If my friends from Ripple Lake didn't hear yesterday, they probably knew by now that I was a brand new homeowner. I told Peg not to call people, but I don't think she understood. She said she wouldn't, but she'd probably caved by now.

Peg knocked at my bedroom door and came in. "Why don't we get over to The Golden Bowl for some breakfast? Then we can go home and pick up our stuff."

I sat up in the bed and squeezed Rosie to my chest. "They're all gonna want to come over here. I don't want them all in my new house. They'll break stuff. They'll steal stuff. They'll think I'm rich now. I just wanna start a new life, Peg. Don't you?"

She sat on the edge of my bed. "Sure, baby, if that's what you want. I'm goin' out to the deck for a smoke. You let me know what you wanna do for food."

"Yeah, The Golden Bowl is good. We'll go soon. I'll get Rosie ready."

"Okay." She started to get up.

I reached for her arm. "Peg, thanks for staying here with me. It's not just because I trust you with Rosie. You're my friend—my *best* friend. We can have a brand new life here. I need you, Peg. I'm starting my new job tomorrow morning, and we'll have real money comin' in, finally. A brand new house, all furnished. Everything we need. There's nothin' we need back in Ripple Lake. Are you gonna stay?"

She sat for a minute, like she was thinking on it. "I got no real family. Messed up with them pretty bad. Two kids that hardly ever call me. But I learned some lessons from it. Been sober almost twenty-five years now." She turned and patted my shoulder. "I love you and Rosie. Don't know what I'd do without ya. It might take some gettin' used to Marberry, but I'd like to stay. You and Rosie are family now. I can take care of her while you're at work."

Peg was an odd duck, a friendly old lady with tons of friends, but she never got close to them. Her kids had been gone for years and years. Don't ever remember a husband. She was the type that kept everything inside. But I could see it in her eyes. She wouldn't leave Rosie and me.

~ LISA ~

It was lunchtime when we got a seat at The Golden Bowl. Service was quick and friendly. Rosie practically dove into a bowl of squash, and she had fun playing in that while most of the townspeople came up to congratulate me on my new house. Peg soaked it all up. She was a neighborly sort. Me, I worried we'd get some unwanted visitors.

A fire alarm blared, and before I could wonder what happened, thick smoke wafted in the front door.

Ashleigh stood in the doorway with a towel over her face. "It's the prayer bowl! Someone set it on fire."

Annie directed people out the back way, but the smoke cleared fast. I picked Rosie up, reached for my uneaten muffin, and headed out with Peg. By the time I made it to the door, the guards had extinguished the fire and Billy had two guys by the scruff of their necks.

I shuddered. "I went to school with those guys, Peg. They're from Ripple Lake."

Her mouth popped open in surprise, and her top denture dropped down. She didn't seem embarrassed as she popped it back in. But maybe now she understood why we needed to be careful.

After that wake-up call at the restaurant, Peg was happy to stick around town and do some grocery shopping. We stocked the kitchen and then grilled hamburgers on my new gas grill on the deck. Peg was all excited for the Amanda James show to start so we could see our new house and how we looked on TV. She put all kinds of snacks and drinks on our new tray tables in front of our new TV, which she set to record the show.

I was curious about how we'd look, but I thought it'd be important to hear Annie's story, too. Even though I'd known her for years, I didn't really know her. And I was interested to find out more about her and The Golden Bowl before starting my new dishwashing job tomorrow.

I put Rosie to bed in her new crib and came downstairs to sit on my new couch with my new baby monitor. Peg handed me a bowl of chips.

"They showed you in the previews, Lisa. You look good. Surprised. Very cute. I think it was after you fainted." Peg took a box of chocolates and a glass of ginger ale and settled into my new recliner. "Everybody on TV is sayin' Amanda James has the real—*the exclusive*—scoop on Debbie Lambrecht's new sister. Annie's not talkin' to anyone else."

"Hmm. I guess once you talk to Amanda James you don't need to talk to anyone else." I started in on the chips. Amanda's voice turned my attention to the television.

"When celebrated designer, Debbie Lambrecht, heard her mother's deathbed confession, her husband—notorious secret agent, David Lambrecht—discovered Debbie's long-lost sister, living in the attic above her restaurant in Maine. Meet Annie Brewster. Tonight! On *Amanda James Now*."

As the commercials started, I turned to Peg and made a face.

She swallowed a mouthful of chocolate with a gulp of soda. "Amanda sure has a way with words. Makes us all sound like a bunch o' hicks."

~ ANNIE ~

Nathan drove me to The Golden Bowl, arriving promptly at 5:45 a.m. I climbed the stairs and put my handbag on a wicker chair. "The bowl cleaned up nicely." I rustled the prayer slips, looking for any charred strays.

Nathan stepped up beside me. "They sifted through all the papers, cleaned and polished the bowl. That incident is behind us now. We won't let it happen again."

"Thanks." As I looked up at him, I noticed Lisa chatting with Billy in the parking lot. I decided to keep my thoughts to myself. Nathan was probably not interested in my comments on prayer or what a cute couple Lisa Quinn and Billy Foster would make.

Since the bowl was still overflowing with prayer slips, I pulled one out. Nathan stood stone-faced and motionless as I read it aloud. "Pray for Peter Fellowes and his work to build the school for disabled kids." I lifted up Peter and his students in a silent prayer then put the paper in my bag.

Lisa bounced up the stairs. "Never been so happy to be at work at 6:00 a.m. on a Monday morning."

I gave her a hug and led her downstairs to the employee lounge. "We'll have some breakfast, and Ashleigh will go through a little orientation with you. Then she'll get you started on training. Every day you'll learn a little bit more—there's a meeting and brief training before each shift. Every employee has an important job to do here. You're part of a team, a family."

I introduced Lisa to two other new employees while Ashleigh served yogurt and fruit, and her assistant put out employee handbooks and pens for each trainee.

I took a cup of coffee, and gave the group an introduction

and welcome to The Golden Bowl. Then I headed upstairs to check on the kitchen.

Buckminster Wynn stepped inside and caught my eye. “Good morning, Mrs. Brewster. Shall we adjourn to your office?” As my stomach rebelled, I wondered what I was in for. Today would be tough enough without facing him.

He laid his briefcase on my desk and stood by the file cabinet. I shut the door and leaned on it, my hand clutching the knob, ready for a quick exit.

Almighty Buck looked down his nose at me. “I had a lovely chat with your accountant, Pinky Gugino. Why would you engage an accountant named Pinky?”

“He’s a very kind man, Mr. Wynn. He’s been doing my taxes for years. He lost part of his little finger—it caught in a car door—and that’s why they call him Pinky.”

“Yes, an untoward incident with a mobster, no doubt.”

Untoward? *Mobster*? “I don’t know, Mr. Wynn. I don’t think we have mobsters in Marberry.”

“I’m sure, Mrs. Brewster, but Pinky lives in the next town over. Did you know he retired twelve-and-a-half years ago?”

I took a seat at my desk. I didn’t want him to see me shaking. “Did he not submit my taxes?”

“He certainly did, Mrs. Brewster. And his numbers were, shall we say . . . creative . . . surely pulled from thin air. I suppose he didn’t want to bother you with all the burdens of record-keeping.”

How could I admit that’s why Pinky and I got on so well? He rarely sent me a bill. Pinky had told me he wanted to help humanity, and doing my taxes was his way of contributing. My mouth was dry as dust. “I relied on his advice. He’s an accountant.”

“Sadly, Mrs. Brewster, that won’t keep you out of prison.”

“Prison?”

“Fraud.”

“Fraud?”

A dark eyebrow, framing steel gray eyes, lifted sarcastically. “Is there an echo in here?”

The coffee I’d drunk gurgled in my stomach. “How can they put me in prison for fraud when I had no idea I was doing fraud? Pinky was taking care of all that.”

“Mrs. Brewster.” He exhaled a heavy sigh. “As a four-year-old watching Saturday morning cartoons I learned this: ignorance of the law is *no* excuse.”

“Please don’t tell Cisco. Please!”

“Don’t tell Cisco? He knew your numbers made no sense long before he ever called *me*.”

I almost fell out of my seat. “He *knew*?”

His eyes bulged, incredulous. “Mrs. Brewster, the man is a mathematical and financial genius. He’s worth billions. Just because he’s so personable and kind, don’t let that fool you. He’s a smart man.”

My voice caught in my throat. “O-of course. B-but why would he offer to help me?”

Buckminster Wynn took the chair at the side of the desk and faced me, his expression now unexpectedly soft and sympathetic. He reached over and put his hand on top of mine. “Mrs. Brewster, there’s a sign over your door that I’m sure is inspired by one of Cat and Paulo’s albums. ‘There’s no place like family.’ You’ve hit the jackpot. Your sister married into their family. And now, you are a member of that family. I know Cisco takes that very seriously.”

He gave me a minute to let that sink in. I couldn’t look at his face. My eyes focused on his hand and the hint of a pinstripe in his custom suit jacket, the Rolex watch that probably cost more than my restaurant. Tears blurred my vision. I felt like a fraud, sitting there in designer clothes I could never hope to afford.

“Mrs. Brewster, let me help you out of the weeds. If I have your cooperation, I’m certain we can turn your business into one that works for you. I understand your vision. We can make it work, but only if you help.”

I cleared my throat. "Thank you, Mr. Wynn. I promise I'll do my best to get things on track. Whatever you tell me—I'll do it if I possibly can." I sniffed in the tears and reached for a tissue with my free hand, conscious of the warmth of his hand on mine.

"Good!" He squeezed my hand and let it go. "The sooner we start, the sooner we'll have everything in order."

I whisked the tissue under my nose. "What would you like me to do first?"

"Call me Buck." There was a twinkle in his eye.

I attempted a smile. "If you call me Annie."

"Deal," he said.

Buck removed his expensive suit jacket, loosened his silk tie, rolled up his starched white shirtsleeves, and went right to work emptying the file cabinet of anything that could possibly hint at numbers or records. He commented that my employee job descriptions and training manuals seemed very strong.

With that bit of encouragement, I dove in as best I could to assist him in putting together a complete picture of where the business stood. Before I knew it, Ashleigh knocked at the door with an offer of lunch, which Buck elected to take at the desk. Minutes later two juicy cheeseburgers arrived.

He unfurled the napkin and tucked it into his collar. "Thank you, Ashleigh. I appreciate fine cloth napkins. This looks delicious." He inspected the food. "Whole grain bun and sweet potato fries . . ." He picked up a slice. "These are baked and cleverly disguised as fries. Healthy. Hmm."

She giggled at me as she awaited the verdict. He took his time chewing but managed a polite smile around the food.

"Scrumptious, Ashleigh, truly! This is an outstanding burger. I've never had a better one." He tossed a slice of sweet potato into his mouth. "Delicious! Top class. My compliments to the chef."

Ashleigh beamed. "I'll tell him. And just so you know—

Annie taught him everything he knows." She winked at me and took off.

"I must tell you, Annie, I appreciate your attention to healthy, delicious food. Your pancakes, for example, are the best I've ever eaten. You've achieved the perfect recipe with a balance of whole grains, and yet they are supremely fluffy. Delectable and healthy. I applaud you."

I nodded. "Thank you. That means so much to me."

But Buck seemed to be concentrating on downing his cheeseburger. I munched on sweet potatoes from my plate and sipped tea. Now that my dastardly secret was out, it was hard not to like him, although I knew nothing about him. Well, other than he was a talented businessman, and he liked cheeseburgers, pancakes, expensive clothes, and cars. That was a start, I suppose.

I excused myself to go to the restroom, got intercepted by customers, and by the time I returned to the office, Buck had disappeared. I sorted through papers for five or ten minutes, but he didn't return. I hoped he hadn't gotten sick from his meal. Another ten minutes passed and I was worried. Sweat beaded on my forehead. I went to find him.

There was no sign of him amongst the crowd in the dining rooms, so I headed to the kitchen. No Buck.

"Psst . . . Annie!" Her whisper was loud, and I turned to see Lisa. "Sorry I left my post."

"Why are you whispering? Are you okay?"

"There's an English guy—all dressed up—going through the garbage. I saw him through my window. I asked him if he's all right, and he said yes. I don't want to make a scene or anything. But I thought you should know. You want me to call the cops? Or I could call Billy if you want. What's his number?"

I bit my lip to keep from laughing. "It's okay. That's Mr. Wynn. He's helping us improve our services."

"Oh. I get it. He's a waste-watcher, too." She proudly pointed to the waste-watcher pin on her apron.

I couldn't help hugging her. "That's it!"

"Kudos to you, Mrs. Brewster." Buck's voice boomed in the small hallway. The door swung shut behind him. "You have the best-looking trash I've ever seen." He wore a devilish grin and large rubber gloves.

I couldn't help bursting into laughter. "Thank you, Mr. Wynn. I'm glad we're doing the trash properly."

"Indeed." He nodded at Lisa. "No silverware, no cloth napkins, no ramekins, no hidden meals. I've never seen such clean trash. And I love your waste-watcher pin, young lady."

Lisa beamed at him. "Thanks. Me, too."

I introduced her to Buck.

Once Lisa returned to her post, Buck removed the gloves and guided me by my elbow back to the office. He picked up his briefcase. "Let's take a bit of a break and visit The Bakery & Sweet Shop. We'll take a tour, sample some sweets, then go along to your retail meal prep facility."

It was a rigorous tour. I did my best to answer every detailed question, but it seemed like an endless quiz. By the time we exited the building, my brain was fried and the moon had risen in the sky.

"I have to say, Annie, you're a remarkable woman. Your facilities and grounds are spotless, your operations, your customer experience is superb. Frankly, I have no idea how you manage to make all these ends meet with so little financial control. How do you do that?"

I looked up at the front porch of The Golden Bowl, softly glowing with tiny white lights. "You see that prayer bowl? That's how. Prayer. I have no idea how I go on from day to day. I know I'm financially illiterate. But God also knows what I'm trying to do for people, and I think that's why he sent me Cisco, and perhaps that's why he sent you to us, too."

"Hmm."

I turned to him. "I have to tell you I'm so relieved to finally get that out. I pretended to be some great businesswoman for way too long. I'm just a chef, a nutritionist trying to feed people, trying to love them and take care of them. I'm no businesswoman."

It was hard to read his expression in the dark. He was silent as we headed back to my office. The restaurant was officially closed, but the staff was still there. My second shift manager, Brianna, oversaw the closing—everything clean and in its place, ready for the morning. As always, she gave a pep talk to her crew before they headed out the door, laughing and chatting.

Buck observed the scene. "Strange. It's like they're energized."

"Brianna is a great manager and a real people-person."

She grabbed her coat and handed me the receipts for the day. "Good day today, Annie."

"Thanks, Bree." I hugged her. "See you tomorrow."

She exchanged pleasantries with Buck, then left.

"Ashleigh will be in at 5:00 a.m. to get the new day started." I took my coat and bag from the office. "That's going to get here pretty fast, so if we're all set for now, I'm going to go home."

"Very good. It's been a breakthrough day, I believe." He took his briefcase. "If I may be so bold, Annie, please be here tomorrow morning with your personal financial records—bank books, retirement accounts, etc. That will help me greatly in dealing with your business situation. As I said, this business is ultimately about you."

I swallowed hard. "I'll do my best." My heart started to pound. It would be a sleepless night.

We stepped out to the porch and found Nathan standing by the prayer bowl. "Mr. Rhodes." I nodded as I approached the bowl in my usual routine.

"Your car's ready, Mrs. Brewster." He stepped aside to give me space.

As I took out a slip, I realized it was another linen paper from Cat. The feel of that paper was ingrained now. I dropped it in my bag wondering how it had survived the fire. Was I the only one retrieving her scriptural messages?

The thought vanished at the sound of Buck's voice. "Hmm." He plucked a slip of paper from the top. "I'll have to see how this works." He winked at me.

CHAPTER 7

~ ANNIE ~

I sat at the kitchen table, staring out the bay window to the back lawn. The white of my Adirondack chairs was all I could see against the black sea and sky. My hot chocolate was growing cold.

My checkbook sat in front of me, unopened. There was no need to review it. I knew the exact amount in the account: $5,035.45. It didn't sound so bad if I ignored the fact that my brother-in-law, David, had given me $5,000 on Tuesday before they left. He said it was for any incidental expenses for the house that might arise during the month. I couldn't help chuckling. How could I be living in a world where $5,000 was incidental? I was living in a world where $35.45 was the extent of my money. Period.

There were no other accounts for Mr. Buckminster Wynn, of Brooke, Lewis & Wynn with offices in New York and London, to review. *Oh dear God*! What would I do? Beg stupidity? I obviously watched the wrong cartoons at age four.

Now I was risking prison. Fraud. *What exactly is fraud*? *I suppose I'll find out*.

I heard the swinging door swish. "Mrs. Brewster, are you all right?"

I turned to see Nathan, who'd been finishing up his night rounds. "I'm fine, Mr. Rhodes. Can I get you a hot chocolate?"

"Sure smells good."

I took that as a "yes" and bounced out of my seat to the stove.

"I don't want to put you to any trouble, ma'am."

Ma'am made me feel even older than my forty-seven years. I caught him watching me intently. Maybe not so old then?

"That's why it smells so great—you make it from scratch."

I had to smile. "That's why."

He shook his head. "I've gotta say, I've never been better fed, Mrs. Brewster. Even the cocoa is real."

"Cocoa?" Billy peered around the wall of the kitchen staircase.

I waved him over. "I'll make plenty, don't worry."

Before I knew, it I was surrounded by six huge guards and Doc, all acting like little boys drinking hot cocoa on a cold autumn night.

My mood brightened, and I remembered Cat's prayer in my bag. As I foraged around to find the slip of paper, I noticed sudden silence.

I came up with the prayer slip.

"What have you got there?" Doc asked.

I looked up at him. "A prayer from Cat. How it survived that fire, I don't know. But I do know this is the paper she used."

"Like a fortune cookie," Billy said.

"Better." I read it aloud. "*Trust in the Lord and do good; dwell in the land and enjoy safe pasture. Delight yourself in the Lord and he will give you the desires of your heart. Commit your way to the Lord; trust in him and he will do this: He will make your righteousness shine like the dawn, the justice of your cause like the noonday sun. Psalm 37: 3-6*"

There was momentary quiet. *Safe pasture*.

"That's a good one, Cat." Doc lifted his cup in a toast to our amazing friend.

"I love her songs," Billy said. "Got her autograph before she left."

I wiped my eyes. *I could use safe pasture, Lord.*

~ ANNIE ~

Tuesday morning at The Golden Bowl was as packed as Monday. Ashleigh waved her hello from the middle of the dining room and pointed toward my office, her wild ponytail bouncing with the movement. Buck was an early bird, too, it seemed.

I opened the door to a chipper voice. "Best omelet ever, Annie!" He raised his coffee to salute me. "If I didn't know better, I'd think you're trying to butter me up."

"That was the plan, Buck, but you found me out."

"Yes, but I *do* have a record of the cook's employment here for the past five years. And there's no other restaurant in town, so where did this delightful meal come from?"

I hung my coat on the rack and decided not to maneuver around him to put my bag in the drawer. If he wanted to sit at the desk, that was fine.

I couldn't help laughing. "At least there's a record of *something* around here."

His smile was so genuine, it somehow relieved the ache in the pit of my stomach.

"Here, hand me your bag and I'll put it in the drawer. I know the drill." He pretended to drop the bag from its excessive weight as I gave it to him.

It was silly, but I was so overtired I got a case of the giggles. I dropped into a chair and put my hands over my face. *Enough*!

The grating of the old metal desk drawer drew my attention. Sometimes it was tricky—like anything else that was long past its prime.

"Hmm."

I watched Buck fight with it, then remove the bag and a large envelope that had jammed in there somehow. He held it up with an inquisitive look.

I squinted at an official looking return address. Light

dawned. "Oh! I was supposed to get that over to Pinky. Those are some tax forms or something. With my sister being here all summer, I guess I forgot. I can run them over today."

The look on his face told me I got that quiz wrong. "I think you should open it first, don't you?"

The stomach ache returned with a vengeance. "Yeah. Yeah, I guess I should." Panic bubbled up. "Why don't you open it? You'll probably understand it more than I would."

He slipped the contents out of the envelope and leaned back in the chair. His lips pressed together as he read. "It's really quite simple, Annie. You're being audited. Friday."

"Audited? Friday? No! We don't even know if Pinky is available. Let's call them and change it."

"I'm sorry. I'm quite sure it's too late to change the appointment."

"Too late? No! I'll just call Pinky."

Buck didn't hide his displeasure. "I've met Mr. Gugino. I can assure you he's missing more than part of a finger."

"But—"

"I expect Maine Revenue Services is a relatively small department that serves a large geographic area. Considering the mess your files are in, I think it best to keep this appointment." His head tilted back, and Buck stared at the ceiling for a while.

Gratitude at his silent contemplation turned to hope that he was conjuring a plan to get me out of trouble. But the silence continued, dashing my hope and spiking my fear. Me and my $35.45 would be heading to jail. What would my parents say? I burst into a sob. "I guess I'm a criminal. I'm a disgrace to my family."

Buck gasped and exploded in laughter. It didn't stop.

My self-pity turned to indignation.

Those steel gray eyes met mine, and his laughter intensified.

Rage dried my eyes.

He wouldn't stop until he finally turned toward the

wall to compose himself. That tactic was only moderately successful.

I got up to leave, turning my back to him.

"May I point out your brother-in-law is an assassin? Somehow tax evasion pales in comparison."

I whirled around. "What do you know about David?"

He wiped the smile off his face. "Fortunately, not too much. Sit down, Annie."

I grabbed a tissue and resumed my seat. I must have looked a fine mess. Blotting my face, I realized I'd broken out in a sweat. David's career choice had been a matter of public fascination for some time now.

"I met them only once—at a business function. It was quite apparent they live and breathe for each other. I was rather taken by that. Jealous, really."

Jealousy—that's what it was, but I'd never admit it. Debbie had the love of her life, despite his inordinately dangerous job. My husband had been a woodworker, a careful man with a careful job. A good solid man taken from me way too soon.

I cleared my throat. "Amanda James brought that passion out to the public quite effectively, don't you think?"

"I do! I was glued to the television every time they were interviewed."

"It's hard to believe they've been gone a week today." I wiped the balled-up tissue over my eyes.

Buck straightened in his chair. "Well, let's get to work so you can plan an Austrian holiday after this audit. How's that?"

I nodded. "Um . . . a little unrealistic . . . but great."

"Good. Did you bring along your personal financial information?"

"Yes. Back in the desk drawer—in my bag."

He retrieved the bag, and I removed my checkbook and handed it to him. To say he looked surprised was an understatement. Or maybe it was consternation. *That, too.*

"I can explain," I said.

"Please do." He flipped the plastic cover open and perused a few pages.

"Do you want the long version or the short one?"

He looked up at me. "The short will suffice."

"I'm broke."

"I should say."

I took a long breath. "Just so you know, $5000 of that balance is David's. He told me to use it for incidental household expenses for the month. The $35.45 is mine."

He lifted his brows. "All yours?"

"Yes, Buck, all mine. Minus whatever taxes I owe on it." I put my head in my hands.

When I looked up, wondering at his silence, he was rubbing his chin. He looked me in the eye. "Well, I'd say the government should consider themselves lucky you haven't applied for welfare."

The growing lump in my throat wouldn't let me reply.

He threw the checkbook back in the drawer. "Why don't we take a little walk and clear our heads? The bakery has some pumpkin bread we need to try." He rose and helped me from my chair and into my coat.

"A little cream cheese with that—"

"And hazelnut coffee," he said. "That will make everything all better."

~ ANNIE ~

There was a stiff sea breeze, but the walk did us good. A quick tour of the bakery kitchen, bursting with trays of jack-o-lantern cookies, goblin cupcakes, and broomstick biscotti would ensure our readiness for the Halloween onslaught. It was hard to believe the big day was tomorrow. It seemed like only yesterday we were planning for Fourth of July.

My confections manager, Karen, took the opportunity to speak to me. "Annie, you're probably not surprised to hear this, but we've been bombarded with calls and emails for blueberry and chocolate chip ice cream. I've been telling them we don't ship ice cream, but people aren't happy with my answer. Should I tell them something different?"

I let out a sigh. "Thanks, Karen. Once Amanda James let it be known that those were Paulo Clemente's favorite flavors, I knew we'd be flooded with orders . . ." I glanced at Buck, embarrassed that, once again, I didn't have things under control.

"As *you* know Annie, I am in the process of revising the website," he smoothly stepped in. "And I'll be taking all of that into consideration for the future, right Annie?" He grinned at my surprised look. We hadn't even gotten to talking about the website yet. At least, I hadn't. Buck was ten steps ahead of me, as usual.

I nodded, relieved that he was helping us. "Yes, so for now—just keep telling them what you're telling them. We're not equipped to ship ice cream at the present time."

"Okay. I did ramp up the production on those flavors, so we've been—barely—keeping up with demand here at the shop. Kids are coming from miles around. It's crazy."

"I know." I patted her shoulder. "Thanks, Karen. Great job."

We took our coffee and pumpkin bread into a small private office. Buck seemed to sense it was best to keep the conversation on the positive side and postpone any more discussion about the audit. It was that obvious, that I was a jumble of nerves.

"Business is brisk again today. Not a table to be had in The Bakery & Sweet Shop. Lines for take-out. Packed dining rooms. And your manager, Gerald, told me this morning that your prepared food orders have skyrocketed since the Amanda James interview. Now they're asking for your homemade ice cream as well. You know, The Golden Bowl is a gold mine."

I took a sip of coffee. "Yes, with the right management."

Buck took his time with a bite of pumpkin bread. "I find it remarkable how organized you are in all your food service operations—all paperwork and licensing in order. And yet your financials are a disaster. How is that, Annie?"

I shook my head. "I don't know. I really don't."

"You haven't paid attention. That's all it is. You've avoided an important part of your business, and somehow some supernatural force has kept it all afloat. Until now."

I pulled my blue cashmere sweater, a lovely gift from my sister, tight around me, wrapping my arms around my stomach. "It's not '*some* supernatural force.' It's the grace of God. Ask Cat. She'll tell you the same thing."

"Yes, I suppose she would. That's all she ever talks about, isn't it?"

I wanted to roll my eyes in sarcastic reply, but I realized the Clementes and Buck were here helping me, rescuing me, by God's grace, so I could continue doing his work. It was time I helped myself by taking their advice. I took a bite of pumpkin bread in hopes of reviving myself.

Buck downed the last of his coffee. "Well Annie, now would be a good time to summon up all that grace. As much as you can muster."

CHAPTER 8

~ LISA ~

First shift on Halloween day was crazy at The Golden Bowl. I barely had time to take a break to see Rosie in her little princess outfit when Peg brought her in for lunch. All the kids were in costumes—and even some of the adults. The waitresses wore tiaras. They offered me one, but it wouldn't stay on, so I hung it up by my sink. It made me feel pretty good. I was already making some new friends. And everyone was so nice.

I didn't mind staying on a couple extra hours to cover for a girl who had a doctor's appointment. But by the time I got home, it was 5:00 p.m. I was tired.

Peg had bought bags of Halloween candy, and we sat out on the deck and dug into it while Rosie napped in the living room.

"It must be thirty degrees out here." Peg took a drag of her cigarette.

I pulled my hat down over my ears. "It's refreshing." I was putting up with this cold because I was a new homeowner with a new deck overlooking the Atlantic Ocean. I sure wasn't going to wait till spring to use it. "And when we go inside, we'll sit in front of our new gas fireplace. And eat some more candy. Did you get enough in case we get some kids?"

"I hid a couple bags in the cabinet."

"Good." I could hear Rosie on the monitor. "Okay, time to go in." I closed the sliding door behind me, threw my hat on the table, and headed to the living room. The bag of candy fell from my fingers.

"Hello, Lisa." My ex-husband sat on the couch holding my daughter, waving her little hand at me. My heart went into my throat. All I could see was evil with his hands on my baby.

I hoped I looked calm. "What are you doing here, Ryan? How'd you get in?"

"Now, what kind of hello is that? I wanted to visit my little girl, and your front door was wide open."

I wanted to scream at Peg. She just didn't get it.

"You know what the judge said. You're not supposed to be here."

He laughed. "Did you hear that, Rosie? I'm not supposed to be here. I'm unfit. And your Mommy is unfit, too. She just doesn't let on."

"Get out of here. Don't make me yell and scare the baby."

"No problem. But I need some money. A hundred bucks should do it."

"You bum. I don't get paid till next week."

"No problem. I'll get it then." He got up and handed Rosie to me. "With interest."

Then he walked into the kitchen, unplugged the coffee maker, and took it.

"You lousy thief! That costs more than a hundred dollars! Give it back."

As he stomped out the kitchen door, Peg peered in through the slider and stepped inside. "At least he didn't get the gourmet coffee cups."

~ LISA ~

Thursday lunchtime I called Peg to let her know I'd be working that night for someone who needed the time off. It was just a little white lie. My manager told me about a special party they were having where you could donate a thousand dollars to charity and then invite other people to do the same. It was called gifting tables, and when you moved along the courses from the Appetizer Table to the Dessert Table, you were not only helping charity, you were making money, too.

It sounded like a great way to make some cash, but I didn't want Peg to know I had a thousand dollars. I hadn't even been paid yet. There was no way I'd let on about that ring—not to anyone. But I wouldn't mind telling Ashleigh I'd scraped it together for an investment for Rosie. With that story, she'd probably understand if I gave the charity a few hundred bucks. That was a lot of money to me.

Annie would know right away exactly where that money came from. But I was pretty sure I could trust her. And if a successful businesswoman like Annie thought this was a good idea, I was in.

Maybe I could buy a car without touching my nest egg. Peg's car would probably last through the winter, and by then I'd definitely get to the Dessert level. I was pretty pleased with myself until I walked into the Miller Room and almost bumped into Terri Monahan.

She reminded me of a vulture with some poor guy in her claws.

"Lisa! Glad you could make it." She angled her victim to face me. "This is Peter Fellowes."

I shook his hand. "Hi. Nice to meet you." He was a good-looking middle-aged guy with wavy dark hair dressed in a sport coat and khakis.

"Glad to know you. We're really making a difference for the kids. I appreciate you coming tonight. Have some food. We'll be doing a little presentation in about ten minutes. You'll see how you can do good—and do good." His smile was kind of sweet.

"Oh, I get it. Make money for charity and make money for yourself."

"Right!" He reminded me of Ted Monahan when he wanted to make a real estate sale.

"Okay. Thanks." I headed for the appetizers. As I made a plate for myself, I noticed the only two guys in the room were Ted Monahan and Peter who ran the charity. A couple of women came over and congratulated me on my new house and introduced themselves. They seemed nice, but I didn't want to get too involved. So after making quick work of the appetizers, I headed to the restroom.

When I pushed through the ladies' room door to return to the Miller Room, I saw Billy in the hall holding the door for Annie.

"Thanks. I'll be maybe an hour and a half or so."

"No problem. I'll be right downstairs at the counter—filling up on cocoa."

Annie disappeared into the room, and when Billy saw me, he held the door and winked at me. A million butterflies kicked up in my stomach, and I think my brain went numb. I couldn't even say a word, and I know I gave him a stupid smile. At least I didn't trip through the door like I did the last time.

Annie was at the front of the room introducing Peter Fellowes. He was a special needs teacher and vice principal at Marberry Academy, where all the rich kids go to elementary and middle school. He was also making his dream come true by raising money and building a special school for disabled kids. While all the women applauded him, I went to the back of the room to make myself another plate of food.

I sat in the back and watched one slide after another showing the progress of the construction. This place was huge, and it looked like it'd be a mansion right on the water. Even better than Marberry Academy.

Then Peter's voice cracked a little talking about how much all of our support meant to him and all those deserving kids and their families. He showed pictures of some of the disabled kids and told some of their stories.

I noticed Annie got a little emotional, sitting in the front row wiping her eyes. She sure was a soft touch. All

I could think about was how much of that $8000 I could keep without looking like a pig. Buck's car sped through my head. I'd love to have one of those, but someone told me you could buy a whole neighborhood for what one of them costs.

Finally, Peter showed some diagrams of how gifting tables work. "This is a fun way to do good for others—and to do good for yourself, too. When you make your $1000 cash gift, you join the table on the Appetizer Level. There are eight seats on the Appetizer Level. When there are eight recruits on that level, older members at the table move up to Soup and Salad, then to Entrée, and finally to the Dessert Level. The person at the Dessert Level takes eight thousand dollars, and the remaining members split into two tables, ready to recruit eight more for the Appetizer Level."

He showed a slide with eight thousand dollars divided up the way Ashleigh had explained it to me. At Dessert you get your $1000 back plus $7000 more. Most people take their original $1000 and another $1000 for their trouble. Then they donate $6000 to Peter's charity. Some people just donate all $8000.

Ashleigh told me Annie was the only one who never took any of the money she made from the tables—she always donated everything to the charity—unless she was strapped for cash that month. You can go through the table again and get even more money. He told us many of the people in the room had already gone through the tables several times.

Then he said most of those members and some "ambitious" new ones do his VIP Table and gift $5000 cash to join the Appetizer Level. *Wow*! That's $40,000 cash when you get to Dessert! I was really tempted to jump in at VIP, but decided I better stick with the $1000 gifting table.

After Peter was done with the slides, some people had questions. A woman in the second row said, "It sounds like a pyramid scheme. Is this legal?"

Peter smiled at her. "Thanks for bringing that up, Donna.

I call this a strategy, not a scheme. It's a great strategy to help people reach their dreams. Everyone wins. And, yes, this is perfectly legal. Not only is it perfectly legal, your cash is tax-free. No need to get the IRS involved. We have attorneys and accountants who are table members. Louise Gugino—her dad is an accountant—she's a dedicated member of our club. She's told me it's helped so many of her friends pay a few extra bills, help their families out, or have a little vacation. And they have the warm feeling you get inside when you know you've done something special for humanity. It's people helping people.

"Let's face it. You may struggle to write a check for $6000 to build a school for deserving kids. But with your membership in a gifting table, you pay only $1000 and you get double the cash back when you recruit just eight people. *Plus* the $6000 to this worthy cause is totally painless. Simple, easy *strategy* to do good for yourself and others. Thanks, Donna!"

Me and Donna and ten other women signed up that night.

~ ANNIE ~

By Friday morning I was somewhat calm about the impending tax audit. Between Buck's reassurances and tireless work—and my unceasing praying—I thought we had a chance of prevailing. I had admitted my plight to Doc and my parents, though it wasn't easy. They all said they would help in any way they could. I asked only that they keep my situation in confidence—and visit me in jail if need be. My attempt at humor went over like a lead balloon.

I watched the sunrise from my bedroom window and read through all of Cat's verses that I'd collected over the past ten days. I dropped to my knees and thanked God that he was in charge. I certainly wasn't.

Then I put a smile on my face and headed out to face the music. I found crowds of customers filling the restaurant and The Bakery & Sweet Shop. When I completed my rounds, I located Buck in my tiny office.

He threw his cloth napkin on the breakfast tray. "Good morning, Annie. The hash and eggs are the best ever. You continue to amaze me."

"Thank you, Buck. Let's hope we amaze the tax man."

"Indeed."

We'd barely organized our folders when there was a knock at the door. I reflexively pressed myself against the file cabinet as though I could make it, and me, disappear.

Buck gave me a strange look as he opened the door. "Good morning. Mr. Curley?"

A large man in a grey wool coat stepped inside. "Jim Curley, I'm with Maine Revenue Services, and as you know, I'll be conducting this field audit today."

Buck shook his hand. "Buckminster Wynn of Brooke, Lewis & Wynn. I'm a consultant to the restaurant industry, and Mrs. Brewster has asked me to represent her today." He gestured in my direction. "Mr. Curley, this is Anne Brewster, owner of The Golden Bowl."

I stepped forward to shake his hand. "Nice to meet you, Mr. Curley. Please call me Annie. Can I get you some breakfast?"

He removed his coat. "Thank you, Annie, you can call me Jim. Coffee would be good."

I hung his coat on the rack and went to the kitchen. By the time I returned with a coffee pot and three mugs, Jim was addressing my consultant as Buck, and they seemed to be having a fine conversation about "marvelous Marberry" and the joys of living in Maine.

Jim drained most of his cup in one swig. "Tell me, Buck, where are you from? England?"

"I was born and, somewhat, raised in the U.S. Now I travel internationally with my job. It's a good life."

"You got that accent just from traveling?" Jim seemed in no rush to attack my pile of folders. Maybe this would be a mere formality.

Buck filled his cup again. "I spent much of my youth and university days in England. My mother is American, and my dad is a Brit. Dual citizenship."

"I see." Jim's second cup of coffee was gone. He slammed the mug on the desk. "You make a great cup of coffee, Annie. We should get started."

The words I'd been dreading to hear.

It felt like a lightning bolt had seared me. I dropped into a metal folding chair that loudly scraped against my file cabinet. Jim cast a questioning glance at me.

I forced a smile. "Sorry. Not enough room to change your mind in here."

Buck cleared his throat and took back his attention. "Tell me, Jim, what triggered this audit today?"

"Oh, it can be a random selection, or there can be an inconsistency, or—"

"Yes, I understand. But what specifically brings you here to The Golden Bowl today?"

Jim furrowed his brow. "Well, frankly, I was auditing another business in Marberry and there was a bit of a red flag. Your name came up regarding some possible irregularity. We decided we should look into this."

"Irregularity?" How could I sound so offended?

~ ANNIE ~

Jim Curley thoroughly enjoyed his lunch at The Golden Bowl along with a lively conversation with Buck about the international business climate. I finally excused myself to hide in the bakery.

I had no idea how this audit was going, but it was painfully slow. Numerous "irregularities" had already been unveiled. I couldn't keep them all straight, though he did his best to explain them. I had the feeling I'd be serving them lunch for months. At least Buck and Jim got along famously. And perhaps my jail term wouldn't begin until after the holidays.

I kept thinking if only we'd brought Pinky in, he could explain everything. But Buck had spent the past days warning me against that. Apparently, Pinky was as useless as I was with taxes.

My confections manager, Karen, knocked at the door and let herself in. She put a blueberry scone and a cup of tea on the makeshift desk in front of me. "You look like you could use this."

I looked up from an insane to-do list I'd prepared. "Thanks. I need to be getting back. How's the blueberry and chocolate chip ice cream doing?"

She took a seat beside me. "It's getting worse. I didn't want to tell you. I know you're preoccupied with the consultant. Mr. Wynn said the new website is supposed to be ready for Monday. With a new department just to do the online orders—that'll take a huge load off us, once we hire new staff. And we'll probably need some new equipment to expand ice cream production. I had to put a message on the phone about Paulo's ice cream availability. And we threw up a message on the website about it, too. But I'm no web designer, so I hope Mr. Wynn's guy gets the job done fast. We've got a ton of people to interview this weekend, too."

Karen took off her glasses and rubbed her eyes. "I don't know how we'll fit in interviews on top of the regular work."

I put my arm around her and swallowed my guilt at creating this monster. "You've done a super job dealing with the onslaught. We'll get it straightened out."

"No problem. Just tell Mr. Wynn we're behind you a hundred percent—and make sure his guy finishes the website."

"I will."

If I'm not hauled off to jail first.

~ ANNIE ~

It was dinner time when Jim Curley stood up to leave. "Annie, I need you to sign this extension of limitations. It's going to take us a while to work with you to determine your tax liability."

"A while?" My voice cracked.

His brow furrowed again. "I'm afraid you have a real mess here. Frankly, your accountant should be shot."

"Oh, it's not his fau—"

Buck grabbed me and twirled me toward the desk. "Here's your pen, Annie. Just sign here. All set."

We escorted Jim to the front door. He turned to me. "Buck told me about this prayer bowl thing." He strode to the bowl and took a slip.

I saw it was Cat's linen paper, and nerves skittered up and down my spine as he read in silence.

"What kind of a scam are you running here?"

"Scam?" My offended voice again.

Jim held up the paper, then read it aloud. "*Give to Caesar what is Caesar's, and to God what is God's. Matthew 22:21*"

A funny sound rattled in Buck's throat.

How could I explain Cat? At this point I was far too exhausted to try.

I managed a smile. "That's a good one, Jim." *Even Jesus had to deal with taxes.*

The Friday night dinner crowd was descending on us, and there was nothing left of me. Buck and Brianna followed me into the office.

"You look like that tax guy wiped the floor with you," Brianna said. "Why don't you go home and get some sleep. Karen told me we've got dozens of people coming for interviews tomorrow. You'll need to be awake for that."

"True." I slouched into the chair to get my bag out of the desk drawer.

Buck took my coat from the rack. "Bree's right. You need to get out of here, and so do I. I'll see you bright and early." He helped me into my coat and escorted me to the door.

"Why don't you join us for dinner tonight, Buck? You must be starved."

"Thanks, but I'll take a rain check on that. I have a few more things to wrap up here. The website will be ready to go live Monday morning, and I need to make certain we have the right people here to deal with the orders and inquiries. I'm going to review the applications now so I'll be on top of the interview process tomorrow. We're cutting it close, but we've already lost a fortune in business since the Amanda James show." He gently pushed me out the door to the prayer bowl. "Good night."

Then Buck was swallowed up in a crowd of guests. I lifted my weary eyes and saw Nathan standing in front of me. "The car is ready, Mrs. Brewster."

~ ANNIE ~

More guilt consumed me when I stepped through my door and smelled hamburgers on the grill. Doc was slicing cheese, onions, tomatoes, and lettuce to top his creations. "Annie!" He looked up from his task, and picked up a towel to wipe his hands. "Join us for burgers and beer."

Billy was assisting with the beer.

"I didn't intend to be so late. I'm sorry."

He gave me a hug and a kiss on the cheek. "No problem, we've got dinner under control here. You look like you could use a break." He led me to the table, and Billy put a glass of beer in front of me.

"This is all I need. I'll be out like a light. We've got a day packed with interviews tomorrow, on top of the regular weekend craziness. But I promise to get you dinner on time tomorrow night."

"Not to worry. I'm going camping with two of my favorite SEALs, Roger and Keith. We'll probably be away a week or so, but we'll be in touch in case you need us.

Nathan approved the plan. We'll leave in the morning. Weather's supposed to be decent."

"You—you'll miss Election Day." *There's a lame excuse*.

Doc chuckled. "I'm not worried about that." He left Billy to the grill and sat with me. "The last thing I want is to interfere with your work—or anything you want to do. Making meals for us is not your job, too, on top of everything else. We know you're busy and preoccupied right now. I don't want to stress you any more than you already are."

I let out a sigh. "Where are you camping?"

"Just around Acadia."

I couldn't help it. Tears poured out of me. *What if it happened again*? I couldn't take another thing.

"Annie!" He reached for my hand and squeezed it. "What's wrong?"

When I finally summoned the breath to speak, words came out in a flood. "Why do you think we have all these guards—all this security? There are wacky people out there, and they've already come after you. Why can't we just be safe here? Why camping? God knows we have acres of land right here. You can camp right here. No one will bother you."

Nathan walked over and gave Doc a box of tissues. He held it while I pulled them out with a vengeance and waited patiently as I had my little tantrum.

"You don't have to worry. I'll have two big ex-SEALs with me on this trip. They have years of experience in protecting clueless people like me. I've seen them shoot. I've seen their medals. I've even tried to work out with them. Impossible to keep up with them—even if I suddenly lost forty years." He smiled and stroked my hair.

I tried to calm down.

"We'll be perfectly fine. And you, young lady, need some rest. Let Wynn take care of The Golden Bowl. That's what Cisco hired him for. And don't worry about the taxes—you're not going to jail. It'd be like putting Mother Theresa behind bars. I have money saved we can tap into to pay off the tax man." He took a tissue and dabbed at my face. "Let's calm down and have some dinner."

I inhaled the tears. "O-okay."

Doc should have been able to enjoy his retirement and go camping—or do anything else he wanted—without worry. But last summer was an eye-opener for both of us. Doc was kidnapped—taken right from his patio and transported across the country where he was held in an old storm shelter for weeks. It took my brother-in-law and his colleagues to find him and deal with the perpetrators. Being a part of Debbie's family was something wonderful, but dangerous, too. Thank God we had a crack security team.

I took a sip of beer. I was exhausted from all the turmoil. Would our lives ever get back to normal?

~ DOC ~

Sitting on top of Cadillac Mountain watching the first rays of sun come up on the East Coast was the closest thing to a spiritual experience I'd had in my life. My camera remained by my side. I couldn't distract myself from the present moment. I couldn't imagine the colors would ever be as spectacular in a photo. Gold, purples, pinks, and blues, changing from second to second, swept me up in the experience, making me an intrinsic part of this miracle. The sun rose in the sky, warming my face, lighting up the rocky terrain of the summit, the colorful trees, and the sparkling ocean below.

Transfixed, I could now see and feel that there is a God, as both my daughters knew.

Annie's belief in God was a given, considering her upbringing in a pastor's home. And then there was her biological grandmother, a woman who painted The Golden Bowl long before Annie found it. Strange, for sure. Annie and Debbie had called it "a God thing," but hadn't spoken much more about it to me. I got the feeling they'd discussed it at length in their time together this summer.

Debbie's strong belief was a mystery to me. Her upbringing must have made her wonder. But then again, her grandmother had some influence in her life, and she was certainly the source of Debbie's amazing artistic ability. Perhaps she'd sparked her belief in God, too.

Then there was Cat, the lyricist and rock star who was drawing the world to God. It seemed no one was unaffected by her. Even her cousin, Debbie's husband, an assassin. God and his ways were most definitely mysterious.

The sun was up, but I remained on the warming rock, the highest point in Hancock County. The wind was still. I removed my jacket and used it as a pillow. The sky was now bright blue, and it mesmerized me.

I wondered why God would put Annie through such turmoil and anxiety, when all she wanted to do was help other people. What's the point? My only thought was that things would be better for her once the consultants and tax men were done. Hopefully, they'd build a solid foundation that would provide for her through her retirement.

With all of Annie's prayers, if God didn't convince her to let go of all the anxiety she was feeling, I would. I'd had a successful career in medicine and invested wisely. I'd see to it that Annie wouldn't have to worry.

~ ANNIE ~

Buck had sectioned off a second floor private dining room to conduct the job interviews. Each pre-screened candidate had a few moments to sit with my managers, Buck, and me. At the end of the process on Saturday we discussed all the applicants and short-listed a dozen people to run our new customer service/order department.

Some of our current servers were on the list of applicants. Since we'd be needing additional servers, regardless of how many would be transferring to customer service, Buck had planned another round of interviews for Sunday.

Buck and I were still refining the list of new employees on Monday morning when Jim Curley returned for breakfast and auditing. He began with a fresh cup of coffee and conversation. "I took that note home. My wife and I had a good laugh over that one. Give to Caesar! A little tax humor there."

Buck joined him in a chuckle, then made a face at me as Jim refilled his cup and led us outside.

"My wife wants to come for dinner some night soon. She's been interested in all the celebrity news since Paulo and Cat Clemente were here." His big fist reached down into the golden bowl for a new prayer.

My heart skipped a beat when I saw it was another from Cat.

Jim read aloud. "*He sent forth his word and healed them; he rescued them from the grave. Psalm 107:20*" He pursed his lips. "Well, that's an interesting one." He glanced up at me with a sharp glint in his eyes. "Maybe you'll be rescued from paying any tax penalties."

"Yes." I swallowed, nervously, trying to smile.

By now, it was obvious I was no use in the auditing process. Even if Jim or Buck took the time to explain something, it was pointless. If I did follow it, I forgot it in minutes. My nerves wouldn't let me focus. So Buck graciously suggested I go about my normal routine in the restaurant, and they would call if they needed me.

Thank God! I ran right for The Bakery & Sweet Shop, bent on having an extra large hot fudge sundae with blueberry and chocolate chip ice cream. Karen would have a few extra scoops for a desperate woman.

Though it was not quite noon, the place was full. The aroma of coffee and confections was enticing. Before I could duck into the bakery's private office, a woman standing in line asked me for my autograph. I couldn't help but giggle. After a brief chat, I ran straight for the office. I needed to look over the orders for the meal prep facility and plan menus for the upcoming weeks.

Karen poked her head in. “Would you like some coffee?”

I swallowed my pride. “I’m going to need an extra-large sundae . . . for lunch.”

After Karen burst out laughing, she placed the order, then joined me at my makeshift desk, an old round table we’d found in the barn before we started renovations.

I was soon indulging in the sweetest of lunches while Karen sipped coffee beside me.

I wiped some stray whipped cream from the tip of my nose. “I can’t believe we could hire so many new staff in the space of two days. They’re top notch.”

She smiled proudly. “That new website and customer service department is exactly what we need. They’ll take some time to get up to speed, but they’re good people. And they really admire you. That’s what makes the difference. The Golden Bowl is the best place to work in Maine . . . or anywhere. It’s because of you. It comes from the top down. People are clamoring to work here, so we can take the best of the best.”

I let a spoonful of blueberry ice cream linger in my mouth. It *was* the best ice cream anywhere. “I can’t do anything without all of you. You make this place run, and you really care. That’s what makes the difference here—employees, and especially managers who really care. I can’t thank you enough.” I could feel myself getting weepy. *Too much sugar*.

“Well, you inspire us. And Mr. Wynn, too. I wasn’t so sure I was gonna like him at first. But he’s a good guy under that designer suit. He really wants what’s best for The Golden Bowl, the customers, and the staff. He did an awesome job on the website.”

“I have to take a closer look. It went live this morning, and I haven’t had a chance to really study it. But I think they got the message right. I loved the photos and videos they used.”

Karen lit up. "It's perfect! We've already had orders for ice cream and baked goods. Mr. Wynn was right. There are people willing to pay top dollar to ship ice cream. We've got orders from all over the country, and Gerald's team is diving right into it. *And* we have inquiries from some big grocery chains. Those are forwarded to your inbox and Mr. Wynn's. So check it out. It's really great. Right now they get an automated response that says we'll get back to them ASAP. But due to a high volume of inquiries, it might take a little time. Makes it sound like we're in demand. And we are." Karen took in a deep breath. "I wasn't so sure before, but now I know you were right to hire Mr. Wynn and his company."

"Well, they know how to generate business. That's for sure."

"They did a great job using the Amanda James' interview and some of the video about the ice cream—and supposedly leaking the news about Cat and the lemon bars. Very clever."

"He is. Well, Buck and his team." I could feel an inopportune blush coming on, so I dove into my sundae. "You make a fabulous sundae." I realized I was speaking with my mouth full. Looking up to apologize to her, I saw Nathan looming in the doorway behind her. The ice cream slid down the wrong way.

As I sat choking, Karen ran for a glass of water, and Nathan came to my aid. I tried pushing him away, my embarrassment too much to bear. I slurped the water and finally managed, "I'm okay." I covered my face with my napkin. *What is it with him*?

He took a seat at the old table that served as a desk and waited. Karen slipped out the door.

I did a final wipe with the napkin. "What can I do for you, Mr. Rhodes?"

He rose from the seat and shut the office door. "Lisa Quinn took a box of steaks from the cold room and hid it under the porch near the trash. Since you have a personal relationship, I thought I should ask you what you want me to do."

The ice cream landed with a thud in the pit of my stomach. Food theft is a common problem in the restaurant business, but it was rarely a problem for me. If someone gave me a sad face they could eat as much as they wanted for free. In my years at The Golden Bowl, I'd fired only two people for stealing food and supplies. Now Lisa?

Emotion welled up. "How could she?"

He had a strange look on his face. "You're a very trusting, kind person, Mrs. Brewster. She strikes me as the type to do whatever it takes—right or wrong."

I let out a sigh. "Lisa's had a rough life. I thought she was trying to turn herself around. Just yesterday she signed up for Wednesday morning group. Why would she do that, then steal?"

Nathan dragged his hand down his face in a gesture of exasperation. It dawned on me how pitiful this was. He was a former SEAL. It had to be a big step down for him guarding a business woman in a tiny seaside town.

I cleared my throat. "I don't mean to whine. I know you're a highly trained security guard—director—with a lot more things to worry about than petty theft." That handsome face was unfathomable. "I'm sorry you're so bored here."

"Ma'am, I'm not bored. I'm trying to do my job. I take it you want to wait until that Wednesday counseling session before confronting her?"

I dared not correct his impression of Wednesday morning group. "That's probably a good idea. Thank you."

"We'll see what becomes of the steaks, and keep an eye on her until you tell us otherwise." He got up and left.

I returned to my puddle of ice cream, fudge sauce, and whipped cream and obsessively fished out the cherry.

CHAPTER 9

~ LISA ~

I sat in the rocker with Rosie in my arms watching the six o'clock news. Peg came in with a slice of cake and sat on the couch. "Rosie's out cold." Peg had a hoarse laugh.

"Yeah, long day, I guess." I turned to Peg. "I did one of the stupidest things in my life today."

She looked up at me.

"Ryan told me I had to steal him some steaks. I took a box and stuck it in a trash bag and put it by the trash. He's gonna pick it up tonight. I feel like a traitor. Annie doesn't need this crap."

"Not after all she's done for you, baby."

I felt sick inside. "Yeah. Ryan said she'd never miss 'em. You can just go in and get 'em free if ya want anyway."

"That's different," Peg said.

"He's tryin' to ruin everything for me." I watched her scrape all the frosting into a chocolate pile.

"He's totally different now. Totally different person. When you guys got married, I thought he'd be a good husband for you. Working two or three jobs. Ambitious, ya know. But it all went up his nose. Everything. Even that good job at the car dealership. Now he'd kill ya as soon as look at ya. Just use ya for whatever he can get. He don't care anymore."

I wasn't going to cry in front of Peg. I swallowed tears and laid my face on Rosie's head. Maybe I'd have to sell this place and move far away, just to get away from him.

~ LISA ~

I was a little nervous about joining Annie's Wednesday morning group. I mean, what do you say to God after twenty years of ignoring him? But I figured it was the best way to start meeting people I could recruit for my gifting table. Who did I know from Ripple Lake with a thousand dollars? Not a soul.

We met at 6:00 a.m. in one of the small dining rooms. Most of the women were members of The Marberry Girls. They met here for coffee, tea, and prayer every morning and then went for a walk on the beach. Afterwards, they were back for breakfast. But Wednesday was a bigger meeting that brought other women in, too. If you had something to pray about, this was the place to be. When I walked into the room I wondered how I let Annie talk me into this.

I sat beside a woman I recognized from the gifting table party. She looked about my age. "Hi. I'm Lisa."

"I know you! Congratulations on your new house. I'm Donna."

We got into a little conversation, and then Annie walked in with Terri Monahan.

Donna whispered, "Terri is here strictly for the gossip. She says she's big on prayer, but really she just loves the scoop on anything going on in town."

"Oh." I was trying to be nice. But I wasn't surprised about her opinion of Terri.

Annie took charge of the room and introduced me and another new member. Then she said today's topic would be about "the desires of our hearts" from Psalm 37. Servers came in with breakfast.

While all the meals were being served, there were some announcements. One of the women got up and stretched her hand out to me. "Lisa, welcome to the group. I'm Bev, and I work in child care. This summer I babysat for a family who donates their kids' clothes instead of packing them up and taking them home. I have some outfits you might like for Rosie. If anyone else is interested, just let me know. Their kids range in age from toddler up to twelve years old."

"Thanks, that's a big help." I couldn't believe she was so nice.

Donna leaned in to me. "It's a really great group. You'll see."

The breakfast was delicious as usual, and I even joined in on the conversation. I usually kept mostly to myself. It felt good to talk with nice people for a change. I couldn't bring myself to talk about the gifting table yet, though. I wondered if Donna was here to recruit, too. "Are you inviting any of these people to the gifting table?"

She turned to me. "A lot of them are already involved. I spoke to some of my old high school friends. Some people at work. I have four so far."

"*Four*? Wow." Now I felt like a slacker. "I'm new in town. Don't know anyone. My old neighborhood . . . people don't have a spare nickel." I left out the part about them spending all their money on drugs, booze, and lottery tickets.

Donna made a sympathetic face. "Well, you could treat it like a business almost. Go canvass businesses and tell them how they can do good by doing good. I think a lot of business people are even doing the VIP Table."

"Hmm. That's a good idea. I'll try that."

After we ate, Annie read a prayer she'd pulled out of the prayer bowl. "*Trust in the Lord and do good; dwell in the land and enjoy safe pasture. Delight yourself in the Lord and he will give you the desires of your heart. Commit your way to the Lord; trust in him and he will do this: He will make your righteousness shine like the dawn, the justice of your cause like the noonday sun. Psalm 37: 3-6*"

Then she passed out copies of the prayer. We were supposed to write our thoughts on the prayer and share if we wanted to. I took my pencil and underlined "the desires of your heart." My thoughts about that were too much of a jumble to write. I listened to what everyone else had to say. Then I wrote, "Trust God."

Before the meeting ended, everyone was invited to share a prayer about the desire of her heart. Donna shared first and turned to me. "Me? I . . . I want to be a nurse someday." I surprised myself with that one.

~ LISA ~

I was home by 3:00 p.m. and found Peg changing Rosie's diaper.

"I'm going shopping for a new jacket. Mine has the lining all torn. Time for a new one before winter really sets in. Wanna come? Rosie's ready to rock." She handed me my baby.

I planted a kiss on Rosie's forehead. "Nah. Thanks anyway, but I thought I'd take Rosie for a stroll around Marberry Square. It's still pretty nice out. We can use the fresh air." I wasn't going to tell her about my gifting table business yet. But since there were so many commercials using kids and pets to sell stuff, I thought people might take pity on me if I went around to local businesses with Rosie. How could they resist my pitch? I was a single mom trying to do good by doing good.

Peg made kind of a weird face. "It'll be dark soon. I'll drop you at the Square, so you'll just have to walk back. But call me if you get tired, and I'll come get you."

"Okay. Thanks."

Fifteen minutes later me and Rosie and our cool new stroller were in a dress shop making my first pitch. The lady was nice, but she told me she didn't have that kind of money, especially since tourist season was over. I guess it was a good excuse.

Then, a woman came out of the dressing room and went right to the register with an armload of stuff. The shop owner gave me a look, but I didn't care. I started chatting with the woman. She loved Rosie. She said she lived around the Portland area, but came up Marberry way to visit family a lot. She handed me her card, and I gave her an invitation to Peter's next party at The Golden Bowl. Then I walked out with the woman so the storekeeper didn't yell at me.

I went into the drycleaners next door, then a toy store. The drycleaner was a maybe, and the toy store clerk was a stupid kid who couldn't understand what I was talking about. I made a note in my little notebook to come back when the owner would be in.

By now, Rosie was getting restless, so I steered the stroller to the gas station and variety store to get her a snack. There were people in line to pay, and the clerk didn't look too interested, but I practiced my quick pitch anyway. A nice looking guy in a dark woolen coat smiled at me. I quickly paid for Rosie's juice and cornered him with the stroller. "Hi." I smiled at him, suddenly forgetting I was probably fifty pounds heavier than any girl he'd date.

He smiled back. "Can I buy you a coffee? I'm interested to hear more about your new business."

"Sure!" I gave him my coffee order and went outside to sit on a bench. I saw he had a really nice car parked at the gas pump. I practiced my pitch in my head and pictured dollar signs. By the time he came over, Rosie had had enough of her juice, and her stuffed toy was keeping her busy.

He barely had a sip of coffee before I was giving him every detail. He seemed to follow the appetizer to dessert thing pretty well. "We're having a little party at The Golden Bowl to introduce people. You can see how Peter's school is coming along and all the good work he's doing. And you can meet Annie Brewster. She's been doing this . . . like . . . since the start. They put on a fun party. You know, The Golden Bowl has great food, and it's free. You just learn all about the gifting table and have great food and meet nice people, and it's fun."

He nodded at me, and I was thinking he'd definitely do the VIP Table.

"Sounds like I need to take a look at this."

"Yeah!" I grabbed an invitation from my notebook and noticed Terri Monahan marching toward us. I had to think fast. I didn't want her stealing my prospect. "Oh, here's Mrs. Monahan. She's one of the leaders in charge. She can tell you, too."

Terri glared at me. "Lisa, I need to speak with you for a minute."

"Yeah. Um." I turned to my prospect. "I'm sorry, I didn't get your name."

He looked up at Terri. "Special Agent Tim Hayes, IRS-CI."

Terri's lips pursed in a weird surprised look. "What?"

He grinned a little. "Do you know Ponzi schemes are illegal, Mrs. Monahan?"

Her lips pressed tighter.

Terri's confused. But my training kicked in. "I don't know Ponzi, but this isn't a scheme—it's a strategy!"

~ ANNIE ~

Terri grabbed my arm as we left the Thursday morning Marberry Girls meeting. "Now that Doc is out of town, we should see a movie tonight. Ted works late most of the time, so there's nothing keeping me."

I stopped at the top of the stairs and noticed her bloodshot eyes. "You don't look well. Are you sure you're up for a movie?"

"I'm fine. Stayed up too late. I'm going for a walk with The Marberry Girls, but you call me, okay? We need to talk. It's been too long."

"I will." *How to fit that in my schedule*? As we headed downstairs I saw Jim Curley arriving for more auditing fun.

"Hello, Annie!" He smiled. "Good morning, Mrs. Monahan. Nice to see you again."

Terri managed a pained smile. "Hello." She brushed

past Jim and mouthed a "call me" gesture as she left.

As Jim and Buck assembled in the office, I went to get the coffee. Nathan met me at the serving station. His voice was low. "Mrs. Brewster, you remember I told you Ryan Quinn picked up that box of steaks around midnight, Monday. What are we doing about that?"

I might have known he wouldn't forget. I tried to mollify him. "I heard he started a job as a custodian at Marberry Academy last week. He was unemployed for months before this."

"He's a punk."

"Okay. Thanks. I'll try and have a talk with Lisa today. Let's just leave it for now. Okay?"

"Yes, ma'am."

My hands shook, and I didn't know why. I guess it was the fear of another day of tax auditing. Nathan took the rattling mugs from me. "I'll take the coffee pot and cups for you." Grateful for his steady hand, I thanked him.

When we reached the office, Buck and Jim were in deep conversation about the election results. Relief came over me as the coffee diverted them from politics. The last thing I needed was Buck offending Jim somehow.

Jim's ringing phone distracted him from all of it, and he accidentally hit the speaker. "Daddy?" The whispered horror in a little girl's voice stopped all of us cold. Nathan turned back into the room and shut the door.

"Kara! Are you okay?"

"He's got the twins, Daddy, and everyone. There's a man with a rifle. He shot the principal, I think. Help us, Daddy. I don't know what to do."

Jim went whiter than a sheet. "Where are you, Kara?"

"In the sink closet."

"What school?" Nathan asked.

"Marberry—Marberry Academy," Jim squeaked. "Stay, stay on the phone, Kara."

Nathan reached for the phone as Buck explained he was a SEAL in charge of our security. "Kara, we'll be right there to get you. Don't move from the closet and stay on the phone with me. I'm Nathan."

He turned on his heel to leave as Billy arrived. "Stay here with Mrs. Brewster. Alert the police."

While Billy was talking to the police department—which in Marberry was all of three officers in the off-season—Jim's round face grew pink, and large drops of sweat formed on his forehead. He struggled for air. "My . . . my daughters . . . my girls are all in there . . ." He lumbered to the door.

Billy blocked him. "Mr. Curley, there's nothing you can do. Just sit tight for now. We'll get the kids out."

But Jim wasn't having it. He raised his hand to strike Billy. In one smooth motion, Billy put the phone down and subdued Jim into the chair. "Don't make me tie you down, Mr. Curley."

Jim burst into tears.

God help us. I grasped Jim's hands. "Let's pray." He looked at me as though I was crazy.

~ ANNIE ~

Half an hour later, the police told Billy the gunman at the school had taken everyone hostage after shooting the principal and her administrative assistant. The new custodian, Ryan Quinn, had apparently let the man into the school, and had been shot to death. His body still lay on the front stairs.

All two hundred students from kindergarten through middle school and their teachers had been herded into the gym of this private school. All but ten-year-old fifth grader, Kara Curley, who remained quietly on the line from the janitor's closet.

Then word came in that Peter Fellowes had used a school van to take his students on a field trip. Peter, his assistant, Louise Gugino, and six children never arrived at their destination in Portland. No one had heard from them. Neither Peter nor Louise were answering their cell phones. None of the students—all special needs children—had phones with them. With that news, I broke down. What had become of them? What would become of the children and teachers held hostage in the gym?

An hour later we sat silently in the office, praying, sipping coffee, thinking, and sweating. Billy's phone rang, and he stepped out of the office to take the call. Jim broke down sobbing again, his tears soaking my unkempt tax records. How meaningless this whole project seemed now. What a waste of time. Of life.

Billy slipped back in and gently closed the door behind him. "Mrs. Brewster, Mr. Wynn, we'll be leaving for home right now. Mr. Curley, the police are on the way. They'll re-unite you with Kara. Mr. Rhodes got her out of that janitor's closet. She's safe and sound. They're working on getting the twins out, too."

As Jim burst out crying, Billy turned to Buck and me. "We'll walk straight out to the car quickly and quietly. I'll help you with your coat, Mrs. Brewster. Please be sure to take your personal belongings."

"What's going on? Why are we leaving?" Buck was first to get the question out.

"I'll explain as soon as we're underway. Let's go."

We exited my office and faced a restaurant full of people. Faces wet with tears. I'd never heard such silence in The Golden Bowl. I'd never felt such an atmosphere of anxiety. Ever. As our guards led us down the stairs, two state police cruisers pulled up.

Jim was directed to the first one. I grabbed his hand. "I'm praying for you."

He turned to me, his face red and swollen. "Thank you, Annie. Thank you." He squeezed my hands in his and left with the officer.

Buck and I settled into the back seat of our car, with our driver and Billy in the front. The police cruiser led us swiftly home. It was so surreal neither of us questioned

Billy until we filed into the panic room in the basement of our house.

I focused on Buck's blank face.

"Billy?" My voice sounded strange.

He shut the door and locked it. "Just a precaution."

"This is no precaution." Buck drew me to his side. "What's going on?"

Billy faced us. "The perpetrator has been identified as Carson Phelps. He and his family have had an ongoing gripe with the president. David Lambrecht shot Adam Phelps years ago when there was an attempt on the president's life in Vienna. So now it looks like Carson Phelps is taking up the cause. He looked straight up at the surveillance camera at the front door of the school and smiled—right after he shot Ryan Quinn. He was obviously sending a message. Now he's demanding Annie Brewster and David Lambrecht show up at Marberry Academy."

"That's ridiculous," Buck said. "We're supposed to turn them over in return for the children?"

"That's his demand."

My heart pushed into my dry throat and my stomach burned in fear.

"And he's waiting for Lambrecht to come from Salzburg?" Buck's eyes bulged as they often did when he was incredulous.

"We've got to do it. He'll shoot the kids if we don't." My knees threatened to give way, but Buck held me up.

Billy eyed us both. "They'll be okay. The state police are there. And Rhodes. They'll take care of this guy, Phelps. We just sit tight." Then he disappeared into an adjacent room filled with computers and all the equipment that monitored every inch of the property, inside and out. A large room beside that one housed every imaginable weapon you could need to defend the place. Our own personal fort.

Buck guided me to a couch and sat beside me. He took out a linen handkerchief and wiped his brow.

"What about Doc?" My voice was a rasp.

"I'm sure he's fine. He's with Keith and Roger in the middle of the woods."

"Doc doesn't exactly have a good track record in the woods. He went off hiking once and got hit over the head. Some lunatic out there in the middle of a pine forest. He never found out who attacked him or why. But he had a heck of a concussion. Lucky he wasn't killed." That thought propelled me off the couch and into the computer room. Billy was obviously in the middle of a serious conversation, but I couldn't tell what it was about. When he signed off, he turned to me.

"Billy, what about Doc?"

"They're on their way. I'm expecting them in an hour or so. They'll be fine, Mrs. Brewster."

"Okay, thanks. I should call my parents."

"No need. They're on their way."

"Okay." My stomach knotted despite his assurances.

I turned back through the doorway and sat in a nearby chair where I'd dumped my bag. Billy watched as I rifled through it to find my phone. As soon as I had it in my hand, he took it from me.

I looked up at Billy in shock. "I . . . I need to call my sister."

"She's safe and sound, ma'am." Billy deposited the phone on his console. "There's no need for you to call now." He busied himself with his computer.

Shock turned to indignation. I looked over at Buck, who had his eyebrows raised in that knowing way he had. "Why can't I talk to Debbie?" *And then it came to me.*

"David's on his way."

CHAPTER 10

~ LISA ~

The minute I heard about the gunman at Marberry Academy, I told Ashleigh I had to leave. I didn't know if she could find another dishwasher, but it didn't matter. I ran home as fast as my chubby legs would carry me. I don't know if I was fuming mad or relieved when I found the kitchen door unlocked. I held onto the counter, bent over, trying to catch my breath. Peg watched me from her seat at the table. Rosie was in her arms, smiling at me.

The startled look on her face faded. "What's the matter, baby? Are you sick?"

I took another gasp of air. "I need your car, Peg. You and Rosie stay here. Lock all the doors. Don't let anyone in. Shut the shades. Somethin's goin' on at the school." I had a coughing fit and used the time to run around and check the doors and windows. By the time I sipped some water and quit coughing, Peg had followed me upstairs. Rosie reached for me from her arms.

"What's goin' on at the school?" She put Rosie on the bed and turned on the TV.

"I don't know. I gotta go." I kissed Rosie. "Don't open the door for anyone!"

I got to the car and screeched out of the driveway in a panic. What did Ryan get himself into now?

I replayed our last conversation in my head, over and over. I had a sick feeling in my stomach telling me he was in cahoots with some nut with an axe to grind. Some guy from away, he'd said. No wonder he was so excited about taking a janitor job. Easy money, he'd said. *Easy money*.

Maybe I'd have to pack up the car, get my money out of the bank, take Peg and Rosie, and make a run for it. *Why am I driving into this*?

Marberry Academy was a private school at the edge of town, in the woods down a bunch of winding roads. People always called it Historic Marberry Academy, I guess because it was a real old building with a beautiful lawn that went down to the ocean. Rich people bussed their kids there from a lot of different towns. As I sped along, I could see a police car blocking the main road to the school. I hung a quick left and bumped along a dirt road shortcut I knew.

Police cars lined the driveway when I pulled up to the school, but there weren't any parents around from what I could see. A cop I recognized from The Golden Bowl grabbed me by the sleeve. "You can't go in there. Get in your car and go home."

I snatched myself out of his grip and ran to the front door. A dollar bill flew into my face and woke me up. Money was flying around in the wind. There was a body on the stairs. "Ryan!"

The shock dropped me to my knees. Two cops hauled me up and into a cruiser.

~ ANNIE ~

Buck turned on the television without opposition from Billy. I watched and prayed as reporters repeated the same information over and over again. The only thing Billy hadn't mentioned to us was that the sea breeze had swept up hundreds of dollars in cash swirling around the body of Ryan Quinn.

Lisa's ex-husband was dead. *God help Lisa and Rosie*. Nathan had called him a punk after he'd stolen a box of steaks from me. Considering he'd been unemployed for so long, I could understand. But now he was accused of admitting the gunman to the school in return for some cash. All caught on the school's surveillance video. *Another tragedy to come out of Ripple Lake*. I stared into space, pondering this wretched situation.

Periodic announcements of the disappearance of Peter Fellowes, Louise Gugino, and their six students captured my attention. There was no new information. It was as though they'd fallen off the edge of the earth. *Poor Pinky*. He must have been in agony, waiting for news of his dear daughter, Louise. She'd devoted much of her life to taking care of him and helping him with his accounting business. She said her teaching assistant position at Marberry Academy was her way of doing something for herself. I'd always admired Louise's selflessness.

Buck's voice made me jump out of my reverie. "No!" He pointed to the TV. The ongoing hostage crisis at Marberry Academy was interrupted with a special report. "The president's been shot!"

Billy walked right past us and let Doc and my parents inside. Keith and Roger remained outside with the rest of our security team.

I was stunned silent. In case no one had heard, Buck repeated, "The president's been shot."

I hugged my parents then Doc who spoke up to be heard over Buck. "It's okay. The bullets got him in his vest. He's going to be fine."

"He's in hospital," Buck said.

Doc turned to face him. "It serves their purposes. They're not telling the public about his injuries—or lack of injuries—just yet."

Mom and Dad sat together on a small couch and sat me down between them. Mom whispered in my ear. "I think Doc'll be an honorary SEAL by the time all this is over."

It was true. Reporters whipped the television audience into a frenzy, but Billy reluctantly confirmed Doc's opinion.

The president was in good condition, admitted to the hospital mostly as a precaution. He'd been exiting a hotel in Washington, D.C. after addressing the National Conference of Educators, when a sniper's bullets hit. Two Secret Service agents were slightly injured.

I headed to our fully stocked kitchen wondering how people could eat while living in a panic room. All I needed was a cup of tea. Doc followed me in and grabbed a bottle of spring water from the fridge.

"They won't let me call Debbie," I said. "I think David is on his way here. Why else would they say we can't talk?"

Doc took a gulp of his water. "Sounds reasonable. The police might be trying to be as conservative as possible—not take any chances. Maybe they think David could be the decoy, and then the SWAT team could get the guy."

My hands trembled as I took out the tea bag, making a mess of the paper wrapping. "I know he's put himself in harm's way a thousand times at least, but if something happens to him here, I'll never forgive myself. I don't have a family depending on me. They should let *me* do that job. The guy said he wanted me there, too."

Doc wrapped his arm around my shoulder. "I'm sure David has done this sort of thing a million times, and he's trained for it. There's no reason in the world for you to offer yourself up to this nutcase." He took the mangled tea bag from me, put it in the mug, and poured the hot water. "Here, let's have a seat at the table and calm down a bit."

Chamomile tea and conversation did the trick. My anxiety lifted enough that I teased Doc about surviving his camping trip unscathed. We returned to the television to find the same reports running over and over. I withdrew into the *23rd Psalm*, and the monotony of my repetitions lulled me to sleep.

When I woke up, I was on the couch, my head on Buck's shoulder. Light from the television was the only illumination in the room. In my grogginess I leaned closer to Buck, and he put his arm around me.

Doc observed us from a recliner.

I sat up and rubbed my eyes. “Is David here?”

“No sign of him,” Buck said.

Fear shot through me. “The kids?”

“They’re still locked in the school, Annie. No one knows of any change. It must be freezing in there. They shut down the power before noon.”

I groaned and tried to focus on the TV. “What’s this?”

Doc chimed in. “They’ve been showing this video continuously for hours now. Nathan helped the principal and her assistant out through their office window. They were both shot, but they’re expected to make a full recovery. Then Nathan climbed in that window and found little Kara in the custodian’s closet. He got her out of there, and she’s safe with her parents now.”

“Thank God!” It was a dramatic video. I praised God for putting Nathan in a place where he could make such a difference. Maybe it was worth the boredom of the job as my director of security.

As clarity heightened, I noticed my parents had gone. “Did Mom and Dad go to bed?”

Doc leaned forward in his seat. “Yes. Why don’t you get to bed, too? Get some rest. I’ll let you know if there’s any important development.”

“What about the president?”

“They say he’s resting comfortably, and they’re looking for a lone gunman. That’s it.” Doc got out of his seat. “Let me help you to your room.”

“David should’ve been here long ago—even if he took a row boat . . .” Buck gave a gentle push at my back while Doc took me by the hands and pulled me from the couch.

“I’m sure David’s in the U.S. by now. I’ll let you know when we hear something. Good night.”

I ambled down a long hall that led to ten small bedrooms. David and his colleagues had thought of everything when they built this place. It was constructed and supplied to keep us safe for months, if need be.

I stared at tired eyes in the bathroom mirror. My hair had mostly come undone from the clip and looked like an eggbeater had tossed it around my head. *That's lovely*. I worked my brush through the snarled mess and was painfully and totally awake by the end of the process. Prayer eluded me. My thoughts and words were a jumble.

I was afraid for David, worried about Debbie, Peter and Louise and those kids lost somewhere, and the hostage situation at the school. It was all too much. And Nathan had jumped right to the rescue.

Knowing Nathan was out there in danger had me even more frightened. An ex-Navy SEAL, he was a superhero to me, but anything could happen. I sent up a plea for protection and safety and decided to go back to the television room.

Buck and Doc were out cold, the TV replaying the same old news again. The door to the control room was closed, but I decided to intrude. My hand on the doorknob, I was about to knock when I heard Roger's voice on the other side. "Lambrecht got Boyd Phelps."

Billy offered his descriptive, though hushed approval. All I could make out were expletives and "ABCs."

What were ABCs . . . and who was *Boyd* Phelps? It wasn't the time to impose myself on Roger and Billy. Their conversation was now unintelligible. Buck had stretched out on the couch, so I pulled a comfortable chair in front of the TV and considered this latest snippet of information. *Boyd Phelps*. *Carson Phelps*. David had shot Adam Phelps in Vienna. *ABC*.

~ LISA ~

It was 4:00 a.m. I sat on a cot in a cell in the basement of the Marberry police station. I'd been crying into my sleeve for hours and hours. They wouldn't let me call Peg or see Rosie. No one knew I was there, because I was a suspected terrorist. How could this happen? Ryan. That's how. I'd probably rot in here.

A cop came and opened the door. “We have two FBI agents here to speak with you.” He took me to a small room with a table and chairs and brought me a glass of water and a napkin to blow my nose. I wondered if I’d need to call a lawyer to get me out of here. But I was innocent, and lawyers cost a lot of money, so I didn’t say anything to the cop.

“Mrs. Quinn, I’m Agent Fuller, I have a few questions for you. For your information, we’re videotaping this interview.” The guy took a seat across from me. His partner watched us from the other side of the room.

My stomach was in knots. “When can I go home?”

“That depends. If you answer truthfully and completely, you may go home today. Now, why don’t you tell us—you’re a dishwasher by profession—how do you have $37,000 in your bank account?”

The pit of my stomach exploded. “I . . . I sold my ring. Terri Monahan paid me $40,000 and I put $39,000 in the bank, and took a thousand in cash, and then I spent another two thousand on . . . stuff.”

The guy had a cold smile. “And then you got a brand new house on the beach?”

I could feel my face twitching and scrunching up. “A-Amanda James. I won the house on her show. She said it’s all mine, and all the taxes were paid, too. That’s what she said.” I rubbed my sleeve over my face. This wasn’t going too good. “I’m not a terrorist, and I’ll pay my taxes. I promise. Just . . . just tell me how much I owe. Okay?”

“Sounds like you’re a very lucky young lady. A forty-thousand-dollar ring and a new house. Ryan Quinn wasn’t the kind of guy to buy you a ring like that, was he?”

I shook my head. “No. I . . . I found the ring. In Annie’s prayer bowl. I work at The Golden Bowl now. It’s a restaurant with a big bowl of prayers, and someone put the ring in there with a note that said, ‘I hope you have better luck with this than me.’”

The two guys burst out laughing. I know my story

sounded crazy. Here I thought finding the ring and winning the house was the best thing ever. But my luck was worse than whoever threw that ring in the bowl. Maybe it was cursed. What could I do? If I tried to run, I wouldn't make it to the door.

"Annie's my boss. She said I could keep it. She said I could keep the ring. Ask Annie!"

The guy quit his laughing. "Annie Brewster is your boss?"

"Yeah. She's the nicest person in the world. She'll tell ya. Maybe she's havin' some tax problems, but she's honest. You can trust her. She'll vouch for me. I promise."

"Okay, Mrs. Quinn, we'll ask Annie Brewster. What do you know about Carson Phelps?"

I stared up at the ceiling and tried to calm down. My heart raced. I was soaking wet with tears and sweat. *Carson Phelps*. The name didn't ring a bell. I looked at the guy. "I don't know who that is."

"You've never heard of Carson Phelps?"

I took a deep breath and let it out. "No."

"Was your husband an associate of his?"

"I don't know. It's been a long time since we've been together. Lately, he's come after me for money. Other than that, he's not interested in me and Rosie."

The guy leaned forward. "You gave him money?"

"Just a couple of times. He stole my coffeemaker and some other stuff. He took money out of my wallet, but I don't keep much in there." I wiped my eyes.

"And he didn't mention any dealings with anyone? Any job?"

I knew I had to tell him. "He said he got a job at Marberry Academy, and he was comin' into some easy money. That's all he said, and I didn't ask anymore about it. I knew he was a bad influence on Rosie, and I didn't want him around. So I did whatever I needed to . . . to get rid of him whenever he came by." Tears started up again. My voice cracked. "Easy money. That's what I thought when I saw him on the stairs with all the blood and the money flyin' around." I put my head down on the table.

~ ANNIE ~

"Mrs. Brewster." I woke up with Billy tapping my hand. Doc, my parents, and Buck were there, too. I was still in the chair. "We're clear to go upstairs now."

"Clear?" I was in a fog. Doc and Buck helped me up.

"The kids are all safe," Doc said. "Nathan and the police got them out. The guy got away from the school. They're still looking for him, but I'm sure he's out of Marberry by now. And the news station said the sniper who shot the president died in a gun battle with law enforcement. So we're safe enough now."

Buck patted me on the back. "Now we can get back to work. Right after breakfast. I'm famished."

He guided me through the door and upstairs. I was a free woman.

Billy was still in security mode. "We'll be staying here, on the grounds, until further notice, Mrs. Brewster, Mr. Wynn."

I *thought* I was a free woman. "Is Carson Phelps really still a danger to us?"

"We're not clear on that yet, ma'am."

"And the children? Peter and Louise? Any word?"

"No word on them, ma'am."

Acid burned in the pit of my stomach.

Mom led the way to the kitchen. "I'll get the breakfast. You take it easy. Sit down, and I'll get you some juice."

"Thanks, I just need a breath of fresh air." I headed out the door.

"Get your coat, Annie, it's freezing out."

I welcomed that cold blast of air to wake me up. Sunrise was underway, and I stepped off the back stair. Nathan stood in front of me. "Nathan! Thank God!" I dove into him, and he wrapped his arms around me.

"Are you all right, Mrs. Brewster?"

His professional voice sobered me fast. I stepped back, and he kept one hand on my arm, presumably to ascertain I was "all right."

"I am, Mr. Rhodes. I'm fine. I'm happy you're okay. So grateful the kids are okay. Thank you, for everything you've done." My voice carried off into the sea breeze. Despite the cold, my face felt on fire.

Not only had I broken my rule and called him Nathan, I hugged the man. Whatever possessed me? I stared at his chest. *What to say*? *What to do*?

"Is . . . is David okay?"

"He's fine as far as I know, ma'am."

"Oh, good." I took an icy breath. "Well, you'll need some breakfast. Come inside. Mom's working on it now."

"Thank you." He opened the door for me.

Buck stood by the window, looking at us, expressionless.

I had a strong feeling he'd seen the entire embarrassing scene. "I'll be right back," I said to whoever was listening. "I need to freshen up." I pushed through the kitchen door and ran upstairs. Maybe a hot shower would wash away these crazy feelings, the embarrassment.

It didn't, but I decided to proceed with my day, ignoring the incident and putting my best foot forward. I put on one of my favorite outfits from my sister, a soft wool jacket and silk blouse in the palest of pinks, paired with comfy navy wool slacks. I brushed my hair up into a clip, and strode purposefully downstairs to the kitchen.

Mom had blueberry waffles and eggs piled high on serving dishes. "Thanks, Mom, this looks delicious." I took the platter of waffles and pushed through the door to the dining room.

"Has anyone heard anything about Peter and Louise and the kids? What could possibly have happened?" I served up the waffles and took my seat. The silence was overwhelming. "And what about Lisa? Her ex-husband was killed. I need to check on her and the baby."

Buck looked like he'd just lost his best friend. Doc gulped his coffee. Dad sat stone-faced, staring into space.

Nathan laid a platter of eggs on the table. "The kids are safe and sound. They found them in the van, not too far from Portland."

I began to shake. "Peter? Louise?"

"They're missing."

"What . . . what happened?"

His eyes penetrated mine. "The kids told the police that Peter and Louise parked the van by the side of the road and told them to stay put. Then they left. They've disappeared."

I put my head in my hands and wept. Mom came up behind me and rubbed my shoulders, trying to soothe me.

"Mrs. Brewster." Nathan's voice was a mix of concern and foreboding that alarmed me to my core.

I lifted my head.

Nathan's face was unreadable. "There are three men on their way over: two FBI agents and Timothy Hayes, Special Agent in Charge of IRS Criminal Investigation in New England."

My mind was a blank. "IRS?"

"Internal Revenue Service, ma'am."

My stomach roiled. "Is . . . is Jim Curley all right? I thought his girls were safe."

Nathan stared at me, his lips unmoving. Mom patted my shoulder.

Buck spoke in a gentle voice. "Annie."

I burst into tears. "Did someone die? I thought they were safe. Peter? Louise? Are they going to die?" Before Buck could come around the table to me, I sank into terror. "*David*? Is he all right? Tell me!"

Buck sat in the chair beside me. "No one's going to die, Annie. They're all okay. All okay." He produced a fine linen handkerchief and patted my face.

We sat in silence for a few moments as I composed myself. My mother's hands continued gently rubbing my back. I glanced from Buck to Nathan to Doc and Dad. "Someone needs to tell me what's going on."

Buck frowned. "Annie, there's a very good chance you could be charged with conspiracy."

"Conspiracy? What do you mean? I thought it was fraud. What did I do? Conspiracy?"

He took his wet hankie out of my hand and wiped his face. "We don't know any of the details. The IRS agent mentioned this in a brief phone conversation with Mr. Rhodes."

Before Nathan could open his mouth, Billy announced our visitors.

CHAPTER 11

~ ANNIE ~

Billy introduced Agents Fuller and Kendall from the FBI, and they displayed their credentials to Nathan. Then he introduced Special Agent Hayes as a member of "The President's Financial Fraud Enforcement Task Force." We all sat in the parlor.

"Mrs. Brewster, I understand you employ Lisa Quinn as a dishwasher. How long have you known her?" Agent Fuller wasted no time on pleasantries.

My heart was in my throat, but I surprised myself with my calm voice. "She's only worked at The Golden Bowl a short time, but I've known her for years. She's from my hometown, Ripple Lake, and she's had some help from my dad's church where I have a kitchen and food pantry. She's a young single mother, you know. I'm so sorry to hear her ex-husband died at the school. Is Lisa okay?"

Agent Fuller's blank eyes and face made the sick feeling in the pit of my stomach even worse. "She's in custody. Do you have any reason to believe she had any prior knowledge of the plot to take over Marberry Academy?"

"Not at all. She's been turning her life around. She has a job with us here. She has a new home, and her daughter is the center of her life. She's been pulling herself up by the bootstraps . . . trying to distance herself from Ryan. Now she's talking about going to nursing school."

"She told us you can confirm that the $40,000 in her bank account was from the sale of a ring she found in a bowl on your restaurant porch."

"Yes. I was standing right there with her at the prayer bowl when she took out the prayer wrapping that ring. She asked if she could keep it, and I said, yes." As I spouted off to the FBI, I watched growing disdain on Nathan's face. He obviously knew the ring was worth much more than $40,000, as well as I did. I made a mental note to confront Terri about it.

Agent Fuller turned to Nathan. "The stories are consistent. We have no reason to hold Lisa Quinn any longer. Send one of your men to pick her up and bring her home. She shouldn't be in any rush to leave Marberry in the near future."

Nathan escorted the FBI agents to the door, and Billy went to get Lisa out of jail.

Meanwhile, Timothy Hayes, Special Agent in Charge of IRS Criminal Investigation in New England, sipped coffee. He had quietly observed my interview with the FBI agents. After they left, he was slow to speak.

"Can I get you another coffee or something to eat?"

"Your coffee is the best I've had in a very long time, Mrs. Brewster. I'll take another cup, thank you."

Mom motioned for me to stay put and went to the kitchen to retrieve a fresh pot.

Agent Hayes leaned forward in his seat. "Jim Curley speaks very highly of you. And that was before your bodyguard saved the day at Marberry Academy."

"Jim's a very nice man."

"Well, I'd say so. He told me you're a very kind woman . . . disorganized . . . and a bit naïve . . . He did his best to try to find an explanation that might exonerate you from some steep penalties. Unfortunately, he found evidence of tax fraud. This is a very serious matter, and it's becoming more serious by the day. Now it's apparent that you're at the center of a Ponzi scheme. There could be enough evidence here for a grand jury."

Buck jumped to the edge of his seat. "Ponzi scheme? What are you talking about?"

Agent Hayes eyed Buck coolly. "Maybe, being from England, you haven't heard of Ponzi schemes, Mr. Wynn?"

Buck's eyes bulged with rage, but before he could answer, Agent Hayes informed us. "Charles Ponzi is famous for using the technique way back in 1920. The Ponzi scheme is a fraudulent investment operation. The original investors in the scheme are paid from new capital paid in by new investors—"

Buck interrupted. "We know what a Ponzi scheme is. Annie doesn't have investments, and she certainly doesn't run one."

Agent Hayes grimaced. "Anne Brewster and Terri Monahan conspired with Peter Fellowes in a gifting tables Ponzi scheme. Witnesses tell me—in addition to recruiting people at $1,000 or $5,000 a pop and misleading them as to the legality and tax implications—Anne Brewster hosted parties where she promoted the opportunity to support Peter Fellowes's nonexistent charity for disabled children, as well as make money for themselves. 'Do good by doing good' was the line. In reality, recruits had little chance of ever seeing their money again, and Anne Brewster, Peter Fellowes, and Terri Monahan walked off with the cash."

Buck turned to me, eyes on fire. "What?"

My throat was parched and my voice sounded strange. "Agent Hayes is mistaken, Buck. Peter is building a school for disabled kids—right on the water. It's beautiful. I've seen the pictures with my own eyes. It's going to be state of the art. We were just starting another round of funding. And it *is* a tax deductible charity. Louise Gugino told me. She checked with Pinky. She said the money is tax-free and everything is legal."

Buck glared at Agent Hayes and then at me. "Annie has given away practically every penny she's ever received. Her personal checkbook—her one and only account—contains $35.45 of her own money. Her business checkbook is hemorrhaging as we speak. Does that sound like a criminal?" Buck turned toward him.

Agent Hayes smiled for the first time. "You make a point, Mr. Wynn."

Mom handed him a fresh coffee, the cup almost spilling from her shaking. "Please understand, Annie would never do anything illegal. I'm sure Peter has a good explanation."

Agent Hayes nodded. "Thank you, Mrs. Auclair. I'm sure he does."

Buck's voice escalated. "Let's put our thinking caps on. Something is amiss with Louise Gugino. She obviously lied to Annie about the legality of the gifting tables. I believe she finagled Annie's tax returns as well. Annie admittedly paid little to no attention to the figures on her returns. She trusted Pinky Gugino as her accountant, and Louise as his assistant. And now Louise Gugino mysteriously disappears with Peter Fellowes. Annie, did Louise have anything to do with your tax forms?"

I wondered why we were suddenly discussing tax returns, but I knew Buck had my best interests at heart. "Louise was wonderful. She always respected my time. She'd bring Pinky's forms right to the restaurant, and I'd sign one after the other. Then she'd leave me with a copy and take the rest to submit. She helped her dad tremendously."

Buck pointed his finger at Agent Hayes. "It's obvious that Louise Gugino altered Annie's tax returns. Annie likely signed a return the IRS received *and* a return we thought she filed. Annie paid no attention. She would never have known. She trusted Louise. Unfortunately."

Agent Hayes grunted. He seemed to be considering Buck's scenario.

Buck stood up and paced. "There you have it. Louise Gugino filed fraudulent taxes and undoubtedly collected refunds. Annie's mistake was—and sounds like it still *is*—one of mislaid trust. Now Louise has disappeared with this Peter Fellowes. Don't you think she's up to her neck in something?"

"It's entirely possible. But tax payers are responsible for checking their returns. And we still have the gifting tables scheme. Mrs. Brewster is up to her neck in that one."

"I'm sure if I talk to Pinky, he'll straighten everything out. He'll know," I said.

Agent Hayes' eyes narrowed. "Pinky Gugino was admitted to a nursing home three days ago. He's not doing well."

The shock turned me into a quivering mess. "Oh! Poor Pinky."

Buck dragged an old mahogany chair over and took a seat facing me. He took my soggy hands in his and looked into my eyes. "Annie, I know you're worried for these people, but it appears they are not your true friends. Agent Hayes told us Peter Fellowes was running a scam. There is no school for disabled children."

I gulped. "He's wrong, Buck. I've seen the pictures. I've watched the construction progressing. Every time Peter came to the restaurant, he'd show us all the photos on his phone. He was so excited. It was a dream coming true."

Agent Hayes shook his head. "Did he tell you where the construction was taking place for the school?"

"In Washington Harbor. It's beautiful. Right on the water."

He made a face. "There's no school going up there. That's Rick Thorne's new estate. The billionaire from New York. He's building his summer home there."

I was becoming indignant. "Mr. Hayes, you haven't seen the pictures."

"I *have* seen them. Terri Monahan gave them to me Wednesday night."

The wind was knocked out of me, I couldn't speak, and my head spun. It dawned on me that Jim Curley must have audited Terri Monahan's jewelry business. He obviously knew her. He'd addressed her by name when we saw him Thursday after The Marberry Girls meeting. More than likely, with that sheepish look on her face, Terri was the one who instigated my audit with whatever flag Jim had uncovered when he reviewed her accounts.

And now this! Terri had given Peter's construction photos to Agent Hayes. Why wouldn't she have told me on Thursday morning? Then I realized that talk about seeing a movie—that was an excuse to get together, to tell me about it.

What about Ted? I caught my breath. "Agent Hayes, you know Terri's husband, Ted, is a prominent real estate agent. He would have known if those photos were false. He never doubted Peter Fellowes."

Agent Hayes smirked into his empty coffee cup. "Ted Monahan all but admitted he knew those photos were fake. He went along with it for the sake of his wife. You and Terri Monahan were well entrenched in this gifting table scheme by the time he caught wind of it. So he made a conscious decision to go along with it. Sounds like he was in the middle of expanding his real estate business and some nastiness with his first wife when this gifting table idea started. Now, Terri doesn't strike me as the meek and mild sort. I'm sure he didn't want to rock the boat in his second marriage. Did he?"

I had no idea what to say.

Buck stood. "Agent Hayes, before you run roughshod over Anne Brewster, I suggest you take a long hard look at Louise Gugino and her father's accounting business. This pillar of society here in Marberry seems to be smack in the middle of this so-called conspiracy. If anything, it's a conspiracy against Annie. Louise filed fraudulent taxes. Louise advised Annie and her friend Terri that this gifting table was legal, and the money was tax-free. Not that Annie ever took a dime of it. I've examined her accounts. I challenge you to tell me how she's profited from any of this."

Agent Hayes stood and handed his coffee cup to Buck. "Still working on that. But I'll let you know what I come up with. Meanwhile, Mrs. Brewster should not be planning a trip to Austria—or anywhere out of Maine for that matter."

Buck looked like he wanted to hit the IRS agent with the cup. "Nonsense! Annie is not a flight risk."

"Good." Agent Hayes turned to me. "Thanks for the coffee, Mrs. Brewster. I'll be in touch."

Buck followed him to the door and practically slammed it behind him. He turned to Nathan, now standing nearby in the foyer. "I need a word with you."

They headed toward the kitchen. I forced myself up on rubbery legs and followed them.

As I went to push through the swinging door, I heard Buck's commanding voice. "Call David immediately. He needs to know what's going on here. Someone has to nip this folly in the bud. Or Annie could end up in the middle of a scandal that family doesn't need or want. Not to mention the serious prison time she'll face if they decide to make an example of her."

"I'll get a message to him ASAP," Nathan said.

Buck let his irritation out in a boom. "Get *him*! We don't have time for messages."

"He's on assignment. I'll do my best."

Buck was like a barnyard dog. "See that you do. I'll call Cisco. Annie's going to need a good lawyer, not some hack from Marberry, Maine."

Nathan rammed through the kitchen door, knocking me to the floor. My last thought before I passed out was that I was going to jail.

~ LISA ~

When the cop opened the door to my cell and said I could go home, I couldn't get up the stairs fast enough. I ran right into Billy.

He took me by my arms. "Hey Lisa, I'm here to take you home. Sorry you had such a rough time."

I busted out crying like an idiot. He put his arm around me and brought me outside to his car. I sat in the passenger seat, wiping my face with my soaking wet sleeve.

I must've looked like a wreck.

He got in the driver's seat and handed me a box of tissues from the glove compartment. "Here, try these."

"Okay." I sucked in the tears and blew my nose so loud it sounded like geese honking. "Is Rosie okay? Peg?"

"They're fine. I called Peg on my way over here. She was really worried about you, but I explained everything."

"Thanks." I wiped my eyes.

"Can I get you a cup of coffee or something?"

"I've got coffee at home. I'll make you some. Okay?"

"Great." He smiled at me, and I forgot all about Ryan stealing my coffeemaker.

Peg met us at the door with Rosie in her arms, and I grabbed them both in a long hug. Billy was nice about taking charge, and he told Peg I needed something to eat. They both went to the kitchen to put together a meal.

I sat on my couch, Rosie pressed to me, her sweet baby smell filling me. My tears wet the both of us. She was starting to doze off. I stared at the flames flaring up from the fake logs in my fireplace, thinking, hoping we were finally safe. I couldn't get the picture of Ryan on those steps out of my head. There was blood all over the place, and he was dead. Gone.

It bothered me to feel relieved about it. Was I a bad person to be thankful that he wouldn't be around to threaten me or Rosie anymore? Life would be different. I hoped it would be better. Maybe eventually, I could tell Rosie about him, when she was older. She wouldn't have to know the awful truth, but I could tell her about some of the good times.

Billy came in with two cups of coffee and Peg with two sandwiches. Peg set the stuff on tray tables. "I'm gonna put Rosie down for her nap now. She didn't get much sleep since yesterday. I'll be with her. Just call me if ya need anything."

I let Peg take her and watched them head up the stairs. I picked up my mug. "Sorry about the coffeemaker."

Billy grinned. "No problem, there's more'n one way to make a good cup of coffee."

"Thank you."

"For what?" The grin stayed.

"For gettin' me out of there. For coffee . . . for bein' so nice to me."

He raised his mug like we were going to toast. "I like you. You're a good person. You're a fighter."

I couldn't believe my ears. *He likes me*. "You're not just sayin' that 'cuz I've got a private beach here?" I couldn't believe I said that.

He spewed his coffee.

~ ANNIE ~

Once Nathan and Buck laid me on the couch, Doc examined me and told me I'd need to take it easy.

I focused on his blue eyes, so much like mine. "Under the circumstances, I don't think I can."

Mom pushed through the group to serve me juice and a scone. "You need something to eat. Have this now. I'm going to start a pot of chicken soup." She stood over me until I took a bite and swallowed some juice.

I turned to Dad, anxiety all over his face, and handed him the glass. "I'm fine, Dad. No worries." I don't think he believed me. Mom went back to the kitchen to make soup. That was Mom's way of coping. Everything was better with chicken soup. I remembered the days when it was. There was no going back.

Buck heaved a sigh. "Annie, get some rest. I'll see to it we get the proper assistance in this matter. You'll need to be well rested to tackle this head-on. But first we need a strategy."

I flopped back on the cushion and repeated Peter's well-used line. "It's not a scheme. It's a strategy." *How had I not recognized a Ponzi scheme? How could I be so stupid? God help me.*

~ ANNIE ~

Late that afternoon Nathan found me in my Adirondack chair, staring out to sea, wrapped in my long, hooded, down coat, covered with my wool blanket. Darkness was rapidly overtaking us. I gripped my coffee mug to keep it from accidentally toppling to the ground as he turned his chair around to face me.

"Mrs. Brewster, Cisco Clemente's legal team from New York is on your case. We don't know exactly when they'll be here to interview you. The expectation is sometime tomorrow, but it could be Monday, even Tuesday."

"Thanks, Mr. Rhodes."

"Is there something I can do for you now?"

"Just answer a couple of questions. Where's Buck?"

"He's at the restaurant. He said you shouldn't worry. He's taking care of everything."

"Does anyone know how Lisa is? Her ex-husband was murdered."

"Billy is still with her at home. I thought it best for him to keep an eye on her and keep the reporters at bay. Last I spoke with him, he said she was stable. They were having some lunch."

"Good. Lisa needs support. I think Billy will be a good friend to her."

Nathan nodded, but had no further comment.

I decided to dig a bit more. "I heard something last night that I was probably not supposed to hear. I was about to knock on the control room door when Roger said David got Boyd Phelps. I thought the guy who took over the school was named Carson Phelps. Is that the same person? And where is David? I thought he was on his way to Maine."

Despite the persistent sea breeze I heard a sigh. "Boyd Phelps shot the president. His brother, Carson Phelps, was the one at Marberry Academy."

Light began to dawn. “So David was never on his way to Maine. He went after the guy who shot the president. Why did the news say that the guy was killed in a shootout with the police? Roger said David shot him, right?”

Nathan gave me a stern look. “Lambrecht did shoot him, but no one will know that. The media was told Boyd Phelps was killed in a shootout with law enforcement. That’s the way they’ll leave it. That’s the way you should leave it.”

“Okay.” *I guess I’m in the secret society now.* “I understand.” I used my “professional” voice, hoping it might instill some confidence that I could be trusted with this privileged information.

It sounded like David was the president’s go-to guy for these pesky problems. *The assassin’s assassin.* I almost laughed out loud. *Not nearly enough sleep last night.*

“So why are there so many Phelps guys running around? David shot one years ago. Then one goes to the National Educator’s Conference to shoot the president, and another one goes to Maine to terrorize a school.”

Nathan remained tight-lipped, and I answered my own question. “It was a distraction. They both wanted the president dead. So they put all the attention on the school kids. They were trying to lure David to Maine.”

“Yes.” There was a slight upward curve to Nathan’s lip.

Emboldened by my brilliant deduction, I kept going. “But David had it all figured out. He outsmarted them all.”

“He usually does.” Nathan actually sounded amused.

“That’s why Billy was talking about ABCs . . . Adam, Boyd, Carson. Right?”

He laughed. “Right.”

“So when can I call my sister?”

“Not now,” he said.

“I bet David is off looking for Carson Phelps. Is he?”

“He doesn’t report to me.”

“But that’s what he’s doing. It sounds like he has a special place in the president’s heart.”

My heart skipped a beat as Nathan smiled at me. "I wouldn't know about that, Mrs. Brewster."

"How did Carson Phelps escape anyway? Didn't you surround the school?"

"We did, but Phelps and his team were in and out of there long before we realized it."

"He had a team?"

"It seems there were three or four of them, at least. They herded everyone into the gym, and bound, gagged, and blindfolded the kids and the teachers. They left recorded messages with their demands and instructions. It stalled us, and gave them time to escape through the basement. Apparently, no one remembered the tunnels from the days of the Underground Railroad. They made their escape in speedboats."

"Hmm. That was convenient." Peter's face appeared in my mind's eye. "How would the likes of Carson Phelps know about the Underground Railroad? The perfect escape." A nagging feeling gnawed at my gut, and I remembered something. "Peter told me about Marberry being a stop on the Underground Railroad. And he would have known exactly where those tunnels were. But he wasn't there to tell Phelps and his gang about that."

"I don't know." Nathan shook his head. "But I'm glad you told me. Anyway, it's too cold out here. It must be time for dinner soon."

"When do I get my phone back? Or are you afraid I'll start some new Ponzi scheme to keep myself busy?"

He grinned. "Both Doc Westcott and Mr. Wynn agreed you should not be on your phone. I'll leave it to them to decide what's best."

~ ANNIE ~

Saturday morning I looked up at the sea of faces staring at us from the front porch of The Golden Bowl. I put on a determined smile as Nathan took my arm and walked me up the stairs. "Good morning!"

Ashleigh met me in the office with a cup of coffee and a barrage of questions. I dumped my bag in the desk drawer and dropped into the chair. “Before we get started, Ash, where’s Buck?”

She took a seat and reworked her ponytail. “He’s in the barn . . . in the customer service center. It’s been nuts over there. Millions of people have called since this all started Thursday. And not just with orders. They were wondering if you were okay. Your name, your picture, and The Golden Bowl are all over the news. They say you’re a hero, Annie. And you are—you and Mr. Rhodes—for saving those kids. Are you okay?”

“I’m fine. But I’m no hero.” Life couldn’t get much stranger. The whims of the public would soon turn in the opposite direction if a grand jury took my case and charged me with fraud and conspiracy. And I had been completely oblivious to it all. Stupidity was my crime.

Ashleigh flipped through her notepad. “Amanda James called twice. I talked to her, and so did Brianna. We didn’t have much to tell her. But she told us to tell you she was asking for you.”

“That’s sweet. But I don’t want to do another interview with her anytime soon.”

Ashleigh made a face. “Well, I talked to your agent, Mr. Harris, and it sounds like he’s got the world lined up to interview you. Buck was happy to hear it this morning. He says all publicity is good publicity.”

“Oh joy!” I picked up my phone and scrolled through hundreds of messages from Joe Harris, Amanda James, and everyone but my sister. No wonder they wouldn’t let me have my phone until Nathan had handed it to me when I reached the office door. The flood of messages boggled my mind.

A text message from Cat caught my eye. “We love you, Annie. God loves you.” My eyes filled, and I choked on the tears.

Ashleigh whipped out a box of tissues. “I’m going to

get you a warm blueberry muffin with butter. You'll feel better."

By the time she returned I'd composed myself. "Just a warm-up on the coffee is all I need. Thanks, Ash."

"Okay then, how about we split it?" Her big blue eyes widened as she bit into her half. "That's the best muffin in the world, right there."

I let out a giggle. Ashleigh could always make me laugh. Oh, how I adored my staff. Even in the midst of all this craziness, they were still so positive and supportive.

"Jim Curley left a message."

We listened to his heartfelt thanks for all we'd done—especially Nathan's heroism in saving his three daughters. I wiped my eyes. "He's such a sweet man. Even if he does give me the willies with his tax stuff."

Ash cracked up laughing. I grabbed my coat and headed to the customer service office.

CHAPTER 12

~ ANNIE ~

The irresistible aroma of cinnamon, blended with nutmeg and brown sugar, greeted me as I entered The Bakery & Sweet Shop. *Mmm, apple crisp*. My appetite was back full force. Karen raced over to hug me. "Oh, Annie! Thank God you're okay. I heard you had a bad fall, on top of everything else."

As I proclaimed my excellent health, she weaved me through the gathering mob of well-wishers. We ended up in my new office that was across from the new customer service center. We took seats in comfortable chairs—an incredible luxury compared to the furniture I'd been making do with for years.

"Buck's in the weeds like he always says. Can I get you something?" She took off her glasses and rubbed her eyes.

"That apple crisp is calling me. No hurry. Rest a minute." I couldn't help wondering why she suddenly called him Buck. Like Mr. Rhodes was suddenly Nathan. My stomach fluttered.

"Sorry. I didn't sleep much last night. This place was Grand Central Station yesterday and again this morning."

"I know. It was tough enough after the Amanda James show. Now this. It's crazy."

"Well, you'll be happy with Tracey, the new customer service manager. She's on top of everything. Buck said he was really pleased with her performance through all this madness. Very professional. And sweet at the same time."

"I liked her right away. We made a good choice," I said.

Karen smiled. "We did! And orders have gone through the roof. Literally. Now Buck has people coming up from New York. He said he thought he could handle this on his own, but with the tax audit and everything . . . and now he's told Gerald the meal prep facility needs to expand. There's just not enough space in the building to accommodate all the growth, he said."

I swallowed a lump in my throat. "He'd mentioned that before, but I thought that was a future plan. It'll cost a fortune to add on to this building, and at this point, I wonder if it's even a good idea. The Golden Bowl is a quaint old farmhouse and barn by the ocean. Expanding it will detract from that image."

Karen nodded. "That's why the team from New York is coming. They're gonna scout out some locations for a separate facility to prepare the food and ship it. Buck said we'll be shipping all over the country on a routine basis. Some major stores want our products. It sounds like a whole different ballgame than servicing some local stores here in Maine."

My head started to pound. "Where is Buck?"

"He's with Gerald. They're working on streamlining everything to make the best use of space in the meantime. But Buck said he didn't want to be disturbed while he's trying to get this organized. I'll go get you that apple crisp and coffee. Just relax and enjoy your new office, and I'll be right back." She closed the door behind her.

I put my head down on a very professional-looking desk. A far cry from the pitiful metal thing in my office under the staircase. I thought of *The Prayer of Jabez* and asked God if Jabez went through such havoc and angst when his territory was enlarged.

I was almost drifting off when Karen reappeared with the best warm apple crisp and vanilla ice cream in the world. After downing that, I decided I was fortified enough to sort through all my messages and emails. It was a ridiculously long, tedious task. Hundreds of requests for interviews from local stations to national and international news shows filled my inbox. I dreaded the conversation as I picked up my phone to dial Joe Harris, representative to the stars. And now Annie Brewster.

He took my call immediately. *Wow*.

"Annie, Amanda James will be back out there in the next five days or so. They'll do a quick update on you and Lisa and the restaurant after the Marberry Hostage Crisis. Wynn tells me you're having a hard time keeping up with the business from the first show. I'm gonna put off most of these offers till you guys get your act together. Meanwhile, I'll send a crew out there to do some promo videos for Thanksgiving and Christmas at The Golden Bowl. We can use stuff like that online and to give out to some of the entertainment reporters following you. Keeps you in the public eye. Then we'll do the major push when Wynn's got you all straightened out there. Okay. Talk soon." He was gone.

That was a conversation?

I pulled myself out of my comfortable new office chair, opened the door, and surveyed my customer service team hard at work in a sparkling new space behind glass walls. Tracey gave me a wave as she headed from one station to another. I marveled at the constant flow of phone calls, but they seemed to be taking things in stride.

My gut told me I should not disturb Buck in his "weeds," but I needed to connect with him somehow. I wasn't sure I was coherent enough for the task. The slight concussion I'd suffered in the fall apparently did have more of an effect on me than I had realized. Despite that, I needed to take some action here.

Buck's plan to enlarge and expand The Golden Bowl, nagged at me. I had no money to my name. I did have the real possibility of facing a grand jury and the scandal that would ignite if they decided to charge me with fraud and conspiracy. What was Buck thinking?

Appropriately enough, I found him in the freezer in the meal prep facility. He came through the door holding a clipboard and pen, with a frigid blast of air forming a frosty halo around him, followed by Gerald, who closed the door behind them.

Buck seemed a bit startled to see me. "Annie! We need to talk." He nodded a "carry on" to Gerald and led me back to my brand new office, offering a wave and a bright smile to Tracey on the way.

I wasn't sure where I was supposed to sit.

Buck walked past the desk and landed on the couch.

"Karen told me you have people coming from New York?"

He glanced at the empty expanse of couch beside him, as an invitation for me to sit, but I twirled a leather chair to face him instead.

"They'll be arriving this evening and ready to work bright and early tomorrow."

"Tomorrow's Sunday."

"Yes," he said.

So much for a day of rest.

I settled into the chair. "Isn't it too early for us to expand the facility here? Maybe all this attention is just fleeting. Maybe it's just a temporary spike in orders. I don't know what's happening with this tax audit thing, the . . . the other thing. How can I risk putting more money I don't have into this business?"

Buck nodded in consideration. "All good observations and questions. We need a plan. We have myriad things to fix here. We have to continue to move forward, and we have to base our decisions on solid facts, as much as possible."

"Agreed." I wiped perspiration from my forehead. "So why don't we slow down a bit, take some time to fix things, and then decide about expanding?"

He made some notes on his clipboard, giving me the feeling he was only half-paying attention to me. "My team is coming up to do the work I cannot possibly fit into sixteen-hour days. We have serious inquiries from the top grocery chains and retailers in the country. Looking at the profit centers of your business, I see The Bakery & Sweet Shop is a goldmine waiting to happen. Your prepared meals, as well."

He looked up at me. "The restaurant is a financial disaster at this point. With your commitment to charity—and the media's focus on you and the restaurant—it makes sense to keep the restaurant as your charitable focus, with the confections and prepared meals businesses as your income producers. For the moment anyway. I have no doubt once we get you out of crisis, we'll make the restaurant profitable as well."

I let out a sigh. "Okay. I feel like I've been taken out to the woodshed."

Buck grimaced a bit. "A necessary trip, I'm afraid."

I swallowed my embarrassment and failure, leaving my voice just a shade stronger. "Did you ever get breakfast?"

He finally smiled. "You're the most caring person I've ever known. No, I did not have breakfast. There really wasn't time today. I realized we need a new production facility ASAP. My people will get the lowdown on all available commercial properties. We'll lay our options on the table and make a decision. In the meantime, we're tightly scheduling the meal prep facility for maximum production."

"Well, I'm glad we don't have to add on to the barn. I think it would detract from the beauty of the property."

"I agree completely. No need to have that on the most expensive real estate in the area. But I do want you to know, I recommend we do the ice cream deals that are in front of us now. Our margins are phenomenal, we have Paulo Clemente on board to endorse it, and his fans are flocking to buy it. We'll be able to donate part of the proceeds to charity without losing our shirts. A great deal all around, so let's jump on it."

I let out a chuckle. "Nothing like ice cream in the winter in Maine."

"Apparently not." He tapped his pen on the clipboard. "I'll get in touch with Ted Monahan. Perhaps he can help us locate the proper space. He certainly owes us a favor." Buck started out of his seat.

I raised a hand to stop him. "Let me order you some lunch. You can't go all day without eating."

"Very well. If you'll join me." There was a sudden gleam in his eye that catapulted me back to my dive into Nathan's arms on Friday morning. Butterflies exploded in my stomach at the thought of Buck witnessing that embarrassing scene. It was a short trip into the misery that followed with the talk about grand juries. My mind and my emotions were out of control.

Maybe Buck was right to ignore the elephant in the room—the threat of a grand jury and a prison term. What could I possibly do about it now? *Best to focus on the job at hand.*

~ ANNIE ~

I returned to the office with two Thanksgiving turkey meals. "Buck, Ashleigh said you'd be proud. We're promoting our Thanksgiving programs with a 'Giving Thanks' lunch special. Not only does it fit in with our gratitude that the Marberry Academy crisis is over, but it reminds people to help out the less fortunate this holiday season. People are donating two extra dollars for every turkey lunch today, and a lot of them are donating even more. The money goes to The Golden Bowl Thanksgiving Fund, and we're keeping close track of that money. So we don't have issues. I might not have to dig into my non-existent savings to fund the project this year."

Buck broke into laughter. "I wonder how that works, Annie. How do you fund your projects with no money?" He took a seat behind the desk and unwrapped his meal.

I took a taste of roast turkey while I shooed away the fear of the grand jury and the sense of failure it encompassed.

Just because Peter Fellowes' charity was bogus—that was no reason to quit my own. And somehow, I had always funded my projects with no money. I had the answer. "Well, it's God's provision."

His dark elegant eyebrows shot up. "Assuming God is involved in all of this, don't you still need money to make it work?"

"Well, sure." *Maybe I shouldn't have brought this up.*

Buck leaned forward over the desk. "Of course! And that money comes out of your salary, doesn't it?"

I felt like crawling under the desk. "I . . . I guess you're right. I don't really take a salary. I live on whatever is left over—or I do one of those rob Peter to pay Paul things."

This past summer I'd totally lost all concept of reality. I'd previously lived in my attic apartment over the restaurant. I'd always lump my food, utilities, and other expenses in with the business. Then Debbie bought the Miller estate for me. All the furnishings, everything, was included, not to mention an elite security team equipped with special vehicles. My ten-year-old car now sat unused in the garage.

David saw to it I had plenty of money for household expenses, and if there were some other incidental things, Doc was always there with the cash. To top it all off, Debbie had given me more clothes and personal care products than I could ever want or use.

I wasn't even conscious of the fact that all my would-be salary went to my charities. *Jim Curley must have been having a fine time figuring all that out.*

"Buck, is it illegal to spend all your money on charity?"

"Let's just say you're generous to a fault."

My appetite for turkey suddenly failed me. Buck had wolfed his down before taking a call from Jim Curley. It sounded like they were old buddies. While they chatted, I dumped my uneaten meal in the trash, guilt rising up as I disposed of perfectly good food.

When he got off the phone, he escorted me from the

office. "Jim's girls are all healthy. They're seeing counselors to help them through the trauma, and they'll be fine. He wants you to know how very grateful he is to you and Nathan, and he'll see us bright and early Monday morning to continue the auditing fest." Buck gave a quick knock and let himself into Gerald's office.

There was definitely an elephant in the room. Buck merrily expanding the business, Jim merrily auditing away. Why? Wasn't I far enough in the hole? Maybe Buck and Jim would join forces to enjoy the fruits of their labor after I was sent down the river. *Too crazy, Annie, you're too crazy.*

Where was my faith? Buck and Jim were both good men. Buck had been tirelessly working on my behalf, and Jim was only doing his job as an auditor. But I had believed in Peter as well and look what happened there. I blew out a deep breath as I went back for my coat. I decided a butter pecan cone was in order. *Nuts are loaded with protein. Good choice*. I needed to walk the beach and clear my head.

November gales can be treacherous on the water. But Miller's Way was a well-worn path. My boots were sturdy. The ice cream cooled my insides as the wind blasted my body. *How did I get myself into this mess? And the more important question—how would I get out?* Buck could sell a fortune in ice cream—or any of our other products—and I'd still give away the money. Why? Was all this giving a good thing or was I doing more harm to myself than good to anyone else? Had giving become a compulsion, or was I truly doing God's work? It was too confusing. All I'd wanted to do was to help people, but look where that had gotten me. In the middle of a Ponzi scheme that could potentially land me in jail.

Darkness descended. I felt so alone.

My phone vibrated in my pocket, and I sheltered by a rocky cliff. "Hello?"

"Annie! Are you okay?"

"Debbie!" Windblown hair and tears blurred my vision.

"I'm okay. Are you okay? Is . . . is David home?" I slid down the side of a rock and sat on the ground.

"He's home now. Everything is fine. I'm so glad you didn't go near that school. That man's brother shot David when we were in Vienna at the business convention, and the president was there to give a speech . . ." Debbie's voice quivered. I pictured her pretty blue eyes shimmering with tears.

I could hear David's voice in the background. "It was just a scratch."

I had to laugh. "What constitutes a scratch?"

Debbie's sarcastic retort was surely meant for both of us. "He could be missing half his brain, and he'd say that." A cascade of giggles told me David had assuaged her momentary upset.

I didn't dare bring up the fate of Carson Phelps. Had David found him already? There was no indication from anyone that he was in custody—or dead.

The conversation turned to the more routine topics of family life: kids, work, health. I hung on every word, and the more Debbie spoke of David and their children, the more her voice came alive.

When I clicked off the phone, I remained by the rocks, my head on my knees, trying to contain my emotion. But tears came in a flood. Carson Phelps removed that ski mask and his hideous smile defied the camera and defiled my brain, over and over again. I cried for those kids and teachers at the school, for Lisa and Rosie and their loss, the administrators who'd been shot, for Peter and Louise and Pinky, for the president and all that awful news video.

Mostly, I cried for me. My sister had her husband, and I did not have mine. My sister had six beautiful children, and I was childless. My sister had a thriving business, and mine was in financial shambles. I was alone. I was a fraud and a failure. *Generous to a fault*. What a joke that was.

"Mrs. Brewster? Are you all right?" Nathan's voice was an unexpected jolt.

I wasn't all right. "I'm okay. Just tired. I should probably get home. I'm not much use around here today."

Nathan was always there when I needed him. But if I ended up in jail, I'd probably never see him again. Another depressing thought.

He offered his hand to help me up, and I looked at him. Was I being foolish or did I see a glimmer of tenderness in his eyes? *Foolish.* I felt like an old lady, whipped and flattened by the salty wind, half-frozen from sitting on the cold ground.

On the drive home, Nathan told me Lisa was okay, and Billy would cook dinner for her. I was happy to hear that a friendship was developing between those two. It was obvious that Lisa had a crush on him. And Billy was a sweetheart, if you could use that term to describe a Navy SEAL who looked like a surfer dude.

When we walked into the kitchen, Mom was hard at work on dinner, Dad and Doc assisting where possible. I claimed a headache and went to my room.

A hot shower and warm flannel pajamas helped the headache. I snuggled under the covers and reached for my phone. An overwhelming urge drove me to investigate the word "fraud." *A false representation by a person or business to obtain money. Deception. Imposter.*

I suppose all those definitions applied to me—even ignoring the gifting tables fiasco. I was wrong to mingle my personal expenses with my business. I lived as though the restaurant and I were one and the same. Up until now, I'd thought that was fine. I'd considered my business a reflection of my personal philosophy and calling and a vehicle for carrying out that work.

But living in the attic apartment in that building, I should have paid rent to The Golden Bowl. I should have taken a salary and paid personal expenses from that. I thought Pinky was taking care of everything, but I never made sure to give him correct numbers to go on. I had no idea what numbers were involved—never bothered to spend the time and effort to figure that out. I'd made a false representation and obtained the money I lived on tax-free. Until now. *Fraud.*

I took advantage of Pinky's generosity and let him figure out the taxes. No wonder Buck said the numbers came out of thin air. They probably did. That was *deception*. That was dishonest. That was *fraud*.

I let everyone from Marberry to Ripple Lake and beyond think that I was so philanthropic. Was it really a kind of addiction to the praise? A way to fit in and be loved? *Imposter. Phony. Fraud.*

That thought cut me to the quick. I didn't know what to do with it. I'd always believed my heart was in the right place. My motives good. Was I wrong?

Now the eyes of the world were focused on The Golden Bowl. Territory was enlarging, but I was crumbling underneath it. I was terrified. How could I get off this train? What had Grammy started with The Prayer of Jabez? What plan did God have for me?

~ ANNIE ~

Sunday morning I couldn't get out of bed. I remember Mom arriving with chicken soup. "You need to rest," she told me as I made short work of the soup. "Just forget The Golden Bowl and everything else and rest."

"That's a little hard to do right now."

She found the remote and turned on the TV. "Oh, it's the Bible story of Jonah. This should be good."

I rubbed my eyes. "It's a cartoon."

Mom paid no attention. She put the remote on her tray and left the room. Trapped with a cartoon on television, I let out a heavy sigh, and my eyelids fluttered.

Jonah appeared as a stick figure caricature robed in iridescent white. He was running away from God as fast as his little stick feet would carry him. Jonah did not want to go to Nineveh, and I sure didn't want to "enlarge my territory." I had enough to cope with on the grounds of The Golden Bowl. Now I'd have some massive production facility to manage, too. Possibly from prison.

"God helps the humble, Annie,"

Russ? My husband's voice was narrating the cartoon. *How strange.*

Jonah took a flying leap off the boat into bright blue water. His silver shoes began to sparkle. But he was quickly swallowed by a huge fish.

I'm in the belly of the whale with Jonah.

"Keep God's priorities, Annie, not yours. Sometimes you're called to do things you'd rather not do . . . but do them anyway, for the greater good. Even when things seem bad for you, remember your greater purpose. Think of others and not only of yourself."

I need to change my attitude, Russ. I do.

Jonah obeyed God and his silver white shoes glowed brighter with each step as he walked to the great city, Nineveh. Only it was odd that he was walking through snow. Snow in Nineveh?

Even though Jonah didn't want to, he'd tell them to stop their evil ways and come to God. Jonah's mission was a success, but he was still angry because he wanted his own way. "Don't make the mistake Jonah made."

You're right, Russ, it's too easy to take my eyes off God. It's too easy to be selfish.

The stick figure Jonah was now sitting on a rock under the sun's heat. He was clearly feeling miserable. Then suddenly a vine grew over him that gave him shade and some relief.

"*And the Lord God prepared a gourd, and made it to come up over Jonah, that it might be a shadow over his head, to deliver him from his grief. So Jonah was exceeding glad of the gourd* . . . Remember that, Annie."

I woke up and realized it had been a dream. And I realized something else, too. God had sent me Cisco, Buck, and all my family and staff, as God had sent Jonah a vine. *Thank you, God.* I prayed that vine would stand.

My dear husband's voice echoed in my head. "Nineveh is greater than a small vine."

I put my head in my hands and wiped the sleep away. Nineveh is The Golden Bowl. And God will grow it in whatever way God wants.

The Golden Bowl was God's work. And I was working on behalf of God. This wasn't about me. I'd been feeling sorry for myself and forgotten the real reason why I had started The Golden Bowl in the first place. To do God's work.

Fear and anxiety had no place here. I looked out my window and saw large flakes of snow falling. "Snow in Nineveh." Laughing, I went to the window, opened it, and stretched out my hand to capture silver white flakes.

Time for an attitude adjustment.

~ ANNIE ~

I felt better by Sunday evening, but decided to stay in bed and rest up for the coming week. When there was a soft knock at my door, I was expecting more chicken soup from Mom.

Dad cracked the door and peered in. "Are you up for a visit?"

I sat up. "Sure."

He helped me fluff the pillows and stuffed them behind my back to support me. "Now you look a little more comfortable." He took a seat on the bed beside me.

"Are you all right, Dad?"

"I'm all right. I'm worried about you. These federal agents, IRS, Maine Revenue . . . well, I don't need to go on."

Fresh tears stung my eyes. "I'm so sorry I caused this mess. I'm praying this doesn't go to a grand jury. It would embarrass you and Mom. And Doc. Never mind the business at The Golden Bowl—what about your church? Would people leave?"

"Annie, God's in charge. Don't worry. Just trust. If people leave, they leave."

"God's in charge, but I haven't been the best steward, have I? Buck says I'm generous to a fault. But it was stupidity, not generosity that got me into this mess."

Dad chuckled and stared into space, smiling, like he was remembering something. His gaze found mine. "When you were in kindergarten, you brought your favorite doll to school one day. You came home with a lunchbox full of cash. We thought you were doing show and tell. But you sold that doll to a friend to raise money for a classmate's leukemia treatment."

"I'd almost forgotten that. The little girl lived."

"She did. And I've never been so proud. How many five-year-olds take it upon themselves to start a fundraiser for a sick kid?" Dad clasped my hands. "So don't tell me about being a poor steward. Anne Auclair Brewster, you have a gift. And you make God—and people—smile."

I started to laugh and cry at once. I couldn't help it.

Dad lifted the tissue box on my bedside table and offered it to me. "Here we go."

"Thanks for the boost. I needed it. But I've really messed up when it comes to money. I've mismanaged my business into a hole."

Dad let out a sigh. "I never gave you much guidance on that subject. I'm not good with money, either. The elders run the business of the church. Otherwise, I'd be in a real pickle. We've been so blessed that they've made wise decisions with our money."

I leaned back on my pillow. "Your church has been blessed."

"Yes, and again, it's a matter of trust. God is our source. Who could've ever thought the answer to our crumbling masonry would be Cat and Cisco? Rock stars in Ripple Lake, Maine? They came to see our church, to meet some of our members, see the soup kitchen at work. When they left we had $70,000. Not just to fix the masonry, but to renovate our kitchen. We paid the final bill this week. It came to $70,000. That's God's provision."

My heart leapt at the thought of God's goodness and attention to the details of our lives. "You're right. I need to trust. Things are getting scary, and I'm scared about letting everyone down. Not just the people who benefit from The Golden Bowl. A scandal could affect Debbie and her design business. Not to mention Cisco. He's putting his money on the line for The Golden Bowl. What must he think?"

"He obviously thinks well of you. He's paying for your legal representation. He knows you're not a criminal."

I sank into the pillow. The burden of anxiety was lifting.

My father brushed wisps of hair out of my face. "Try to get some rest. Let Buck and his team do their jobs. They'll get the business on an even keel, and then you'll have the systems and the help in place to cope with everything. You've been going nonstop all on your own . . . well . . . since Russ died. I think you took your grief and turned it into action. It was a help to people around you, but I think you forgot yourself along the way. You need to take a little time to yourself." He kissed my forehead. "Get some sleep."

"I will."

He closed the door with a gentle click.

Nonstop since Russ died. I guess Dad was right. I'd never really taken the time to grieve. *I just might have that time in federal prison.* Almost instantly I realized that negative thought had no place in my head. It was time to trust. God would get me through this.

CHAPTER 13

~ ANNIE ~

On Monday morning, despite the season's first serious snowfall, a throng greeted me at The Golden Bowl. As Nathan and I made our way through the crowd up the stairs and to the front porch, people patted us on the back and thanked us. Why were they thanking me? They had to have meant it for Nathan. He was the hero of Marberry.

The prayer bowl called to me, and I was excited when I drew out another of Cat's prayers. *I am the vine; you are the branches. If a man remains in me and I in him, he will bear much fruit; apart from me you can do nothing. John 15:5.*

My breath caught in my throat. *Thank you, God.*

Nathan gave me no time to contemplate the thrill of the message. He nudged me through the door. Wild applause, lights, cameras, banners, and Amanda James at the center of the mob shocked me.

Amanda hugged me, laughing at my bewilderment. "I'm so glad you're okay, and Marberry Academy, students, and teachers, are still standing." She turned to the crowd. "Shall we offer a toast to Mr. Nathan Rhodes?" There were cheers from the crowd, raised glasses of juice and mugs of coffee. Then Amanda and Nathan disappeared into a large group of well-wishers.

Peg and some of my staff were sitting at a table with Lisa, who was bouncing Rosie on her knee. I ran over and caught her and her baby in a bear hug. "I'm so happy you're here! I'm sorry for everything you went through—so sorry for your loss."

Her arm tightened around me. "Thanks, Annie. It's over and done. Rosie and me are movin' on. It'll take time to get over everything. But at least now we don't need to live in fear all the time. And the police said Ryan died instantly from the gunshot. So that was as good as it can be . . . under the circumstances. I guess."

Amanda joined us, dragging Nathan by the sleeve. "Let's order some breakfast. I'm starved." She took a seat offered by a staff member.

I put my hand on her shoulder. "I'll get your order in right away. Do you have something in mind?"

"Blueberry pancakes, what else?" She smiled up at me.

"Done!" I delivered the order to Ashleigh, then peeked into my office. "Buck! Good morning."

He looked up from his paperwork. "How are you feeling today?"

"Better." I shut the door behind me and nerves fluttered my stomach. That Friday morning incident stuck in my head. *Should I confront him*? *Be strong, Annie*. I let out a frazzled breath. "Buck, are we good?"

He furrowed his brow. "Good?"

"Yes. You and me—are we good?"

He looked puzzled. "As in . . . is everything all right between us?"

"Yes, is everything all right between us?"

"Everything is fine. Why do you ask?"

Acid surged upward from the pit of my stomach. "Oh . . . just because of everything that's happening. What should I do about Amanda James? I really don't want to sit under those bright lights again with her. Do I have to? And the lawyers from New York—are they coming today?"

Buck grinned. "The lawyers will be here later today and will keep a very low profile. They'll probably interview you tomorrow. But they have most every detail, so no need to worry. As to Amanda, no need for a formal interview. You'll be showing her around your new commercial facility. I'm sure they'll be filming you for Sunday's show."

I grabbed the doorknob to support me. "What?"

"Ted Monahan took us right to the perfect building—an old fish processing plant about six miles from here. The owner is anxious to sell, as it's been vacant for quite some time. He agreed to Cisco's terms for a very quick closing. Cisco's cousin—the one with the construction company—" Buck snapped his fingers.

"Raphael. He does business all around the world—they do massive projects." The acid burned my throat.

Buck smiled. "Yes, Raphael Dominguez. I've worked with him before. Top class. He knows what he's doing, and he already has one of his VPs out here to oversee the sale and renovation. There'll be a crew in there by Thanksgiving. And the town is well aware *you*, Annie Brewster, are the one responsible for good jobs for local construction workers—and soon even more food service jobs. I believe Amanda James will alert the world to that fact, too. Cheers." He raised a mug in my direction. "By the way, once you tour the building today, your signature of approval will seal the deal. Cisco will go forward with the purchase."

I hoped my smile didn't look fake.

Fraud.

Yes, it was time for an attitude adjustment. I couldn't listen to that negative voice anymore. I'd just picked out that prayer about the vine from Cat. And Buck's news was good. Good news for a good cause. As Jabez would say, I'm blessed indeed.

When Jim Curley came through the office door, he had a huge smile on his face. I was drawn into his bear hug. "Annie, I can't thank you enough."

He finally let go of me and shook Buck's hand vigorously.

"Really, Jim, I'd like to keep my hand," Buck said.

Jim laughed like Buck was the funniest comedian on

earth, threw his coat on the rack, and took a small paper from his briefcase. He read Cat's prayer aloud. "*He sent forth his word and healed them; he rescued them from the grave. Psalm 107:20*"

He placed it back in the briefcase and closed it. "Mr. Rhodes found Kara in that utility closet and carried her to safety. Then he went back in with the SWAT team and rescued the kids and their teachers. Rhodes made sure to tell my twins that Kara was fine and even went to the hospital to see them."

Buck nodded. "He's a hero, for sure."

Jim stepped toward me. "Annie, you're a hero, too."

"Not me. I sat out the battle in a bomb shelter."

"I mean, what you do here. You take care of people in so many ways. You never look for anything in return. You're a true hero. And when the chaplain came by and read that same verse, it hit me like a ton of bricks. I just want to thank you. I took my family to church yesterday."

"I'm so glad." Joy filled my heart, and I thanked God it was back.

Jim took a seat and rubbed his hand over his head. "I'm sorry, but I have to go through all your cash register tapes."

Buck rolled his eyes.

"I'll get the coffee," I said.

Within hours we were at the new building with Amanda and her crew. Buck introduced us to Carlos, the man from Dominguez Construction who would give us a tour of the site of The Golden Bowl's newest facility. He and Buck expected it would be operational early in the New Year.

As Amanda asked many of the same questions that were running through my head, we followed Carlos around the building. He'd already hired people to clean out the place—one of the conditions of the sales agreement. It was impressively spick-and-span for a vacant building pretty much in the middle of nowhere.

When the camera crew finally packed up and we headed out, a strange feeling came over me. *Look what happens when I just get out of the way*. Cat's prayer filled my mind.

Trust in the Lord and do good; dwell in the land and enjoy safe pasture. Delight yourself in the Lord and he will give you the desires of your heart. Commit your way to the Lord; trust in him and he will do this: He will make your righteousness shine like the dawn, the justice of your cause like the noonday sun. Psalm 37: 3-6

I looked up at a crisp blue sky. I wasn't a fraud—just a foolish woman who needed to smarten up. This was a just cause, a desire of my heart—to improve life for my neighbors here in Maine. And God would make it shine like the dawn. Gratitude and joy welled up inside me.

That night I didn't have to worry about a rigid interview under bright lights in my parlor. Amanda and I fell into a natural conversation over dinner at my kitchen table. By the time we were done, it was time for her to fly off to New York. My fear was gone. I knew she'd do right by The Golden Bowl—and by me—even if things turned sour with an announcement of a grand jury investigation.

~ ANNIE ~

First thing Tuesday morning, Cisco's legal team arrived at my home and spoke with me, Buck, my family, and our security team—in private, and as a group. They seemed extremely professional, and at the same time there was an air of genuine care and concern about them. They could not make guarantees, of course, and the charges were potentially very serious, but they assured us I would receive the best legal counsel money could buy. No doubt, Cisco was paying a fortune for this assurance.

Shortly after they left, Buck drove off in his high-powered sports car that was the talk of the town. I could never remember the make, but everyone practically swooned over it. Nathan and I followed in his dust. I suspected that gave Buck a certain satisfaction, given that he and Nathan weren't exactly the best of friends.

When I got to work Jim Curley was at my desk once again. Since I was useless to him, after almost half an hour of witnessing his tedious calculations, I decided to excuse myself. "I'll be in the customer service office, working on my orders."

Buck stopped whatever he was doing on his tablet and stood up. "I'll head over with you. Jim, I'll bring you back something from the bakery. I have a craving for a blueberry scone."

Jim glanced up at us. "Sounds good. Make that two."

A cold blast of air greeted us as we left the building, but it felt good. "Should we be leaving Jim all alone?"

Buck turned up his collar to shield his ears from the wind. "He has my number on speed-dial, and Ashleigh can supply him with pots of coffee and whatever else he wants. As to the deeper question—Jim has already done his damage."

We worked our way through crowds. As many people as I'd normally see on a summer Saturday. I watched a bus pull into the parking lot. "This is totally unbelievable. All these people. Customers. Here."

"And that's the key. Customers. *Paying* customers. That's what we're getting from all this publicity. From Amanda James. Not freeloaders just looking for something for nothing."

"Most of the people who get free food are legitimately in need. I know I was wrong to let things get off track with the accounting and the gifting tables, but I'm not changing my mission."

Buck held the bakery door open for me. "Heaven knows we can't change the mission."

A gang of teenagers pushed by us, almost knocking me down. Buck grabbed me by the arm and tugged me inside. "Aren't they supposed to be in school?"

"I think so." I accepted the handkerchief he offered and dabbed blueberry ice cream off the front of my coat. Blue stains now marred a white linen monogrammed hankie that probably cost as much as any coat I'd worn before my sister's kind donations. "I'll get this back to you tomorrow. I have something that'll take these stains out." *I hope.*

Buck waved his hand about the handkerchief. I had a feeling he had plenty more where that came from. He walked ahead to Karen's office. Noticing Terri Monahan out of the corner of my eye, I quickly followed.

Terri headed straight for me. There was no avoiding her this time. "Let's go to a movie tonight. Girls' night out. We could both use a little break. How about it?" She closed the door behind us, shutting out the racket of the customers.

Buck smirked as he took a seat at the table and opened his binder.

I turned to him, hoping for some kind of excuse. "I'm not sure my finances will allow that, Terri."

Buck choked on laughter. Terri didn't believe me.

He took out his wallet and handed me a hundred-dollar bill.

My eyes popped. "What's this?"

"Just a little gift. Go see a movie. Take a break."

~ ANNIE ~

When Jim Curley left that afternoon, he hugged me and shook Buck's hand again. He told us he'd be back in the morning to continue the audit. I accepted the news with grace. Heaven only knew how many numbers there were left to go through. And I decided to leave it that way. God was in charge. Not me.

Terri arrived at my front door minutes after I got home. She walked into my bedroom and stood in my bathroom doorway as I threw water on my face. "What movie do you want to see?"

I grabbed a towel. "I don't care. I'm afraid I'll fall asleep in the middle of it."

"How about dinner then? Café Bella?"

"How about Café Annie?"

Terri's jaw dropped. "Aren't you exhausted after a day

at The Golden Bowl? Now you're going to cook?"

"It's easier than driving thirty miles. And who knows who'd be listening in on our conversation. Besides, I enjoy cooking. I haven't been doing a lot of it lately, between Mom spending so much time here, and Doc's and Billy's new fascination for cooking. So it'd be fun to whip up a nice Italian meal. What do you say?"

"I'm in. I can help with chopping or peeling."

"Fine." As we adjourned to the kitchen, I tried to forget that elephant in the room, the very real possibility we could both go to prison over Peter's gifting table scheme. But I knew there'd be some uncomfortable conversation tonight.

Doc and our security team were thrilled at the prospect of Chicken Marsala. Terri and I had ample assistance with the cooking. Then we retreated to an elegantly set table in the dining room, while the men feasted in the kitchen.

Terri gave her phone one last look then threw it in her bag. "Amanda James is a sweetheart. She did a great job talking up The Golden Bowl . . . and Marberry in general. It was nice of her to revisit everyone she had on the first show. I think she'll make Lisa a real sympathetic character, and Rosie's so cute! I bet the cops don't give Lisa any more grief. And Ted looks so handsome and professional on TV."

She paused long enough for me to agree. After that, Terri talked non-stop through the salad course. It was like nothing had ever happened. Sudden silence spurred me to look up.

Terri was sipping her wine and staring into space. "It must be fun to have a bunch of bodyguards wherever you go. Have you gotten used to it?"

"I guess. If I wasn't used to it before that Phelps guy showed up at Marberry Academy—well, I am now." I decided to get the difficult conversation over with. "I have a bone to pick with you."

"Oh." The wine seemed to be mellowing her. "I'm sorry. It just slipped out. Before I knew it, Curley was writing you up. I didn't mean to sic him on you."

She admitted it! Relief loosed the knot in my stomach a bit. "I wondered about your strange behavior when we ran into Jim Thursday morning. You were audited, too?"

Terri looked apologetic. "I didn't mean it. I'm sorry. He was telling me all these things weren't deductible, and I used you as an example. It just got us both in hot water." She poured another glass of wine.

I whisked an empty glass in front of her. "One for me." *Probably not a good idea.* I was sweating already.

Terri leaned over the table toward me. "Remember the time Pastor Mike—your dad—talked to us at Wednesday morning group? On forgiveness?"

I needed to bite my tongue. "Yes."

"Good." She swallowed half a glass of wine.

Good? Good? The stress and the upset returned to my stomach. That was all the apology I'd get. *That's Terri.* I twirled my glass on the table. My hands wouldn't be steady enough to get it to my mouth.

Terri picked at her salad. "You know, Ted lowered his commission on the building for your new kitchens. Cisco Clemente got an awesome deal on that place. Are you paying him rent or what?"

"Terri." My voice was too loud and shrill. She had a definite talent for bringing out the worst in me. We could both be locked up in a federal penitentiary, and she's worried about getting the scoop on Cisco Clemente.

I could see her gulp. "Yeah?"

Two could play at this elephant-in-the-room game. I hissed out a whisper. "You gave Lisa a raw deal on that ring. We both know it was worth a lot more than forty thousand. If you make two hundred thousand on it—"

Terri interrupted. "Excuse me, I sold it for one-fifty."

I leaned back in my seat. "That's still not fair."

"It's totally fair. You're not gonna guilt me into giving her another dime. So who do you think threw the ring in that bowl to begin with?"

I tried to exhale my frustration. "I told you, I don't know."

She twirled an olive on a toothpick. “Buck.”

“What?”

“I think it was Buck.”

“No!”

“Annie, the guy’s got more money than God. He drives a Lamborghini. Who drives a Lamborghini in Maine? Rich people buy them and keep them in airtight garages. And look at the way he dresses.”

I stared at her, stunned. *Lamborghini! That’s the make of that car*. And now the truth was right in front of my face.

Terri popped the olive into her mouth and pointed her toothpick at me. “And he’s sweet on you. That’s for sure.”

“N-no.” That sounded feeble, even to me.

It was probably the look on my face that propelled Terri into the kitchen to fetch the main course. My legs felt like rubber, and the last thing I wanted was food. Deep down inside, I knew Buck had thrown that ring into the prayer bowl. Who else had that kind of money, that kind of extravagant taste?

On a gut level, I understood when you have such a prized possession as a made-to-order sports car—and you drive it through the elements over the rural roads of Maine—it shows a certain rebelliousness. He had the money to afford that. Despite the wealthy people I’d met of late, there was no one else who showed a propensity to do something like that. Like it or not, it had to be Buck.

I fought the urge to imagine the circumstances that would bring Buck to throw the ring in the prayer bowl. That was none of my business. I took a deep breath and exhaled slowly. *Let it go*. Maybe he did it to draw publicity to the restaurant? Another breath. *Let it go*.

Terri appeared with two plates of Chicken Marsala. “I was lucky to get these last two servings away from the guys.” She laid the plates on the table. Then she poured more wine. I didn’t stop her.

“I hate to bring this up, but we have to talk about this gifting tables thing.”

I stared at my plate, thinking I'd be sick. "I know."

She sank into her seat. "Ted is scared. He says we don't have a leg to stand on. He told me he knew that the Washington Harbor property wasn't Peter's. He knew it was that billionaire's summer home. He never told me—until the other night. He said we were in too deep before he realized it. Then he thought we could keep it quiet."

She gulped some wine. "I mean, you have all your own charities and programs to talk about, so Peter's was just another charity to you. It wasn't talk about the money. It was talk about the kids. With me, it was always talk about the money. Ted knew that. Early on, he advised me to keep it quiet. And it worked to attract more people, believe it or not. Everyone wants in on a great deal when it's a secret—exclusive, you know. That's why I almost popped a gasket when Lisa Quinn was running around town mouthing off."

She went for the last of the bottle. "Anyway, I wanted to tell you that Agent Hayes from the IRS cornered me, but the next morning everything went crazy with the hostage thing at Marberry Academy."

"What did Agent Hayes say to you?"

"Ugh." She swiped her hand at the air. "Like I said, Lisa Quinn was running around town to every business mouthing off about the gifting tables. One of the shop owners called me to complain. I rushed off to find her and, lo and behold, there she was sitting on a bench, baby carriage beside her, pitching to some guy. He definitely looked like a businessman, and no one I'd ever seen before."

Terri pushed her plate away, food untouched. "He introduced himself, and I knew we were up the creek. I mean, I know you never made a dime off the gifting tables, but I pocketed some decent cash. And I never reported it on my tax returns. It sounded like he wanted to pit us against each other to get information. But in the end, we could both end up in prison."

She grabbed her glass and finished it off. "He came

back to our house that night. Ted and I were talking to him for hours. It was midnight when he finally left. Never got a minute of sleep that night. Or since, really."

I propped my head in my hand. "Did you contact a lawyer? Did you tell anyone else?"

"No. We didn't know what to do. I wanted to wait and talk to you in person. Especially since Peter and Louise disappeared. It's too scary." She went for the bottle again, shaking a final drop into her glass. "I know I probably shouldn't drink so much."

But she removed a new bottle from the wine rack, and I made a mental note to ask Nathan to drive Terri home tonight. *No need to take chances.*

Terri gripped the bottle like she'd never let go. "Then Buck showed up, and since he knew pretty much everything, we discussed it with him. I don't know if that was a good idea or not. But the guy seems trustworthy. Anyway, it's obvious he'd do anything for *you.*" She gave me an acidic smile.

"He told us he'd refer us to a New York lawyer—a top class one, he said. A different firm than you have. It sounds like he's offered to pay at least a retainer until we find out if a grand jury is taking the case. And if they arrest us. The lawyer came up and spoke with us. He seems more than qualified. But we're in deep trouble, Annie."

CHAPTER 14

~ ANNIE ~

Tuesday morning, I huddled with a pot of coffee, alone in my office. The headache I'd had since last night took its time dissipating. I wondered about Terri. She'd always seemed to take pleasure in stirring things up. It certainly diverted my attention from Lisa's money, and her "sicking" Jim Curley on me. But now, the pot was stirred way more than even Terri could stand.

And with all the trouble brewing, here I sat contemplating Buck and the ring. I'd spent too much time already wondering about the history of that ring. And so what if Buck did toss it in there? That was his concern. He was a business associate. That was all I was to him, too. Cisco's money, and staying in his good graces—that's what was important to Buck. He'd do whatever was necessary to get the job done, including turning on the charm. Buck was no fool. He wasn't called Almighty Buck for nothing.

I wondered why I'd never dared ask him any personal questions. I knew nothing about him that mattered. I knew more about even casual acquaintances. Most people told me all about their families—and even some of their hearts' desires—in the first few minutes of conversation at The Golden Bowl.

I supposed Buck was an intentional mystery. Just like Nathan. There was something emotionally dangerous in getting to know them.

Jim Curley knocked and entered the office. "Mornin'

Annie. Made some good progress yesterday, but I'll probably be another week or so on this audit. Just so you know."

I dragged myself up with a squeak of the old chair. "I'll get you some coffee. How's the family?"

"Great, thanks."

"We've got some delicious blueberry muffins today. Can I get you one?"

"Heated with a little butter. Thanks."

Ashleigh accosted me in the kitchen. "The postmaster is complaining again about the volume of mail. Roger's been picking it up every day. But he's saying now you'll need to come get it twice a day. What've you guys been doing with all that mail?"

I propped myself against the counter. "It gets screened and checked, and then the hate mail gets destroyed. The prayers go to the churches. It's way too much for us to put in the bowl. The pastors and prayer groups pray over them every week, then burn them. What else can we do?"

"Sounds good to me," Ash said. "I don't mean to keep adding to your worries. I just thought you should know."

"Of course. I've missed too many of the morning meetings. I'll try to be better about that. And any time you have a concern, please don't hesitate to bring it up to me. I know it's crazy now, but we'll get it all organized. Buck's on top of things. He knows how to deal with a growing business."

Ashleigh's ponytail bounced with her enthusiastic agreement. "Well, this is growing like wildfire. And I love Buck. He makes almost all of our meetings. He's real nice and professional. Everyone loves his accent." She plated Jim's blueberry muffin and grabbed a fresh pot of coffee. "I'll take this to Mr. Curley."

"Thanks."

After making my rounds of the restaurant, I checked with Jim before heading off to the customer service building. I found Buck in my office, just getting off the phone.

"Annie! The new packaging is ready for your approval.

My team did a brilliant job. I think you'll be more than pleased." Buck leapt from the chair, took a carton from the desk, and directed me to the couch. He landed there beside me, the large corrugated box between us.

"This is the 'Giving Thanks' turkey dinner package." He took a golden—almost a deep pie dish—container out of the box and handed it to me. "That contains the meal, and the paper wrap . . . look at the graphics and the text."

I lit up inside. "Oh, Buck!"

He beamed. "Debbie's rendition of The Golden Bowl. It's beyond my expectations."

My eyes filled. "She's so talented. It's gorgeous. How sweet of her! She's so busy with her designs, her family, and yet she took time to paint this for us."

"Reminds me of Currier and Ives," Buck said.

I dabbed at my eyes. "Yes! It's gorgeous. I love it."

"With your approval, this artwork will become part of your logo. We'll have it on our menus, all our materials, website, everywhere. Somehow Debbie captures not just the physical features of the building and grounds, she makes you *feel* The Golden Bowl, the spirit of the place. Your sister is amazing. Truly."

Buck was right. But then Debbie's artwork always evoked emotion. As Cat often said, she was Spirit-led.

The story of The Golden Bowl was tastefully featured on the box, along with our charitable mission. I read aloud, "*What are you grateful for today? Use this golden bowl to hold your own daily thoughts of gratitude.*" I gazed up into his bright eyes. "I love it!"

He pulled out more. "Each one is a different meal and a different suggestion for using the container for their little prayers. The story is consistent. The packaging is simple, elegant. It shows your quality, your uniqueness, your altruism."

My headache was gone, my heart filled with joy once more. "Buck, it's perfect."

~ ANNIE ~

That evening I looked forward to relaxing and retiring early. When I came through the kitchen door with Nathan, the smell of beef stew beckoned. Doc and Billy looked up from their posts.

"You're right on time." Doc lifted a cookie sheet full of dinner rolls from the oven. "We're ready to sit down. Summon the troops, Nathan."

"Yes, sir." Nathan helped me out of my coat, hung it in the closet, and disappeared to gather the rest of his men.

I washed my hands in the kitchen sink. "You two are quite a team. I'm sorry I didn't get in early enough to cook for you."

Doc winked. "Not a problem. Billy and I are getting pretty good at this." He dumped the rolls into a basket and covered it with a towel. "But I'm happy to report, Millie will be handling the Thanksgiving dinner. They'll be here Wednesday afternoon and staying through Saturday."

"Mom's holiday meals are the best. I can only imagine what she'll be able to accomplish in this kitchen. It's three or four times the size of hers in Ripple Lake."

We brought bowls of stew and baskets of bread to the dining room. Our security team was at the table, utensils in hand. They practically inhaled the meal.

An hour later we were chatting and enjoying The Golden Bowl's rocky road ice cream when Nathan's phone rang. Buck and my lawyer were on their way.

Somehow, I knew it wouldn't be good news.

When they came through the door, I managed an offer of coffee and dessert as Doc took their coats. Both refused. We settled in the parlor.

As Buck jumped back up and paced, my lawyer came out with the news. "It concerns Peter Fellowes. The police found a letter in his desk drawer in his classroom at Marberry Academy. It suggests he left in a hurry."

Everything in me trembled. "A letter?"

"I'll read it to you." She produced a notepad. "Annie, things are getting too hot. Time to go. Meet me at our place Friday. We'll finally be together for good. You said you'd give up The Golden Bowl. Do it. Friday."

I gasped for air. Hot tears burned my eyes.

My lawyer's voice was soft. "They've confirmed the note is in his handwriting."

Buck stopped in his tracks. A questioning gaze met mine.

I put my head in my hands and sobbed. *Who would do this to me*? *Who could hate me that much*?

"Annie?" The lawyer's voice woke me up. "Do you know anything about this? Was there anything between you and Peter Fellowes?"

I raised my head. I could barely see. "Nothing. I know nothing about a letter. There's nothing between Peter and me. Nothing but that charity we were trying to fund. Why would he write that? Who would want to do this to me?"

~ LISA ~

My mind wouldn't turn off—too many flashbacks. Annie'd told me my health insurance would pay for a counselor for me after the attack at the school, but I didn't need a shrink. I needed justice for Ryan. Even though he wasn't the best husband and father, he didn't deserve to get murdered. I was hoping the cops would find that killer soon. Then my brain could rest.

Meantime, I decided to work some extra hours. I could use the money. But I wasn't too with it. Brianna was helping me wrap up everything to close on Tuesday night. I knew we all wanted to go home, but I couldn't get out of my own way.

She finally let everyone go and sat me down with the last two cups of cocoa. I smiled as she piled the whipped cream high.

"It's good to be manager." She giggled. Then she sat down with a serious look on her face. "I can't say I know what you're going through, but I know it's got to be the worst. I'm sorry. Is there anything I can do to help?"

"Nah. There's nothing anyone can do. But thanks." I scooped up a spoonful of whipped cream and let it melt in my mouth. "I keep having flashbacks of Ryan dead on those steps. Then every five minutes on TV they keep showing that killer taking off his mask and smiling for the camera. Can't stop thinking about it. I know Ryan wasn't the best, but he didn't deserve that. I hope they get that scumbag."

Brianna's freckly cheeks got pink. "I keep watching that video over and over again, too. I knew I'd seen him somewhere, and when I caught a glimpse of it on the news again tonight, it hit me—"

"You've seen him before?"

"Yeah. I'm calling Annie as soon as we're done here. She needs to know. I'm afraid to show up at the police station. I mean . . . the way they arrested you and put you in jail just because you were married to Ryan. It was scary."

Billy and Roger's voices in the hallway stopped Bree. Then Billy peered around the corner at me. "Can I see you home, Lisa?"

My brain went numb again. "Sure." I guess Brianna's smile woke me up. "But Bree needs to tell us something about that scumbag that shot Ryan." I turned to Brianna. "You can tell Billy and Roger. They're SEALs. They'll know what to do. They're on our side."

The two guys sat ready to listen.

Brianna started. "That Carson Phelps—the guy smiling at the camera—I finally figured out where I'd seen him. My cousin wants to buy a bar, and there was a rumor Twist might be for sale. So I went with him to make sure he didn't put an offer on that dive. That's where I saw Carson Phelps. I'm positive it was him. That same obnoxious smile. He was sitting with Louise Gugino."

Billy looked at Roger and back at Bree. “Louise, huh?”

“I know Louise likes her liquor, but she was cozied up to the guy. She looked startled when she saw me. I waved, but I think she was too shocked to wave back. Do you think he kidnapped her and Peter?”

Billy leaned forward. “When did this happen?”

“Oh. Probably a month ago or so. Do you think that’s any help?”

“I think so.” Billy grinned, and took out his phone to make a call.

As he started to get up, Bree stopped him. “Um . . . there’s one other thing I want to tell you.”

Billy plopped back in his seat. “Yeah?”

“I don’t know if this is anything, but Peter Fellowes got kidnapped with Louise, or maybe they weren’t even kidnapped. Nobody seems to really know what happened to them.”

“They’re still investigating. But if you saw something, it could really help.”

She scrunched up her face a little and, with her freckles, she looked like a kid. “It’s not that I ever saw anything. It’s just a weird feeling about him. He was always talking about his charity for disabled kids, and Annie and Ash and a lot of the others at The Golden Bowl were chipping in money to help out. I gave him a few bucks here and there, but with two kids, I couldn’t do any more than that.”

She took a sip of her cocoa. “Anyway, my husband works construction, and I told him about the special school that Peter was raising money for. So he went to Peter and asked him for a job. Peter kept yessing him to death, but he never even got to meet the contractor. He never even got the contractor’s name. It was weird. Peter came up with one excuse after another. Finally, my husband gave up asking.”

“That’s interesting,” Billy said.

“Yeah. I don’t know if it helps any. I’m just not so sure Peter’s as charitable as everyone thinks. But thanks to Annie and Buck, my husband has a job now, renovating the new production facility.

"That's great." Billy stepped out to make that call and then came back in to walk me home.

Billy was such a gentleman, he remembered I was working late, and he knew I always walked to work to save gas. Not that Marberry was a tough area like Ripple Lake could be, but you never know these days. Who would've ever thought some madmen would take over Marberry Academy? But it happened.

It was a chilly walk with the wind whipping off the water. I didn't mind with Billy beside me, though.

Peg and Rosie were already asleep. So we had a quiet cup of coffee in front of my fireplace. Billy was great company, a real friend to me. And yeah, I had a crush on him. I tried not to let it show. But being a Navy SEAL, he probably figured it out.

~ ANNIE ~

My lawyer left. Buck and Nathan disappeared downstairs, and Doc sat with me on the couch, his comforting arm around me. I'd cried all the tears I had. I was out of emotion, out of ideas. I was a shell taking up space. Doc was out of soothing words.

My phone rang, and we both jumped.

"It's Debbie!" Life returned to my body. "Are you okay? What time is it there?"

Debbie's voice was hesitant. "It . . . it's almost 5:00 a.m. David's leaving—all the guys are going with him. He said it's okay to tell you."

"All of them?" My mind wasn't working.

"Yes, the five of them. They're going to get Carson Phelps, the man who took over the school." I heard the tears in her voice. "The president asked them as a personal favor. David said it's okay to tell you, but you shouldn't tell anyone else. And it's okay for us to talk while he's gone, because he knows it's important to me. But . . . but you might have to go into your bomb shelter again, depending on what happens." Her voice was weak. "Promise me you'll do that if they tell you to."

"Of course I will, sweetie. Don't worry about me."

"I did some paintings for you. I'm sending the pictures to your phone."

I remembered the packaging I'd seen this morning. It seemed eons ago. "I love the packaging. It couldn't have been more perfect. Thank you!"

She sounded like she was in a fog. "These paintings are much more important. Cat said it's all about favor and blessings for you, Annie. You just have to take a leap of faith. It's in the paintings. I'm going to go now and kiss David good-bye."

She was gone and the photos arrived in my inbox.

"Is she all right?" Doc asked.

"I don't know." The first photo appeared, and it was Jonah in silver white shoes trudging through snow. The second photo—Jonah leaping from the boat, shoes aglow. It was my dream. How did Debbie do this?

Buck appeared through the door leading to the panic room, his phone to his ear. He stood in the foyer, deep in conversation.

Nathan approached us, now dressed in the same clothes he wore the day I first met him. He pulled up that old mahogany chair and straddled it.

Doc smirked at him. "Going slumming?"

"Heading out to do some research. We got a tip that might turn out to be a break in the case." He turned to me. "Mrs. Brewster, your manager Brianna told us she remembered seeing Carson Phelps at a bar with Louise Gugino about a month ago. She said they were cozied up together. Her words. I believe that's very good news for you. There's no reason she'd be with him unless it was trouble."

My shock came out in a high-pitched, "Oh."

Before Doc could offer an opinion, Nathan turned to

him. "I'm told Mrs. Brewster received a call from her sister, letting her know David Lambrecht and his team are heading back to the U.S. to get Carson Phelps."

Doc's face lit up. "That's more good news. I'm confident they'll do it. If they could find me in a hole in the ground in the middle of Oklahoma, they'll find this Phelps character."

"No doubt." Nathan grinned. "But anything can happen in the meantime. So Pastor and Mrs. Auclair will be arriving tonight and staying until we're certain the threat is over. Mr. Clemente has asked to have guest rooms here for Mr. Wynn and that VP from Dominguez Construction. Just as a precaution."

"That's a good idea. Circle the wagons," Doc said.

"Yes, sir." Nathan addressed me. "Mr. Lambrecht informed me his wife and other family members will be in touch with you. He asks that there be no mention of their mission here and to tell you his wife has no knowledge of the charges you're facing. He prefers you keep it that way, as she tends to worry, and that's not helping her health."

"I understand, Mr. Rhodes. Thank you."

~ ANNIE ~

It was 3:00 a.m. when, from my bedroom window, I watched Nathan return home. Sleep had been fitful despite the encouraging news. By 2:45 I'd decided to crack open the window and sit there to pray, hoping the sounds of the sea and the breath of salt air would lull me to sleep. It hadn't. So after seeing Nathan's return, I decided to get ready for my day and head downstairs for an early breakfast. Baking something scrumptious would probably help take my mind off everything.

I pushed through the kitchen door to find Buck sitting at the table, coffee in hand, presiding over a pile of papers. He was still in the same clothes, sleeves rolled up, collar open. "Did you ever go to bed?"

He glanced up. “Good morning, Annie.” He checked his watch. “Looks like it’s too late for sleep now. I’ll do a few refills on the coffee instead.”

I put on a fresh pot. “What has you pulling an all-nighter?”

“I’m finally getting some confirmation of my theory. Louise Gugino pushed a number of your vendors into that gifting table scheme—telling them in order to do business with you they’d need to join at the $5000 level. Then re-join every six months or as often as she could press them. Of course, she told them this was all at your insistence.”

I shook my head in shock. “Why? What did she have against me?”

Buck joined me at the counter. “I don’t know. Perhaps it was nothing. Perhaps she simply saw you as a way to get money.”

I gazed into steel gray eyes. “Gullible. You’re saying I’m gullible.”

His bold stare, the curve of his lip, told me that’s exactly what he was saying. *He’s right*. I turned to the coffee pot. What was the point of arguing?

Fueled with a new cup of coffee, Buck returned to the pile on the table. I poured mine and stood over his shoulder. “I don’t know how you can deal with tax forms at this hour, never mind during the day.”

He pointed to the bottom of some of the pages. “Your copies—and the originals that were filed—have no evidence of your accountant’s signature. No evidence a tax preparer was ever involved. Very strange, unless your accountant was filing fraudulent returns. And of course, she did. Your so-called copies from Louise show totally different numbers than the returns the IRS received.”

I decided oatmeal apple crisp would soothe my nerves and building ire.

~ ANNIE ~

Work was non-stop all day. By dinnertime I was wiped

out. Buck was still going, after untold pots of coffee. My managers had everything well in hand, and Jim Curley had gone for the day. Nathan had been happy to escort me home, but he'd only been a tiny bit forthcoming on the investigation. He'd merely said things were encouraging.

While my parents and Doc took over the kitchen, I bundled up and headed to my Adirondack chair with my blanket and a thermos of tea. I stared out to sea and fell into a prayer of gratitude for all that people were doing for me.

Terri Monahan's voice carried from the back stair. "I don't understand how you can sit out here in the freezing cold."

"Hi, Terri."

She took the chair next to mine. "My lawyer called. It sounds like they're pointing the finger more at Louise now. We're not in the clear, but things are looking better. Did you hear the same?"

"Yes." I took a sip of tea. "Why would Louise do this? What made her hate me so much? She was always so nice to us, from the time Russ and I moved to Marberry. I remember she'd bring us pies—blueberry, apple, cherry. Pies every day. She was always so sweet."

Terri sniggered. "She hated you. From the minute you moved to town. She'd be nice to your face, then talk behind your back somethin' fierce. Especially at the beginning. Once she figured out how to use you in the gifting table thing, she stopped most of the backbiting. The hate came out in a more profitable way."

"Why would Louise talk behind my back, and then bring pies? I don't get it."

Terri's dark eyes gleamed in the dim light, anxious to fill me in on the gossip. "The pies weren't for you. The pies were for Russ. Louise wanted your husband."

"Oh." I turned to the blackness in front of me, surprised I wasn't surprised. I remembered Russ was always polite but quite formal with Louise. Not warm and friendly like he was with everyone else. Kind blue eyes were winking at me from heaven. "Russ was a great catch."

"Yeah. And how stupid was she to try and compete with your baking?"

A small giggle bubbled up, drowned in the roar of the ocean. It became full-blown laughter. "Her pies were awful."

"What?" Terri snorted in my ear, catching the mood.

I lost my breath in a belly laugh. "Terrible . . . her pies . . . yuck . . ."

Terri burst into cackling laughter. That was it for me. My thermos hit the ground and I doubled over.

I couldn't stop.

When Nathan stood before us to announce dinner, the two of us were in a fit, rolling in our seats. Over pies? It felt good for a change. I didn't even mind my lapse of propriety in front of our Director of Security.

CHAPTER 15

~ ANNIE ~

They say laughter is the best medicine, and I guess that's exactly what I'd needed. Thursday morning I was rested and refreshed, ready to face Joe Harris' camera crew. They filmed the hearth decorated for Thanksgiving, then transformed The Golden Bowl for Christmas. Wreaths went up on our windows and doors. Lights twinkled on the evergreens around the buildings. Fresh cut Christmas trees were placed strategically in the dining rooms and in The Bakery & Sweet Shop. Their scent, mixed with the aroma of cloves, cinnamon, cardamom and other spices that we used in our holiday baked goods, created an irresistible atmosphere. Lines formed out the doors.

Reporters arrived to cover the holiday preparations at The Golden Bowl. Buck expertly kept me from saying much of anything to them. I did a lot of waving and smiling.

Before the crew left, they lined my staff up for a photo by the front stairs of the restaurant with a throng of customers behind us. I was directed to the center of the line, flanked by my managers. As the photographer asked us to say "cheese," Jim Curley came from behind me with a kiss on my cheek. The crowd burst into applause and cheers. Even Nathan was laughing.

~ ANNIE ~

At home Mom was gearing up for Thanksgiving, though

it was a week away. She enjoyed my help as her baking assistant, so I volunteered for a couple of hours after dinner. Then we made hot chocolate for the entire gang now living in my house. There was little talk of my brother-in-law and his cohorts, or what progress had been made in finding Carson Phelps. Although the news stations continued to mention the story, they were as clueless as I was.

When my head hit the pillow, I was out. No dreams about Carson Phelps, grand juries, or enlarging my territory. I woke up early enough to call my sister. No big news on that front. At least she was calm. Apparently, she'd heard from David, and he and his team were okay.

The sunrise was just beginning when I stepped outside and down the stairs to the beach. The wind was light, the colors of the sky and sea spectacular. It was here where I most clearly felt the presence of God. I smiled up at the first rays of sun.

My gaze settled on the whitecaps, as the energetic tide rolled to shore. Sunshine glistened on the waves, making them look almost like glass. A few hardy seagulls circled above, their cries disappearing into the relentless roar of the ocean. To me, the smell of the beach on cold mornings defined fresh. I inhaled lungs full of glorious salt air, and the bite shocked me from drowsiness.

A hissing sound became my name. "Annie!" The wind was playing tricks. "Annie!" I turned around to find my bodyguard, Keith, standing behind the short hedge that marked the cliff's drop to the beach. He wasn't calling to me. Simply watching over me.

"Annie!" It was a voice.

As I turned again, a ray of light directed me to a crevice in the rock.

A hand motioned me to come. "Annie."

I drew closer and my heart thumped. "Peter?" My whisper disappeared with the breeze. His face was bruised, swollen. His body collapsed limply into the wet sand. I glanced back at Keith. He hadn't moved. I slowly approached the crevice.

"Peter?"

"I'm so sorry, Annie. I didn't mean to hurt you. It got out of hand."

"What happened?"

"Did you find the note? He made me write that note. But I do want to be with you. I just didn't know how to say it."

"Peter, what happened?"

"He shot me, but it missed—just grazed me. I fell overboard. Phelps. It was Phelps. Don't call the cops on me."

"Peter—"

"Just come with me. I do love you. Always have."

An arm grabbed me, and I was suddenly behind Keith and his automatic weapon. The rest of the team stormed the beach.

Hands behind his head, Peter eased out of the cleft in the rock, as he was told. The guards grabbed him and shoved him facedown on the sand. As they searched him for weapons, he repeated, "I can explain." They handcuffed him and pulled him upright. Sunlight highlighted his battered face.

My stomach ached. "He needs to get to a hospital."

"Yes, ma'am." Nathan put his hand on my back and guided me to the stairs.

I tried looking over my shoulder, but he was intent on keeping me from seeing what was going on. He told Keith to escort me up to the house.

"Just relax, Mrs. Brewster. No worries," Keith said.

Easy for him to say. I tried to turn, but saw only the horizon as we walked up the lawn and through the screen door. "Whew! I'm parched."

Keith had an easy smile I couldn't quite understand, considering the circumstances. "Comin' right up." He escorted me to a seat at the kitchen table and poured me a glass of water.

Facing the bay window, I craned my neck to see if

there was any activity outside. “Can I go upstairs?”

“Yes, ma’am. But now would not be a good time to call anyone.”

“I understand.” I pushed through the swinging door and met Buck at the bottom of the stairs in the foyer. It looked as though he’d just finished a workout, his towel perfectly draped around his neck.

“Good morning, Annie, are you all right?”

I let out a sigh. “Peter Fellowes . . . he showed up on the beach. He looks like he’s been beaten. Mr. Rhodes has him outside. I think he’s questioning him.”

“Splendid!” Buck turned toward the kitchen.

I tugged at his sweatshirt. “They don’t want anyone out there. What are they going to do to him? He needs a doctor.”

Buck seemed unconcerned. “Well, we have a doctor. Perhaps Doc will take a look at him once Rhodes gets what we need from him.”

Two hours later, Peter was at the kitchen table eating toast and scrambled eggs as fast as Mom could make them. He must have downed a gallon of water and juice. Doc had treated the cuts and bruises, and Dad had seen to it he had clean, dry clothes.

Aside from a few sheepish glances, he didn’t profess his love for me or ask us to let him go. FBI agents arrived and took him into custody. Nathan left with them.

As we watched them drive away, I thought about the note Peter had left in his desk. I’d memorized and pondered those words since my lawyer first read them to me: *Annie, things are getting too hot. Time to go. Meet me at our place Friday. We’ll finally be together for good. You said you’d give up The Golden Bowl. Do it. Friday.*

Buck clapped his hands and startled me out of my musings. “Well, that was a fine start to the morning. Are we ready for another fun Friday at The Golden Bowl?”

~ LISA ~

The weekend was wild at The Golden Bowl. Tourists and townspeople showed up because of all the publicity from Amanda James. *Amanda James Now* would air on Sunday, for a follow-up on Annie and her famous family, and all the people Amanda had interviewed on the first show.

There was a lot of excitement, and the pretty holiday decorations made it even better. A dusting of snow covered the grass and trees, so it looked like a movie. All the visitors were taking pictures and buying stuff. We almost ran out of some meals, and the bakery shelves were empty by closing time.

Annie called it a frenzy.

Everyone was in a good mood because Thanksgiving was coming up, and most of Marberry survived the takeover of the school. TV news bulletins reported that Peter Fellowes had been found. He was being held because they weren't sure if he was in cahoots with Carson Phelps. *Wow*. I was shocked to hear that. It was pretty strange because Louise Gugino was still missing.

When Billy offered to cook me dinner tonight, I turned over my kitchen with a big smile and told him I'd eat anything but turkey. He set to work on grilling some steaks. We stood out on the deck in the freezing cold. But being with Billy and inhaling the smell of those steaks, I was just fine.

"So why did Louise Gugino get away, but they caught Peter Fellowes?" I was dying to pick his brain on the Carson Phelps case. "Where did they find Peter?"

He gave me his "that's classified" look.

"Okay, Billy, you gotta spill it. I was in the middle of everything. I'm not gonna tell anyone, but I need to know."

He busied himself with the grill.

"Ya know I was there when the IRS big shot practically arrested Terri Monahan. Peter Fellowes is up to his armpits in it, 'cuz he was right there with Terri in this gifting table strategy. And it sounds like it's a *scheme* now, not a strategy, like he told us. It sounds like some guy named Ponzi is at the head of it." I wiped sweaty hands on my apron, proud of myself for speaking up, but nervous about making a Navy SEAL I had a crush on mad at me.

He grinned at me, and I had to sit down. At least he wasn't mad at me.

"Just tell me. Is Annie okay?"

He leaned down and kissed the top of my head. "Annie's okay."

He kissed me.

~ ANNIE ~

Sunday evening, my parents, Doc, Buck, and I shared bowls of popcorn and watched *Amanda James Now*.

When the credits rolled, Doc chuckled. "You couldn't have done a better ad for The Golden Bowl if you tried. Be prepared for a crazy business day tomorrow."

For the first time in a while, I was at peace with that thought. There was so much uncertainty in my life, but my restaurant—my business—was one thing worth all the effort. This weekend my reward was watching the smiles on kids' faces, families having a wonderful time enjoying The Golden Bowl—all the delicious foods we offered, friendly people, scenic grounds, and invigorating salt air. Best of all, many of them took the time to learn about the prayer bowl and talk about the power of prayer.

Tonight it hit home for me as Amanda took her audience on another tour, a deeper look at the people that make The Golden Bowl so special. My staff was my family. I couldn't have been prouder.

After the show I excused myself and retired to my room. Settling in the window seat, I watched brilliant moonlight shimmering on the waves. *No Peter, even if I loved you, I could never give up The Golden Bowl.*

~ ANNIE ~

Early the next morning, I came through the kitchen door to find Doc video-conferencing with Debbie and the kids. I nestled over his shoulder, and they laughed and shouted when they saw me. My niece, Sabena, told us, "Papa is still at work."

Debbie seemed in reasonable spirits, undoubtedly holding it together for the children. We discussed Amanda's show. Then she prattled on about making a Thanksgiving dinner to celebrate on Thursday, despite the fact it was not a holiday in Austria. I told her I'd email the recipes she'd requested.

My heart went out to her. It was so obvious she was distracted over her husband's absence. But we were ordered to avoid discussion about the real concerns. More of that "elephant in the room" stuff.

The sudden disappearance of my nephew, Danny, from the screen did not bode well. Of any kid I'd ever known, he was the most prone to mischief. If he was left to his own devices for more than a second, there'd be trouble. Our conversation came to a quick conclusion.

Doc closed the laptop. "She still calls me Dr. Westcott."

I took the chair beside him and patted his arm. "She'll come around, Doc. It's just going to take time. Between her husband, her kids, and her business, she's under a lot of stress. Not to mention, she's still getting over the death of her mother."

Doc grimaced. "Marion was your mother, too. Your birth mother."

A sour feeling gurgled in my stomach. "I never knew her, and frankly, she never wanted anything to do with me. Her death only affected me because it affected Debbie."

"I think Debbie gave you a one-sided view of Marion. Maybe that's why it's hard for you."

My jaw stiffened. "It's not hard for me. I know I was

spared some misery when she gave me to Mom and Dad. I had a wonderful childhood. Debbie wasn't so lucky."

Doc rubbed the irritation off his face. "You make up your own mind. But I want you to know Marion was a beautiful, lively, young woman when I knew her. Full of life. George Aldridge sucked the life out of her. And he almost succeeded in doing that with Debbie, too."

I put my hand on his arm. "I'm sorry. It's been a hectic, emotional six months—a lot to process. Right now, I have enough to deal with the living. I'm sure my birth mother is happy now in heaven with Grammy. That's what's important."

~ DOC ~

I wouldn't let on to my daughters, but it was tough watching them go through all this grief. I put on a heavy jacket and gloves, and headed out to the beach. Billy caught up with me before I made it to the stairs. "You okay, Doc?"

"I'm okay. Just concerned about my daughters. Thought I'd take a walk to help work things out. Not that there's much you can do when your child marries an assassin."

Billy grabbed the railing and landed in the sand, turning to face me. "David Lambrecht is a good guy. Basically . . . I mean he goes after the bad guys. You need guys like him."

"I agree. I just don't need them married to my daughter."

Billy's answer was a smirk.

As we headed north, the sandy beach became cobblestone. He busied himself throwing rocks into the ocean, distracting me. Just like a kid.

I decided there was precious little I could do to improve Debbie's situation. My thoughts turned to Annie, and I realized there was nothing I could do for her either. I took to throwing rocks at the water, too. "Yeah, this solves exactly nothing. But it feels pretty good."

~ ANNIE ~

The predicted craziness was in full bloom when I walked through the door of The Golden Bowl. Buck was trying to preside over a meeting to discuss the new computer system while employees were pulled in every direction. He finally settled on instructing Ashleigh and me.

By the end of the morning, my head was spinning. I went upstairs to my tiny office to check on Jim Curley before heading off to The Bakery & Sweet Shop.

He gave me a weak smile. "I've tied things up and—reluctantly—filed my report. I included all of your extenuating circumstances and all the charitable work you do. But, as you know, it's not my decision what happens from here. You know the IRS is already involved, too. That's another ball of wax."

"Yes. That much, I know, Jim. I appreciate all you've done for me."

The frenzy of activity only increased as Thanksgiving approached. Preparations for the holiday dinner at The Golden Bowl, Dad's church, and four other soup kitchens I'd committed to, required all hands on deck. Everyone was more than generous with their time, talent, and money to make it a truly meaningful celebration of gratitude.

By the time I trudged through the door on Thursday evening with Buck, Doc, and our entourage of guards, I was exhausted. Mom and Dad were working on our own meal after serving up the noontime dinner at their church in Ripple Lake. Despite my endless work on turkey dinners all week, there was something special about the smell of Thanksgiving dinner coming from my own kitchen.

A quick shower revived me, and soon we were all seated around the dining room table. "Well, we're eating fashionably late. I can't believe it's almost 8:00."

Dad offered up a prayer of thanksgiving, and Buck raised his glass in a toast.

Doc said, “Let’s eat!” and everyone dug in.

Mom smiled over at me. “I hope there’s enough food.”

Dad chuckled. “I don’t think we need to worry about that, Millie. There’s enough for an army here.”

Mom glanced at our security team around the table, filling their plates as though it was their last meal. She turned to Dad. “We do have an army here.”

Chewing muffled the laughter. Once the hunger pangs were assuaged, conversation began. Mom accepted a chorus of compliments to the chef.

She took the spotlight off her culinary skills. “Annie, Debbie called us at the church this morning and wished us all a very happy Thanksgiving. She held up the phone so all the kids could yell their greetings—very cute. But I think she was feeling a bit down.”

Doc nodded in agreement. “I think so, too.”

“Yeah. I spoke with her this morning, too. She said David had just called, and he was fine—the guys were all fine. But they’re not home, and she had no idea when they would be. She was weepy. I felt so sad for her. I didn’t know what to say. But at least they have a big crowd of extended family to take care of each other.” I dabbed my eyes with my napkin. *Quick with the tears, like my sister.*

Mom gave me a sympathetic nod. “Debbie said they’d all be celebrating the holiday with Raphael and Cindy Dominguez. She said they have a massive home. I can only imagine. He’s made a fortune in construction all over the world.”

Buck lifted his glass in the direction of Carlos, Raphael’s VP. “A toast to the incredibly talented and generous folks at Dominguez Construction. We are eternally grateful to you for the new meal prep facility for The Golden Bowl.”

Carlos smiled broadly and downed his wine. “It will be the finest in all the country.”

Mom waved her fork at him. “I’m so excited, Carlos. I hear there’s going to be a kitchen area for Annie to teach classes. I can’t wait!”

I smiled and nodded, having no idea about classes. Was this something Buck had dreamed up? And how could I fit another thing into my day? Here we go, enlarging my territory again.

I turned to Buck. His politely happy expression was in place, which could mean anything.

~ ANNIE ~

Two weeks passed with long days at The Golden Bowl and customers coming out of the woodwork. The new software system was keeping track of finances and food costs. The learning curve was even more challenging with all the holiday distractions. Buck said, "Ideally, we would implement the system during a less busy time of year. But necessity dictates we do it now."

There was no further official word about the IRS investigation by Agent Hayes. My lawyer spent just a few moments on a conference call with Buck and me. We were told with the search continuing for Louise Gugino and information provided by Peter Fellowes, the possibility of a grand jury would most likely not happen until after the holidays.

When Buck clicked off the speakerphone, I sat back in my chair. "That's supposed to be good news? Will life ever get back to normal? Don't they understand how stressful it is to live every day wondering if you're going to prison?"

Buck's gaze circled my new office with the professional, comfortable, ergonomically correct furniture. Outside our door sat a host of customer service employees, making sales soar for The Golden Bowl. Their CEO, Annie Brewster, fraud, could be leaving them for the penitentiary any time. I wanted to bolt for the prayer bowl. What else could help but prayer? I pictured myself rifling through each slip of paper, scouring the bowl for a word from Cat. If I knew anything, it was that God spoke through Cat Clemente. *Safe pasture*.

I watched Buck drag his hands across his face. If he was trying to wipe away frustration, it didn't work. "All we can do, Annie, is keep moving forward. If, God forbid, you—" His voice choked up, and I saw a momentary glimpse of fear.

My heart pounded.

There was a knock at the door. Buck managed, "Yes."

Nathan entered and closed the door behind him. "Carson Phelps is dead, and Louise Gugino is in custody. The men who helped him take over the school are dead or in custody."

I thought I'd fall out of my chair. "David?"

"Lambrecht and his team got them. They found Phelps and Gugino on a yacht in the Gulf of Mexico."

"David's okay?"

"Fine, ma'am. They'll be questioning Louise Gugino. Hopefully it will mean an easier time for you."

After Nathan left, Buck and I sat in momentary silence. It dawned on me that "an easier time" meant that I was still on the hook. I could still be charged in the gifting tables conspiracy.

"Buck?"

He looked at me. His smile at the good news had disappeared. "Yes?"

"I could still go to prison."

Fear flashed in his eyes. "We'll fight tooth and nail for you. Don't worry. You'll be fine. Let's get back to work and let the lawyers do their job."

A while later, Tracey, our customer service manager, and Karen, The Bakery & Sweet Shop manager, showed up to let us know about the celebrations going on all around The Golden Bowl, not to mention the calls and online communications that were bombarding the customer service office.

When Billy stopped in to report that a news team had pulled into the parking lot, Buck came out of his work haze.

My phone rang. "It's Debbie!"

Buck stood. "Stay here. I'll take care of all this hoopla.

Talk with your sister and relax." He left with Billy.

"Debbie! We just heard the news." I plopped onto the couch and curled my legs up under me.

"David's okay. He called me. Everyone's okay." Her voice melted into a sob.

"It's okay, sweetie. You can let it out. I know how hard all this is on you. You've been so strong. But he'll be back home. I bet he's on his way."

Her cries turned to heavy strained breaths. "No . . . not yet."

"But soon," I said.

She exhaled into the phone. "A few days, I think." I could hear her trying to compose herself. "He . . . I don't think he likes not working." Her voice sounded like she was under water. "I know he's happy to be away from General Pearson, but I still think he misses work. I think maybe the president found something else for him to do." I could feel her tears starting again. "It's almost Christmas." The deluge began.

CHAPTER 16

~ LISA ~

I had a hard time staying at my dishwashing post, with all the excitement going on around me. That scumbag, Carson Phelps, was dead. Who was smiling now? Me!

As I danced around my sink, Billy came up behind me, and I almost jumped out of my sneakers. He put his arms around my waist.

"You're the woman of the hour. Wanna talk to the reporters?"

He let go, and I spun around to face him, a little off balance. He steadied me in front of him with his hands on my shoulders.

"Reporters?"

He grinned. "They're dying to talk to you."

"What if I say something stupid? Does Annie want me to do it?"

"Annie's busy in her office. But Buck thinks it's a good idea."

"Okay. Will you stay with me? Make sure I don't say anything stupid?"

He laughed. "Okay. But you'll be great. Really."

So Billy stayed behind the cameras while I sat by the fireplace, still wearing my Golden Bowl apron and waste-watchers pin, answering a bunch of questions. Mostly I ranted about Carson Phelps and how happy I was that he was dead. I spent a lot of time talking about dancing on his grave. I told them I'd bring Rosie and Peg, and all my friends, and anyone else who wanted to go. I named all the dances I'd do there—the twist, the hustle, even the hokey pokey.

That got everyone laughing, so I named a bunch more dances I'd heard of, but didn't know how to do. Egged on by my friends, I gave the reporter a goofy smile. "Yeah, you should come, too. We'll do the foxtrot and the tango and the mashed potato. Take that, Carson Phelps—Maine potatoes on your head."

When it came to Louise Gugino and Peter Fellowes—I was happy they were alive. I had no idea how they got mixed up in the whole thing. And if I knew, I sure wouldn't say.

Billy was smiling by the time I was done. And so was I. Then everyone in the restaurant—staff and customers and me—boogied out the door and down the stairs. The cameras got it all.

~ ANNIE ~

The next few days were surreal. I had no inkling of what happened with Louise Gugino. No one seemed to know anything about what she'd told the authorities. No one could—or would—tell me what she'd be charged with.

Peter Fellowes could have been swallowed up by a black hole, for all I knew.

The news media continued to buzz about the story, but there were precious few facts in their reports. The entertainment and news magazine shows spent even more time on it. Every reporter had a different angle, a different spin. Despite the minimal information, it was hard not to watch, hoping I'd glean some little fact or helpful theory.

Much to my chagrin, Lisa and her "dancing on the grave" interview went viral. People created copycat videos of "dancing on the grave." Reporters clamored to interview her. Billy and Roger were assigned to keep her and her family safe.

I had no energy to sit with Lisa and discuss her reaction to Carson Phelps' demise. With her sad background, I wasn't surprised she'd reacted that way. Many of our neighbors also cheered for vengeance. At least she wasn't burying her feelings. I kept her in my prayers, knowing God would work in her life, and somehow all this would be transformed to something good.

Buck and my super-agent, Joe Harris, kept Amanda James and the rest of the interview requests at bay. They spun every inquiry into a story on The Golden Bowl. Sales records were set each and every day.

My parents returned home to Ripple Lake, so Dad would be able to take care of his church and congregation. Their security guards took care of Mom and Dad.

Debbie and I spoke at least once or twice a day. There was never a peep from the media about David's involvement in the takedown of Carson Phelps, and David kept his wife in the dark about what he was doing. Debbie's anxiety rose. At last he and his team returned home four days after they found Phelps.

Three days after he returned home, Debbie put on a brave voice and told me David was leaving again. She surmised he was thinking about taking a new job. It sounded like she had no idea what or where that would be.

His silence was overwhelming for her . . . and for me.

~ ANNIE ~

It was two weeks before Christmas and snow was swirling around my Adirondack chairs. Doc and I sat at the kitchen table, he with a cardiology journal and a cocoa, me with my thoughts. I was too tired to go to bed.

I'd long since refocused from the definition of "fraud" to "conspiracy." That was far more frightening. What made it worse was Buck's silence on the matter. I realized his mad focus on making The Golden Bowl the business of the century was his way of ignoring the situation. He remained in the customer service office long past closing every night. I had the feeling the skyrocketing sales figures were his only comfort.

I didn't dare call the lawyer, and when she called me, it was all so non-committal. The charges and possible consequences could be very serious. But no one knew how serious . . . yet.

My tea was cold again. I dragged myself up from the table and headed to the stove. "It's going to be a tough winter, Doc."

My security team came through the door with a blast of cold air. "We could sure use some hot cocoa, ma'am," Billy said.

The six of them gathered around me in our new nightly routine. "Hot chocolate for everyone," I said.

It was like a feeding frenzy.

"How many people have walked into my house unannounced since I left?"

We all jumped in place. "David!"

I thought Nathan would faint. "You're the first, sir."

David's smirk did nothing to alleviate the horror on the men's faces.

"The first that you know about," he said.

In the silence, I rushed into David's outstretched arms, and we exchanged kisses on the cheek.

Doc shook David's hand. "Great to see you! What brings you to Maine? Is Debbie here?"

"No, Debbie is at home. I had some business in Washington." David turned those inscrutable brown eyes on me. "A certain tax matter."

I swallowed the lump in my throat. "Tax? You went to the President of the United States with my tax problem?"

"Under the circumstances, it was the simplest solution."

I realized my mouth was hanging open. I cleared my throat. "Circumstances?"

"Yes, the president is honoring you at his Lame Duck New Year's dinner. He and his wife will be giving out commendations. You'll receive something for your wall—or your drawer depending on your politics."

"Commendation?"

"You're welcome." That endearing smirk. "Now is there any hot chocolate left?"

From fraud, to commendation from the president, to state dinner, to hot chocolate? Life was stranger by the minute. I took a breath. "Plenty of hot chocolate." I returned to the stove.

"Good." David took out his phone. "Mr. Wynn? David Lambrecht. Annie's celebrating some good news this evening with hot chocolate." He addressed me. "Any biscuits or something to go with that?"

"Whatever you like," I said.

He returned to his phone. "You'll be fed. How soon can you be at the house?"

It sounded like Buck would waste no time responding to David's summons. Once the phone went back in David's pocket he addressed Nathan. "Rhodes, I need a moment." He looked over at me. "Annie, I'll get my bag."

"Great, the room you and Debbie had this summer is ready and waiting. I'll put out some fresh towels for you."

Nathan followed David out to his car. His men stood still, frozen around the kitchen stove.

As the door swung shut, Billy let out a low whistle. "So just how screwed are we?"

By the time I checked on the bedroom, put out towels, and headed down the hall to the stairs, I heard Buck and David in the foyer. I stopped to listen.

Buck had true joy in his voice. "Thank you, from the bottom of my heart, for getting Annie out of this tax mess—this Ponzi conspiracy. Things had been looking pretty bleak. However did you manage it?"

David, always calm and precise, was such a contrast. "I spoke the truth to the right person. It's as simple as that. That mission statement on the back of her restaurant menu isn't just words—it's her life's calling."

Buck seemed surprised. "You told the President of the United States about Annie's mission? Amazing!"

I was surprised David would have remembered the mission statement from the menu. Such a small detail for someone like him. But then again, his job had to be all about details.

Buck's voice softened, and I strained to hear. "'Feed people—body, soul and spirit.' She does that every day. Your sister-in-law is a very special woman."

"She is," David said. "She spends her life taking care of everyone else. She doesn't deserve this strife over one poor business decision. She thought the accountant was helping her cause. She trusted him to do a job. She trusted his daughter—his so-called assistant. If she's guilty of anything, it's being too trusting."

Buck interjected, "And she ended up with $35.00 to her name."

I couldn't take the embarrassment of going down that garden path, so I sprang from the hallway as though I'd been rushing along, and headed down the stairs.

David's familiar grin told me my ploy wasn't working, but Buck did look surprised. "Let me take your coat, Buck."

"It's a bit damp from the snow." He removed the overcoat, and Doc appeared in time to take it.

Buck's dark suit was as fresh as it was when he'd arrived at The Golden Bowl early this morning. I had to wonder. "Do you ever wear jeans?"

"Jeans? Of course. Why do you ask?"

"Well, it's 9:30 at night, and you're still in a business suit."

"I was working on some figures. I don't think you realize how much work we have to do to get this place turned around."

Doc waved us into the kitchen. "I recommend the hot chocolate, Buck, but you might want something stronger."

The four of us settled at the kitchen table with drinks and snacks. Doc had easily convinced the men to join him with a beer. I quizzed David about the family, and he repeated most everything Debbie had told me on the phone earlier.

Buck's $35.00 comment nagged at me. "David, I'm sorry about the $35.00 bank balance. I hope you know I'm extremely careful with the money you give me for the house. I'd never waste it."

"I know. I'm not concerned. You're always thinking about other people—always generous—above and beyond. Debbie's the same."

"Thanks." I had to change the subject before I got choked up. "Does Debbie know you're here?"

"No. I have a surprise for her."

"Oh?"

David grinned. "I'm taking you home for Christmas, Annie. I haven't a gift for Debbie yet—no time for shopping. So you and Doc will do very nicely, I'm sure."

"What?" I thought I'd fall over.

Doc laughed. "We couldn't have a better present."

David gave Buck a look as though they were in cahoots. "Buck will hold down the fort until Christmas, and he'll have your managers ready to take care of things until you get back. We'll leave tomorrow morning."

I was overwhelmed. "Oh, David! That . . . that's so kind, but I . . . I couldn't possibly."

"I'm not taking no for an answer. Buck says it's doable. We'll need to be in Washington for New Year's Day anyway. So take a holiday. You certainly deserve it."

My head was spinning. "That's too long to be away." My eyes started to water.

Buck took my hand and squeezed it, much the way he did the day he explained the mess I was in with my business. The warmth of his touch distracted me. "Annie, you're going to be taking a national stage to plead your cause for your charities, your call to prayer. You'll have to hand over daily management issues to your staff. You can't do everything. This is the start. Take some time for Christmas with your family. Enjoy it. Recharge yourself. Then you'll be ready to meet the president and first lady, receive that award, and put in another plug for your cause. You'll come back to Marberry ready to work. And your staff will be here, proudly carrying on at The Golden Bowl."

I used my free hand to wipe my eyes. "Buck, you should be a politician."

~ ANNIE ~

After everyone went upstairs, I spent a few minutes cleaning up the kitchen. Being busy was what I needed. I felt like I might float away with the relief of it all. No grand jury, no charges, no prison sentence. I giggled at the dishwasher. *I'm free*! And I was going on holiday to visit my sister. I'd get to step into her world for a while. The excitement made me dance around the room with my sponge.

Thoughts of meeting the president and first lady stopped me in my tracks. What could I possibly say to them? How could I plead my cause? I'd most likely be tongue-tied. Why would they want to hear anything I'd have to say?

What about the others? What would happen to them? Louise? Pinky? Peter? What about Terri and Ted? Questions propelled me up the stairs.

As I entered the hallway I noticed the door to Debbie's art studio was open, a shaft of soft light glowed on the carpet. I peered inside.

"Come in, Annie." David held one of Debbie's paintings, a bemused expression on his face—the one I'd only seen when he was with her. He waved me to a seat by the window, shut the door, and sat in an upholstered chair facing me. He put his wife's artwork aside. "I expect you have more questions." Those inscrutable eyes were back.

"If you don't mind me asking."

He smirked. "I'll let you know if I do."

"What about Terri and Ted?"

"They don't get to meet the president." He grinned.

My stomach released a squad of butterflies. I pressed on. "No . . . no charges? They're free?"

"No charges. As long as they keep their mouths shut, they'll be fine. From what I understand, that could be a deal-breaker with Terri Monahan."

It took a moment for that to translate as a joke. The light bulb went on, and I started laughing, then crying, with relief.

He got up and found the tissue box, then handed it to me. "You and Debbie have a few things in common."

He resumed his seat and focused on one of Grammy's paintings on the wall as I composed myself.

"David, what happened? I mean . . . what . . . how was Carson Phelps involved with Louise and Peter? Why did he invade Marberry Academy?"

His eyes fixed on mine. "Unfortunately, this . . . celebrity . . . that has happened to me and my family has continued to explode. It has a considerable downside. My family—and extended family—have become targets as well. Carson Phelps and his brothers had some resentment toward the president. It makes no difference what it was, I was charged with protecting the president in Vienna. I did that, and Adam Phelps died in the process."

He grimaced. "After that, the remaining Phelps brothers extended their grievance to include me and my family. When the world learned you and Debbie are sisters, you were sucked into the vortex. I'm sorry about that, Annie. All I can do is my best to protect you, without trampling your ability to live your life as you see fit. I apologize for the fact that life as you knew it is over."

"No apologies necessary. You may recall I was living in the attic above my restaurant."

His smirk almost went to a smile. "I thought it was a nice, cozy place. The view unbeatable."

I smiled. "It does have a great view."

His unfathomable eyes were back. "Long story short, Phelps arrived in Marberry along with thousands of tourists to see what he could dredge up. He quickly found Louise

Gugino. Her criminal tendencies made a perfect match for him. Peter Fellowes was a cog in the wheel. He started out with good intentions to raise money for a school for special needs children. But Louise deftly ensnared him, then you and Terri, in a fine conspiracy. I'm sure by the time she met up with Phelps, she saw the writing on the wall. Things were about to get too messy. He gave her a way to walk away with the money, and it served his purposes perfectly. Anything he could do to stir up trouble for you was fine with him. Fraud and conspiracy charges were satisfactory. And then there was the likelihood I'd come after him. That's what he wanted."

"Wow." I took another tissue. "It's like the Wild West."

"Sometimes."

"And Peter—did he know? I mean, he must have known those pictures were that millionaire's estate."

"Louise had him hooked early in the game. He thought he was going to be a philanthropist, but he liked the money too much. By the time his conscience kicked in, he was in too deep. So when Louise introduced him to Phelps, he had to go along. He told Phelps about Marberry Academy and the Underground Railroad tunnels that were left under the building. Phelps had him write that note to put another nail in your coffin."

I blew out a breath. "So Louise and Peter purposely took those kids in a van to make a getaway while Phelps and his gang took over the school?"

"Yes. They ditched the van and walked to a small boat they'd hidden nearby, then met up with Phelps and his men on the yacht. Peter found out that was the end of the line for him. Fortunately, he survived the beating and the dip in the ocean."

"He told me Phelps shot him, but missed, and he fell overboard."

"Lucky for him."

"Why did he come back to Marberry?"

"Where else could he go? He had nothing. He thought you could save him."

A tear fell down my cheek. "So sad." I blew my nose. "What's going to happen to Peter?"

David shrugged. "I suppose he'll make a deal. They'll probably go easy on him. You mustn't worry about it."

I dabbed at my eyes. "Okay." I realized I was completely exhausted. I wasn't sure I could move, but I had to. "It's late. I'll let you get some sleep."

He took his phone from his suit jacket pocket. "I'm calling Debbie. I'll tell her I'll be home tomorrow night, but I don't want her to know I'm here. Your visit is to be a surprise."

"Okay. Are they awake?"

He looked at the time. "It's six in the morning there. Danny's probably re-routed the Salzach River by now."

Exhaustion fueled my laughter. My nephew's antics were just that crazy.

~ ANNIE ~

By morning the weather cleared, and my parents came to the house for breakfast, accompanied by their security guards. They embraced me in a hug with tears of gratitude for the happy news that their daughter would not go to prison. Mom was so emotional she hugged everyone from David to Doc to Buck and Carlos. She insisted on making breakfast, but was too shaken to be much use. She and I took over the kitchen while the men gathered in the dining room to discuss this latest development.

David had invited them to go with us to Salzburg. Dad felt strongly that he needed to be with his congregation for Christmas, and Mom was afraid of flying.

I thought if I could change Mom's mind, Dad would give in. "Mom, you've never even been out of the country. Why not come with us? Austria is beautiful. When would you ever be able to afford a trip like this? Debbie will be so thrilled to see you. We'll have a blast."

Mom had pancake batter and blueberries everywhere.

"That's just what I'm afraid of—a blast. Even those private planes can crash. God help us. Besides, I *have* been out of the country. Your father and I have been to Montreal more times than I can count. You know that."

"I know. But that doesn't count. Canada's right down the street."

There was no changing Mom's mind. So Dad would be impossible.

After breakfast, the luggage was loaded into the SUV, and we all drove to The Golden Bowl. Mom and Dad wanted to see the Christmas decorations and take some prayers from the bowl to the prayer group at Dad's church.

I said a tearful goodbye to my staff. Buck and my managers—even some of my customers—told me not to worry. "Go! Have a good time," was the refrain.

David helped himself to some treats for the family from The Bakery & Sweet Shop. Not surprisingly, he cleared us out of lemon bars. "My Christmas gift to Cat," he said. Then he took a five-gallon barrel of our homemade blueberry ice cream and every blueberry scone in the store. "For Paulo," he explained. Doc made sure to add another barrel of chocolate chip, so as not to disappoint the rock star. Several more boxes of scones "for everyone," bags of holiday candies for the kids, and David pronounced, "We're done."

My manager, Karen, blushed as he took out his wallet. I stepped in. "David, your money's no good here."

He held up hundred dollar bills. "Did Maine secede from the Union without telling me?" He wouldn't take no for an answer.

We headed out into sunshine. Light swirls of snow dusted the grounds, sparkling like the inside of a snow globe. David, Doc, and Billy loaded the car.

"I've got to take a prayer from the bowl before we go." I ran up the stairs, and they followed me. After taking a prayer slip, I invited Doc and David to choose.

I could see shock on David's face. "It's Debbie's." He showed us a swirled heart and rainbow design in pastels.

"Oh, it's gorgeous! I've never come across one of her prayers." I took the card and read, "Remember, nothing can separate us from the love of God." It was a reminder Debbie had given us a number of times over the summer, and I knew that verse had a special meaning for them.

David cleared his throat and stashed the card in his pocket. "Time to go."

Buck appeared on the porch and escorted me down the stairs. "I have another prayer for you." He put a small envelope in my hand. "I'll see you in Washington. Merry Christmas."

"Washington? You're going to the White House, too?" I could feel the blush rising.

"I am. I'm hoping to accompany you to the dinner, if that's good with you."

"That's good with me, Buck." I stared down at the envelope and decided rosy cheeks might be okay. *Let him think what he will.*

He nudged me toward the car. "I'd say David is in a rush to get home. Have fun with your family. Enjoy the holiday."

"I . . . I will. You, too."

Mom and Dad waved and blew kisses. My staff and customers joined in with laughter and song wishing us a Merry Christmas.

I had a case of the giggles by the time Doc and I were seated in David's SUV for the trip to Bangor. Keith jumped into the front passenger seat. Nathan and Billy went ahead of us in another black SUV. I'd never had such a sense of importance as the tiny motorcade swept out of the driveway past a waving crowd of staff and customers.

We were almost to the airport before I had the nerve to open Buck's card. It was a luxuriously simple holiday card. As I opened it a cream-colored paper slipped out, and I recognized it as one of Cat's prayers. It had to have been the first one he took when he joked about the prayers working. I'd never seen him take another one.

Forget the former things; do not dwell on the past. See, I am doing a new thing! Now it springs up; do you not perceive it? Isaiah 43:18-19

As we pulled up to Cisco's private jet, my heart was pounding.

CHAPTER 17

~ ANNIE ~

It was after midnight, local time, when we landed in Salzburg, Austria, and an hour and a half later when we pulled up to David and Debbie's home. It was as secure as it was stunning. Set in a winter wonderland in the foothills of the Alps, the little family village they'd created was breathtakingly beautiful and private. The Clemente and Lambrecht homes nestled impressively against a pastoral backdrop.

From the garage we entered through the kitchen door. "Are you hungry? Thirsty?" David asked.

"No thanks," was the unanimous reply. We'd been well fed on the plane.

David had not told Debbie about our arrival, so his family was asleep. He was extremely protective of her, not only because of the risk due to his job and their celebrity. Debbie had a weak heart from twenty years of battling anorexia and bulimia. So David made sure she got proper rest and nutrition.

Everyone said they'd saved each other's lives, and I thought it was true. Debbie made him feel the love of God, and pulled him out of a sordid life. Circumstances had brought his dirty laundry out in full view of world media. But she'd redeemed him—her love made his life worth living.

I admired the lovely carved staircase. My husband Russ would have appreciated all the work that went into this gorgeous home. A security guard helped me with my luggage—up the stairs and down the hall. Doc and I had adjacent rooms across from Nathan.

As I unpacked, I noticed a message on my phone. It was Terri Monahan screaming at me in relief. Her lawyer had called and informed her and Ted that it was all over. No charges. "My lawyer said it's thanks to you. He said not to say another word about it. I promise you, we won't."

I put the phone on my nightstand. "Merry Christmas, Terri."

Looking out my bedroom window, *Silent Night* came to mind. The moon and the stars lit up the snowy landscape. I melted into a soft featherbed and thanked God I'd have breakfast with my sister in the morning.

Giggles and the pitter-patter of children's feet woke me, and Nanny Shirlene's voice stirred me from my bed. I opened the door to her loud whisper. "Auntie is trying to sleep!"

I smiled down at my niece and nephews—two miraculous sets of triplets. Little Sabena jumped into my arms. "I'm going to be six!"

The boys all spoke at once—each with a different story I needed to hear. It was as though we'd never been apart.

In short order we all settled on my bed, and I heard the plans for birthday festivities for the youngest triplets and Christmas, too. The excitement was intense.

Out of the corner of my eye, I noticed the pale pink of Debbie's robe. She jumped on the bed with gleeful giggles, and we were in each other's arms. We laughed till we cried. David and Doc appeared in the doorway, and they were pelted with kids. Doc had an armload of them, and tears in his eyes.

I drew Debbie into a hug and whispered in her ear, "This dream's been in Doc's heart for decades—to have his girls and now his grandkids. To have a real family. I can't thank you and David enough for inviting us into your home at Christmas."

Debbie and I were both quick with tears. She stretched

out her arms to Doc and got up from the bed. In an instant she was in his arms and bawling into his chest.

David took the kids downstairs for breakfast. The decibel level became tolerable. Doc stroked Debbie's hair, patted her back and spoke soft, soothing words. I saw a few tears drip onto his cheeks, too. When Debbie finally pulled away, she wiped her face and looked up at her father.

"Dr. Westcott, can I try calling you Doc?"

Doc's face lit up and his voice cracked a bit. "That would be wonderful, Debbie." He tugged her into his arms again.

By the time we arrived downstairs, the children had eaten, and breakfast for the adults was served in the dining room. Nathan had already helped himself to the buffet and sat at the far end of the elegant table. We joined him and introduced Debbie. David explained that the men would spend the day working on a training exercise. Then Nathan would be free to enjoy the rest of the holiday vacation as he pleased.

I pointed to a graceful gold bowl in the center of the table. "Debbie, I can't help but notice your beautiful bowl."

She giggled. "I decided we needed one when we came home from Maine. So David got this one for me. Now we put our prayers in there, and everyone takes at least one out every day."

A surge of happiness went through me. "That's fantastic. It's a great way to teach the kids about prayer."

She smiled. "Yes, and David and me, too."

To put it bluntly, I was shocked that David would take part in that routine. Maybe Debbie caught my surprise.

She blushed. "Well, David cheats a little."

He grinned at her and took a bite of his apple.

Doc looked puzzled. "How can you cheat at praying?"

David shrugged.

Debbie let out another laugh. "Well, I guess it's not really cheating. He types them up in advance. Usually he copies the same prayer to fill a page, prints it out, and gives it to me. Then I put it through the paper cutter. So he gets lots of mileage out of one prayer."

I burst out laughing.

"Sounds pretty efficient," Doc said.

Nathan nodded.

"Yes." Debbie turned to her husband. "David is efficient. But his prayers are from his heart. I know that. God knows that."

He took her hand, and once again I noticed that look in his eyes. Debbie was certainly the center of his world.

The sweet moment was interrupted when Sabena trotted in and climbed onto Doc's lap. She looked up at him with a purposeful face. "Papa says only God knows why we have so many grandfathers."

The table erupted in laughter.

Debbie was bright red, her hands clasped over her mouth.

David shook his head. "I admit, I was a bit frustrated after the hundred questions this morning."

Debbie recovered her composure. "They call everyone grandfather: Cisco's grandfather, Papa Roberto, and Cisco's father, and David's father, and Daddy . . ." she began to stutter a bit, "and now . . . Doc." She turned to David. "Is that why Sabena wrote out a prayer this morning to bless all her grandfathers?"

"That's why." David winked.

"That's why," Sabena echoed. "It's in the bowl now. But God knows, even if no one picks it out yet."

Sabena tilted back over Doc's supportive hand. She looked like a miniature of her mother. "Can we go sledding now?"

Doc was animated. "That sounds like a fine idea. Let's get some warm clothes on and go outside to play."

As we got up from the table, David took me aside. "Debbie wants to work on a painting. Would you mind joining us in her studio?"

"I'd love to."

I followed them upstairs, and David opened the door to the ultimate artist's studio. My eye immediately went to three paintings awash in the morning light near floor-to-ceiling windows. "It's your painting—The Golden Bowl!" I stood in front of a familiar version of the restaurant and prayer bowl. "You based the packaging on this one?"

"Yes." Debbie smiled. "I'm so glad you liked it."

Emotion welled up. "Oh sweetie, I can't thank you enough. It's absolutely gorgeous."

David stood by the other two. "Annie, what I don't understand—and maybe you can shed some light on this—why do these paintings have jewelry overflowing the prayer bowl? Are these prayer bowls or just gold bowls on a table?"

I saw Debbie chewing her lip, evaluating the canvases. "I'm not sure why that came out. But this one shows the front porch of the restaurant and even though the prayer bowl is far away, there's definitely jewelry sticking out of there."

She sat down and pointed to the one with what looked like the prayer bowl teeming with expensive jewels. The bowl was set on a mahogany table. "This one feels like the same prayer bowl. Just more close up." She began to work on it.

I turned to David. "I have no idea why Debbie would paint jewelry. But it does look like The Golden Bowl."

"All right. I'll leave you to figure that out. I'm going to head out with Nathan." He kissed his wife. "Have fun."

I took a seat beside my sister to watch her work. It wasn't long before a chill went down my spine. "Why are you putting a diamond ring on that table?"

The concern in my voice stopped her. She put down her brush and faced me. "I don't know. Sometimes I get these feelings, and I just paint. Like I told you last summer. It's a little bit weird, I know." Her eyes filled.

"I couldn't tell David. I know he was upset because this was bothering me. I shouldn't have shown him, but he always likes to see what I'm working on. Sometimes my paintings seem a little bit strange."

I could see her gulp as she pointed to the mahogany table. "This is a casket. Not a table." Shaky hands wiped the tears. "Why am I painting a casket? What is it now? Who is it?"

"Sweetie, I'm sure it's nothing bad," I said, trying to reassure her. Meanwhile my breakfast was churning in my stomach.

"I have that feeling. That feeling I always have. I need to call Cat. Don't tell David, okay? He worries about me too much."

"I understand." But I didn't understand. My sister's penchant for painting prophecies seemed to be inherited from our grandmother. A gift from God. But it could be frightening at the same time. I put my arm around her. "David told us last night we're going to the Clemente's for dinner tonight. Maybe we can ask Cat then?"

"I'd rather we just go over there now."

"Of course."

We carefully wrapped the canvases, and the guard loaded them into the car. He drove us the short distance down the rural road to Cat and Cisco's home. My head was spinning, trying to take in all the spectacular sights on this glorious winter day. The mansion came into full view. "It looks like a castle! Wow. It takes your breath away."

Debbie smiled. "Cat's so modest, but Cisco wanted to build a dream home for her. It was a surprise."

I chuckled. "That's some surprise."

"Yes. It works out well though, because it's plenty big enough for his business, and they have a music studio, too."

We pulled up a long driveway and into a secure garage. Cat met us in the kitchen with hugs, kisses, and a pot of tea. She was one of the most successful musical artists in the world, a lyricist beyond compare, and a constant presence in the media, regardless of the fact that she lived in a castle in Austria.

She stood before us, joy radiating from every pore, literally barefoot and pregnant. Despite the glamorous world she inhabited, I rarely saw Cat dressed in anything but jeans—and no shoes. I felt like we'd been friends forever.

She was so petite, I couldn't resist commenting, "You're all baby! You look like you're going to deliver any minute. And you're only five months along?"

She let out a giggle. "Yes, five months. But I *feel* like it's nine. The doctors tell me to rest. I'm tired of resting." She put a teapot and some pastries on a tray. "Cisco will be back from London this afternoon, in time for our celebration. Let's have some tea—and lemon bars." Cat's grin reminded me of her cousin David's.

One of our security detail carried the tray to a sunny sitting room with dazzling views of snowy mountains. Cat poured the tea while he helped Debbie prop the paintings on chairs for display. He left, and we settled into luxuriously comfortable couches. Debbie smiled as I squeezed heavenly soft pillows.

I laughed. "Sorry, I can't help fondling your furniture."

Debbie patted the back of the sofa. "It's down. Isn't it wonderful?"

When I came out of my contemplation of the stunning furnishings I noticed Cat was taking a close look at the paintings, her fingers lightly touching the bowl, the ring, and the mahogany table.

She took a seat across from Debbie and me, her face solemn. "Her husband had given her an expensive ring when they were married. He was a jeweler in New York. He often traveled for business, but when he returned, he would give her a gift of jewelry. Quite by accident she learned that he'd been unfaithful—on many occasions. She confronted him, but his behavior never changed. Bitterness consumed her, but she never divorced him. Eventually he left her."

I stared into Cat's deep blue eyes, spellbound. Sadness crept through me. Confusion gave way to sudden fear that lurched my stomach. "Buck?" *Oh dear God*! "Is it Buck?"

"What?" Debbie sounded shocked.

"Buck—he threw that diamond ring in the prayer bowl. He's so rich—he—well, he can be careless with expensive things. Is he going to die? Please don't let him die, Cat."

"Almighty Buck?" Debbie's voice pitched higher.

My mind spun into overdrive fitting Cat's words to Buck's sad past in the midst of such wealth. No wonder he was such a mystery. No wonder he was reluctant to talk about his past, his personal life. He let greed get the best of him and then unfaithfulness destroyed his marriage. *When was Buck in the jewelry business*?

"Cat?" Debbie startled us both.

Cat popped out of her reverie and turned to Debbie.

Debbie's voice was pleading. "I don't know who she is, Cat. Why is the bowl of jewels on a casket? Did she die? Did she ever have happiness?"

Cat's face went white. "There was no love. No peace. I'm so sorry. She passed away last summer." She bowed her head, as if in prayer.

"Buck's ex-wife?" I began to sweat. "Lisa pulled that ring out of the bowl. That's how it started. Poor Buck. He must have been so sad inside, so guilt-ridden, he put the ring in the prayer bowl."

Cat's eyes widened. She turned to me. "It wasn't Buck. It was Nathan who put the ring in the prayer bowl. After his mother passed away. She raised him with a deep distrust of people. I think he's given up on finding a wife. He's already had two divorces, and a third shattered marriage."

My mouth hung open, but there were no words.

"That's so sad," Debbie said.

My entire body was on fire with embarrassment. I knew my face was bright red. I shook my head as though that would remove it. *I called Buck sad and guilt-ridden. Nathan put the ring in the prayer bowl*?

Finally, incredulity at Cat and Debbie took over my thoughts and prompted me to speak. "Jewels? Where does that come from, Debbie? You paint a bowl of jewelry, and Cat knows the story that goes with it." I remembered the paintings of Jonah she'd sent to my phone, along with Cat's explanation.

"It happens all the time," Debbie said. "Cat is very gifted."

"And you are too," I said. "Just like Grammy."

Debbie made a shocked face. "Ohhhh! But you're just like Grammy, too. You're an entrepreneur, just like Grammy. You founded The Golden Bowl." She let out a chuckle that relieved some of the tension.

After finding out about Buck and discovering Nathan's secret, I wasn't about to disabuse her of the fact that I was no businesswoman. No doubt she now knew David had to get me out of tax trouble, through the President of the United States, no less. But that was just the tip of the iceberg of my entrepreneurial failings.

I had my own list, but heaven only knew what more Buck would find as he wound his way through The Golden Bowl. I doubted I was smart enough even to figure out the list. But today, in the lap of luxury, I wanted to pretend. So while Debbie and I waxed poetic in our mutual admiration society, Cat quietly sipped tea and nibbled on a lemon bar.

We finally ran out of nonsense, so we helped ourselves to pastries and tea. I did feel a little better.

"I hope Nathan can have some time to rest and rethink things while he's here. Maybe he'll feel better when he gets back to Maine," Debbie said.

"I hope so." I didn't know what else to say.

"God is good," Cat said.

"Yes." Debbie smiled. "I can't wait until your cookbook comes out, Annie. Make sure you give us the recipes for the blueberry scones and lemon bars, please."

With a burst of laughter, I choked on a scone. A fit of coughing and gulps of tea and water finally did the trick. I smiled at the ceiling. "Cookbook." I giggled. "That's all I need."

I noticed Debbie's guilty glance at Cat. Jonah the stick figure in silver white shoes ran through my head. What did they know that I didn't? I turned to Cat.

Those eyes locked on mine. Every cell in my body paid attention. "Annie, you must use your God-given power. You are blessed to be a blessing to others. But you're under attack. That tax audit is one example. Don't let Satan limit your effectiveness. Don't give him a foothold. You know God is looking for people like you. You know he works in and through you. Step into all God has for you."

Tingling traveled from my head to my feet. My gut told me Cat's words were true.

"Holy Spirit is with you."

"Thank you."

"'God opposes the proud but gives grace to the humble.' Read 1 Peter 5. God is the source of all power. He gives power and resources to humble people in order to bless others. He's giving you power and resources now. Praise and thank him for that. Walk in his will. Keep your eyes on God. He'll give you the wisdom and discernment you need."

"Thanks Cat." Sudden realization that Cat was well aware of all my foibles—and how they could limit my effectiveness—brought more tears pouring down my face. She knew I was sloppy with my finances, and I basically lied about it, letting Pinky take the blame. She knew my entire salary disappeared into my charity projects—that I was "generous to a fault," as Buck said. It was a big fault.

Debbie leaned over to hug me, and Cat brought a box of tissues. I must have soaked them all. We sat in silence for a long time. I hoped and prayed I'd be able to change my ways and learn to be responsible for my finances around my charity work and my personal life.

Cat and Cisco were superb stewards of the money God had blessed them with. They gave away millions upon millions every year to worthy causes. They paid attention to the results their charitable investments achieved so they could make the wisest decisions and get the most benefit for every dollar spent. I thanked God I had their help in going forward with The Golden Bowl.

Debbie got up, took a portfolio from her oversized bag, and flipped through some sketches. "This is the dress I want to make you for the White House dinner party."

Cat said, "You'll be stunning. Debbie's design and your smile. You'll charm the president and everyone in Washington. I'll leave you to your consult." She took the opportunity to work on the music for their Christmas concert to be held in Salzburg, and televised around the world.

Debbie and I spent hours involved with sketches and color swatches and discussion of fabrics. I was floored by her ability and flair. "Your talent is incredible, sweetie."

"We look almost exactly alike, so I have no problem designing for you," she said with an impish grin. She made a final flourish to the skirt and propped the sketch on the seat. Standing back we looked at the drawing, then at each other. She nodded her approval.

"It's perfect, Debbie. I'm so excited!"

"Annie, glad you're finally here." I turned to see Cisco coming through the door with Cat and David.

He embraced me in a gracious hug, kissing the top of my head. "It sounds like you can use some time off."

I looked up at piercing blue eyes. He was probably even taller than David. "I'm so excited to be here. What a gift!"

We sat in a small circle, and he pointed to Debbie's sketch. "It looks like Debbie will have you ready to meet your public."

I exhaled a nervous sigh. "Well, at least I'll look good as I bumble around the White House."

Cat and Debbie let out a simultaneous, "You'll be fine."

A maid came in with tea and blueberry scones. Cisco grabbed one and lifted it in my direction. "We wrangled a few of these away from Paulo. Otherwise, he wouldn't have offered to share."

I couldn't help smiling. I could understand why Cisco was so successful. He had a way of making everyone feel at ease. No doubt he'd do the same thing with his business associates. Then go in for the kill. I decided I'd better nip that business conversation in the bud. If I didn't take some semblance of control, I might end up on the floor.

"Cisco, I have to offer you a big apology for all the difficulties and confusion with my business. I obviously have been a bit math-challenged to say the least. I can't thank you enough for all your help and understanding . . . and frankly . . . paying for my legal bills. I was so stupid to get involved in Peter's gifting tables idea. I shouldn't have been so blind. I should have recognized it was a Ponzi scheme." Emotion caught in my throat, and Debbie pulled herself out of David's embrace to encircle me with her arm.

Cisco leaned forward, "No apology necessary, but thank you. We knew there were challenges and unexpected problems. But The Golden Bowl is worth all the effort. Cat and I are thrilled to be a part of it. And Buck is, too."

My stomach quaked a bit. "Thank you. Buck's been such a huge help. He's indispensable. He knows what he's doing, and he's been so gracious and supportive. I've never seen anyone work so hard."

Cisco smiled. "Buck's a good guy. I had a talk with him today. Now that the threat of legal action is out of the way, we can move forward. What I need to know is—do you still agree with growing this business and charity? The potential is limitless, but it needs to be your vision."

The prayer of Jabez rolled in my head with my stick figure Jonah prepared to take a leap of faith. When I opened my mouth, I was afraid I'd have no voice. But the words poured out with clarity. "I want The Golden Bowl to be everything God wants it to be."

Debbie patted my shoulder, and Cat's eyes were as bright as her smile.

Cisco looked at his wife, then at me. "Amen." He smiled.

CHAPTER 18

~ ANNIE ~

After a wonderful evening at Cat and Cisco's home with all the extended family, I was wiped out. When I made it back to my room, there was a large box on the bed with a holiday ribbon securing it. Debbie's joyful, "Merry Christmas, Annie! A little early," came from the doorway as I opened it.

"Oh, sweetie! The Leap of Faith paintings!" There was Jonah in his original silver white shoes. "Wow! They're even more beautiful in person."

"I can't thank you enough." I hugged my sister.

"I hope you put them somewhere that reminds you how wonderful you are. And how blessed you are."

"I have just the spot for them in my bedroom. I'll see them every morning when I open my eyes. Thank you."

"There's one more little thing under the tissue paper."

I reached into the box and pulled out a small package done in red tissue. My jaw dropped as I saw the calligraphy with an artistic border, reminiscent of Grammy's work. "The Prayer of Jabez! It's magnificent. Oh, wow. Thank you." I kissed her. "How did you know? I mean, Grammy said this prayer for us every day. Did you know?"

"I woke up from a dream with a verse in my head, and when I looked it up, I remembered Grammy said it over me sometimes. That was a long time ago. Daddy got pretty mad if he heard her. He thought it was mumbo jumbo. But I think it's a perfect prayer."

"It is." I squeezed her hand and met her eye-to-eye.

"Your dad . . . George—he loved you the best he could. But you know how much more you're loved. And Grammy knew it. She prayed this for the two of us every day. Miracles have happened."

"Yes."

I was so stricken by Cat's words, Debbie's paintings, and Grammy's Prayer of Jabez, that I barely slept that night. Then the thought of Nathan, the story of the ring, and my mortification over Buck kept turning in my mind. Once I grappled with my embarrassment, Nathan's bitter story left me heartsick. I couldn't think of any way to help him—only prayer.

When Sabena let herself into my room and jumped on the bed at 5:00 a.m., it was almost a relief. "Auntie, Nathan's getting a medal for his suit jacket. Like Papa's. We're visiting the president to get the medal with him."

I sat up in bed and pulled her into my lap. "Really?"

"Yes, Mama says he's a hero, and he saved all the children at school."

I took the opportunity to cuddle up with my niece and tell her the story of Nathan's heroism at Marberry Academy.

~ DOC ~

My body still hadn't adjusted to the time change, so I gave up on sleep and decided to make myself an early breakfast. I took the long route through the halls, down the stairs to the front foyer, then around toward the kitchen. As I entered the dining area, I came upon Debbie sitting in a window seat, propped up by a mound of pillows. A shaft of light from the window glowed around her. She looked like an angel.

I pulled a chair toward her, and she put her book in her lap. "This is a first, finding you alone in the peace and quiet."

She responded with a chuckle. "Good morning, Doc."

I kissed the top of her head and noticed her devotional.

I pointed to her book as I took my seat. "I've been wondering. Have you always been religious?"

"No." She gave me a shy smile and shook her head. "My parents always insisted we go to church."

I couldn't help a burst of laughter, then quickly muffled it in a cough. It occurred to me Debbie had a completely different perspective on most everything. It was charming. It certainly had captivated her husband. About all he could do was smile when she came out with these things. She seemed used to it.

She gave me time to compose myself, then began with a soft stutter. "D-daddy was always very concerned about appearances. I think it was important to my parents to look religious. Sometimes, I'd sit in church and ask God if he was real."

Her stuttering signaled her uneasiness, and I tried to tread lightly. I realized I'd need to approach her gently if I was ever to win a place in her heart. "Hmm. Well, I wondered how you came to believe in God. I mean, Annie was brought up in a pastor's home. I didn't realize your parents were . . . churchgoers."

She stared at her lap for a while, then looked up at me. It was the first time I truly felt her look me in the eye. "When I was nineteen I had a heart attack on Christmas Eve, and I went to heaven and saw Grammy. Just for a few seconds, I think. But it changed everything. I know God loves me. I never knew that until then. I haven't told anyone outside my family. I never told my parents. I didn't think they would have understood anyway."

She played with the fabric of her skirt as I tried to wrap my head around this news. The fact that she didn't seem to consider her parents part of her family was not lost on me. I remembered David pulling her prayer card from the bowl at the restaurant, the emotion on that normally stoic face. I remembered the words on the card. "Nothing can separate us from the love of God."

Her voice made me realize I'd spoken aloud. "Yes,

Grammy's words to me came from scripture. She told me, 'Remember, *nothing* can separate you from the love of God.' Then I woke up in the hospital."

I squeezed her hand. I had no more words. I wondered if she was literally an angel sent from heaven. She went back to her book, silently reading, while I watched the light through the window form a halo around her.

~ DOC ~

It was the following evening when we had the pleasure of attending a Christmas concert by Paulo Clemente and his band at the Large Festival House located in Salzburg's Altstadt, or Old Town. The audience of about two thousand were invited guests, mostly business associates and employees of the family's various businesses, and they filled the place. The event was primarily planned as a television special for the English speaking countries where the band was wildly popular. That explained the cozy venue. They were scheduled to give a concert in German at a larger hall shortly before Christmas.

The band made a fortune on the rights to these events and donated most of the money to their charities. Fortunately, for Annie, Cat and Paulo had announced this was a warm-up for The Golden Bowl Tour, which would begin next summer after the birth of Cat and Cisco's first child. The Golden Bowl and Annie's charitable programs would receive global publicity and some major funding, as a result.

The world beat a path to Paulo Clemente's door for a reason. Not only was he a composer and musician beyond compare, his distinctive tenor voice demanded your attention. "A voice to die for," the press called him. With Cat's lyrical talents they churned out hit after hit.

Each of the musicians and singers in the band were charismatic personalities in their own right. Personally, I'd say the "secret agent" connection didn't hurt either. As a matter of fact, the band rose to stardom right around the time our favorite assassin appeared in scandalous headlines around the world. No doubt they'd amassed a fortune at least partly due to David.

Regardless, screaming fans appeared wherever they were. So security was tight as Annie and I joined our extended family in a comfortable box overlooking the stage. The entire hall glowed with golden light, like we were sitting in a golden bowl. The scent of evergreen boughs evoked memories of Christmas long past.

Cat performed one of her biggest hits and brought down the house. She looked tiny in the middle of that stage, but she had the crowd wrapped around her little finger.

"Tonight, I want to tell you about my friend, Annie, a woman who spends her life feeding people—body, soul and spirit. Her restaurant, The Golden Bowl, is in the little town of Marberry, Maine in the United States. It's been blessed with a staff of people who truly care about their mission. People who work hard every day to bless others with a delicious meal, and encourage them with friendly conversation and a helping hand whenever and wherever needed.

"The Golden Bowl has become a symbol of the awe-inspiring power of prayer. We're invited to leave a prayer and take a prayer from the large gold bowl that sits on the front porch. Great things are happening in Marberry, Maine. The poor are fed, the sick are healed, needs are being met, and love is winning. Love is lighting Annie's little town and beyond because of one small prayer.

Oh that You would bless me indeed, and enlarge my territory. That Your hand would be with me, and that You would keep me from evil.

"Jabez had the courage to pray it more than two thousand years ago. Annie's grandmother had the courage to pray it over her grandchildren. A little prayer with a big impact.

"Tonight, I challenge you to pray. You are called to be Salt and Light to the world. As golden light floods this building, light up lives. Light up this world. Leave a prayer and take a prayer from the golden bowls you see as you leave tonight. Take your own golden bowl out to your community. Start with your personal prayer. Watch what happens."

The audience did exactly as Cat asked, and prayers filled the gold bowls around the building. I spotted gold bowls everywhere we went, and when the concert was broadcast in the United States and Europe, news headlines and social media encouraged the world to take the mission of The Golden Bowl to heart. It couldn't have been a better Christmas message. I couldn't have been more proud and happy for Annie.

After the concert, we spent several nights at The Mönchsberg Hotel, owned by Cisco's grandfather, who everyone called Papa Roberto. Named after the hill that bordered the city, it was one of the most historic and elegant hotels in Salzburg's Old Town. I thoroughly enjoyed their VIP treatment, not to mention the convenient location for exploring a picturesque city all dressed up for the holidays.

I was fascinated by the baroque towers and churches, and the Festung Hohensalzburg, one of Europe's largest castles, which overlooks the Old Town. Of course, we toured Mozart's Birthplace and investigated the shops along Getreidgasse, a medieval street. I enjoyed photographing all the old wrought-iron signs and narrow cobblestone alleyways that made me feel like I'd taken a step back in time. Inspired by my daughters' enthusiasm, I took photos of every golden bowl we found in the course of our little tour. Debbie created a unique collage for Annie to display at The Golden Bowl in Marberry.

Naturally, we had to check out the variety of restaurants, taverns, and cafes that offered traditional meals. Annie and I especially appreciated the cafes, with décor from lavish baroque to homey wood paneling. The coffees, cakes, and pastries were "divine" according to Annie, and I agreed. She told me she'd take the inspiration back to The Bakery & Sweet Shop at The Golden Bowl.

The people-watching was fun, although most of the

time we were the center of attention. My daughter's family members were world-famous celebrities, so it was understandable. Annie and I adjusted to that fact as paparazzi pulled any stunt they could to get a prized photo.

Upon our return to the countryside, the days were a blur of fun—playing in the snow with the kids, sightseeing, painting with Debbie, and getting up close and personal with our rock stars as they created more soon-to-be hits. It was an experience of a lifetime.

~ ANNIE ~

All the excitement culminated on Christmas Day. With so many kids and constant activity, I was worn out by 10:00 p.m. As I retired to my room, my phone rang. *Buck*! I closed my door and landed on the bed. "Hi!"

"Merry Christmas, Annie."

"Merry Christmas! Where are you?"

"I'm in London for the holiday. I left Maine late last night. Christmas Eve went extremely well at The Golden Bowl. Just wanted to let you know. Ashleigh, Brianna, Karen, and Tracey will have everything in hand when they reopen tomorrow. Gerald will be between the two facilities for a few weeks. But it's all good."

I sighed into the phone. "I can't thank you enough."

"You're very welcome. Your business has turned the corner, and much quicker than anticipated. You've done it, Annie. You've made a positive change."

Positive change? "It's all your doing. I tried to do what I was told and stayed out of your way. You get the credit. And my endless gratitude."

"Thank you. You're most kind. I'm sure your prayers were instrumental in our success."

Positive change. Buck rarely mentioned prayer. And I really hadn't changed. "Um . . . Buck, you know that hundred dollars you gave me for a movie with Terri?"

"Yes?"

"I gave it to Dad's soup kitchen for Thanksgiving dinner. All of it."

"No movie?"

I pressed on with the bitter truth. My compulsion was apparently still not under control. "Terri and I decided to cook at home. I should have given you the money back, or at least asked you if it was okay to donate it. You said it was a gift."

"It was."

"Thanks, I just didn't want to see a movie."

"You just didn't have the right company."

"Oh? Terri?" It dawned on me. "Oh." Instant heat flushed my face.

"I hope you're having a nice holiday."

I sputtered into the phone. "I—I am." Then babbled, "The kids are at a fever pitch, they're so excited. And it's a thrill to see where everyone lives. It's a winter wonderland here. The concert was—well, it was so incredible I can't even begin to tell you. And Salzburg is so quaint. I miss home, but I know I'll cry my eyes out when I have to leave here. So . . . so how is your holiday?"

"Relaxing. But I'll be in top form when I see you in Washington. Looking forward to my first trip to the White House, and with such enchanting company."

I couldn't help giggling. "It'll be fun." My mind began to race. I wondered if he was calling just to give me an update, or did he, maybe, miss me?

"It will. I'll see you soon." He was gone.

Hmm.

I found Buck's holiday card in my handbag, tucked in an envelope with all of Cat's prayers I'd plucked from the bowl. I took it out and examined it. The elegant design and greeting was embossed on the finest of paper. Buck's handwriting said simply, "Merry Christmas, Annie!" He signed it, "Buck." Simple. Nothing to read into. I felt like I was in high school.

In the years since Russ had died, I'd kept my focus

on my charity work and my dream of establishing The Golden Bowl. I'd certainly been lonely, but never considered finding someone new. But in the past few months, my life had been one continuous whirlwind of progress for The Golden Bowl and twists and turns that I hadn't foreseen.

Buck was flirtatious one moment, and just friendly the next. But how did *I* feel about Buck? I was certainly attracted to him. He was handsome and charming, and he just swooped into my life and weathered the storm with me, handling everything with his charm, wit, and dedication. It was hard to resist him. But did he feel the same way about me? Who knew? It was all too confusing.

I quashed an urge to ask Cat and Debbie what they knew of Buck's personal life. After that embarrassing incident with the jewelry painting, I didn't want to look even more pathetic.

~ DOC ~

Christmas night I was in no rush to go to bed. I sat near a huge, fragrant, perfectly decorated tree, endless ravaged boxes beneath it. Nathan relaxed in a leather chair nearby. He lifted his beer in my direction. "Another Christmas gone."

My watch told me it was just after midnight. I raised my glass. "My best yet. I hope you've enjoyed it."

"I have."

I let out a sigh. "I've got my daughters in my life. My grandkids. All healthy. Like Cat said, we've been blessed." I took a sip of beer. "And we've been blessed to have you and your crackerjack security team protecting us. We've learned some hard lessons about all the crazy, sick, greedy people out there. So having you to keep us out of trouble has been a wonderful gift."

"Thank you." Nathan almost smiled.

"I can't tell you what a relief it is to have Annie free of those fraud and conspiracy charges. It's been like having an axe hanging over our heads. Now maybe she can settle down and enjoy life more."

"I hope so."

His expression made me wonder. "Do you see some trouble you're not telling me about?"

He cast a glance at me, then focused on the soft light of the Christmas tree. "Sometimes trouble is right in your own circle, right in front of your eyes. Sometimes you think you know people, but you don't. I think the world of Annie Brewster. She's probably the sweetest person I've ever known. I'd never want to see her get hurt."

I leaned forward in my chair. "You think she might get hurt?"

He turned from his contemplation, and his eyes met mine. "I think she's a bit too trusting. That's all."

"Too trusting of someone in particular?"

I could see him squirm. "Just . . . in general."

~ LISA ~

Christmas in Marberry was my best one ever. We'd been through a tough time with Ryan before he was murdered. But even with everything that'd happened, I had hope. We had a brand new house with brand new furniture, money in the bank, and I had a steady job I liked. I had some new friends that were real friends. And Santa Claus actually came this year.

I watched Peg with her new tablet at the kitchen table, Rosie on her lap clapping as they played my dancing on the grave video. *Again*!

"This one's got close to sixty million hits, Lisa," Peg said.

I laughed. "Yeah, that's 'cuz you and Rosie watched it fifty million times."

Billy brought over a tray full of ice cream sundaes. "As good as The Golden Bowl," he said.

I grabbed one. "Yeah, that's 'cuz the stuff's from The

Golden Bowl." I downed a spoonful of the creamy caramel "Mmm. You could get a job with Karen. They could use you at The Bakery & Sweet Shop."

He took a seat beside me and dug his spoon into my sundae.

"Hey! You've got your own." I swiped at his hand.

"Don't be stingy. I wanna try the butterscotch."

Peg got up. "No fighting. I'm putting Rosie to bed. You can have my butterscotch. I'm gonna turn in." Peg and Rosie waved good night and headed to the stairs. "Merry Christmas!"

We yelled back, "Merry Christmas!" Then I turned to Billy. "Let's sit in front of the fire by the Christmas tree."

He grinned at me. "Okay."

I sat on the couch and curled my leg up under me. I could feel the sugar kicking in already. "I've never had a Christmas tree and a fireplace to sit by at Christmas. So I want to take advantage this year." I dipped my spoon into my sundae. "Yeah, this is heaven."

Billy grunted his approval. He was ready to start on Peg's ice cream.

I stared into the fire wondering how he could eat two sundaes and not gain an ounce. *Oh yeah.* He ran twenty miles before I ever thought of waking up in the morning.

My leg was going to sleep, and I kicked it out from under me, slamming his leg. That got his attention. "Billy, if I lose fifty pounds would you date me?"

"Huh?"

I hiked my shirt down over my stomach. "Sorry. I meant to ask if you have a girlfriend, first."

He shook his head, grinning. "No, I don't have a girlfriend. Yes, I was thinkin' of asking you out. But you don't have to lose fifty pounds. . . I like you fine the way you are. It's that I didn't really know what to do. I mean, we always end up cooking here. You have Rosie. And it's probably better than fightin' off paparazzi. Maybe we could try a movie. No offense, but by the time they get to

Marberry, they're already on TV. I like to ski. But—well, we could go cross country at Annie's. No one'd bother us."

I was so shocked, I didn't notice I'd dumped the sundae in my lap.

~ ANNIE ~

By New Year's Eve I was a wreck as we all boarded Cisco's plane for the trip to Washington. Almost everyone in their large extended family was going—except for Cisco and Cat. Cat's advanced pregnancy prevented her from flying.

Buck met us at the hotel in Washington. We had a brief toast and celebration of the New Year, then retired for the night. It had been a long trip, and fortunately, I slept like a log.

New Year's morning we had a leisurely breakfast, and then Debbie invited me to join the rest of the women in the spa. By the time we were ready to get dressed for the evening, I felt so relaxed and pampered my nerves barely bothered me. My violet silk gown fit like a glove, and the hair and makeup transformed me into a woman I didn't recognize.

Doc made a fuss over how pretty I looked. He took my arm and led me down the marble staircase to the parlor the family shared. I was conscious of how the dress flowed about my legs as I moved, surely a reflection of the designer's skill. My sister led everyone in applause.

Buck reached for my hand, a twinkle in his eye. "You look beautiful, Annie."

When we arrived at the White House, I was awed by the stately beauty of the building and grounds, aglow with festive decorations. The first lady stretched out her hand to me, then clasped mine in hers. "I'm happy to meet you, Annie. I'm so impressed with The Golden Bowl. I can't wait to see your show!"

I babbled something at her, and Buck stepped up for his ten seconds. Meanwhile, the president addressed me.

"Annie, nice to meet you. Thank you for all the fine work you do. You make a big difference in the lives of your neighbors in Maine."

I stumbled over a "thank you," and didn't hear a word Buck said, but they seemed to be having a fine little conversation. I focused on standing and walking on heels that were way too high for me.

We were seated at the table, my smile still plastered in place, before I had any ability to think or communicate. David helped Debbie to a seat beside me, and Buck took his place on my other side. "Um . . . Buck? What show?" I noticed David's smirk and turned to Buck. "It's like the cookbook and the classes, right?"

Buck winked at me. "Yes, my dear. Just like the cookbook and the classes."

"Okay." I fumbled with my napkin and decided to stash it in my lap. Joe Harris, super-agent, appeared in my mind's eye, cigar in hand. "I have a feeling we might not be on the same page with this."

Buck sipped some water. "What does your page say?"

I cleared my throat. "My page says it might be something to consider for the future. What does your page say?"

Buck smiled. "My page says the contracts have arrived for your TV show and book deal. You have a lovely studio ready and waiting in your new facility. The world-famous fashionistas, Glori Coulson Dusseault and Debbie Lambrecht, have agreed to guest on your first show. I think my page is much more fun than your page, actually."

Debbie giggled beside me.

~ ANNIE ~

One or two glasses of wine helped enormously in coping with the evening, and even negotiating my designer heels on the dance floor. Buck was such a good dancer—and charming company—I forgot my business cares and had a great time.

By the time he escorted me to the suite, my up-do was a little down, but my spirits were high. "What an amazing night with the president and first lady. I'm sorry to see them go."

He chuckled. "I can see why you don't serve liquor at The Golden Bowl."

I let out a sigh and listed in my shoes. Buck righted me before I hit the wall.

I looked down. "I really need to climb out of these things." I carefully lifted my foot, balancing with my arm on his. "I think she super-glued them to my feet."

Buck escorted me to a seat in the parlor and gallantly unstrapped the shoes. "There." He grinned. "Now, do I get entrepreneur Annie Brewster back?"

"Oh! You sure do. That feels wonderful. We should've done that hours ago."

He stood over me laughing.

I wiggled my toes. "I think I'm finally getting the circulation back to my brain."

I watched him cover his mouth. "Oh go ahead. It's okay if you laugh at me. I'm not cut out to be a supermodel. But it was fun to pretend tonight. Just don't tell Debbie I don't have the stamina for their evening wear."

He pressed his lips together to stop the laughter. "I'll take that secret to the grave."

"Thank you. You're so kind. Now help me up and push me toward my door."

The following morning the family met in a private dining room for breakfast. After some eggs and toast, Buck invited me to a quiet drawing room for coffee and conversation.

"After Rhodes receives his medal, I'll be off to New York for a few days. I have a new restaurant opening there, and the owner is insisting I oversee the project personally. I may be delayed getting to Maine. But things are well in hand at The Golden Bowl, so no worries. Once I finish up in New York, I'll be back to Marberry for a while."

"For a while?"

His gaze held mine. "I have to be in Tokyo by the first of February. I expect to be there for a month or so. This project has been scheduled for some time—long before Cisco called me to Maine. But I'll be in touch with you during that time, and I expect you'll be fine without me there. We'll be adding some new employees for you. That should take a lot of the stress off you and free you up for other things."

Somehow, Buck's assurances didn't completely console me. "Other things, meaning a TV show and a cookbook?"

"Yes. Cisco told me you had a few conversations about your vision for The Golden Bowl and the future. The alliance is well underway since the concert in Salzburg. Business has exploded. There's no other word for it. *Exponential* growth."

"Exponential growth?" The thought of Buck in Tokyo while I tried to cope with a business explosion sent my stomach on a roller coaster ride.

Buck didn't seem to notice my nervousness. "It sounds like you, Cat, and Cisco agreed that growing the business from Maine would be the best plan. I concur. Having your businesses and charity work based there makes it easier for you. You wouldn't have to travel unless you want to. I think the franchise concept could play into it down the road, but for now, I see it as a gold mine right where you are in Marberry."

I pushed my tea aside. "I guess the idea is to branch out from Marberry by using the media. I didn't really understand what Cisco was getting at, until he said Cat and Paulo would start The Golden Bowl tour early with the Christmas concert. That way we can fund all the charities."

"Absolutely," Buck said.

"Well, I didn't know I was going to be the center of attention. I mean—a TV show? It scares the heart out of me. I don't know anything about doing television."

Buck put his coffee cup down and reached for my hand across the small table.

"Annie, you did a phenomenal job with Amanda James. Think of that as your very successful screen test. Not only do you have The Golden Bowl, you have the golden touch. Everyone wants you, and they're paying good money. Take Cisco's advice, and you'll be able to fund a multitude of charities. Sensibly, of course."

"Of course."

Once he had my agreement, his hand left mine. Watching him sip his coffee, I began to wonder at the gesture. Was it just his way of getting what he wanted, or was he signaling interest in me? The same frazzle of feelings I'd experienced with his Christmas phone call came over me now. I decided maybe I could send him a signal of my own . . . Besides, the experiment might be fun.

I moved my hand to gently cover his free hand. One elegant, dark eyebrow went askew, but I ignored it. "Um, Buck, just what is the format of this TV show?"

His lip twitched. "It's not etched in stone yet, but I believe it will center on recipes and stories from The Golden Bowl." He cleared his throat. "You'll have celebrity guests to chat and cook with." He stared at my hand on his. "Harris . . . has . . . he's got at least a dozen guests lined up . . ."

"And the book?"

"The book?" Baffled eyes met mine and glanced away. "The same . . . format."

I couldn't continue my experiment another second. I pulled my hand away.

Buck gulped his coffee, returned the cup to the saucer with a gentle clink, then leaned back in his seat. "I won't be gone long, Annie. Don't worry about the show."

What just happened here? I'd need some time in my Adirondack chair to sort it all out.

Later that morning we assembled back at the White House to witness the president bestow a Presidential Medal of Freedom on Nathan. Lights flashed as he shook the president's hand and accepted one of the highest honors a person could receive. After a few words from the president and government officials involved in education, we all attended a luncheon held in Nathan's honor.

I was surprised to see the very same camera crew that filmed The Golden Bowl for our holiday promotion. Come to find out, Joe Harris had arranged this as well. When I mentioned it to Debbie, she giggled. "Welcome to Joe's marketing machine. If the paparazzi don't get it, Joe will."

~ ANNIE ~

After a couple of days touring Washington, Doc and I headed back to Maine with Nathan. My extended family flew back to Austria. It was a tearful good-bye, but I missed home. Mom and Dad were cooking dinner in my kitchen when we came through the door. It was good to be home.

We had a hearty pot roast dinner with our security staff. Dad offered a prayer of thanks for Nathan, and Doc offered a toast. Conversation covered our holiday adventures in Salzburg and Washington.

I retired to my room and sat in my window seat with a stack of mail to sort through—mostly holiday cards. I came across an envelope with a Marberry PO Box return address and sliced it open. It was a plain card from Peter Fellowes.

Dear Annie, I want you to know how sorry I am that I caused you so much pain. I guess I started to believe my own pitch. I convinced myself with more money, I could make that building happen. I thought it was just a little exaggeration. I know a lot of people lost money. I'm sorry. I should have turned Louise in to the police instead of going along with her. I thought I could make it work, but I couldn't. You're a wonderful woman, and I've always loved you. Please pray for me. Sincerely yours, Peter.

My thoughts on Peter were interrupted by a knock at the door. "Mrs. Brewster?"

"Come in, Mr. Rhodes."

He flung open the door and called to me across the

room. "Terri Monahan is here to see you."

Terri squeezed around him and ran to me. "Annie!" She threw her arms around me and yanked me off the window seat. My cards dropped to the floor. Nathan left.

We landed on top of a pile of mail. "I can't thank you enough. It's over! No charges. Nothing." She burst into tears. "When my lawyer called, I couldn't believe it. But it's true."

My eyes watered. "It's true. Thank God."

She hugged me again. "My lawyer said Cisco Clemente paid my legal fees. All I have to do is pay back some restitution—you know so some of the women like Lisa Quinn get their money back. That's it. I don't even know where to contact him to say thank you. My lawyer said it's not necessary."

I pictured a mailman trying to deliver a thank you card to Cisco's castle in Austria. *Not going to happen*. "He's incredibly generous, Terri. I'll make sure to call him and thank him for you."

She dabbed at her face. "It must be nice having billionaires on speed-dial. Sounds like you had a great time in Salzburg. Thanks for leaving me those messages. Three weeks of phone tag. But you must've been busy with your family. Actually, Ted and I decided to get away for a few days, too. It was a nice break—a nice celebration. We went to Sanibel. Ted wants to retire there."

Wet tissues fell to the floor. "Sorry." Terri bent down and came back up with used tissues and Peter's card. She made no apology for reading it. "Wow. I always thought Peter was sweet on you."

I grabbed the card. "You think everyone is sweet on me."

She laughed. "I guess so. You have that sweet face. That sweet smile. That sweet voice."

"Okay, Terri, you don't have to flatter me—if that's what you're doing."

"Do you know what's going to happen to him?"

"No. I suppose there'll be a trial. I hope we don't have

to testify. I don't think Peter is a bad person. But he made a mistake thinking he could handle that money and build a school. He seemed so dedicated to helping disabled kids. I don't think he was lying about wanting to help. But I don't understand what really happened."

Terri let out a sigh. "That's the way the guy was. Take the easy way out when the going gets tough. Run away. I'd say that's what he thought this time, too."

"What do you mean, 'this time'?"

She made a face. "Well, he left his wife when they had a baby girl with Down Syndrome. You'd think some guy dedicated to teaching special needs kids wouldn't flip out when he had his own. He got a divorce and moved a thousand miles away to take a job at Marberry Academy."

You could have knocked me over with a feather. "How did you find that out?"

Terri looked me in the eye. "Louise had one too many glasses of punch at one of Ted's open houses. FYI: I think she was drunk when she arrived. She told me about Peter being divorced, and that he swore he'd never get married again. She'd baked him a few pies, too."

I couldn't stifle a chuckle.

"Anyway, I pried the whole story out of her. I thought the guy was a jerk, but the gifting table idea was irresistible. I should've told you the scoop on Peter, but you would've talked me out of the gifting table. You only do business with saintly people like you."

"Right." Little did Terri know, I had a weakness for stray people. I probably would have fallen for the gifting table scheme even if I'd known Peter's history.

~ ANNIE ~

I thanked Billy profusely for shoveling a path to my Adirondack chairs and digging them out of the snow. I tossed a thermal chair pad onto the seat and landed there with my thermos and my thoughts. I pulled my hood around my face with a woolen scarf. The intricacies of the wrap allowed me to sip my coffee. Not exactly glamorous, but functional. January could be fierce along the coast of Maine, but I was ready for it. Fleece, down, wool—whatever layers it took, I was prepared. I needed this time alone with my thoughts and prayers, with God.

My first thought was of gratitude. Not only for the spectacular hues of sea and sunrise before me, and the coffee warming my insides, but especially for safe travel through the storm of fraud, conspiracy, and painful revelations these past months. *Safe pasture.*

I noticed a string of clouds along the horizon and remembered Cat's prayer, "every cloud's a flag to Your faithfulness." *Thank you.*

Names and faces floated through my head, and I prayed for each one. I didn't know what else to do for Peter Fellowes. Money had caused us both problems in different ways. Underneath all the difficulties, I believed he was a good person who made some bad choices. I made a mental note to send Peter's wife a gift to help with expenses for herself and her child.

Then there was Almighty Buck. Buckminster Wynn of Brooke, Lewis & Wynn with offices in New York and London. The terror I had when I first encountered him had turned to a deep warmth and gratitude—tinged with more than a tiny bit of fear that he could consult his way out of my life. *I'm not ready for that, Lord. Can't you cut his trip to Tokyo short*?

A thud in the chair next to mine startled me. As I turned my head, my hood did not cooperate.

"Pretty sunrise, Mrs. Brewster."

I grabbed the scarf and hood away from my face, and I thought my eyes would freeze wide open. "G-good morning Mr. Rhodes."

He took a swig of coffee, and I wondered if we were supposed to silently admire God's handiwork or have a conversation. It seemed like there was a perennial elephant in the room with Nathan. *Even little Sabena calls him Nathan. What's wrong with me*?

"That was a pretty amazing trip to Austria." He was still gazing out to sea.

"Yes." I wasn't sure if I was supposed to comment or remain quiet. Maybe he was talking to his higher power, too.

"You have a wonderful family, Mrs. Brewster."

My mouth took that as a signal to go without considering my brain. "I hope you didn't miss your family too much over the holidays." I bit my lip before I could start on his mother's passing.

He faced me. "I don't have a family, so I appreciate being included in yours for the holidays."

My heart crept into my throat. "Oh, I'm so sorry to hear that. I mean—you don't have siblings?"

"No. I was more than enough for my parents." He grimaced.

"I'm sorry. I know it can be challenging to be an only child. I couldn't ask for better parents, but there were times when I prayed for a sister to grow up with. I suppose Debbie was an answer to that prayer in a strange way."

He smirked. "You waited a lot of years for that prayer to be answered. But I guess it was." He wiped the back of his hand across his mouth.

I giggled. "Debbie was the best answer I ever could have had. Everything works out for good if we trust God. That's what Dad always says, and he's right."

He chuckled. "Maybe so. I never saw that presidential pardon coming."

I almost choked on my coffee. "Me either." That was the extent of our conversation. But we continued to sit and admire the ocean and the sky for a while longer.

CHAPTER 19

~ ANNIE ~

My return to The Golden Bowl was triumphant. The breakfast crowd was in full swing, and I received a standing ovation when I came through the door with Nathan. Everyone shook my hand and thanked me for my dedication to improving life for neighbors in Marberry and beyond. The new commercial kitchen facility was nearly complete, creating good jobs for construction workers who might have had a hard time finding employment this time of year. Now, there was more hiring for food service jobs. Tracey had already added more customer service staff. Buck had orchestrated everything perfectly, made sure to give me credit, and shouted it from the rooftops.

I retreated to my tiny office under the staircase and cried with joy as I squeaked the desk drawer open to put my bag away. The chair creaked its familiar song as I sat down. It was good to be home.

Buck was right. If it meant The Golden Bowl would be successful, if it meant our mission of feeding body, soul, and spirit, and our message of the power of prayer would spread, it was certainly worth my effort to write cookbooks and host a TV show.

Where to begin? My phone rang. "Hello?"

"Annie, good to hear your voice."

"Buck! How did the restaurant opening go?"

"A few minor bumps, but all in all a major success. We're pleased they're pleased. I'll be here in New York a few more days, then a quick trip through Connecticut for two or three days and up to Maine."

"Oh. We miss you, Buck. Hurry back."

"Well then, put some prayers for good weather in your gold bowl, and get started on your cookbook."

"I will." Then he was gone.

~ ANNIE ~

January weather was in full swing. Buck was delayed in New York and Connecticut. Despite a bitter winter, business continued to grow at The Golden Bowl. The new facility ran like a dream. Our territory was enlarging without a doubt. With enthusiastic new—and old—employees and state of the art technology, the business hummed, and I had time to work on the cookbook.

It was the last Monday of the month when my phone woke me. "Buck?" I sat up listening to the wind howling, the shutters rattling.

"Annie, I'll meet you for breakfast."

"Where are you?"

"Just driving into Marberry."

"You're driving a Lamborghini in this weather?"

"No, I have my SUV. Would you like me to pick you up? Or is Rhodes the only one allowed to drive you?"

"Come to the house. I'll make you some breakfast."

"All right. See you soon."

I padded around the room trying to see out a window. All were plastered with snow. Hopefully, the driveway would be plowed.

Half an hour later Buck came through the front door with a blast of snow. He reached for me, and I was in his arms. He kissed my cheek.

"I can't believe you drove up here in this stuff. It's a wonder you didn't get stuck in a drift."

He pressed me tighter to him. "I wouldn't have done it for any other client. I've missed you."

My heart melted, and I told myself I wouldn't get weepy. I pushed back a step. "I missed you, too. I'm glad you're here. Let me take this wet coat and get you some coffee. I've got a fresh pot all set."

I busied myself hanging the wool coat to dry. When I found him pouring the coffees I burst out laughing. There stood the distinguished Buckminster Wynn, of Brooke, Lewis & Wynn with offices in New York and London, clad in a pair of jeans. They were fancy designer jeans, perfectly pressed, but jeans nonetheless.

He turned to me, a quizzical look on his face.

I took a seat at the kitchen table and squelched the laughter. "I never saw you in jeans before. You look great."

He smirked. "Well, it seems you like the rugged type, so this is my ode to rugged."

I tried to keep a straight face. "A very admirable one." It was no use. I burst out laughing.

Buck deposited the coffees on the table and sat waiting for me to compose myself. He lifted his mug. "Cheers."

"Cheers. It's great to have you back here." I took a sip. Maybe it was the laughter. Maybe it was the relief of finally having him back. Sudden boldness overtook me, and I went with it. "Tell me about yourself. I want to know my real friend, Buck. And I don't mean how you make restaurants work, point of sale, or food costs—or even Almighty Buck of Brooke, Lewis & Wynn with offices in New York and London. I mean I want to know about *you*."

He made a face. "You've heard the Almighty Buck thing, hmm?"

"I was told that's what they call you. Not that I know who *they* are. I assume, your clients."

He set his cup on the table and focused on it. "If you want to know about me, I guess Almighty Buck does sum it up. My god is money. That's what I focus on, that's what I get. It's been comfortable—a bit lonely at times—but comfortable." He looked up at me, as though he wondered if I thought less of him.

I swallowed whatever ball of emotion was welling up in my throat. "Maybe we could both stand to step out of our comfort zones."

He grinned. "Maybe."

"Do you have a family?"

"My parents. They're alive, healthy, living in London."

"Siblings?"

"I have a younger brother—haven't seen him in years. He lives near Portland, Oregon with a wife and three children. Probably a dog. He has a software business."

"I take it the dog could have passed on."

Buck smiled. "Yes, it's been some time since I've heard about the dog."

I had to press forward with my interrogation while I had the nerve. "Do you have a wife? A girlfriend?"

He seemed surprised. "Never married. I lived with someone for twenty years or so. I wasn't interested in marriage, and I told her from the start. She eventually decided to find someone else. I believe she did."

"Why would you stay with her if you didn't want to marry her?"

He lifted his eyes to the ceiling, as though he'd find the answer there. "Convenience, I suppose. I did care for her. We were useful to each other. We could have intelligent conversation. So many business functions—well, you need someone on your arm." He grinned. "I've satisfied myself with casual relationships. Sounds rather sad, doesn't it?"

"Yes." The tightness in my throat intensified.

"I haven't seen you wear a wedding ring." Buck's voice was tentative.

I put my hands on the edge of the table, thinking the best excuse for no jewelry would be my job. *Simple*. "It was one of the worst days of my life. I dove into the water and came up without my rings. I'm sure the tides have taken them around the world. I lost them five or six years ago."

"I'm sorry. You've never spoken to me about your husband."

"We got married right after college. Russ was my knight in shining armor. He'd do anything for me. He was so talented. When we bought the property that's now The Golden Bowl, he did the transformation. All that beautiful woodwork, the stonework. He did the plans for the barn, but he died of a brain aneurism before he could do the work. He's been gone almost eleven years now." My hands trembled as I lifted my cup to my lips. It made an awkward landing on the table.

Buck reached over and put his hand on mine. "I'd say we've both had our share of difficulties, but I wake up every day now and remember it's a new day. That prayer I took from your prayer bowl. That woke me up a bit. It said God's doing a new thing. We don't need to live in the past. Life can change for the better. Why not take a leap of faith?"

Jonah the stick figure in bright silver shoes ran through my mind, ready to leap off that boat. My breath caught in my throat. Buck's hand quickly moved away.

Doc pushed through the kitchen door. "I smell coffee . . . Buck!"

~ ANNIE ~

Late that afternoon I was sprawled on the couch in my office in the barn with my notebooks, pens of many colors, and my thoughts. The recipes for my new cookbook were simple to assemble. The stories from The Golden Bowl were a bit more challenging to write.

With a quick knock at the door, Buck let himself in and landed on the couch holding a folder stuffed with paper. He flipped the pages for my benefit. "These are the considerable deals I've negotiated for The Golden Bowl. We have some lucrative contracts with the top retailers and grocers in the country. Gerald and Karen are executing well. Money is coming in. I have the restaurant in my sights next. I have no doubt we'll be able to turn that into a profitable venture, assuming you take my advice.

We're already seeing positive results with the new computer system. And I have considered your mission and your principles in my plan."

I couldn't help a sarcastic smile. "That's very kind of you. Thank you."

The file landed on the floor with a thud, and he reached for my hand. *Not the hand thing again*. If anyone was going to be first to do that, it should've been me. That would have given me the upper hand, so to speak.

Buck had a strange look in his eye, one that insisted I return his gaze. "Annie, over the course of our time together, I've grown to treasure our friendship, such as it is. Considering our conversation this morning, I feel I can be so bold as to express myself plainly."

A rising bubble of emotion filled my throat. I croaked out an "Okay."

"I've been through encounters with a secret agent *assassin* who could snap my neck before I knew what was happening and a *billionaire* who could make or break my consulting business. I assured both that my intentions were honorable. Now, I expect no less frightening episodes with your *two* fathers and *SEAL Team Six*. I saw what they did to Peter Fellowes, by the way. Before I begin that daunting process, I wonder if you have any interest in me at all."

I noticed a tiny bead of sweat on Buck's forehead. I opened my mouth to speak, but a nervous burst of laughter came out.

He slouched back in the seat and stared at the ceiling.

The warmth of his hand on mine reminded me how much I'd missed him. Was I capable of that leap of faith? My comfort zone had become too comfortable, despite the loneliness.

My smile had disappeared, leaving my face red hot, the lonely ache permeating my heart. There was something in me that wouldn't let down my guard. My weak voice belied my determination to get back on an even keel. "I'm sorry. I had no idea you had any conversations about me with David or Cisco. I mean *that* kind of conversation."

He sat up and looked me in the eye. "I find it interesting Cisco picked this up from phone conversations, and you were right here with me. Can't you see I care about you? I was stricken from the moment I met you in that pitiful little office."

Tears poured down my cheeks. It felt like my breath was gone. He took the box of tissues from the desk and silently handed it to me.

It was a while before I found my voice. I reached for his hand and caught him by the sleeve. "I care about you, too. I do." My throat closed up again.

"Good. That's a start. That's all I ask." He took my hand and brushed it with a kiss. "I'll go about my business here, and perhaps we can have dinner together this evening."

I nodded my reply. Whatever words I had were trapped in a ball of emotion blocking my throat.

He picked up his folder and left.

My Adirondack chairs were buried under a blizzard, so I closed my eyes and stretched out on the couch. Overwhelmed. My prayer had no words, but I knew there was only one place to turn with my confusion, my joy, and my fear.

When I looked at the time, it was after 6:00 p.m. I freshened up and went in search of Buck. I found him with Karen and The Bakery & Sweet Shop staff going over ideas for the online store. He looked up from the makeshift desk and smiled at me. "Hello, Annie. Sales of our baked goods are soaring. We're nailing down some special Valentine packages for online customers that should take us to the stratosphere."

I leaned on the doorframe. "Awesome. Thank you."

He winked at me. "By the way, feedback on the jeans has been very positive."

Everyone laughed. Karen chimed in, "Now, Buck really fits in at The Golden Bowl." The staff pronounced him an honorary citizen of Maine.

~ ANNIE ~

Doc thought it a little odd, but I arranged dinner for Buck and me in the privacy of our home's library. After serving a hearty beef stew to Doc and "SEAL Team Six," as Buck called them, we adjourned to our private meal.

Buck uncorked an appropriate red wine and poured two glasses. "To us." He raised his glass.

"To us." Not wanting to break out into a beet-red sweat, I took a tiny sip. I served the stew along with a crusty loaf of French bread and butter.

We fell into conversation about Paulo Clemente, whose music played softly in the background. A nice neutral topic. I was feeling less daring about asking personal questions as I'd done this morning.

Buck complimented me on the meal, and I thanked him. *What to say*?

"So tell me, Annie, have you any plans to visit Austria again?"

I cleared my throat. "Well, no plan, but I do want to go back. I'm hoping everyone will be back here for the summer. They said they would, but we don't have a date set."

"Undoubtedly, The Golden Bowl tour will happen. Every city is lined up, starting with Boston on June 30th. They're not selling tickets yet, in case there should be some issue with Cat and the baby. But I'm sure things will go as planned."

"I'm sure they will." I slathered butter on my bread and returned it to my plate. "Buck, when is your birthday?"

He raised an eyebrow. "Is that a subtle way of asking me, what's my sign?"

I let out a laugh. "Um, no, it's a subtle way of asking when I should have your birthday cake ready."

"December 30th."

"Oh no! We missed it. Why didn't you tell me?"

"No need. But I do have yours, and there will be cake, at the least."

I made a face. "I suppose you've been staring at the date every time you picked up one of my tax forms."

"Yes. March 1st."

I could feel the blush. "Well, that was sneaky. We could have celebrated your birthday in Washington."

"Indeed. The president and first lady would have been thrilled." He smirked. "It would have been a bit too awkward, I'm afraid. But I have no complaints. I had a great time with you in Washington."

"Me, too."

He raised his glass. "Let's see what the March winds blow in to Marberry."

"Cheers. Just don't drive your Lamborghini up here in March. You need to wait until May, I'm afraid. Even then we can have rough weather." I wondered if Buck would even be back in the U.S. for my birthday.

A knock at the door interrupted us. Doc poked his head in. "Annie, the storm is finally over. I'm going outside. Don't worry about your Adirondack chairs. I'll help Roger and Keith shovel them out."

My brow furrowed. "It's nine o'clock at night. There must be two feet of snow out there. You don't need to shovel."

"No worries. You two have a nice evening." Doc clicked the door shut.

I put my head in my hands. "Ugh!"

Buck chuckled. "It looks like Doc doesn't approve of me, either."

I shook my head. "It's not you."

~ DOC ~

Roger and Keith did the bulk of the shoveling. I was pretty useless in comparison, but I needed to get out the frustration. I didn't hear Nathan come up behind me.

"Doc? Why don't we go inside?"

I straightened up in a hurry. "I thought you were watching Annie."

"She's gone to her room. Alone."

I let out a frosty sigh. "Well, let's get back in the house. Make sure he stays where he belongs."

Nathan's white teeth showed a rare smile in the dim light. Laughter from his two cohorts followed us to the back stairs.

"I'll make the coffee—decaf," I said. By the time we sat at the kitchen table, it must have been close to midnight. I took a sip and collected my thoughts, as the coffee warmed me. "You've been holding out on me. You know something I don't know about Buck. Now that Annie seems interested in him on a personal level, well, it's important that I know. So tell me."

Nathan wasn't much different than my son-in-law, David. You would know only what he wanted you to know. He sat there calmly, the ultimate poker face.

"I'm not an idiot. Christmas night, I knew your comment about Annie being too trusting of someone close wasn't pulled from thin air. There was a reason. I'm betting that reason is Buck. What's going on?"

Nathan looked me square in the eye. "You have nothing to worry about, Doc. Cisco and David had words with Buck at Christmastime. They're aware of his feelings for Annie, and I'm sure he's aware we're looking out for her."

"So what is it with Buck?"

"I take my orders from David Lambrecht, and he's okay with Buck. So I'm okay with Buck. If that changes, I'll keep you informed."

I stood up and stopped myself from coming across the table at him. "You'll inform me now!" That poker face slipped for an instant, and I knew. "It's you. You're in love with Annie."

He stood up to face me. "I care about your daughter. She's the most kind and trusting person I've ever known. But that's where it ends. That's where it has to end. As to Wynn, he's got a playboy reputation. But he's on notice.

He's not going to take advantage of your daughter." He picked up his cup and put it in the dishwasher. "I'm going to get some sleep. Good night."

I sat back down and stared at the table. *Joe Harris—he's the one to ask.* A short phone call later, I had a clear explanation of Buck's playboy reputation.

~ ANNIE ~

It was not quite 4:00 a.m. when I went downstairs to the kitchen, my head whirling. Buck and I had had a fine dinner together and a polite good night hug. He'd remained on his best behavior, cognizant of Doc's apparent concern and Nathan's watchful eye.

I couldn't sleep. Buck had stirred feelings I'd buried long ago, but circumstances weren't conducive to a new relationship. Not now.

I'd only recently met my biological father. Doc didn't seem anxious to include someone else in the family. We were still straightening out all the relationships. My life was busy with work, and Buck had a hectic travel schedule with his job.

Sure enough, Doc came through the kitchen door. "The coffee smells great."

"Morning." I poured him a cup.

He kissed my temple and reached for the coffee. "Have a seat."

I poured my cup and followed him to the table. "Is something wrong?"

"No, nothing wrong. But it looks like you and Buck are getting a little cozy, and I have to tell you—just take it slow. Please."

I let out a breath. "We are. Don't worry about me."

He rubbed the back of his neck. "You don't know anything about him. He's on his best behavior with you. Cisco's paying him a fortune to overhaul The Golden Bowl. The guy has money—he's smart—but that's not everything.

You . . . well, you're a sweet angel. Too trusting. Men like that prey on women like you."

I tried to keep a straight face. "Okay. I understand."

He pointed his cup at me. "I don't think you do. The guy carouses with women half his age. He's one of those love-them-and-leave-them types. Fine if you want to have dinner together once in a while. But nothing serious, please."

I put my head down on the table and felt his hand patting my back.

"I couldn't sleep. I had to tell you. I'm sorry. I know you're a grown woman, and I told you I wouldn't tell you how to live your life. But I can't stand by and watch you get hurt."

I sat up, hoping my face was not as bright red as I knew it had to be. "I appreciate that. It's okay."

He took a gulp of coffee, like he was fortifying himself, then looked at me. "Why don't you give Nathan a chance? It's obvious he cares for you."

I almost choked on my coffee.

CHAPTER 20

~ ANNIE ~

I checked the temperature before bundling myself up to spend some serious time in my Adirondack chair. Twenty-three degrees wasn't too bad, considering. I pulled on warm boots and grabbed my blanket, chair pad, and thermos before heading out the kitchen door.

"Mornin' Mrs. Brewster." Nathan extended his hand to help me down the back stairs. "The chairs are shoveled out. Watch out for slippery spots when you get up to come inside."

"Thanks." I could barely meet his eyes. Doc had floored me with his comment earlier.

Nathan escorted me to the chair.

"There's fresh coffee in the pot. I'll be in soon to make some hash and eggs for breakfast."

"Thank you, ma'am." He returned to the house.

I peered through my carefully arranged scarf and hood to find the beginnings of sunrise. "God help me." I mumbled the prayer over and over again. Things were clear as mud. More territory enlarging. More angst.

"Annie!"

I turned to find Terri sliding toward me. *Not now*.

She plopped into the chair beside me. "Word is you and Buck got together last night. So?"

I thought steam would come out my ears. "Word is wrong. Buck and I had dinner together. That's it. So you can straighten out whoever spread that gossip."

Terri was not daunted. "I just had coffee with Doc. He told me Buck came up from New York yesterday morning in that storm. And I saw him bouncing around the bakery yesterday. All smiles. I told you he's sweet on you. Doc agrees."

I shook my head, but my hood and scarf wouldn't let me. "Doc needs to keep his opinions on my personal life to himself."

She let out a heavy sigh. "I told him the same thing. He needs to mind his own business. It's like that prayer we did in Wednesday Morning group. *You* have to decide the desires of your heart."

For once, Terri had helped me. *The desire of my heart.* I'd announced it to Cisco only a month or so ago. "I want The Golden Bowl to be everything God wants it to be." That's what needed my focus now.

Clouds etched in gold told me God is faithful. The sunrise was spectacular.

~ ANNIE ~

Buck and I worked hard that week. Orders came flooding in, signaling a Valentine's Day business beyond my wildest expectations. We celebrated his last day in Marberry with cross-country skiing, and a delightful picnic lunch. The weather cooperated perfectly. Doc and my security team were gracious and obliging.

After dinner that Sunday evening with Doc and the team, Buck and I took dessert in Debbie's art studio. My mind returned to the conversation I'd had here with my brother-in-law. David would have been the last person on earth Doc would have chosen for his little girl. Fortunately, for those two, Doc was not in the picture when they'd met and married. There was not a couple on earth more perfect for each other than Debbie and David.

Buck turned to me from the window overlooking the glorious moonlight on the water. "I know this week hasn't been easy for you. Time will tell if this new thing God is doing includes me in your life—in a real way. Perhaps it's for the best that I'll be traveling a good deal for the next few months. We'll have a bit of perspective, I suppose."

I didn't know what to say. "I suppose."

When he left the next morning, I handed him a thermos full of coffee and some scones for the road.

"I'll be in touch." He hugged me, and his kiss fell on my forehead. He shook Doc's hand, took his bag, and walked out the front door.

Doc went back to the kitchen while I watched Buck drive off. Then I let the tears come.

~ ANNIE ~

Aside from a quick phone call letting me know he'd arrived safely in Tokyo, it was almost a week later when Buck called to tell me Tokyo was fun, but lonely. The project was already behind schedule. He was happy to hear things were humming along at The Golden Bowl.

I'd busied myself in the Valentine's Day build-up. My new bookkeeper from Brooke, Lewis & Wynn was keeping me on track and reassuring me my charities would see some serious money from our efforts. I looked forward to giving Cisco and Cat a great report.

I began each day in my Adirondack chair, praying, praising God for a series of magnificent sunrises and all the wonderful things happening at The Golden Bowl. The weather had turned a bit milder than usual.

"Mrs. Brewster."

"Good morning, Mr. Rhodes. I'll be in in a minute to start breakfast."

He dropped into the chair beside me. "No hurry, ma'am." Leaning forward, his elbows on his knees, he stared out at the horizon.

I couldn't concentrate, and I had no idea what to say.

He sat up and turned to me. "I'm glad Lisa Quinn

got that ring out of the prayer bowl. I didn't think much of her at first. But I was wrong. She's a good person."

I smiled. "She is. What changed your mind?"

He almost blushed. "She came to me yesterday and asked what Billy would like for his birthday. Then an hour or two later, he asked me about what he should get her for Valentine's Day. I guess she's on a diet now."

I chuckled. "Down ten pounds as of Saturday, I hear."

"That's the word." He half-smiled and went back to scanning the horizon.

I decided to get up and go make breakfast. He helped me up, and I slid into him. "Sorry." I looked up at him, and his brown eyes focused on mine.

"Mrs. Brewster, I know it's not my place to comment. But Wynn isn't half good enough for you."

I got lost there in those brown eyes for a moment. I had no idea what to say, how to interpret those inscrutable eyes. I said nothing.

I looked away. "Blueberry pancakes for breakfast today. Your favorite, I think."

He took me by the arm, guiding me safely over the icy spots, and up the stairs into the house.

~ **ANNIE** ~

February 13th was a long day at The Golden Bowl. Already exhausted from filling endless orders, my staff and I worked from dawn until midnight to push out every last one and get ready for the next day. I barely had an ounce of strength left to encourage them for the upcoming last-minute barrage on Valentine's Day.

Upon arriving home, I plodded up the stairs and fell into bed, asleep before my head hit the pillow. My phone startled me from a dream about a roomful of chocolate hearts. I reached for it, but I wasn't awake. "I'm done with hearts."

"What?"

"Too many broken ones. Can't fix 'em. Try melting."

"Annie?"

I noticed I was on the phone. "Hello? No more orders. You'll have to come by today before I sell out."

"Annie."

I sat up realizing I was still fully clothed. My wool coat twisted about my torso, making movement uncomfortable. "I've gotta get these boots off."

"Where are you, Annie?"

I tried to reach the boot zipper. No luck. "Gotta get the clothes off first."

"*Annie*?"

I dropped the phone.

I managed to untangle myself, undress, and make it to the bathroom. As I stepped into the shower, it occurred to me that I'd been on the phone. *Buck*?

By the time I found the phone in a tangle of bed sheets, there was only a voicemail from Buck. "Happy Valentine's Day. I hope you're all right. Please call me, and let me know."

I noticed the clock. I was late for work. I'd call him from The Golden Bowl.

I flew down the stairs in time to greet the town florist at the door—though you couldn't see him with all the bouquets he juggled. He stumbled into the foyer and through the kitchen door. Keith and Roger followed him with more.

"Mitch, are you sure these all belong here?"

He settled them as neatly as he could on the table. "All yours."

Doc laughed out loud. "How about a cup of coffee, Mitch? Looks like you could use one."

"A quick one sounds great." Mitch sorted through a fistful of cards, then carefully placed them on the flowers. "Got it. The right card with the right person. Sorry they got a little roughed up coming up the steps."

Doc put coffees on the table for everyone. "So who are these Valentines from?"

Mitch shrugged his shoulders. "My wife says a lot of

them are from rock stars. I oughta get your autograph, Annie." He took a long gulp of coffee and handed Doc the empty cup. "Thanks. Gotta run. Got a banner day, here. Happy Valentine's Day."

Doc inspected the bouquets, picked the card from a pretty pink and white arrangement and handed it to me. "At least I know this one is from me. I picked it out yesterday." He hugged me. "Happy Valentine's Day."

"They're beautiful." I read the sweet card, and stood on tiptoes to kiss his cheek. "Thank you."

He quickly plucked a red envelope from a lovely bouquet, bursting with color. "Nathan picked this one—from him and the guys. They each signed the card, I think."

"How thoughtful." I opened a heart-shaped card. "To Annie, our sweet Valentine. Aww."

"The others—I don't know," Doc said.

"Well, let's find out." I purposely avoided a stunning arrangement of perfect red roses in a crystal vase. "Cat and Cisco . . . Debbie and David . . . Paulo and Ellen . . ."

"Well, I guess, we know who this is from," he grumped as he handed me the card. "Who else would get you red roses in a vase like that?" He grabbed another cup of coffee.

I smirked. "That would be Buck." I opened the card and read silently: *Missing you, Annie. For the first time in my life, I want to come home. Love, Buck.*

~ ANNIE ~

After a quick piece of toast amidst all the flowers, Nathan came into the kitchen to escort me to The Golden Bowl. I handed him an egg and cheese sandwich. "Sorry for the rush this morning, Mr. Rhodes, it's been madness all month. I can't wait to sleep-in a little bit tomorrow." I threw on my coat and kissed Doc on the cheek. "Have fun today." I bolted through the kitchen door.

"Take it easy," Doc said.

Nathan overtook me and held the front door. "Thanks."

I smiled at him. "And thanks so much for the gorgeous flowers. And the card. Very sweet!"

"You're welcome." He flung open the car door, and I jumped in. "We appreciate you, Mrs. Brewster. You've been very kind . . . to all of us."

The sudden softness in his expression captivated me. Then he slammed the door. So much for Doc's theory that Nathan was interested in me.

As we drove off, and I tried to compose a sentence that would inspire Nathan to express his feelings without sounding nosey, my phone rang. I sighed as I dug for it in my bag.

"Popular lady," he said.

I laughed. "Right." It was Joe Harris. "You're up early."

I heard a heavy puff of his cigar. "Sorry, forgot to tell you the camera crew'll be there today for Valentine's. They'll use the video on newscasts and some of the entertainment shows. And we'll update the website with it, too. I tried gettin' them out there days ago, but that didn't work out. Sorry. I know it's a crazy day for you."

"No problem, Joe. Thanks. I hope you have a nice Valentine's Day."

"Yeah. Hot date tonight." His laughter was gruff. "So I talked to Buck the other day. Sounded miserable. And I thought he'd be tearin' up Tokyo."

"Oh. I hope he's okay." *Huh*?

"Yeah, I gotta run. We need to talk about those interview requests I've been holding off. Talk to you soon."

I slid the phone back into my bag. "Well, that was the longest conversation I've ever had with Joe. Today is full of surprises." I pulled out Buck's card and a tear welled up.

I looked up to discover we were in the parking lot, and Nathan was staring at me. "Surprises can be good." His expression was unreadable.

We entered The Golden Bowl to pandemonium. Ashleigh attempted to answer a reporter's questions, while a throng of people waited to be seated. Our elderly hostess looked frazzled, but her smile remained in place. The cameras turned on me and the reporter followed me to the office. Nathan detained him. "Mrs. Brewster needs a moment, please."

That began a morning of endless tours and interviews with the media. My staff was going full steam coping with the crowds. But the restaurant and The Bakery & Sweet Shop looked beautiful with fresh flowers tucked into every corner. Things were going smoothly, considering the volume of customers. With Valentine's Day falling on a Saturday, it meant even more business for us.

By early afternoon, I felt like a dishrag. *Enough*. I bundled up, grabbed a scone and hot tea, then headed out to the beach. Sunny, deep blue skies made it a perfect day to sit on a bench and enjoy some quiet time. I thought I might manage a call to Buck, though I had no idea what time it was in Tokyo. Calculating the hours was pointless. I was math-challenged at the best of times, let alone when I was tired.

High tide and a Nor'easter swirling around out at sea cast impressive waves against the rocks. I watched in awe and smiled at God's glory before me. *The desires of my heart*. I decided I was too drained for much of a conversation with Buck, but I could send him some photos. Maybe it would bring him home sooner. I stepped out on the rocks to get the perfect shot.

A voice on the wind called, "Annie!" In that instant I was swallowed up and thrown into the Atlantic. My body tossed and slammed against the angry sea, knocking me unconscious.

~ LISA ~

My scream was bloodcurdling, even for me. I'd just met Billy, Keith, and Roger out on the back porch for a break from nonstop dirty dishes, when all of a sudden Annie got swept away by a huge wave.

"Call 911!" Billy and the other SEALs jumped off the porch and ran to the water. Mr. Rhodes got there right away, and then he disappeared, too.

I ran inside bawling. The 911 operator said they were already on the way. Ashleigh started jumping up and down crying, and we all ran out to the beach. By the time we got there, the four guys were way out in the water. I could hardly breathe with all the tears, all the fear. I heard sirens in the distance, coming closer.

It took a long time—maybe half an hour—but they fished Annie out alive. The guys got out alive, too. Annie was unconscious, and they took her straight to the hospital by helicopter.

Everyone poured back into The Golden Bowl, and our hostess started saying a prayer for Annie. People offered their own prayers, and pretty soon, it was one big, long prayer for Annie to be okay.

Later that afternoon, I got a call from Billy. I ran into the office to find some quiet. "Billy, are you okay?"

"Fine. Annie's gonna be okay. She's conscious now. Doc's here with us. They're gonna keep her a day or so, but she'll be okay."

"Did she break any bones?"

"She has a concussion, a broken arm, and a couple of broken ribs. But she's in good shape, considering."

Whatever sound came out of me, I don't know if it was laughing or crying. Relief. I could hear Annie's voice in my head. "Praise God!"

"Yeah." Billy laughed.

My voice was giving out. "You were pretty awesome out there, Billy Foster. You're my hero."

It took a minute for him to say something. "Aww, shucks." He laughed. "So now you have to be my Valentine."

"Yep." I think my heart skipped a beat. "Doin' the Valentine dance now."

~ ANNIE ~

I woke up from a doze when Nathan took a seat beside my bed. "Didn't mean to startle you, Annie."

"Mr. Rhodes. You saved my life," I whispered. "Thank you. God bless you . . ." My eyelids, heavy from sleep and pain medication, closed—my body, my mind, completely spent. Jonah the stick figure in bright shoes ran through my head and into the chilly Atlantic. *A leap of faith.*

The next time I woke up, my parents and Doc were hovering over the bed. Mom gripped my hand, and I saw the pain on her face. "Anne Auclair Brewster! What a scare you gave us. What were you doing on that rock? What would we do without you?"

My mouth was dry, my voice sounded like sandpaper to my ears, but I needed to console her somehow. "I'm sorry, Mom. I love you." That was all I could manage.

When I woke up again it was morning, sunlight shone through the window. Nathan stood at the foot of my bed, his eyes fixed on me. "Good morning, Annie. It's Sunday."

"Good morning, Mr. Rhodes."

"The doctors are happy with your progress. You'll probably be able to go home tomorrow."

I couldn't put my finger on what was wrong with this picture. "I miss my Adirondack chair. Hope tomorrow things get back to normal—whatever that is."

His smirk didn't inspire confidence in that hope. "You need rest."

My eyes focused on flowers stacked everywhere. Get well. Valentines . . .

He called me Annie.

Late in the afternoon on Monday, February 16th, I sat propped on the couch in my parlor. It was good to be home. Tiring, but good. Doc hovered over me.

"Nice of those girls to come by," I said. In truth, I was relieved they'd finally left. A contingent from The Golden Bowl plus Terri was more than enough to contend with.

"You need your rest," Doc said. Then we heard yelling from the front doorway.

Buck blew in the door and rushed over. For all his speed, he landed softly beside me and gently embraced me, kissing my cheek. "Thank God you're alive." It sounded as though he inhaled tears. When he finally set me back on the pillow, I could see his eyes were bloodshot and wet, his clothes disheveled, as though he'd been wearing the same suit for a week.

All my strength was gone, my brain overwhelmed, my throat too full of emotion to speak. My eyes filled.

~ LISA ~

When I got home from Annie's house, I found Peg pulling a sled around the front yard with Rosie cheering her on. She headed over to the driveway. "How's Annie?"

"She's doin' pretty good. She's happy she broke her left arm . . . if she had to break an arm. They said it's a clean break, so it should heal up good. She looks kinda banged up—black and blue—and a big scrape on her forehead. They said she needs rest because of the concussion." I picked up Rosie and kissed her.

"Well, it's a miracle she came out alive. All that prayin' worked. I put some prayers in the bowl for her today. And I mailed a card. Hope it cheers her up."

"Good. Billy said he's comin' for dinner."

"He's already here. Brought some steaks. He's in the kitchen. That boy's a keeper."

"My hero!"

After dinner, I put Rosie to bed, and Peg went to her room to watch TV. I hunted around in the freezer for the ice cream I hid there three days ago. "I told Peg not to touch it. It's my Valentine splurge."

Billy came up behind me. "Little chocolate hearts in honey vanilla." His hand went right to it in the very back of the freezer. "Two scoops."

"Yes! I've been waitin' all month for this."

He reached in and grabbed a quart of chocolate. "I've been waitin' since lunch for this."

I stuck my tongue out at him, and he laughed. We sat on the couch in the living room with our desserts. I sat sideways and put my legs over his. "Ya know, it's a good thing I like you a lot more than ice cream. Otherwise, I'd never lose an ounce."

He grinned. "Sounds like I have a big future as a weight loss coach."

I laughed. "That's a cool job. Probably not as cool as the one you have now, though."

"I guess." His face changed a little.

"You must've been really scared when Annie went in the water. I thought she was a goner."

"Yeah. When it happens, you focus on what you need to do. But afterwards, well, it can get a little tough sometimes. Anyway, she's gonna be fine."

I put my empty dish aside. "I don't know about Buck and Mr. Rhodes, though."

"What?"

"When we went to visit Annie—when we left out the front door—Buck pulled up and jumped out in a real huff. Mr. Rhodes went over to him and said something, and they got into an argument rushing up the front walk. Those two were really goin' at it. Swearin' up a storm. I thought Buck was gonna slug Mr. Rhodes."

"Yeah." Billy didn't look surprised.

"What's goin' on? Why didn't Mr. Rhodes call Buck?"

"The guy's my boss, Lisa, I can't talk about him."

"Well, Terri says Mr. Rhodes is sweet on Annie. I know Buck is. They've been hiding it, but I could tell. Now everyone will know. Won't be long before Terri has it all over town. You think Mr. Rhodes and Annie have a thing?"

Billy let out a big sigh. "Not my business."

I laughed. "That's as good as a yes." I tapped my finger to my lips. "Hmm . . . Who do I root for? Buck's a good guy—and he's rich. But, Mr. Rhodes—well, he's a SEAL."

Billy looked me in the eye. "Let the better man win." Then he went back to his ice cream.

~ ANNIE ~

When Nathan carried me up the stairs to my room, I thought Buck would burst a blood vessel, and I'd die in agony. My entire body felt like shattered glass. I couldn't wait to get another pain pill into me.

Doc did everything he could to block Buck. "Annie needs to rest now. Can't you see she's so overtired she can't even speak? Why don't you get your bag and unpack? You can take the room you had last time if you want to stay."

Buck held his tongue, but trudged up the stairs after us. Nathan and Doc settled me on the bed while Buck stood watching, leaning on the doorframe, his face sullen, his arms crossed.

I had no energy to speak, and the tension cutting the air sucked the life out of me. I remembered Buck's prayer. *God is doing a new thing*. I wished I knew what it was.

After I was perfectly positioned on perfectly fluffed pillows, the down comforter trying to comfort me, Doc said, "You need your rest. Get some sleep now." He kissed my forehead, and they left the room.

I heard Doc's voice in the hall. "What's your problem, Buck?"

"I heard about Annie's accident on the television news. Why did no one call me?"

I heard Nathan throw Buck against the wall. "Don't you think we had a few concerns other than calling a restaurant consultant?"

It sounded as though Buck lashed out at Nathan, and ended up on the floor.

All I could do was cry.

~ ANNIE ~

Later that evening, Mom brought chicken soup, and Dad and Nathan helped me position myself in front of the tray table. I had no appetite. "Mr. Rhodes, why did you hit Buck?"

Mom looked aghast. Dad seemed stunned.

Nathan faced me. "I made a mistake. I shouldn't have hit him. I apologize."

My stomach roiled. "What happened?"

He shook his head. "I let my personal feelings get in the way, Mrs. Brewster. It was wrong."

"What personal feelings?" I was way beyond diplomacy.

But Nathan was not. "I'm sorry, ma'am, this isn't the time to discuss it. You need to get well." He turned on his heel and left.

I dropped the spoon and looked up at Dad. "Is Buck all right?"

He patted my shoulder. "I'll go check on him. Please eat something."

I was only moderately successful in getting the soup down. Dad returned with the obligatory, "Buck is fine. He should rest."

It was around four the next morning when I heard Buck say, "Good morning."

Keith's voice sounded in the hall. "Morning, Buck. Rhodes told us Mrs. Brewster is not to have visitors."

"Such a surprise." The door opened and Buck pushed through.

"It's all right, Keith! Please."

He let Buck in. "Five minutes, Mrs. Brewster." He closed the door.

Buck sat on the edge of the bed, and as I struggled to sit up, he lifted me tenderly into his arms. "How are you feeling?"

"I'm okay. Just sore," I fibbed. "I can't believe no one called you. I'm so sorry about the way they're treating you." My throat was closing again. I took a purposeful breath and tried to smother the grimace that caused.

"All I care about is that you're all right. If you want me to stay, I'll stay. If you want me to go, I will."

"I want you to stay. But what about Tokyo?"

His smile lit up the dim room. "Always concerned for someone else, Annie. That's what makes you so irresistible." He planted a soft kiss on my lips. "It's high time for a new thing. Apparently, your God saw all this coming. Someone needs to be concerned about you. I'd like that someone to be me. I'll plead my case when you're feeling better. But, as for Tokyo, I told my partners it's time for them to do some work."

I wanted to get to another kiss, but my brain had some strange wiring, I guess. "So there's really a Brooke and a Lewis?"

He smirked. "There is. I take it you never checked our website. You'll find their photos."

"Never thought of it." I went for another kiss.

Buck kissed me back. "Seems there's an upside to a concussion," he said.

With that comment, a heavy knock on the door preceded Keith's immediate appearance. "Rhodes is coming up the stairs." He had Buck by the scruff of the neck and out in the hallway in an instant.

But it wasn't fast enough. Nathan's voice boomed down the hall. It didn't sound like Buck was going to back down.

I had to get between them to prevent certain disaster. I attempted to throw myself out of bed. I landed indelicately on the floor. Keith saw this clumsy maneuver, and his expletives were louder than Nathan and Buck's put together. The three of them were on top of me arguing about who was going to take care of me.

"What's going on here?" Doc was beet red with anger.

"Doc! Thank God." I couldn't take another thing.

I was immediately deposited on the bed, everything fluffed and righted again. Stabbing pain that accompanied every breath since I'd broken my ribs escalated. Mom appeared with a tray, and I winced at the thought of having to eat again.

"Gentlemen, your breakfast is ready in the kitchen. I'll sit with Annie while you take the time to talk. Mike will be happy to pray with you, I'm sure."

Keith made a face behind Mom's back, like that was bound to happen. But they left peacefully. For that I was grateful.

Mom was upset, but kept everything to herself. She put on a brave face for me. At this point, it was just as well. I was low on energy, out of ideas on how to rectify the situation. Not that I understood what the situation really was. But Buck was definitely the new elephant in the room.

I did the best I could for my mother. I ate a good breakfast. I guess most mothers are the same. She finally smiled.

Doc arrived with his phone. "Debbie's anxious to talk with you." He handed it to me and escorted Mom out the door.

My sister was bubbly. "You're going to be fine, Annie. You just need rest. Don't you worry about anything. Almighty Buck is taking care of The Golden Bowl while you're recovering. Cisco just spoke with him. Mr. Brooke and Mr. Lewis are taking over their business in Beverly Hills and London and Tokyo. So we'll have no worries at all at The Golden Bowl. Almighty Buck can take care of the east coast. It's just a short trip away if something needs his attention in Marberry."

I didn't want to admit to my sister—or even myself—that I needed his attention. Buck's prayer was spot on. It was time for a new thing.

CHAPTER 21

~ ANNIE ~

It turned out both Cisco and David had a conversation with Buck and Nathan. Apparently, they spoke the same language. There was a truce. At times an uneasy one, but a truce nonetheless.

Since Debbie and David were the true owners of my house, and they had given me final say, Nathan and Doc accepted Buck as a guest in our home. There certainly was enough space for him to have his own wing.

Buck could now spend time with me as I allowed, without being harassed or beaten. Civility returned to my home.

I convinced Buck I'd be okay if he went about his business in New York. He kept in close touch with The Golden Bowl and with me on a daily basis. But he visited Marberry only on weekends.

Conveniently, my birthday fell on a weekend. Buck surprised me with a call on Thursday morning. "I'm in Marberry as we speak, and I'm all yours till Monday."

"Well, come on over, and I'll make you breakfast."

When he arrived, he insisted on cooking. He was adamant about doing everything for me, while I rested. It was difficult for me to accept, but recovery was slow. And trying to do everything one-handed made it slower.

My biggest wish was to sit out in my Adirondack chair again. The weather was mild, Doc was agreeable, so Buck helped me bundle up and head out with a thermos of hot chocolate to face sea and sky again. He lowered me gently into the seat and took the one beside me.

I took a satisfying gulp of salt air. "Spring is in the air."

He chuckled. "You don't say. I hate to tell you, it's still winter."

A rogue wave broke high on the cliff. "Whoa!" The memory of being consumed by such a wave overtook me. Buck must have had the same thought. He reached for my hand, cupping his over mine.

"I guess I am crazy. I was trying to take pictures of the waves breaking on the rocks on Valentine's Day. I was going to send them to you, so you'd miss Maine and come home again." *Why did I have to use the words from his card*? "I guess I did manage to get you home."

"I would have come with a phone call."

"Did I mention I have a tendency to do things the hard way?"

He grinned. "I noticed."

I let the bold Annie take over. "Why did Joe Harris tell me you were miserable in Tokyo?"

His eyes widened a bit. *I must have touched a nerve.* "I missed you. That was a new feeling for me. I've never cared for anyone the way I care for you. I'm trying to be honest and plain about it."

"Honest and plain isn't your usual way?"

That funny sound rattled in his throat. "In many ways, it is. But not *all* ways." His eyes met mine, and he glanced away. "I'm human. And Rhodes is probably correct. I'm not good enough for you. And neither is he, I might add."

"How so?"

He stared off into the horizon and shook his head.

"Doc told me you date women half your age. Is that true?"

He turned to me. "That's true."

I know I made a face, not meaning to. "Do you really think that surprises me?"

His eyebrows raised, but he didn't answer.

"I know I'm a little different, but why wouldn't most women want to be with you? You're a great guy, and most women love money. Even all the talk shows I've had to endure lately say a woman's number one concern is security. So if your god is money and their god is money—why wouldn't they want you? And let's face it, if a guy has a choice, he's going for the youngest and the prettiest. Maybe that's news to Doc, but not to me."

He smirked at me. "You are a little different, Annie."

I smirked back at him. "I'm assuming you mean in a good way. Now can you help me with this thermos? I need a sip of cocoa before it freezes."

He assisted me in my chocolate fix and resumed his seat. "The point is, I'm no longer interested in 'most women.' I'm interested in you."

I could feel that hot blush giving me away. *Just go with it*. "That's good with me, Buck."

~ ANNIE ~

It was a quiet weekend, and Buck took the opportunity to plead his case. Part of that was delving into the particulars of my charities, and some of Cat and Cisco's that he thought would interest me. I saw he could well be a conniver, if given the chance. He knew my weak spot, and made an airtight case for how he could help me make The Golden Bowl a preeminent charity.

But Buck was definitely worming his way into my heart, as Doc had worried.

My birthday dawned with freezing rain and sleet. Despite lovely flowers and gifts, my disappointment showed as I stood at the kitchen window mourning a day lost in my Adirondack chair.

Buck coaxed me to the kitchen table and placed a folder in front of me. "I have a little birthday surprise for you. Open it." He sat beside me, resting his arm on the back of my chair.

There was a check made out to me from The Golden Bowl. "Buck! I got a paycheck."

"You did. Your first one, I believe. The first of many. Happy Birthday."

"What a great present!" It dawned on me that I received this check after doing nothing for two weeks. Another lesson in getting out of my own way and letting God take care of things. "God's provision."

"You've worked hard for your reward."

"That's what you do—work each day on what's in front of you—what you're called to do. Trust God to lead you and show you the way. Trust God for provision. Simple as that."

"Indeed." He stroked my hair. "You do make a case for God. I've been listening—since that 'God is doing a new thing' prayer. Now I hope there is a God."

"Hope's a good thing, Buck." As I examined the check, I suddenly remembered Cat's words to me when we first discussed Almighty Buck. *Don't worry, Annie, you'll be able to help him.* I *had* done a small thing to help him. Cat was always right. God was at work here. Emotion filled me as I said a silent prayer of praise and thanks, asking God to continue his work in Buck.

He took a paper from the folder. "And speaking of hope, this printout shows you how the funds have been portioned out. You have a contribution to your new retirement account, another to your new savings account, another to taxes, another to your charity account, and even a tithe, as you call it. This check is now yours to spend as you see fit."

"Wow! Money left over." I was impressed. "This is incredible. We can do this every month now." Gratitude filled my heart. "I've never been so organized about money."

He chuckled. "Just remember to pay your personal bills."

We spent the day in the family room in front of the fire, talking and eating some impressive meals he whipped up in the kitchen. Friends from The Golden Bowl delivered a cake baked to his specifications. Everyone sang a chorus of Happy Birthday, including my sister and the kids on videoconference from Austria. Then another from our favorite rock stars.

Monday morning I became weepy over breakfast. I blamed it on my medication. Buck was needed in New York. I didn't want him to put his business at risk over my whims.

When Buck left, I turned to see Doc by the kitchen door, shaking his head. I decided to avoid an unpleasant conversation and went upstairs.

~ DOC ~

It was a Monday morning in mid-March when Annie prepared to return to work. As was her usual habit, she started the day in her Adirondack chair, bundled up in front of a colorful sunrise. I hoped her prayers would include a "word" from God about keeping her distance from Buck. Not that I really had anything against the guy. As a matter of fact, he did a remarkable job of educating Annie on her personal and business finances. For once in her life, Annie had bank accounts and something to put in them.

But, the playboy label was enough to give me pause, and I had a strong feeling there was something Nathan wasn't telling me. I didn't need Pastor Mike to assure me that Annie needed someone of faith for a potential partner.

I took a seat at the kitchen table and observed Annie through the window. I guess I couldn't be too hard on Buck. My own faith in God was tenuous. Most of my life, I'd conveniently classified myself as agnostic, my way of not investigating the hard questions. But with the revelation of Debbie's near death experience, Annie's strong faith, and just knowing Cat, I had to consider the possibility of God. I attempted a sip of my steaming coffee.

I suppose my hesitation over Buck looked suspicious to Annie. She probably thought I wanted to have her attention to myself this early on in our relationship. And that had some truth to it. But, in my heart, I wanted what was best for my daughter. Was that Almighty Buck?

Nathan had hinted at his interest in her. But it was probably not a smart idea to push that. After all, he was in a business that could make problems for a relationship. And he had a poor track record with marriage.

Speak of the devil, Nathan barreled through the swinging door and headed for the coffee. "I spoke with David Lambrecht. I'll be taking a few days off." He put his cup on the table and took a seat.

"R and R on a beach somewhere?"

"Sadly, no." He focused his gaze on Annie, still in her chair.

Curiosity got the best of me. I decided to push, but he volunteered before I could get out a question.

"I'm going to New York."

An alarm went off in my head. "Something to do with Buck?"

He smirked. "Just a side trip."

I leaned across the table. "I need to know what's going on."

He turned to me, his face expressionless. "You will, if I find anything."

~ ANNIE ~

I was excited about returning to work today, but the joyous peace of sunrise made me linger in my Adirondack chair. The sound of the kitchen door slamming turned me around. *Must be time to go*. I was surprised when Nathan took the seat beside me. He'd been more distant than usual over the past weeks. I waited for him to scan the horizon and speak if he was going to.

The Prayer of Jabez filled my mind. I thanked God

that business at The Golden Bowl continued to skyrocket, and our charities would see more help. The business was blessed indeed, and the territory was definitely continuing to enlarge—without me there, working my fingers to the bone. No doubt, God's hand was with us. Maybe Buck was right. It could be a preeminent charity.

I contemplated the last line of the prayer. *And that You would keep me from evil.*

Nathan's voice jolted me from my thoughts, and I turned to catch those unfathomable eyes. "I checked with David Lambrecht and cleared this with him. I'd like to take a few days off. Is that all right with you?"

"That's fine. Is everything okay with you?" My face was going red. "I don't mean to pry."

"Everything is fine, ma'am. Roger will take over until I get back. I'll be leaving today."

I had a bad feeling in the pit of my stomach. "Where are you going?"

He turned to me with a pained smile. "I'm going to finalize my divorce. I won't be gone long."

"Oh." I felt my morning coffee surge back into my throat. "I'm so sorry."

"Don't be. It's a step forward."

My bold self took over before I could muzzle her. "I know you threw the ring in the prayer bowl. You must have been in such pain." The coffee choked me into silence. Embarrassment was turning me sixteen shades of red.

I saw the realization in his eyes. "Cat?"

I nodded.

He let out half a laugh. "She's somethin' else. That's why they invited me to Christmas. She told Lambrecht she wanted to speak with me. I've never met anyone like her."

I nodded and found my voice. "She's amazing. I believe she's a prophet."

He smiled at the sky. "Whatever she is, she knows everything. Lambrecht told me she's been this way ever since she was five—almost killed in a plane crash."

"Yes, she lost her parents, her baby brother, and David's brother in that accident. She was badly injured. Internal injuries so severe, the doctors said she'd never have children. It was a true miracle when she got pregnant."

"Really?" He seemed stunned. "The way Lambrecht explained it, well, it sounded like she got a bump on the head and came out psychic."

"David was the one who pulled her out of the wreck. He wasn't physically hurt, but the emotional damage was done. Cat had an experience of God that day. But the family obviously doesn't want that public."

He shook his head. "No one will hear it from me." Then Nathan fell silent staring out to the horizon.

Coffee bubbled around in my gut. I worried that he'd feel betrayed by Cat. Did he think Cat and I had been gossiping about his life? I had no idea what to say.

I watched him rub his face. He probably was aggravated with me.

"Mrs. Brewster, I know about your sister, too."

The coffee clogged my throat, but I pushed through it with a strange sound. "What?"

He faced me. "She paints clues, prophecies. Lambrecht told me. I saw some of her work."

"Oh. I can't tell you what a relief it is to hear that."

He grinned.

My hand automatically landed on his arm. "I was afraid you'd think Cat was a gossip. She'd never—"

"I know. You don't have to worry. I get it. She says what she needs to say to help someone. I know all she wants to do is bring people to God. I get it. There's not a mean bone in her body. But I guess things get a little weird when your sister starts painting."

I laughed. "Yes, I've experienced that weirdness first hand."

We fell into silence for a few moments, gazing at the sky.

"Mrs. Brewster," Nathan's voice startled me, and I faced

earnest brown eyes. "You're every bit as amazing as Cat and your sister. You have a gift when it comes to helping people, feeding them, just like your menu says. You make them think about God and prayer. You make people smile—inside and out." He stood. "I just want you to know."

~ **ANNIE** ~

Roger accompanied me through the crowd of well-wishers gathered outside The Golden Bowl, and then through the door to applause. I stopped to speak with everyone, so grateful for their support. Out of the corner of my eye, I noticed Ashleigh growing increasingly impatient. I curtailed my chatting and led her into the office.

She bounced around a new, comfortable-looking chair. "Buck insisted you use this new office chair. It's ergonomic and everything. It'll probably make you heal faster."

"How sweet." I dropped into the chair hoping it would lower Ashleigh's anxiety level. "Very comfortable. It does take up a lot of space, though."

She began waving her hands around, fanning her face. "Paulo Clemente said hello to me! He said, 'Hi Ashleigh.' He called me by name. Ashleigh. It's like he really knows me."

I stifled a laugh. "What else would he call you? When did you talk to him?"

"His wife, Ellen, was calling on the videoconferencing. He was there with her. He actually said hello to me. And he smiled at me. He has a great smile. And his eyes are the bluest. You can even see it on the screen. He's really shy though. You can tell."

I interrupted with a laugh. "Ash, it's like you're fourteen again."

She collapsed into the squeaky chair and heaved a big sigh. "Sorry. I've got a serious crush on him."

I nodded. "Am I supposed to call Ellen?"

It took a second for Ashleigh to recall Paulo's wife. "Oh, yeah. She said she wants to talk to you and Lisa."

~ LISA ~

Billy startled me when he put his hand on my shoulder. "You need to meet Ellen."

I almost dropped a dish. His tone of voice sent a shiver of jealousy through me. I don't know why. I had a thought Ellen might be a beautiful girlfriend from his past.

"She's on videoconference with Annie . . . in her office. Let's go."

He tugged at me, all excited, and I barely had a chance to get my gloves off and smooth my hair. *Great! I'm gonna look like a mess in front of some supermodel named Ellen.*

Seconds later, I was huddled in front of the screen with Billy. Ellen looked a little bit like Brianna, with a cute, freckly face and pretty, light brown hair—straight with bangs. She had friendly blue eyes you couldn't help but like. I hoped she wasn't Billy's ex-girlfriend.

Before I could open my mouth, Ellen gave a big smile and wave and made a big deal of Billy.

He couldn't have smiled any bigger. "Hi Ellen! This is Lisa." At least he had his arm around *me*.

"Lisa, I'm glad to meet you. I heard you're interested in going to nursing school."

"Yeah, someday." I remembered I should be polite. Maybe it'd impress Billy. "Nice to meet you, too." I pulled my shirt down over my stomach. Not that she could see me. But I knew, even though I was down thirty-six pounds, I could exercise till the cows come home and never look like her.

"Can I borrow Lisa for a couple minutes?" Ellen asked.

Billy's smile wouldn't quit. "Sure. I gotta get back to work."

Annie was already at the door, and Billy shut it behind

them. Now I was really confused. I knew I'd seen this woman somewhere before, but I couldn't remember where.

Ellen took a sip of water or something. "I loved your story from the minute the world met you on Amanda's show. Then when Annie told me you were interested in nursing, well, I had to meet you. I hope you don't mind me taking you away from your work for a few minutes."

"No problem."

She smiled.

Then I remembered exactly who she was. "Ellen Clemente. You're Ellen Clemente!" My eyes popped and my mouth hung open in shock. The wife of the rock star, himself.

She giggled. "I'm sorry, I should have introduced myself."

"Oh wow! I can't believe it took me this long to figure out who you are."

Her smile was *gracious*. That's the word. I learned it from Annie.

I couldn't think what to say to her. "Amanda James said you're a Georgia peach." *Peachy is gracious. Kind of.* "But you don't sound like you're from the South."

She pushed her bangs out of her eyes. "I spent most of my life in California. So I don't have much of an accent."

"That's where you guys met. I know the whole story. I have all the albums, too."

"Thank you." Her mouth kind of quivered a little around her smile. "It means the world to Paulo and me to have such incredible fans."

"You guys are awesome. Wow. Talkin' to you is like—one of the highlights of my life."

I think she actually blushed. "You're sweet. Thank you. I just want to take a couple of minutes to talk to you about something I'm doing."

"Sure."

"I've been working on a program to help train nurses who go to work in underserved areas. So far we've helped people in Europe and Africa. There are still a lot of underserved areas in the United States, too. As you probably know, Maine is on the list of states that could use more nurses. To be frank, your desire to go into nursing coupled with your growing fame would make you a great candidate to participate in my program. So many people have tuned into your videos online, and you've done a great job in front of the cameras. We could use your help in gaining more visibility and funding for our charity."

I probably looked dazed and confused.

She brushed her bangs back and tried again. "What I'm saying, is that we can pay for your nurse's training, if you agree to work in an underserved area and help us grow our charity. I'd love to have you on board."

I could hardly believe my ears. "Sure! I'm on board, for sure."

After my call with Ellen, I had to find Billy. I made it through the door and crashed into him. He took me by the shoulders. "How did it go?"

I had to yell above all the noise in the restaurant. "I'm gonna be a nurse!"

"Cool." He hugged me.

I cried so hard, I soaked his shirt. Then I said into his chest, "Ellen Clemente's gonna pay for my nursing school. It's like she's giving back, 'cuz Paulo paid for her nursing degree. She met him when she was just a poor nobody. Like me." When I finally peeled myself off him, I looked up at a sign above Annie's front door. "There's no place like family." That was the name of one of Paulo's albums—and it sure applied to The Golden Bowl. I started bawling all over again.

~ LISA ~

Annie found me at my post. "Congratulations! I'm so thrilled for you—nursing school."

"Yeah, and it's all because of you. Everything. I'm

taking one of those little plastic gold bowls—from the packaged meals—and I'm gonna put my prayers in it every day. I'll show Rosie how to do it when she's old enough, too. I'm gonna be a gold light. You just wait and see."

She hugged me. From the sound she made, I think she was touched.

"Don't worry, Annie. I'm keepin' my job at The Golden Bowl. Ellen said I can work and go to school, too. I'm gonna work it all out."

All of a sudden, it all hit me, how my life had turned so completely around. "It's all because of you. I got that ring out of the prayer bowl. The house from Amanda. A great job and real friends here at the restaurant. I met Billy. I'm losin' weight, gettin' healthier. Rosie has a real life. And now I'm gonna be a nurse."

"On a wing and a prayer," Annie said.

"A wing and a prayer?"

"It means you're not necessarily prepared for it, but you go for it, you do it hoping you'll succeed. And you have succeeded."

I laughed. "On a *ring* and a prayer."

She brushed the hair out of my face. "I couldn't be more proud of you." I could see tears in her eyes.

A weird feeling came over me, and I blurted it out. "I'm the one—I stole your steaks. I'm so sorry. Ryan wanted them, and I let him push me into it. I know that's not an excuse—it was wrong. I'll never do anything like that again. I promise."

She took a step back and looked at me with shock on her face. "It's okay. I understand." She smiled. "I'm so glad you told me." Then she hugged me.

When I got home after work, Peg was sitting in front of the TV with Rosie asleep in her arms. I shut the door as quietly as I could and put my gold bowl on the coffee table.

She got up and laid Rosie on the couch, then came over and gave me a long hug. "Congratulations, baby. I'm so proud of you. You're gonna be a nurse!"

I laughed. "Word travels fast."

She let out a raspy sound. "It does when Terri Monahan is around. She just happened to be at The Golden Bowl today."

"I don't know all the details, but I can go to school near home. Ellen Clemente told me Maine needs more nurses. So I qualify for her charity to pay for it. I'm psyched, Peg."

"Me too, baby, me too." She hugged me again. "Let's celebrate. I'll make us a good dinner."

~ DOC ~

After Annie left for work that morning, I puttered around, getting more and more aggravated as the day went on. I phoned Cat. I was a bit shocked when she took my call right away.

"How are you, Doc? You seem distressed."

"I'm sorry to bother you, but I'm concerned about Annie, and let's face it, you're the only one who can tell me what's going on. At least I've learned that by now."

She sounded amused.

"I know. I know you're half a world away, and I live in the same house. But you know things. They don't call you a prophet for nothing. And Nathan did have a talk with David about going to New York. I bet Cisco knows about it, too."

"Then why ask me? You've already sent Nathan on his mission."

"I'm worried about my daughter. Buck is here every weekend now, and Annie talks to him at least once a day. I don't want her hurt. She's too trusting. Someone needs to protect her."

I could hear her sigh. "Have you heard *The Prayer of Jabez*? Annie's grandmother prayed that prayer daily for both her granddaughters. It's a very special memory Annie has of her Grammy. Debbie created some artwork around it as a Christmas gift to Annie."

"I remember seeing it. You talked about it at the Christmas concert." I walked through the halls to Annie's room and let myself in. "It's hanging here on her bedroom wall." I read it out loud. "Oh, that You would bless me indeed, And enlarge my territory, That Your hand would be with me, And that You would keep me from evil. Chronicles 4:9-10"

"If you think about it, you'll see God is working that blessing in Annie's life. God is guiding her and enlarging her territory. God's hand is with her as The Golden Bowl impacts more and more people. Annie has been blessed to be a blessing to others."

I couldn't be patient another second. "That's all well and good, but I'm worried about her relationship with Buck. The guy's a playboy, to put it as nicely as I can. I don't want him to use her and walk away. I don't want her hurt."

Cat's voice was unruffled. "Doc, please read the last line of the prayer again."

I groaned and looked back at the artwork. "And that You would keep me from evil."

"You mustn't worry about Annie. The Precious Blood protects her."

"Okay." I walked out of the room, shut the door, and leaned back against it, staring into space. *How to deal with a prophet*?

Her giggle startled me. Had she read my mind? "Cat?" It was a plea.

"Don't you think Buck and Nathan are smart enough to know they're not ready to be married? To any woman, never mind Annie."

I rubbed my eyes. "Nathan—probably. Buck—no. He's determined to have her, and he's thinking he's going to get her before Nathan does. I'm sure on some level, he's jealous of Nathan—he's a SEAL, a hero, saved Annie's life, saved an entire school. And frankly, Nathan could beat him to a pulp in five seconds flat. But Buck probably thinks he's some great catch, too. He's rich, got the great

New York apartment, big shot consultant. God's gift to women. If I told Buck to see a shrink—or a pastor—he'd laugh at me."

Cat was matter of fact. "Doc, please read the last line of the prayer again."

I kicked the door. "I don't have to read it. You have it stuck in my head. 'And that You would keep me from evil.' So . . . you're saying not to worry about Annie. God's gonna take care of Buck?"

"That's God's job, Doc. He's at work in and through Buck. And Nathan. And Annie. And you. Be still and know."

"Yep." I sighed, and realized there was nothing more I could do. *Que sera, sera.* What will be, will be. I think that's the expression. Not that I'd have to like it. "Okay, I'll let you go. I'm going to get a thermos full of coffee and try being still in that Adirondack chair, Annie loves so much. Who knows, maybe the Big Guy'll talk to me out there."

~ ANNIE ~

I dallied in my office in the customer service area, eating butter pecan ice cream and marveling over my new financial notebook. It was a physical ledger I could hold in my hands, not just a bunch of numbers on a computer screen. Like Buck had shown me on my birthday, it turned mere numbers into real life. I recognized this would make the difference for me.

Buck had organized everything for me so meticulously I could now continue it on my own. Well, I did realize I should discuss it with him or my new accountant periodically. I decided on the quarterly dates that would work for me and logged them in. Now, I felt like a responsible adult. *God is doing a new thing.*

Really, I should have understood from the start that, in effect, I was an employee of The Golden Bowl, and should have taken a salary. If managing the business finances were beyond me—and it shouldn't have been with the right accounting help—at least I could have managed my personal finances more responsibly. Thank God, I finally understood what I needed to do to keep myself organized and up-to-date with bills, taxes, charity, and even savings. For me *and* for my business. My new notebook had it all right there at my fingertips.

My phone buzzed, interrupting prayers of gratitude. "Buck!"

"Greetings from sunny Florida."

"Florida? You're all over the place. I thought you were in New York."

"Another road trip, my dear."

I giggled. I could get used to being called, "my dear."

"How are you? Where are you? I hope you're not still at the office."

"Um . . . yeah! I'm fascinated with my new notebook. I love it, and it really looks like I'm solvent."

His hearty laugh made me giggle all the more.

It occurred to me I had more than one desire of my heart. But what was God's opinion on that? Clear as mud to me, but Cat probably knew.

As Buck laid out his idea for another cookbook with the theme of recipes and blessings from The Golden Bowl, I thought how God was always doing a new thing. If I'd learned anything since picking The Prayer of Jabez out of the golden bowl, it was that worry was a waste of time. God's hand was with me. Taking a leap of faith and trusting—stepping into what God was doing—that's what would bring me to the desires of my heart.

Buck's enthusiasm filled my heart with joy. I couldn't wait to see what God would do next.

CAST OF CHARACTERS

The Golden Bowl:
Anne Auclair Brewster (Annie), owner

Staff:
Ashleigh (Ash), Manager, First shift
Brianna (Bree), Manager, Second shift
Karen, Confections Manager, The Bakery & Sweet Shop
Gerald, Manager, Food Prep Facility
Tracey, Customer Service Manager
Lisa Quinn, Dishwasher

Annie's Family and Extended Family:
Dr. Craig Westcott (Doc), birth father
Pastor Mike Auclair, adoptive father
Millie Auclair, adoptive mother
Debbie Lambrecht, sister, fashion designer, artist
David Lambrecht, Debbie's husband, Annie's brother-in-law and security expert who put together Annie's security team.
Cat Clemente, David's cousin, rock star lyricist, philanthropist, prophet
Cisco Clemente, Cat's husband, billionaire businessman and philanthropist
Paulo Clemente, Cisco's youngest brother, rock star, composer
Ellen Clemente, Paulo's wife
Grammy, deceased maternal grandmother

The Consultants:
Buckminster Wynn (Almighty Buck), Brooke, Lewis & Wynn
Joe Harris, Agent, entertainment industry
Amanda James, Journalist

The Tax Professionals:
Jim Curley, Maine Revenue Services
Special Agent Tim Hayes, IRS, Criminal Investigation

The Security Team:
Nathan Rhodes, Director of Security
Billy Foster
Keith
Roger

The Townspeople:
Peg, Lisa's babysitter/friend
Terri Monahan, Jeweler, Marberry Designs
Ted Monahan, Coastal Real Estate
Carson Phelps, David's nemesis
Peter Fellowes, Vice Principal and Special Needs teacher, Marberry Academy
Ryan Quinn, Lisa's ex-husband
Louise Gugino, Pinky's assistant and teaching assistant, Marberry Academy
Pinky Gugino, Accountant

ABOUT THE AUTHOR

Ordinary people in extraordinary situations fuel Maeve Christopher's imagination. Keep asking "what if" and "why," and the plot thickens. What could be more fun?

Maeve's new series, ***The Golden Bowl,*** is set on the scenic coast of Maine. This unusual restaurant caters to the body, soul, and spirit. A large gold bowl on the front porch gives the establishment its name and invites patrons to leave a prayer and take a prayer. When they do: lives change.

Maeve lives in beautiful Massachusetts with too many characters and a number of messy subplots. She loves to hear from readers. Subscribe to Maeve's newsletter for exclusive content, contests, special offers, and more at http://maevechristopher.com

Made in the USA
Middletown, DE
25 April 2017